THE SWEET TASTE OF LOVE

"No!" Was that her own voice she heard? "No, Bryce, don't stop...not now...not...*ever!*" In some deep, nether region of her brain Brittany knew what she'd said was wrong, knew it branded her shameless...wanton, but her conscious thoughts were too filled with the things he was doing to her body, too consumed with the white-hot fire that blazed wildly through her limbs, too lost in his nearness to care...

With a groan, Bryce swept her up into his arms and carried her to the bed. "Please..." she whispered. But she was long past coherent speech. She thought only with her senses now, and all of them were screaming for Bryce's touch, for more of the joy that was coursing hotly through her body.

And then there was his mouth. Moving his warm lips over her own with mesmerizing thoroughness, Bryce worked Brittany's lips apart to let his tongue slip between. Then he slid it along their opening, teasing her senses ...sending her reeling. Tongue meeting tongue, they tasted each other and found sweetness, and Brittany only wanted more...

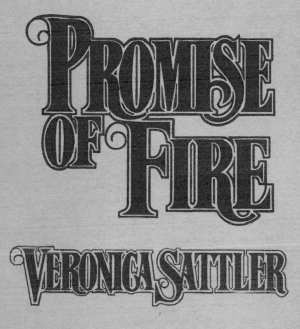

PROMISE OF FIRE

VERONICA SATTLER

ST. MARTIN'S PRESS/NEW YORK

To Adam
This one's for you, kid—
Love,
VS

PROMISE OF FIRE

Copyright © 1989 by Veronica Sattler.

ISBN: 0-312-91769-4   Can. ISBN: 0-312-91770-8

Printed in the United States of America

First St. Martin's Press mass market edition/December 1989

10 9 8 7 6 5 4 3 2 1

PROLOGUE

Somerset, England, 1743

A MONOTONOUS DOWNPOUR OF CHILL November rain pelted the thatched roof of the tenant's cottage. Inside the tiny one-room structure, the combined light from a single rush lamp and the ill-fed fire on the hearth failed to penetrate the gloom; it was almost midnight, and the rain had endured for hours.

The fretful eyes of fourteen-year-old Ben Tremaine searched those of his father across the narrow cot where a young woman lay writhing in pain.

"She—she ain't goin' t' die, is she, Pa?"

Donald Tremaine's weary brown eyes moved from the thrashing figure of his daughter on the cot and met Ben's. The long hours of worry were revealed in the lines of Donald's careworn face and heavily slumping body. Sadly, he shook his head.

"I fear she may, Ben. 'Tis beyond me ken whut t' do fer our Beth, lad, an'—" Suddenly the older Tremaine's face grew taut with anger. "Curse Biddie

Newill fer comin' down wi' th' ague! Whut's a midwife good fer, if she don't come when ye need 'er?" His face twisted with bitterness. "An' curse th' devil whut done this t' Beth, too! Yer sister wuz a good gel, she wuz. 'E 'ad no right t' use 'er th' way 'e did!"

Tremaine's work-roughened hand clenched into a fist as he shook it upward. "Lord 'r no lord, Edmund Avery, ye're a black'earted devil, an' ye deserve t' pay fer whut ye done!"

A moan from the cot brought Tremaine's attention back to his daughter, but young Ben's thoughts had wandered at the mention of the name Avery. Suddenly the boy moved toward the door.

"Where're ye goin', lad?" queried the father anxiously. He gave a quick glance to the opposite side of the hearth where his four youngest children—all boys—lay sleeping in a single bed, and he lowered his voice. "'Tis a wicked night t' be out in, an'—"

"Th' Lady Olivia!" exclaimed Ben. "*She* might ken whut t' do fer Beth! *She's* an Avery we kin *trust*!"

Donald pondered this for a moment, remembering all the kindnesses meted out over the years by the older sister of the man he'd just cursed. Yes, Lady Olivia Avery might, indeed, come to assist one of her older brother's humble tenants with childbirth. Indeed, she'd helped with the birthing of the twins three years ago—and last year, when his wife had breathed her last, she'd been present, though unable to help poor Addie.

But Donald was hesitant to send Ben for Lady Olivia tonight for one powerful reason. It was her younger brother, Edmund Avery, who'd brought Beth to this end. Got her with child after forcing his way with her, he had, and then left her to fend for herself. And it was Lord William Avery, their older brother, who owned the land the Tremaines worked and lived on. Two kinder souls than Lady Olivia and Lord William didn't exist. Tenderhearted, they were, and caring—not at all like that blackhearted brother they lived with! What would it do to their gentle natures to learn what Lord Edmund had done?

Just then, another moan of pain from the cot interrupted Donald's thoughts.

Ben heard it too. "Pa?" he implored as his hand went to the latch of the door.

Donald hesitated for a brief moment longer, his worried glance moving to the swollen body of his daughter, then back to Ben.

"Aye," he nodded. "'Tis th' Lady Olivia, then. Fetch 'er quickly, Ben! It don't seem we 'ave much time."

Lord William Avery, Marquis of Clarendon, hurried to the door that joined the bedchamber of Anne, his invalid wife, to his. Opening it carefully, he saw that all was quiet. The nurse he kept on round-the-clock watch snored steadily in the chair near Anne's bedside, and—

There it was again! And this time he realized the noise that had awakened him came from down the hall, outside their chambers. Quickly, he hurried toward his outer door and opened it.

"Oh, William, 'tis you! We did so hope not to awaken you." The kindly face of his sister appeared concerned as she peered up at him over the taper she held to light her way. He saw she wore a heavy cloak that appeared to have been donned hastily over her night rail.

"Olivia, what—?"

"'Tis the Tremaine boy, Ben," Olivia told him as she moved toward the stairs. "I'm needed at their cottage."

It was then, as he followed her, that William noticed two figures standing quietly at the base of the stairs. One was his steward, Linton, looking sleepy in nightcap and gown; the other he recognized as the oldest Tremaine boy.

"Ben," said Lord Avery, "what's amiss, lad?"

The boy pulled respectfully at his forelock as he'd been taught, then blurted out, "'Tis Beth, yer lordship. She's wi' child an'—an' she's 'urtin' awful bad. Me—me pa fears she ain't goin' t'—t'—"

"Good heavens!" Avery exclaimed. "Beth . . . *with child*?" He glanced at his sister as they descended the stairs. "Why, she's only a child herself! I had no idea . . ." He fixed his gaze on Ben as they reached the lower hallway. "Why wasn't I informed of this?"

William Avery prided himself on taking a personal interest in all those who fell under his care, from the house servants, to the stable help, to the tenant farmers and their families who lived on his vast estates. This concern went far beyond the sense of duty and responsibility that had been passed down to him by his father, the last marquis. William truly cared about these people who were in his charge. He knew each of them by name, as well as the dates when most of them had been born, or christened; he knew when they were wed, and to whom; and, when their times came, Lord Avery was present at graveside when they were laid to rest. He knew their habits: their fondnesses and dislikes, their joys and disappointments, their hopes and dreams.

So it came as something of a shock to him that lovely little Beth Tremaine—*why, she couldn't be more than sixteen!*—had gotten herself with child and was now in labor. Of course, he reminded himself, he had been rather privately involved of late; Anne had long been an invalid, but in the last half-year or so, her health had taken a turn for the worse. . . .

"Well, lad?" he was saying as he helped Olivia fasten her cloak. "Can you explain why I've only now learned of your sister's condition?" His gaze fell on Olivia's face. "Olivia? Did you know of—"

"Oh, please, yer lordship!" cried Ben as he took a step forward and twisted his sodden cap in his hands. "*No one* knew of—of Beth's . . . shame." He lowered his gaze to the floor and shifted his weight uncomfortably to the other foot as he murmured the last word.

Donald Tremaine had been adamant about keeping Beth's plight as secret as possible. She'd been relegated to doing only indoor chores from the time her pregnancy had begun to show. The entire family, even the little ones, had kept mum about her condition, vowing to protect her from prying eyes and wagging tongues. For Beth, aside from being the eldest, was the only daughter and had functioned as the woman of the house ever since their mother's passing. It was only when her labor had begun to turn difficult that the midwife had been sent for, and of course that had proved futile. . . .

Thoughts of the midwife reminded Ben of his father's curses not a half hour earlier, and he immediately recalled the other who'd been cursed that night: Lord Edmund Avery, his lordship's younger brother—*he'd* brought Beth to this pass! Suddenly all of Donald Tremaine's admonitions over the past weeks and months to keep silent, fell like trees in a storm before the boy's youthful sense of outrage. Overwhelmed by the injustice of it all, Ben blurted out what he could no longer contain:

"'Twas Lord Edmund whut done this to 'er, yer

lordship! 'E *raped* our Beth an' forced 'er t' become 'is—'is—"

"*What say you, lad?*" the marquis questioned anxiously as he leaned forward to peer into Ben's tormented face.

Olivia, too, reacted with shock. "Ben! You do not mean to say—"

A groan escaped Ben's lips as he looked up at the two of them, tears beginning to stream down his freckled face. "I know I shouldn't a said nothin', yer lordship, yer ladyship.... Pa told us nary a word wuz t'—"

"Then it *is* true!" William exclaimed angrily. He looked at his sister. "'Tis my fault. I warned Edmund to keep his hands off the lass when I caught him looking at her in that way of his..." His thoughts turned inward as he murmured, half to himself "...like some terrible predatory beast, eyeing its prey...." He shook his head, then met Olivia's stricken gaze. "But I was so wrapped up in my own problems, I failed to make sure my admonitions were adhered to!"

Suddenly William sprang into action. "Linton, fetch my cloak and have the carriage brought round!"

"It awaits without, m'lord," said the steward as he moved toward the end of the entry hall where a cloak was always kept ready for the master.

"Good, good," murmured William as he turned back toward Olivia. "I'm coming with you. Have you your bag?"

Olivia nodded, moving toward the front door. "'Tis already in the carriage."

Olivia's bag contained a number of medicines and simples, along with a varied assortment of bandages and splints which she had found useful over the years when she'd been called on these errands of mercy to aid the tenants of the estate.

William grabbed the long black cloak Linton brought forward, throwing it over his shoulders as he followed her to the door. Almost as an afterthought, he paused and drew Ben Tremaine along with him. "Come, lad," he murmured, "we're off to see to your Beth."

A short while later, the three arrived at the Tremaine cottage.

Donald pulled respectfully at his forelock after he opened the door. "Yer ladyship, thank God ye've come! I've been—*yer lordship*! I wuzn't expectin'— that is, I—"

"Nothing could have kept me away, Donald," the marquis told him, "not once I'd learned who needed help..." He fixed Tremaine with a serious look. "And why," he added solemnly. His gaze moved toward the cot where Olivia was already bending over Beth's restless form. "How is she?"

"Exhausted, for one thing." Olivia motioned Ben forward and quietly began giving him instructions. "Ben, fetch the kettle. We'll need some hot water..."

As Olivia and Ben worked side by side, the marquis drew Donald to a far corner of the room and spoke to him in lowered tones.

"I'll not mince words about what brought me out here with Lady Olivia tonight, Donald. The lad made it clear enough that my wretched brother Edmund is to blame for Beth's—"

"Ben 'adn't ought t' 'ave told yer lordship naught about it!" Tremaine struggled to keep his voice subdued. "Yer lordship 'as enough t' worry over, whut with 'er ladyship's delicate 'ealth an'—"

"Let me be the judge of what I'm to worry over,

Donald," returned the marquis. "And don't go blaming poor Ben. If you'd seen his face, as I did, when he spoke of his sister's pain—"

A pitiful shriek from the cot across the room drew the attention of both men. There they saw young Ben standing at the head of the cot gripping his sister's hands while, at the opposite end, Olivia worked furiously under a thin blanket which was draped over the girl's raised knees.

"Push, Beth, push!" they heard Olivia exclaim. "That's it, sweetheart. . . . Now, once again . . ."

A second shriek faded to a groan as Olivia's shadowy form moved to block the view. Seeing Tremaine's anxiety-ridden face, William sought to focus his attention elsewhere.

"I also want you to know I believe it was proper for Ben to tell me what he knew," he told his tenant. "As my younger brother's guardian and lord of this estate, I have first responsibility in the matter." Here William paused to lower his voice yet further; his tone bore a quavering note of anguish. "I only regret I didn't involve myself far sooner."

A sudden thrashing about on the cot forestalled Donald's response as both men's glances were again drawn to the tableau across the room. Suddenly the lusty howl of an outraged infant split the musty air in the cottage, and they saw Olivia straighten and move from the foot of the cot.

Raising her voice over the healthy infant bawling, she pronounced, "'Tis a lad . . . a healthy young son, Beth." In the next instant she was handing the child to Ben, who seemed to know what to do as he began to clean and swaddle it, while Olivia turned her attention anxiously back to its mother.

While Olivia worked, the two onlookers crept closer, each of them darting concerned glances back and forth between Ben's careful ministrations and what seemed to be Olivia's increasingly frantic ones.

Within a few minutes the infant's howling diminished and then ceased altogether as the newborn found his tiny fist and began to suck on it, then drifted peacefully off into slumber.

The marquis cleared his throat awkwardly as he and Donald peered down at the contented bundle cradled in Ben's arms. "Aye, Donald, a fine lad, by the looks of him. And lusty with health, too. Look at the size of him!"

Donald forced himself to acknowledge this with a nod, but privately he was far from jubilant. He kept thinking of his poor daughter's shame and of all the pain she'd endured to bring this tiny new human into the world, and not least among his thoughts was the worry over how he was going to do right by the babe, or any of the rest of his children, with no wife to care for them and yet one more mouth to feed.

Just then Olivia approached, a look of concern etched on her kindly features.

"How is she, Livvy?" William inquired softly.

"Resting quietly, and out of pain, thank God," said Olivia, "but as to how she—"

Suddenly a half-choked sob wracked Olivia's slender frame. "Oh, William! 'Tis the bleeding. There's far more than there should be, and, God help me, *I cannot stop it!*"

Both men froze at the ominous revelation, Donald's face going white, while William stared at his sister in a mute appeal.

"Is there—is there nothing to be done?" he managed to whisper at last.

A weary shake of Olivia's head accompanied her broken words. "The babe was overly large, and—

and Beth's such a wee thing...." A pair of tears traced twin paths down her cheeks.

At that moment they heard Ben's voice in a hoarse whisper. "Yer lordship, Beth's askin' fer ye!"

William glanced at Donald, then back at the boy. "You must be mistaken, lad. Surely 'tis your father she's asking for. She—"

"Nay, yer lordship," protested Ben. "She kens ye be 'ere, an' 'tis ye she's askin' fer."

Glancing once more at Donald, William hurriedly moved to the head of the cot. Once there, he was shaken by what he saw. The once inordinately lovely face of Beth Tremaine was barely recognizable. A visage that had always shone with youthful vivacity now appeared pale and lifeless. The fine skin was tautly drawn over her delicate cheekbones, and eyes that had always sparkled happily from their green depths now gazed up at him with a hollow, hopeless look. Her bloodless lips, which had always been rosy ripe and given to ready smiles, parted with what seemed to be great effort as she began to speak.

"Yer...lordship..." A ghost of a smile flickered across her face, reminding William for an instant of the youthful beauty that had once been there. "I...I thank ye fer...fer comin'...'twas kind of ye on such a night, an'—"

"Shh, lass," murmured William. "You must save your strength."

Wearily, Beth shook her head, a few dark, limp curls sticking to her sweat-dampened cheeks as she did so. "Nay..." she whispered. "Too late...fer me ...now..."

William began to protest, but with a surprising burst of strength, the young woman cut him off. Then she went on to tell him the truth of what had happened: how Lord Edmund Avery had waylaid her one night on her way home from helping with the evening milking, and forced her to submit to him, then threatened her with having her family turned out if she told anyone of the deed. In an astonishingly calm voice, she traced the events of the year and a half that followed, describing Lord Edmund's repeated uses of her body, always shrewdly calculated to take place when others were not nearby, of the coldness with which he greeted the news that she was with child, of his retreat to the London town house immediately thereafter. (At last, William knew what was at the bottom of Edmund's sudden absence from the country estate—an absence that had lasted inexplicably for more than six months.)

When at last she had finished her tale, William took one of her hands—*how cold it was!*—and looked into her face with deep compassion. "Beth," he said quietly, "you're telling me all this for a specific reason, aren't you, child?"

Weakly, Beth nodded, then began speaking again, but this time William had to strain to hear; Beth's strength was fading fast, her voice a thin thread of sound that was barely audible. "Th' . . . th' babe . . . I pray ye—*beg* ye—t' care fer it, yer lordship. . . ." She glanced wearily around the shabby cottage. "'Tis . . . 'tis its only 'ope . . ."

Tears were streaming down William's face as he nodded. "I understand, sweetheart, and—" Bending low over her ear, he squeezed her hand and whispered, "I promise."

Suddenly Donald Tremaine was bending over her from the other side of the cot. "Beth! Bethie! Ah, lass, don't leave us!" he sobbed, as William withdrew from her side and embraced the weeping Olivia.

They saw Beth whisper a few inaudible words to her distraught father, saw the pale lips cease moving, then watched in mute pain as Donald Tremaine slumped sobbing over the still figure on the cot.

Moments passed before Olivia moved to comfort the now weeping Ben and William pulled the father away from Beth's body.

"She—she asked m-me t' name 'im Bryce!" sobbed the bereaved older man. "'Twas 'er mother's father's name, an'—an' she loved 'er grandpa so when—when she wuz a wee lass!"

Lord Avery nodded, dry-eyed and in control now. "Bryce it shall be. I shall speak to the vicar tomorrow, and—"

Suddenly, a look of resolution crossed William's face. "No, not the vicar. 'Tis the bishop I'll summon for the baptism."

"The bishop!" murmured Olivia, surprised.

"Aye," asserted her brother, "the bishop. For hasn't it always been the bishop who's named an Avery in the eyes of God and the faithful?"

He went on, to tell them of the momentous decision he'd reached as Beth's dying words echoed in his mind. With Donald's permission, he vowed to take Beth's son, his blood nephew, and raise him as his own, with the full privileges of an adopted son. And since his invalid wife had borne him no children, nor could she be expected to in the future, if the lad turned out well—and why should he not?— he fully anticipated making Bryce Tremaine Avery his legal heir!

Soft cries of wonder and astonishment greeted his announcement. The older Tremaine was more than happy to be relieved of his private worry over having one more mouth to feed, and young Ben was overjoyed, welcoming the news without a trace of envy.

Beth had been dearest to him of all his siblings, and the knowledge that her last wishes were to be carried out so grandly filled him with a sense of rightness.

Only Olivia failed to be awestruck by her brother's words. Turning to him with a tearful smile on her face, she said, "Your goodness has always been apparent, William. You are as kind as our brother is cruel. God bless you for it."

But only to herself she added, *And God protect us all from the cruelty of his wrath when Edmund learns he's no longer the heir—and why!*

CHAPTER 1

Fredericksburg, Virginia, 1773

BRITTANY CHAMBERS BIT HER LOWER LIP IN an unconscious gesture of dismay as she looked out her window at the lane below.

There goes another one, she thought. *Drat, he's been at it again!* The lip-biting gave way to an outward thrusting of her delicately pointed chin as dismay became disgust.

The objects of her silently hurled thoughts were walking side by side, heading, she knew, for the Horse's Head Inn down the lane. The tall, portly man on the right was Timothy Chambers, her father, a wealthy merchant and owner of the Horse's Head; on his left stalked a periwigged scarecrow she knew was yet another would-be suitor, come to gain permission to call on her—the nineteenth this year—and it was only June!

Tossing her coppery mane defiantly, she whirled from the window and began to pace a familiar path between the cherrywood Queen Anne tester bed at one end of the chamber and the bonnet-topped, curly maple highboy at the other. Arms folded across her high, young bosom, a mutinous set to her jaw, Brittany began to murmur aloud.

"Will it never end? This constant endeavor to see me wed? Will Father never give it up? And I always thought he was such a bright fellow!"

Her pacing halted for a moment as she considered what she'd just voiced aloud. No, that was not entirely fair. She knew, if she were honest with herself, that Timothy Chambers was operating with only the best intentions toward her, his firstborn child. He truly sought Brittany's welfare. It was just that his notions about what constituted that welfare were so different from her own! And it was not that her father was lacking in intelligence; it was merely that he was also *not* lacking in stubbornness! Or perseverance! Nineteen! Lud, 'twas a wonder that he continued to come by any eligible men, considering the dozens she'd managed to disperse in the five years since she'd turned sixteen, the age at which her stepmother had first deemed it appropriate for her to seek wedlock!

A chuckle escaped Brittany's beautifully shaped lips and her iris blue eyes twinkled mischievously as she reflected on the route she'd taken to "disperse" all those suitors.

"Look at me, now! I'm Brittany Chambers," she chortled into the Chippendale looking glass on a nearby wall. "Behold, the fiercest virago that ever wore skirts. 'The Virgin Shrew' they call me roundabouts, so fierce of temper, no man would wed me!" She made a furious face into the glass, baring her small, perfect white teeth as she let out a hiss.

But the hiss quickly faded and bubbled into a peal of lilting laughter as Brittany pirouetted gracefully.

And had any of those who called her "shrew" taken the trouble to look closely, even when she was at her screeching worst, they'd have caught the hint of laughter residing in her lovely slanting eyes. For Brittany was not at all the termagant she appeared to be.

Highly intelligent, with a strong streak of independence, she had adopted the cloak of a shrew (and not without a good measure of humor at the expense of those she'd been able to dupe by it) in order to achieve a modicum of freedom.

Well aware that most women in her society were allowed little or no self-rule, that they passed from the control of fathers to husbands without any interval of independence, Brittany had resolved not to succumb to such inferior status, not under parental rule and not in the marriage bed!

In the case of the former, she had succeeded in carving out an endurable, if not happy, existence: try as he might, her father was too weak to stand up to her contrived fits of temper (being by nature a peace-loving man), and the rich inheritance she'd recently come into through her late mother's will gave Brittany an independent financial status. In the case of the latter, she had long ago determined not to wed (and see her financial source of independence pass— by law—to her husband) unless, by some rare stroke of luck, she could find someone who would allow her to manage her own money—and life—without laying claim to them.

Brittany's lighthearted pirouette diminished to a small, graceful skip as thoughts of her immediate problem intruded. The "scarecrow" would have to be dealt with—and soon! As she recalled the skinny, stoop-shouldered appearance of the man, her eyes narrowed in calculated contempt. This one had to be Althea's doing!

"At least Father's choices have all been pleasing to look upon," she mused aloud. "But then there was that well-larded colonel from New York last Whitsuntide who turned out to be a cousin of Althea's father . . . and let me not forget the prune-faced dotard my *dear* stepmother met at the St. Cecilia's Day musicale and invited to dinner!"

Her pacing resumed as she contemplated the woman Timothy had married two years after his first wife's death, when Brittany was only four. Althea Chambers was the one person in Brittany's life who could erase the hint of laughter in her eyes. A cold woman, except where her daughter, Melody, Brittany's half sister, was concerned, Althea put most of her energy toward using her husband's hard-earned wealth to achieve a higher social status than the one she'd been born to.

A modest miller's daughter, she'd seen her opportunity on the day the wealthy merchant had come to settle some accounts with her father, and had pursued Timothy with all the tenacity of a hound on the scent of a hare.

Not an unattractive woman—at least, when she smiled, though this was none too often—she had found the lonely widower an easy conquest. Even Brittany had been taken in at first by her repeated assurances that she would be a good mother to his four-year-old child. And if in the months that followed the wedding, Althea had not been the affectionate parent her prenuptial overtures had promised, no one but Brittany seemed to notice. Timothy, always deeply involved in his business ventures, had been too preoccupied to see more than the surface things. In their house, with its staff of

servants, things ran smoothly; his daughter went
about in clean frocks and with neatly braided hair;
meals were well cooked and served on time. As for
Brittany, she learned to hide her disappointment, as
she had her slow-to-heal grief over her mother's
death, and forced herself to be content with the love
and affection of the one parent who did care—when
he had the time to show it.

But then, a year after the wedding, Melody had
arrived. Sweet, golden-haired Melody, an angelic gift
from heaven who had no equal in Althea's eyes.
From the time of her own child's arrival, Althea had
ceased to have any use for Brittany at all.

Fortunately, Brittany mused, Melody was truly a
dear. And a good thing it was, too, that she loved
her younger sister for the sweet thing she was. For if
Melody had not been such a lovable child, it might
have been easy to grow to hate and resent her for the
favoritism Althea showed—not to mention the com-
parisons her stepmother constantly made between
them, in which Brittany somehow always came up
short.

A frown puckered Brittany's smooth brow as she
contemplated Melody's situation in the light of the
present status of things. Melody had turned fifteen
in May of last year, a few weeks before Brittany's
own twentieth birthday. Almost immediately, Althea
had initiated a campaign to see her daughter formally introduced to society, an introduction that had
but one aim: to secure for Melody an "advanta-
geous" marriage.

But it was here that Timothy had finally delved
beneath the surface of things as they applied to the
family's welfare. He had at last put his foot down
where Althea's wishes were concerned, saying he
would not allow his younger child to wed until her

older sister had been "happily walked down the aisle."

Oh, and the fierce emotional outbursts *that* had caused! Althea had wept and pleaded with him for hours, saying it was unfair—that poor Melody would go to her grave an aged spinster if she had to await Brittany's nuptials, for what man would have the redheaded shrew?

Timothy, well aware of the hellish temperament his older child had developed (although obtusely unaware of its cause), had countered that the very circumstances Althea cited made it all the more imperative for the family to unite in its efforts to find Brittany a husband first—indeed, they must regard it as their chief priority!

Failing to breach Timothy's stubborn insistence (and, Lord, he could be stubborn!), Althea had icily retreated to her chamber and remained there, "indisposed," for days afterward.

Melody, too, had succumbed to a flood of emotion, a rare thing for someone normally so docile. Wailing that she would "dry up on the shelf," she had followed her mother's example and retired to her chamber, refusing even to eat for two whole days, and when hunger at last forced her to emerge, she had moped about for weeks afterward, a martyred look on her pretty but wan-looking face.

And Brittany's reaction had been nothing short of turbulent. Rising from her place at the dining table after Timothy had made his startling announcement, she had stormed about the room in such an agitated fashion, the servants had run for cover, Preston, the butler, predicting to Mistress Henley, the housekeeper, that they'd be in need of yet another new set of china before the day was out.

"I tell you, I have no need to wed!" Brittany had

shouted. "I'll soon come into my portion from Mama and can handsomely support myself—*for life!*"

"But, Daughter, there are other needs a woman has that propel her t' marry!" Timothy had countered. "What of children? What of love and companionship?"

"What of them?" Brittany had raged. "There are women aplenty who have lived quite contented lives, though childless. And as for the rest, I have you to love me, have I not? And scores of companions, should I require their company. There's Mary Ambleton, who never tires of joining me for a brisk ride; there are Elizabeth Trevor and the Lee girls, not to mention several others of my former classmates at Mistress Sharpe's School for Young—"

"Young females, all of them, and soon t' be wed themselves!" Timothy's voice had begun to rise in volume to match her own. "Do ye imagine they will continue to seek out yer company when ye're the only spinster among them? Good heavens, lass, use the good sense ye were born with! Think of the long stretch of years to come, when all those ye've mentioned are gone, in one way or another. Who, then, will keep ye from the creepin' loneliness of old age?"

Brittany's lower lip had thrust forward petulantly. "Better the loneliness than the loss of one's freedom," she said at last.

"Freedom! Now I've heard it all," Timothy had responded, "but I shan't hear any more. No, Daughter," he'd added, reaching for his clay pipe on the pipe rack and heading for the door. "My mind's made up. I'll not rest easy until ye're married, so marry ye shall, and there's an end t' it."

He'd made his way from the room then, refusing to discuss the matter further, and in the weeks and months that followed, he had been true to his word, parading a seemingly endless stream of young "eligibles" before her unwilling presence.

Thus far, Brittany, had succeeded in thwarting him, scattering them all with her well-rehearsed viper's temper and biting tongue—and she'd had a grand time doing it, if she did say so herself!

Again, her thoughts returned to "Sir Scarecrow," as she'd already dubbed the latest. Aye, Althea's doing, for sure.

At that moment there was a knocking at the bedchamber door. A nasal, high-pitched voice followed: "Brittany, your father wishes to see you in his office at the inn."

"Speak of the devil!" Brittany muttered to herself as she recognized Althea's none too dulcet tones. "Very well, madam," she called, "I'll attend him at once."

"Mind you, take your abigail with you," Althea told her. "There may be no more excursions about the town unattended. Last Tuesday's episode was quite enough!"

Brittany stifled a chuckle as she recalled the "episode" in question. For her twenty-first birthday, Timothy (likely at Althea's instigation) had gifted her with her own personal maid. Her name was Tansy, and she was a young black woman of about Brittany's age: a slave.

Brittany had been outraged. "Our family's never owned slaves," she'd asserted. "So, what in heaven's name has possessed you to take up such an abusive practice now? And to present her to *me*, of all people! You know my views on the sacredness of personal liberty!"

"But, Brittany, dear," her father had protested, "Old Nancy's been gettin' on in years—too old t' squire ye about—and this poor girl just lost her mis-

tress t' the dropsy. She'd have been sold downriver t'
heaven knows what kind of a fate, had we not
bought her. And you must not go about unattended,
my dear. We thought ye 'd be pleased."

A sly look had briefly flitted across Brittany's face
as she'd given her reply. "Very well then, Father, if
you truly wish to please me, I'll accept . . . on one
condition."

"Eh? What's that?"

"I'll accept the girl as my companion-abigail—just
as soon as you free her and hand me her freedman's
papers."

"*Free her!*" Althea had gasped. "Why—why 'tis
outrageous . . . unheard of . . . and—and expensive!
Wastefully expensive!"

"Nevertheless, those are my terms," Brittany had
declared.

Recognizing the deviltry in her eyes, Timothy had
hedged. "Well . . . I don't know . . . I'll need some
time t' think on 't. . . ."

"Very well, Father," his daughter had replied, "I
shall go out back to meet the woman while you
begin to do your thinking. . . . But, pray, do not tarry
too long. Until she is a free woman, I shall refuse to
have her attend me . . . and, of course, you know
how I love to go out and take the air."

Brittany had gone out into the yard to meet the
young woman then, and she'd been delighted to
find Tansy to be bright, fairly articulate, and person-
able—and about her own age! But as the two young
women became acquainted, the hours had ticked by
without any response from Timothy.

It was then that Brittany put her "reserve plan"
into action. Instructing Tansy to remain in her
chamber and familiarize herself with Brittany's

"things," she'd donned a walking dress and surreptitiously let herself out of the house—alone.

Five hours later, when she returned home from her "stroll," word of her "outrageous" behavior had preceded her and Timothy and Althea were waiting.

"The whole of Fredericksburg's abuzz over your being seen indecently about, unescorted!" Althea had fumed. "Timothy, tell her."

"Indeed?" Brittany had queried. "Tell me what, Father?"

Timothy had long been in the habit of making a swift escape when he saw the current look in his older daughter's eyes, but this time, he knew he was trapped. "Er . . . I . . . shall go t' my solicitor's office in the mornin', Brittany. I don't expect it will take him too long t' draw up the freedman's papers."

Althea had been outraged, but it had done her no good, for Timothy had at last made his devoutly desired escape, and the matter was settled.

Brittany's thoughts tumbled back to the present. Because of a legal entanglement, the papers were taking a bit longer than anticipated to be finalized. She hadn't yet told Tansy about what was happening and had enjoined the others to keep silent as well. She wanted to surprise Tansy with her freedom when it was an accomplished fact.

"Please send Tansy to me," she said through the closed door. (It was a familiar means by which she and her stepmother communicated these days; neither had any wish to look upon the other any more than was absolutely necessary.)

As the older woman's footsteps receded down the hall, Brittany smiled and reached for her bonnet. "Now we'll see about father and his scarecrow," she muttered challengingly.

CHAPTER 2

CAPTAIN BRYCE TREMAINE GAZED AT THE sleek lines of his schooner, the *Lady Beth*, as she lay at anchor in the clear waters of the Rappahannock. Beside him on the dock, first mate Will Thatcher read his thoughts.

"Aye, she be a grand un, Cap'n—a real lady. Carried us safely all the way from the London 'Ole wi' nary a mis'ap, she did, and them two gales we 'it wuz wicked!"

Bryce turned and grinned up at the weather-beaten face of the man who was not only a trusted ship's officer, but also his closest friend. Heavily muscled and swarthy, with a cleanly shaven head, Will sported a gold hoop in one ear and towered over the younger man, who was himself a couple of inches past six feet.

"Now, what would a crusty old salt like you know about a 'real lady'?" Bryce taunted good-naturedly. "I'm not sure you've ever even met one."

Will's scowl said he was deeply affronted. "'Ere, now, and didn't I 'ave the honor 'o bein' intr'duced t'

yer own dear aunt, the Lady Olivia 'erself? *O' course*
I've met a real lady!" He stooped and easily hoisted,
then shouldered, the heavy oak sea chest they'd
share while off the ship. "And there be no denyin' a
ship kin be a lady, too," he added as both men
started for a cobbled thoroughfare neatly posted as
William Street.

"Oh, I've sailed aboard enough 'ores in me time t'
ken the difference," Will continued, trying, but not
quite succeeding at lowering his big, hoarse voice as
he used the indelicate metaphor. "Take the *Molly B.*,
fer instance, the bilge bucket wot I first sailed on as a
cabin boy. Why, that—ahh," he grinned, "but that
be another tale . . ."

Both men turned right onto William Street.

"Anyways, as I wuz sayin'," Will continued, "the
Lady Beth's a true lady, deep down, under the skin—
just like yer poor dead mum wot ye named 'er
arfter."

At the mention of this, Bryce's eyes, which had
been a clear and untroubled green while they were
talking, took on a darker hue that hinted at some
half-buried pain; they focused on Will with a sudden
intensity.

"Take care, my friend," he murmured softly,
glancing briefly about them. "I would remind you to
guard your tongue." But the crowds in the thoroughfare—which was packed with everything from
sailors in striped jerseys, to busily scurrying, worka-
day pedestrians, to mounted men, obviously gentry
—seemed oblivious to the conversation of the two
tall men as they made their way to the next corner.

"I'd not have this mission jeopardized by a carelessly dropped word or name, Will," Bryce told him.

Will nodded. "Ye kin trust me, Cap'n," he added

soberly. "I ken the importance o' secrecy in the mission."

Bryce felt the chill of purposeful determination settle over him, much as it had the day he'd learned Edmund Avery was still alive and not lost at sea, as William and Olivia had given out to all who knew them. For years, both as a young boy and as a man fully grown, he'd endured the nightmares—the vivid images in which his mother lay dying before him and begged him to avenge her, only to be replaced by a ghostly Edmund Avery who mocked him from a watery grave, triumphant in the knowledge that the sea had robbed Bryce of the chance to honor Beth's dying plea. But Avery was not dead. Now the years of nightmares would soon be over. . . .

"'Ere be Caroline Street," Will was saying as they approached the next corner. "The Risin' Sun Tavern be but a short ways t' the right, accordin' t' Abner." Suddenly Will looked uncertain as he considered Abner Morton, their boatswain and a lifelong resident of Fredericksburg before he'd taken to the sea, who'd provided them with a few suggestions for lodgings before they left the ship.

"Aye," grinned Bryce, "and the Rising Sun was the first choice on his list. Are you game to try it?" An arched eyebrow underscored the amusement that accompanied Bryce's question.

Will paused, then cleared his throat noisily. "Ah, suppose we 'ead fer 'is *last choice* . . . the 'Orse's 'Ead, wuz it?"

Chuckling, Bryce nodded. "The Horse's Head it is, then. It should be up ahead, on William, if I recall the directions."

Will mumbled a few choice epithets to himself as they crossed Caroline Street. For all his good nature, Abner Morton was a man noted for his poor taste when it came to the important things in life, as Will saw it. With uncanny consistency, Abner drank the weakest ales, ate the most atrocious combinations of foods, paired off with the ugliest women. And then there were his careless personal habits. Why, one day the captain had been forced to order him doused with seawater to assuage the stench that . . . *arghh*, Will thought, thank God the captain had reminded him!

Suddenly a commotion a slight distance ahead of them interrupted Will's thoughts. A dozen or so people had gathered in front of a handsome brick building that faced the street. Hanging above the building's main entrance, at a right angle to the street, a red and blue sign bearing the outline of an equine profile and proclaimed: The Horse's Head Inn.

The two men glanced at each other, then increased their pace in the direction of the inn. Other passersby joined them, drawn by the growing crowd.

Perhaps it was because of Thatcher's huge size, or the subtly communicated but unmistakable look of command in the green eyes of his companion, but for whatever reason, the crowd parted for them as they reached its edges, and they soon had a front row view of what was going on.

A tall, portly man sporting a white, well powdered periwig came rushing through the large doorway. From the cut of his clothes, he appeared well groomed and prosperous, but the periwig tipped incongruously to one side of his head as he attempted to cover his ears and duck behind a short railing near the entranceway.

A shrill screech from the confines of the building accompanied the man's movements, followed by an airborne missile that just missed the periwig and proved to be a tankard of ale which was far from empty. Its contents sloshed over the bricks of the narrow walkway abutting the street, liberally dousing the shoes of a pair of unfortunate onlookers who happened to be in the way.

"I'll not wed him—I'll not!" a furious female voice asserted from somewhere just inside the darkened doorway. "I'd sooner see myself *dead* than tied to that wretched scarecrow! 'Tis an insult, d' ye hear?"

The outraged soprano carried easily into the street where the portly man groaned and shook his head, further disarranging the periwig. Several of the bypassers began to laugh, even as others gathered to enjoy the spectacle.

"Brittany, my pet," the besieged man implored from his half-crouching position, "I beg ye, please reconsider. The man's rich as Croesus! What matter if he be a bit lean in the shank? He—"

Another shriek, and then a second projectile, this time a pewter porringer, found its way out the door. Several onlookers ran for cover.

Standing somewhat to the left of the doorway and therefore in a more fortunate spot—at least for the moment—Bryce and Will looked at each other. Will's face held a bemused look of inquiry; Bryce shrugged.

As both turned their attentions back to the doorway, they saw a movement within the shadows there, and then a flash of color. At last a figure appeared.

She was medium-tall, lithe and willowy, with coppery red hair that seemed to fight the restraints of the narrow indigo ribbon tied at the nape of her neck. A face that at first glance might have been said to belong to an angel was saved from that assessment by a pair of flashing iris blue eyes. They dominated the perfect oval of her face, playing imperfect counterpoint to the high, delicate cheekbones, a finely chiseled, straight nose that was neither too long nor too short, and a beautifully proportioned mouth whose lush, exquisitely curving lips were currently drawn in a straight, angry line. And everything about her echoed this straight, angry line. Her lovely, well-proportioned limbs, evident even beneath the indigo and mauve striped walking dress she wore, were also straight... and angry. The slender, graceful neck that rose above her snowy cotton fichu appeared rigidly straight... and angry. Indeed, the best that might be said about her stance as she stood there glaring at the hapless man in the crooked periwig was that it was uncommonly straight... and angry.

There was an unnatural silence in the street as she continued to stand in the doorway in wordless fury. Then someone in the crowd to the rear of Bryce and Will gave an embarrassed cough. This seemed to free the young woman's movements and she took a couple of steps forward. Several in the crowd backed quickly away, but she only paused, then glanced over her shoulder.

Moving quietly into sight behind her was another young woman. She wore a gray servant's dress with an immaculate, starched white mobcap over her downy black curls; her skin was the color of creamy chocolate.

A slave, Will thought disgustedly, even as he fought the enraptured sigh that rose to his throat at the sight of the beautiful black woman. But he noted with approval the proud bearing and the disdainful expression on the African's face. It totally matched in hauteur and dignity the mood of her astonishing mistress, although this one said not a word.

"Come, Tansy," the redheaded virago was saying. She paused to bestow a final glare of indignation on

the gentleman who'd been on the receiving end of
her tirade, then sailed off in the direction of some
stately homes further down William Street. Following in the wake of her billowing skirts and petticoats,
the black woman named Tansy made an equally
graceful, equally haughty, exit.

Following their departure, and only once the
women were well out of earshot, the people in the
crowd began to depart, their movements punctuated
by guffaws, chuckles and outright laughter.

One man clapped the periwigged gentleman on
the shoulder, saying, "Sharper than a serpent's
tooth, eh, Timothy?"

Another elbowed his neighbor. "Best show in
town, the Chambers hellion!"

A third was not as kind. "Come, come,
Chambers," he chortled, "'tis time t' give 'er the
back o' yer 'and! If 'twas me own whelp, she'd'a
been set arights with a birch rod long ago!"

The laughter continued for a few more moments,
then died as the crowd began to disperse. Timothy
was led back inside the inn by a sympathetic looking
man in a bottle green waistcoat.

Will turned toward Bryce only to find him staring
silently in the direction in which the two women had
gone. "Er . . . Cap'n?" he questioned.

Bryce was shaking his head now, slowly, as if in
rapt appreciation. "Magnificent," he murmured
softly.

"*Magnificent?*" queried a startled, somber-clothed
man who happened to overhear him.

Will turned and nodded at the man, for he'd been
about to voice the same question.

Bryce's eyes glowed with a green light. "I've never
seen such spirit in a woman," he told Will, ". . . or
such *beauty!*"

The somber-suited man was indignant. "Aye, she's a beauty, all right. I'll give her that. But magnificent? Spirited, you say? Only as the devil's own mistress is spirited, sir!"

At last deigning to pay attention to their unknown companion, Bryce faced him. "Who is she?"

"Why, 'tis Brittany Chambers, daughter of poor Timothy Chambers, owner of the Horse's Head, here." He directed his thumb behind him, at the solid, expensive looking brick structure. "Everyone for miles about knows who *she* is! 'The Flaming Hellion,' they call her, and worse!" He paused and seemed, for the first time, to take in the seafarer's garb of the two men. "You're obviously new to these parts or you wouldn't be asking such a question."

"Aye, my ship made port only a couple of hours ago," Bryce answered. "But, tell me, sir, since details about this Chambers woman seem to be common knowledge, what is it that causes these outbursts of, ah, temperament?"

The gentleman chuckled. "Why, anything that fails to suit her fancy, I'd wager!" Then, seeing that this was not specific enough to satisfy his interrogator, he sobered, adding, "But, truth to tell, sir, Mistress Brittany Chambers and her temper are notorious in Fredericksburg. She has been sought after by most of the eligible men in the area for some time. After all, she is a beauty, and rumored to be an heiress with a handsome dowry—left to her by her late mother, I believe.

"But, sir, she has scorned them all, these would-be suitors, claiming none is man enough to suit her, to the everlasting chagrin of her poor, long-suffering father."

"That'd be the man we jest saw addressin' 'er, then," Will put in.

"Aye," nodded the man enthusiastically, warming to his subject. "And a shame it is, too, for the merchant, who is far from penniless himself, being successful in a half dozen or so endeavors, you see... ah, well, I forget myself.... As I was saying, Timothy Chambers is indeed unfortunate, for he has another daughter, though no sons, and this younger lass is a lovely, soft-spoken, and properly obedient child whom many would gladly wed. But, alas, Timothy has sworn to see the elder girl wed first!" Another chuckle. "I cannot fault him for his reasoning, however. A man wishes to see all of his female offspring taken off his hands, and who would choose the shrew when the lamb was readily up for the taking?"

Will murmured his concurrence while Bryce stood with slightly raised eyebrows and digested this. Then, after thanking the somber-coated gentleman, Bryce motioned for Will to join him in entering the inn.

"Wot a tale!" Will murmured wonderingly as they entered the massive common room. "D' ye still think 'er magnificent, me friend? Arfter all, a shrew's a shrew!"

"Aye, Will," Bryce nodded, then lowered his voice as he spotted their host, Chambers, over in one corner, "but one might take some advice from Shakespeare's Petruchio."

"Eh? Wot's that?" queried Will, as he followed Bryce to a free table near the one where Chambers was conversing animatedly with the man in the bottle green waistcoat.

Bryce kept his voice soft as he neared the table, but there was a devilish gleam in his green eyes. "Shrews, my good Will, can be tamed."

CHAPTER 3

ANNIE BUTLER HAD WORKED AS A BAR-
maid at the Horse's Head for several months and
was quite content with her position. Master Timothy
was a fair employer who paid the staff's wages on
time and never stinted on the amount of well-pre-
pared food he allowed his employees; and where she
was concerned, he managed to close an eye to any
"side" business she was able to negotiate with the
male customers—as long as she was discreet, kept it
to the confines of her own chamber, after hours, and
didn't let it interfere with her regular duties.

It was this side business she definitely had in mind
now as she eyed the two tall men who had just
seated themselves at the trestle table near the hearth.
Her experienced eye told her they were seafaring
men, probably a sea captain and his mate, newly arrived in port after a long voyage, judging by the
length of the younger one's hair; it had an unton-
sured look about it, as if it had been weeks since
he'd seen a barber.

Not that this detracted from his stunning looks,

she thought to herself with a lusty shiver. *Gor, but I'll wager 'e's a reg'lar ruttin' bull betwixt th' sheets!* she thought to herself as the other man, the one with the shaved head, motioned to her for table service.

Annie straightened the mobcap above her yellow curls and glanced quickly downward to make sure her ample breasts were well displayed; they swelled above her stays in the low-cut dress which practically demanded its wearer don a fichu, but which she deliberately wore without that primly concealing triangular scarf. Annie smiled. She could actually feel her nipples hardening as she continued to stare at the raven-haired young sea captain with the wickedly green eyes.

As she approached the trestle table she saw him grin at his mate, revealing a pair of deeply slashed male dimples that were deliciously at odds, somehow, with the high cheekbones and harsher planes of his chiseled face; a flash of even, white teeth in his tanned face completed the picture of male beauty that looked too good to be true. Annie felt her knees go weak.

"Two tankards o' yer finest draught, lass," the swarthy complected giant said.

Annie found it difficult, but she tore her gaze away from his companion long enough to answer. "Aye, sir," she said in her most sultry voice. Her brown eyes flew immediately back to the incredible piece of masculinity next to him, but mirrored instant disappointment when the captain failed to give her a glance.

"Er . . . ah, very good, sirs," she stammered, "ah, will—will that be all, sirs?" Her gaze continued to spear the raven-haired wonder.

"Lodgings fer the night as well, lass," said the giant, "but I expect we'll be seein' yer employer about those." He nodded at the pair earnestly conversing nearby. "That be 'im wi' the bloke in the green waistcoat, right?"

"Aye, sir," Annie mumbled, wondering what was wrong with her heretofore man-attracting voice. The captain still hadn't focused on her. He seemed more preoccupied with her employer and his friend, Thad Newton, at the next table. How was she to ply her wiles on him when he appeared not to notice whether she lived or breathed?

Sighing with disappointment, Annie bobbed a curtsy and went for the ale.

Will watched the sway of skirts about her ample hips appreciatively, then chuckled. "The wench 'as eyes fer ye, lad," he said to Bryce. "O' course, I ken 'tis nothin' new t' ye, Cap'n, but I, fer one, 'ave been far too long wi'out a woman, and—"

"Shh..." whispered Bryce, motioning him to be still. With a brief inclination of his head he drew Will's attention to the conversation at the next table.

"Alas, a full cargo awaitin' transportation downriver, and my captain abed with the ague!" Timothy Chambers was saying. "And the man was t' transport Brittany along with it, for her aunt's plantation neighbors Avery's. Now how am I t' find someone trustworthy and capable enough t' accomplish this?"

Bryce froze. *He'd been right!* It *had* been the name Avery he'd overheard a moment ago! Avery... it had to be *Edmund* Avery whom Chambers referred to— his blackguard sire—and his *prey!* Listening patiently with what looked to Will like the coiled tension of a leopard about to spring, Bryce waited for Chambers to continue.

"I tell ye, Thad," said Timothy, "'tis the lass that concerns me. She's drivin' me t' Bedlam! Even the cargo's importance pales in significance. I must find a way t' get her t' Amelia's home. 'Tis the only chance she has of findin' a husband. 'Tis certain there's none left hereabouts 'twould offer for her, with the reputation she's made for herself!"

"But, Timothy," Thad countered, "what makes you think she'll fare any better downriver?"

Chambers sighed. "'Tis my one hope, old friend. My sister's overly fond of the lass and has always had a calmin' way with her. She's her godmother, ye know, and I've written her and received a reply that she's willin' and hopeful she can manage the business of managin' Brittany. God knows that's more than I've been able t' do!"

Suddenly Timothy slammed his tankard of ale on the table.

Annie, who'd returned with the ales Will had ordered, jumped as she set them down in front of Will and Bryce, forgetting her plan of bending low in front of the captain to try to entice him with her cleavage. She gave her employer a nervous glance and skittered away.

"Damnit, Thad!" Timothy swore. "I declare, I'd give the proceeds from half my cargo on the *Louise* t' someone who'd be willin' and able t' take it t' Edmund Avery's plantation and escort my daughter t' her aunt's in the bargain! 'Tis that desperate I am!"

Bryce glanced at Will, fighting to control his excitement. His look said he could not believe his luck! It *was* Edmund Avery! Not only had Chambers saved him from days, perhaps weeks, of searching for his prey, he'd practically served Avery up on a silver salver. At the least, he'd presented Bryce with a ploy for getting close enough to work his revenge on the man he'd sworn to kill.

With a brief nod at Will, Bryce rose to his feet.

"Excuse me, gentlemen," he said as he approached the other table, "but I fear I couldn't help overhearing your conversation. Allow me to introduce myself . . ."

A half hour later Bryce and Will were accompanying Timothy Chambers to his ship. The *Louise* was a sloop whose shallow bottom allowed her to sail inland by way of the various rivers that fed into the Chesapeake Bay from Virginia: the Potomac, the Rappahannock, the York, and the James. With an interest born of his experience at sea, Bryce noted her gleaming hull and pristine, well-maintained decks, and his opinion of Timothy Chambers rose several notches. In the world of business and trade Chambers was obviously successful—well in control of the different enterprises that comprised his mercantile pursuits; it was unfortunate that he couldn't claim as great a proficiency when it came to managing his domestic affairs.

Ah, well, thought Bryce with a sudden gleam lighting the green of his eyes, *perhaps I may prove to be of some help to him in that arena*. All at once he found himself savoring the image of a headful of tossing red curls, before a comment from Chambers brought him back to the matter at hand.

"Matt Durham's been takin' her back and forth betwixt here and the eastern shore for me for three years," Timothy was saying as they approached the dock where the medium-sized sloop rested in the early summer sunshine. "In all that time I've never known the man t' complain of as much as a headache, but when they put into port two days ago, 'twas his first mate at the helm. Poor Matt's been abed in his home on Charles Street ever since. 'Tis the ague, his physician says, and so far, though he's

bled him and physicked him, nothin' seems t' have
helped. I paid him a visit yestere'en, and the poor
fellow looks worse than when he arrived."

Small wonder, thought Bryce as he and Will followed Chambers across the gangplank and onto the
Louise's deck. In his time, he'd seen enough of the
kinds of damage physicians could do with their so-
called curatives. Bleeding patients with their instru-
ments or attaching scores of those disgusting leeches
were only small examples of the senseless butchery
he'd seen perpetrated by these fools who called
themselves men of science. Why, he'd seen better
medicine practiced by witch doctors on some of the
islands he and Will had visited on previous sailings.

". . . so glad ye happened t' come along,"
Chambers was telling him. "And ye're sure yer own
ship won't suffer from layin' idle whilst ye're about
my business?"

Bryce thought of the several tons of cargo, largely
textiles and some fine Ceylonese tea, that were at
this moment being transferred into the hands of a
factor he'd contacted months ago through the marquis's solicitors in London. Of course, neither he nor
the marquis expected to make a profit on these
goods, the tea especially. It had belonged to the East
India Company, which numbered not a few of Lord
William's friends among its members. Prior to Parliament's lightening of the duty on tea imported into
the British Isles, it had been among the seven-years
supply sitting in warehouses on the Thames. But
now that Parliament had permitted tea to be shipped
at full duty to the American colonies, he'd been able
to do his adopted father's friends a favor by taking
some of it off their hands for this enterprise, and
provide himself with a cover for the trip in the bargain. And as for his crew, they were an able lot,

handpicked by Will and himself, and he had no doubts that the operation would go smoothly. Moreover, if it did not, if some minor details were overlooked here or there, what did it matter? The commercial aspects of this voyage were merely a subterfuge, after all; his true business was about to begin now—on the *Louise!*

"I'm sure, sir," Bryce said to Timothy as they headed for the quarterdeck. "My men have their immediate orders, and what orders remain to be issued as a result of this, ah, change in plans can be taken care of tonight and tomorrow. You're certain you don't wish us to cast off until Wednesday's early tide?"

The time he referred to was two days hence, and for Bryce's money, it was two days later than he preferred to be sailing. He'd waited months for the moment when his revenge would be at hand, and at this point each additional delay began to seem like an unendurable obstacle. Reminding himself that it wouldn't do to display any unseemly eagerness concerning what was to appear a routine business venture, he checked the impatience in his voice, adding, "I mean, sir, given what my mate and I, ah, witnessed earlier, are you sure you wish to wait that long to have your daughter safely under way?"

"Ha!" exclaimed Timothy. "If I had my way, sir, this ship would have sailed yesterday!" Suddenly the older man looked sheepish. "But, truth t' tell, Tremaine, I'm afraid I haven't yet, ah, discussed the trip with Brittany."

Bryce quirked an eyebrow as he digested this bit of news. "Oh?" he questioned, meeting the merchant's uneasy look. He knew something of the time women usually required to prepare for a trip, even a brief one. Lady Olivia had figured prominently in his life as he was growing up, and even that gentle lady, who'd never been given to putting more demands on a situation than the occasion warranted, frequently took days to plan and pack for a journey of any appreciable distance. And if Olivia needed considerable advance warning, he could only imagine the time Chambers's volatile redhead would require —or the sparks that might fly when she wasn't given enough of it!

"Now, I know what ye must be thinkin', sir," said Timothy, reading the look in his eyes. "I mean, I'm aware that ye witnessed that little scene at the door of the Horse's Head earlier, and I tell ye, sir, I can only count myself fortunate that ye were not put off by what it taught ye of my daughter's, er, temperament."

The merchant's look became more thoughtful. "But ye see, Captain Tremaine, Brittany—ah, how shall I put it? Ye see, my daughter's not always that way . . . not always such a—a firebrand, I mean.

"'Tis only this courtin' and marryin' business that seems t' have the lass so upset." A wistful look entered Timothy's hazel eyes. "Why, I remember times in the past when months would go by, and the most explosive sounds she'd utter would be lovely bursts of laughter at things she found t' amuse her from time t' time. Ah, 'tis a sweet child she was when she was a wee thing—in the early years, when my Louise was alive . . ." Timothy's words trailed off, and he was left gazing into the distance, where puffy white clouds floated lazily above the sun-speckled waters of the Rappahannock.

There was a moment of silence before Will, who was standing just behind them on the deck, cleared his throat, saying, "Ahem, oh, aye, sir, but that would 'ave been some time ago, years, in fact."

Timothy's eyes cleared and he flushed briefly before replying with a nod. "True, true. But, gentlemen, I still would ask ye not t' be too hard in judgin' the lass. There's far more t' Brittany than meets the eye. She's a good child at heart, with naught but kind words and compassion for those less fortunate than she. Did ye spy that pretty little blackamoor with her today? Well, the creature's a slave I gave her for her twenty-first birthday recently. But tomorrow I'm signin' papers of manumission for her—at Brittany's insistence! The lass abhors slavery and will not be a part of it in any way."

He chuckled. "'Twill cost me some domestic peace with my wife, Brittany's stepmother, but not as much as 'twould have cost me with the lass, had I refused!"

Bryce had been listening to Chambers's ramblings with half an ear, regarding them largely as the kind of sentimental drivel one would expect from a fond parent, but at this latest, he found himself intrigued. He was about to pose a question, but was cut off by a comment from Will.

"D' ye mean t' say yer daughter 'as opinions about such things as slavin'—about *politics*?"

Timothy chuckled again as he turned and leaned against the ship's railing, regarding the big man.

"Aye, that and more! She was blessed with a quick mind, my daughter. And she puts it t' good use. Taught herself t' read when she was barely three, she did. Of course, I balked and said 'twasn't seemly in a female child, but her mother, God rest her soul, would have none of it. Made me promise, on her deathbed, that I'd keep the child well supplied with books, and so I have . . ."

Suddenly Chambers looked abashed. "Of course, there's some 'twould say 'twas all that book-learnin' that turned her head." Sadly, he shook his head. "Who's t' say? Sometimes I think, if perhaps I'd had more time t' spend with her whilst she was growin' up—"

"This aunt of hers," Bryce interrupted, "you say she has a way with your daughter? That she'll have a softening influence on her?"

"Aye," returned Timothy, "or so I hope. Amelia is..." He groped for the right words. "Unique...a very special woman. I'm thinkin' if anyone can get through t' the lass, 'tis she. She's always been Brittany's favorite—at least since her mother passed on, and Brittany's been hers."

"Well, then," Bryce grinned, clapping him on the shoulder. "What are we waiting for? I'd say 'tis high time you informed your daughter of this upcoming visit to her favorite aunt!"

CHAPTER 4

"NOW, DEN, DIS BE DE LAST O' DEM," SAID the diminutive black woman, as she carefully added a blue gown to a trunk at the foot of Brittany's bed. Straightening her small frame, she eyed the willowy figure of her mistress, who was busily stuffing some books and papers into a valise on her dressing table. "Miz Britt'ny, ah sweahs, we done packed fo' dis visit in brain-sizzlin' time!"

Brittany raised her head and chuckled. "Well, brain-sizzlin' or not, Tansy, 'tis a remarkable job, and we owe it all to you and your capable hands. I'd never have managed without you, you know." Brittany's eyes grew warm as she regarded the petite woman; she grew fonder of Tansy as each day passed and they got to know each other better. "Thank you," she added softly.

Tansy shrugged, still awkward at accepting thanks from a white person. Although this had been happening on a regular basis since she'd come to serve this young mistress, the black servant still found it

astounding. Never in her life had she been thanked
for anything before, let alone for doing some task
that was just an expected part of her duties. On the
contrary, in her previous position, she'd more often
been the recipient of a swift cuff on the side of her
head when she failed to perform adequately—or
swiftly enough.

"Yas'm," she murmured belatedly, forcing her
gaze upward to meet Brittany's. This, too, was something new for Tansy. In the past, during her years as
a slave on the Smith plantation, where she'd been
born, she'd been ordered to keep her eyes lowered
when addressing a white person. But on her very
first day of service under this new mistress, she'd
been instructed otherwise.

"Tansy," the young redhead had said that day,
"whyever won't you look at me when I'm speaking
to you—or when you speak to me? Is...there a
problem of some kind? I mean, I once knew a lady
who was born cross-eyed, poor thing, and didn't
wish to call attention to her...defect, but I've caught
enough of your glimpses to know that's not the case
here, so what is? What's wrong?"

"Nothin', mistress," Tansy had murmured, recalling now how she'd still fixed her eyes on the ground
in replying, at the same instant wondering what
could be wrong with the new mistress for not knowing basic master-slave etiquette.

"Well, if nothing's wrong," Mistress Brittany had
returned, "why won't you look at me?" At that,
she'd taken a step forward, seized her new slave
firmly but gently by the shoulders, and added,
"Tansy, look at me."

Tansy recalled she'd never felt more confused in
her life. *Look a white woman in the eye?* And *close up?!?*
Why, it just wasn't natural!

"Tansy...?" the white woman had persisted, at the same time tilting her head to try to catch the slave's gaze. "What's the matter?"

Forcing her voice past the lump in her throat, Tansy had mumbled, "'Tain't nothin' de mattah, mistress... 'cep'... 'cep'...

"Except what?" the redhead had encouraged, still doing her darnedest to force the eye contact that Tansy was equally doing *her* darnedest to avoid; after all, hadn't Mammy Ruth, the senior houseslave at the Smiths' Big House, warned her a hundred times when she was still a little pickaninny, what might happen if she disobeyed this rule? Why, she might be struck *blind*! Or worse, her eyes might fall out of her head!

But the new mistress wasn't about to be put off. Oh no! She was, as Tansy had since learned quite thoroughly, as hang-dog-stubborn as they come, once she got a bee in her bonnet. "Tansy," she'd finally asserted, "I order you to look at me, or, if you can't, to tell me the reason why!"

Well, there it was. There'd been no escaping then. Tansy had gathered all her courage and, after taking a deep breath and exhaling it forcefully, she'd responded. "B-black folks ain't s'posed t' look white folks in de eye."

There'd been a moment of horrible silence, followed by Mistress Brittany's amazed reply. "Says who?"

Now, by this time Tansy had grown so flustered that she now blurted out brashly, "Sez all de white folks ev'rywheres—an' black folks too!—*Don't you know nothin' 'bout slav'ry?*"

Of course, after she'd uttered this blasphemy, she clasped both hands over her mouth and, in horror at what she'd done, darted fearful eyes at her mistress, thus succeeding in doing the very thing she'd been struggling to avoid!

But instead of the fury—or God knows what else
—she'd expected to find on the white woman's face,
Tansy was astounded to find only *laughter*. Mistress
Brittany was laughing so hard, there were tears in
her eyes!

"Oh, Tansy," she'd chuckled, "forgive me, but you
see, I've never owned a slave before and—" Suddenly her face had grown somber. (Tansy knew, because she now found herself *eye to eye* with the
young white mistress and *nothing bad had* happened!)
"Tansy," the white woman continued, "I've never
heard of anything so demeaning. You may be entirely correct, that I don't know anything about slavery, and that's a body of ignorance I shall have to
correct—though not in the way that you might expect. But I do know one thing. I cannot have such
dehumanizing behavior be a part of my relationship
with another person.

"Tansy, I want you to disabuse yourself of that
horrible notion of subservience from now on. Do
you understand? From this moment forth, you are to
look me in the eye when we address each other—
and no exceptions. Now, what do you say to that?"

Tansy recalled that she had begun to gaze at the
ground again during this long speech, but there was
a tone in Mistress Brittany's voice that was different
from any she'd heard before from a white woman.
The white men she'd encountered may have touched
on it, but never the women. It held authority, for one
thing, but along with that there was a good measure
of respect and self-assurance. And more important,
there was honesty—Tansy could not ignore it.

So she'd raised her eyes and met the blue ones
squarely. "Yas'm, ah'll do it," she said.

Now, as she recalled those moments, Tansy
smiled. When she first learned she was to be sold to

strangers following the old mistress's death, she'd been terribly frightened. After all, she'd had a hard enough time learning her "place" at the old plantation. Hadn't Mammy Roth told her all her life that she was born too proud and "uppity" for her own good? That she was too quick-tongued and prideful to ever make a proper houseslave, and that would bring her trouble?

But then she'd found herself plopped down here, with a mistress who had bigger and more troublesome notions than *she* had—about slavery and a whole lot more! Oh, Tansy knew she was still a slave, and that, if she dared to let herself think about it, was why she couldn't consider herself truly happy, but at least here under Brittany Chambers's roof, she was able to breathe a bit more freely; here she was actually treated like a person and not just a *thing*. Why, Mistress Brittany even asked her *opinions* on things —things that really mattered, and she *listened*, once Tansy had finally been able to force herself past her shock that she should be asked, and began to venture a few shy, thoughtful responses to such questions.

Almost as if she was reading Tansy's mind at that moment, Brittany now put forth just such a question.

"Tansy," she queried, "what do you think Father has in mind for me, to be sending me off to Aunt Amelia's this way?"

Tansy was busy securing the lock on Brittany's trunk, but she made a point of pausing to bestow a level, dark-eyed gaze on her mistress. "Don't 'spect it'll be nothin' new, Miz Britt'ny," she said thoughtfully.

"Meaning . . . ?"

Tansy sat back on her heels and, to Brittany, suddenly looked very wise for her years. "De leopard don't change his spots," she pronounced solemnly.

"Go on," murmured Brittany, intrigued now.

Tansy glanced at the ceiling for a moment, trying to gather her thoughts and put them into words.

"Dis Miz Amelia," she began at last, slowly, "she be yo' fav'rit fambly lady, right?"

Brittany nodded.

"An' you be mo' yo'self when you be 'roun' her, right?"

Again a nod.

"An' she be livin' on a big plantation wid a fancy Big House an' she got plenty rich friends 'n' neighbors she kin aks t' come 'n' visit a spell, right?"

Brittany nodded again.

"Well, den, 'pears t' me she be jes de one t' take on de husband huntin' job fo' yo' daddy. Aftah all, yo' daddy bin soundin' happier 'n a pig in mud lately, evah since he done tol' you you wuz goin'. Ah 'spect he done sent yo' aunt a lettah tellin' huh she gotta find you a *man*, an' ah 'spect yo' aunt done tol' him she'd do it!"

"Tansy," exclaimed Brittany as she extended a hand to help the black woman to her feet, "you're a wonder! 'Tis exactly the suspicion that's been nagging at the back of my mind, and *if you share it*, I just know it must be true!"

Brittany whirled to face an elegant Queen Anne chest of drawers on top of which, in a tiny frame, rested a miniature of her father. "Why, you crafty old devil! I might have known you'd be up to your same old tricks with this. Well, it just won't work, Father. We're on to you."

She glanced over her shoulder at Tansy. "Oh, I'll go to Aunt Amelia's," Brittany continued. "In fact, I wouldn't miss it for the world. Wait till you meet her, Tansy. She isn't the least bit stuffy or 'proper,' like some people I could name."

Both women glanced at another miniature on the chest, this one half hidden by some porcelain figurines and a perfume bottle. It was a portrait of her stepmother, given to Brittany by Althea for her last birthday.

"Aunt Amelia's a lovely soul," Brittany continued, "and even if she has promised Father to help find me a, uh, ball and chain, I know she only intended it as something in my best interest. But once I tell her my side of the story, I'm sure she'll desist. She'd never try to force me to do something I was set against.

"And then there are Toby and Tony." Brittany reached toward the bed for her bonnet, a graceful, deep green, feathered creation that matched her traveling gown. "They're my cousins. They're twins, just two years younger than I, and ever so much fun! We three spent a lot of time together as we were growing up, and—"

"Brittany!" called an anxious feminine voice from the other side of the chamber door. "Mama says you're to come downstairs at once! There's a man downstairs who says he's to escort you to the ship, and Father sent him, so you'd better hurry!"

Brittany pulled a face at the door but was careful to keep her voice even as she answered her sister. After all, Melody was a sweet thing, even if she was a bit insipid. It wasn't her fault if Althea encouraged her to fill her head with "feminine" nonsense, and discouraged her from ever reading a book or a newspaper. And it was even less her fault that she docilely did everything she was told; after all, Althea had taken sole charge of her beloved offspring's upbringing.

"Tell them we'll be right down, Melody dear," she called, "and send Peters up for my baggage, please."

She glanced at Tansy. "Father mentioned something about hiring on a new captain for the voyage. It seems old Captain Durham's abed with the ague. I hope the new man's a conversational sort. 'Twill relieve the boredom of the voyage to have someone new to talk to." She paused and dimpled. "Of course, knowing Father, he's likely chosen the man for his nautical skills, without a thought for wit or charm.

"Ah, well," she sighed, smiling at Tansy after giving her bonnet a final pat before the looking glass and heading for the door, "at least I'll have you to converse with, Tansy. Who cares if this new captain is a bore!"

Bryce watched as Will supervised the transfer of the last of their personal belongings to Chambers's sloop. They'd left the *Lady Beth* not an hour before, satisfied that her able crew had everything in hand, and now it only remained to await Chambers and his daughter, and they could be off.

"The second mate says Chambers left 'ere not 'arf an hour ago," Will told him as he approached the quarterdeck where Bryce stood. " 'E be on 'is way t' meet 'is daughter and 'er escort, says 'e." Will gestured over his shoulder with his thumb at the second mate.

"Excellent," breathed Bryce, scarcely able to believe they were at last to begin the final leg of this journey that meant so much to him.

Sensing his eagerness, and knowing nothing good would come of their mission if Bryce didn't remember to exercise his usual control, Will suggested they retire to the captain's cabin and relax over "a wee dram" of something while they waited for their "redheaded cargo." Bryce readily agreed.

"So, ye be all fired up and champin' at the bit, eh, Cap'n?" Will chided as the two of them found comfortable seats in the handsome, well-appointed cabin.

Bryce cocked an eyebrow and gave him a mildly

deprecating look as he accepted the brandy Will poured him from the flask they'd brought aboard. "You know, Will, 'tis unlike you to use non-nautical metaphors. Surely you could have accused me of 'unfurling all my sails' or . . . ah, I have it, 'weighing anchor without—'"

"Ah, now, Cap'n," Will interrupted with a grin, "ye ken I meant no 'arm by it—and ye must agree, 'twould be fool'ardy t' be appearin' overeager."

"I do agree," Bryce replied smoothly, "but I disagree that you should be fussing over me like a mother hen this way—or should I say, 'like a boatswain over a barnacle'?" He paused to swirl the brandy about in his snifter as he warmed it in the palm of his hand, then raised it to his nose to inhale the fine aroma. "Ahh, excellent French, this," he continued. Then, "And I insist that I was not appearing 'all fired up,' as you so ungallantly put it."

But Will was not about to give up, for he had serious misgivings about the deadly business they were about. Indeed, he'd had them from the moment Bryce had confided in him regarding his vengeful plan. And he'd done his best to try to dissuade his friend at the outset, but Bryce had been adamant. So in the end he'd gone along, as he'd known he would. Bryce Tremaine had earned Will's lifelong devotion and loyalty the night he'd saved him from impressment at the hands of a gang of thugs hired to waylay unsuspecting sailors and kidnap them for forced service in the Royal Navy; beyond that, Bryce had gone on to save him from a knife in the back during the scuffle that ensued in that London back alley.

That night had marked a turning point in Will's life, and he had only Bryce to thank for it. The bastard son of an impoverished seamstress on the island of Jamaica, Will had watched his mother die of the

wasting disease when he was but seven, and following her death, had immediately hired on as a cabin
boy on a ship bound for London. From there it had
been a hard, if instructive, seafaring life, with never
an extra farthing in his pocket, for, as he'd seen it,
without family or ties of any kind, he'd had nothing
to plan for, and less to save for.

But, following the incident in the alley, he'd gone
to work for Lord Bryce Avery, and it was the best
thing that had ever happened to him. Ten years his
junior, the lad soon became like family to him, the
family Will hadn't realized he'd always yearned for
until he found it. And in most things the two men
saw eye-to-eye. Will had certainly understood his
friend's bitterness over the sire he'd supposed dead
when that confidence was imparted by Bryce over a
tankard of ale one quiet night aboard ship, a few
years after they met. So now, even though he worried about the wisdom of the current enterprise,
given the danger it put Bryce in, he could do no less
than give the lad his full support, given Bryce's seri-
ousness of purpose. All that was left for Will now
was to do all he could to ensure that the mission was
successful, and that Bryce remained safe.

And it was with this in mind that Will pursued the
current subject. "Mayhap not so fired up *above*
decks, me lad, but *below*. Aye . . . I caught the gleam
in yer green eyes as ye stood on that quarterdeck,
Cap'n. Ye may *think* ye kin hide it, but ye can't fool
old Will. And if *I've* learnt t' read ye, ye never ken
when there might be another sailin' past ye wi' the
wit t' read yer charts." He ended with a satisfied
nod, daring Bryce with a look to challenge the appro-
priateness of the nautical metaphors he'd used, and
taking a huge swallow from his own snifter.

Bryce understood the look and chuckled. "Very

well, my friend, you've made your point, and 'tis well taken. From now on, I'll take more care." He took a sip of his brandy, regarding the subject closed.

"By the by," said Will, "have ye 'eard about the uproar some o' these colonials are in, since they learnt that the lightenin' o' the tea duty does *not* apply t' *them*?"

Bryce nodded. "I caught something of it down near the other end of the docks as I came from the *Lady Beth*. There was a small but angry crowd gathered . . . mostly factors and other such middlemen, I'd wager. By permitting tea to be shipped here at full duty and allowing it to be sold directly to retailers, Parliament has managed to eliminate colonial middlemen and undercut their prices.

"A couple of men in the crowd stopped me and asked what my cargo was, for they'd seen our Union Jack. Their tone was ugly."

"Wot did ye tell 'em?"

Bryce grinned. "The truth."

Will winced. "*Ye didn't!* Why, lad, we'll be lucky if they don't take it in their 'eads t'—"

"Hold on, hold on," laughed Bryce, always amused at Will's readiness to worry over him. "I also concocted a fantastic tale to the effect that, through a bit of luck, I'd stumbled on my cargo *very* cheaply, so that I could afford to deal with middlemen and still turn a profit. Inside of a minute I had five offers to buy it, sight unseen."

"Ahh," murmured Will, nodding as he took another swallow of brandy. But suddenly the swallow became a sputtering cough. "*But, Cap'n!* Ye *didn't* come by the cargo cheaply! Ye'll be *losin'* on the venture!"

Bryce regarded him with steady eyes. "Just *which* venture were you referring to?" he questioned softly.

Will took a deep breath as if to continue his protest

and then paused, sporting a grin. "O' course," he nodded. "I almost fergot ye wouldn't give a bloody damn if ye lost yer fortune, as long as our true venture succeeds." He shook his head, "But 'is lordship—"

"Lord William will care very little about profit, either. He is perfectly prepared to stand for any losses to his East India friends, so long as what he believes to be the real aim of this voyage is fulfilled: that I use it to fill letter after letter to him full of information on current events in these colonies—events he's dying to know about in detail, so he can continue to make speeches in the House of Lords, speeches that are rationally opposed to what he believes is His Majesty's unfair 'bleeding' of the colonies."

Will grinned. "'E's a bloody radical, yer adopted father, fer all 'is soft-spoken ways."

"Who would be appalled to hear himself so characterized," chided Bryce, smiling softly, remembering with fondness the man he regarded as his true father. "Lord William may have a few, ah, forward-thinking ideas, but he is a staunch advocate of the rule of law. He would never begin to think of effecting any changes except through utterly legal channels.

"And speaking of Lord William and my promise to him, I intend to pen my first letter to him tonight. I don't suppose you've picked up any other information about the docks and taverns—something that might enlighten him?"

Will scratched his chin thoughtfully for a moment. "No, but I did catch some scuttlebut 'is adopted son might wish t' 'ear."

"Oh?" Bryce took another sip of his brandy.

"Aye," grinned Will. "'Tis about our 'cargo.'"

Cocking his eyebrow in the familiar gesture that denoted interest, Bryce waited for him to go on.

Will chuckled. "From wot the townsfolk tell, she

be a reg'lar *'ellion*, that one. Lord bless us, the tales they told!"

"Really?" murmured Bryce over his snifter. He appeared singularly unimpressed, perhaps even bored, Will thought.

"Very well, my fine laddie, try this one on fer fit." Will leaned forward almost conspiratorially. "One o' our 'ellion's first suitors wuz a member o' this 'Ouse o' Burgesses they 'ave 'ere. Chambers 'ad a ball in 'er honor and intr'duced 'em. But when the poor bloke danced wi' the red'ead, she pr'nounced 'im a *'orrid* dancer and pr'ceeded t' screech t' the 'eavens each time 'e supposedly stepped on 'er foot."

Bryce chuckled. "Well, Will, perhaps you shouldn't be too hard on the chit. Some of these country reels can become a bit wild and hard to follow, and if her partner—"

"Bilge water!" Will snorted. "'Twas a minuet! But then, listen t' *this*! The next 'un wuz nothin' less than an earl—one o' *ours*! Chambers selected 'im cuz 'e wuz a fine dancer. And wot did our red'ead do? She called 'im a 'dancin' fool'—*t' 'is face*, mind ye, and sent 'im on 'is way."

Another chuckle. "Did she, now? Well, I—"

"'Old on there, laddie, there be more." Warming to his subject, Will continued eagerly. "Then there wuz the colonel she challenged t' a 'orse race, and when she beat 'im, she swore t' all 'oo'd listen she'd 'ave no man wot couldn't best 'er on 'orseback.

"So 'er father fetched up a lieutenant they said wuz the best 'orseman 'mongst all King George's colonial troops, and—"

"Don't tell me," Bryce interrupted. "The chap bested her and she had a fit of the vapors."

"Vapors, nothin'! She 'ad a fit o' shriekin'—yellin' that 'e 'ad 'is nerve t' beat 'er and topped it off by shovin' 'im bodily int' a 'orse trough! Put that in yer pipe and smoke it, laddie!" He noted with satisfaction that by this time the chuckles had disappeared from Bryce's demeanor, to be replaced by a somewhat incredulous stare.

"Aye," nodded Will, "and *we* jest signed on t' be the young *sweetin's* escort!" He reached for his brandy and finished it in one gulp.

Bryce gave him a smile that appeared more grim than humorous. "Well, I cannot say we weren't warned . . . a *horse trough!*"

Fortified by the brandy, Will's mood became a great deal mellower, and he threw Bryce a merry, mischievously questioning look. "Wot now, me lad?"

Bryce shook his head. "You know, Will, these tales are so outrageous, I can hardly give them credence, but—"

"I spoke t' *dozens* o' locals, Cap'n. There wuz *witnesses!*"

"But if they are to be believed," Bryce continued smoothly, "I would say that Timothy Chambers has chosen his daughter's escort well."

Blinking in astonishment, Will waited for him to continue.

"My friend," said Bryce, clapping him firmly on the shoulder, "I promise you, I shall have her meekly obedient by the time we reach our destination. For one thing, you must remember that we are not her suitors. For another, there's never been a woman yet I've not been able to handle." He pushed out his chair and headed for the door, then turned to add over his shoulder, "And I've no intention of this Brittany creature being the exception."

CHAPTER 5

"AND YE'LL BE SHARIN' THE CABIN WITH yer abigail," Timothy told his daughter as they crossed the plank with Tansy behind them. He nodded as a couple of crew members recognized him and gave respectful greetings. "Ye've sailed with me often enough t' know space is precious aboard ship, so I'll thank ye t' remember that."

"Aye, Father," Brittany's tone was dutiful, though her mood wasn't. She'd already received an earful from Althea before leaving the house, and it stretched her patience now to have to listen to more unnecessary reminders from her father. But, knowing that in a very short time she'd be free of such lecturing, she forced herself to remain cheerfully compliant.

"As ye know, 'tis the cabin I always take when I accompany Captain Durham on a voyage. 'Tis nearly as spacious as the captain's and has two bunks. Ye'll recall ye shared it with Melody the last time ye traveled downriver t'yer aunt's."

"Aye, Father." Brittany rolled her eyes heavenward and heard Tansy smother a giggle.

"Well, here we are," said Timothy. "I wonder— ah, Captain Tremaine! I was just about t' ask—"

"So sorry I wasn't on the deck to meet you as you came aboard, sir," said Bryce as he strode from the doorway of the captain's cabin. The two men shook hands as Will Thatcher emerged from the cabin and watched thoughtfully.

"I should like t' introduce ye t' my daughter, sir. Brittany, this is Captain Tremaine. He'll be yer escort t' Sweetbriar."

Brittany gazed up into the handsomest male face she'd ever seen. She'd been paraded before a great many handsome men in the last couple of years, and this one wasn't just handsome—he was . . . *beautiful!* Thick, casually curling black hair covered a well-formed head, and an amalgam of planes and angles shaped a face that boasted high cheekbones, a straight, well-balanced nose, and a strong, square jaw. The chiseled mouth was wide and purposeful— denoting strength in spades! *And his eyes!* They were bottle green and set under straight, thick brows as raven as his hair, but beyond that, there was the look in them right now: it held secrets, that look—and promises of some kind, too . . . and a history—of a life fully tasted, yet questing for more, and suddenly Brittany felt a frisson of fear; she felt she could lose herself in those eyes if she allowed it, and nothing had ever made her feel that way before.

Yet she made herself hold his gaze before gracefully stretching forth her gloved fingers, which he took with a hand that was surprisingly gentle as he bowed over them. And as he accomplished this courtesy, she had a moment to appraise the rest of him.

He was large and powerfully built about the shoulders and chest, and his upper body tapered to a hard leanness that was gracefully evident in the

way he moved. Brittany was reminded of the sleek,
powerful lines of a big jungle cat she'd once seen in a
picture book. Tremaine's was an athlete's body, and
she found herself wondering what endeavors he
pursued that made it so. She had a split second vision of him climbing high into the rigging of his
ship, as she'd often seen her father's sailors do; she
imagined him astride a horse, for surely those were
an equestrian's long, well-muscled legs so snugly
encased in skintight breeches and tall boots; and she
fanced she saw him as a swimmer, cutting through
the waves with long, powerful strokes.

Bryce's voice cut into her thoughts with its rich,
deep tones. "Permit me to introduce my friend and
first mate, Will Thatcher. He'll be accompanying us,
Mistress Chambers."

Brittany was glad to have the second introduction
as a diversion, for she'd suddenly found her head far
too full—uncomfortably full—of detailed impres-
sions of the captain.

"How do you do, Mister Thatcher?" she smiled
pleasantly. And as Will performed an awkward bow,
she turned and gestured behind her. "And now you
must allow me to make an introduction of my own.
Gentlemen, this is my ladies' maid, Tansy. She'll join
us on this trip."

Bryce nodded politely to the servant and was in
the process of returning his attention to his chief passenger when, out of the corner of his vision, he
caught Will making a most elaborate bow in the
black woman's direction. He stifled a chuckle. Will
had always had an eye for a comely wench, and the
blackamoor was quite fetching, but what was really
amusing was the incongruous picture they made;
Will, all six and a half feet of him, indeed, all eigh-

teen stone of him, bowing over this petite creature who barely reached his chest!

But it was time to begin work on the hellion. Of course, she appeared sweet and docile enough at the moment. Mayhap all the tales were just... Well, there was one way to test the waters.

"Ah, Mistress Chambers," he said, offering her his arm as he turned toward the cabin she would be using, "that's a lovely bonnet you're wearing."

"Why, I thank you, Captain," Brittany smiled. "I designed it myself, with the help of a modiste in Richmond, of course."

"Ahh," Bryce grinned, then paused as if to study her more closely. "'Tis a shame it hides your hair, though. I much prefer it—ah, your hair, that is—flowing unbound in all its glory about your lovely shoulders."

Brittany paused too. "I beg your pardon?"

"I said—"

"Yes, I heard what you said, but—sir, have we met before?"

Bryce resumed walking, much as if she hadn't spoken, and Brittany was forced to go along.

"At least you don't powder it." Bryce continued. "'Twould be a shame to cover such luster with rice powder..."

There was an awkward silence and in it Brittany could hear the others—her father, Will, and Tansy—traipsing perfunctorily along behind them. *What on earth has possessed this man?* she thought wildly. *To be making these familiar references to my person, when he scarcely knows me! And Father hasn't uttered a single word about the impropriety of it!*

Had Brittany been privy to her father's thoughts that moment, she would have been even more upset. The older gentleman had had a few moments to view his offspring walking beside the tall captain, and he was at once struck by what a handsome couple they made. Suddenly all his matchmaking instincts began to blossom.

A sea captain? he asked himself, shutting out their conversation as he let his imagination roam. He was aware that Tremaine owned the ship he captained, and that told him the man had some property; he was a merchant—much like himself. One could do worse than marry one's daughter off to such a man . . .

With new eyes, he brought his attention back to the pair before him as they approached the door to the cabin.

"Green suits you, though," Bryce told Brittany as they faced her cabin. "I daresay, 'tis probably your best color—with the exception of a certain shade of blue, that is—a shade to match your eyes."

Better and better, thought Timothy, but his daughter's response brought him up short.

"Indeed?" Brittany's tone was icy.

Timothy groaned aloud. There she went again! She was going to ruin it before they even got started.

"Father, is something amiss?"

Timothy knew there was, but he could hardly confide his thoughts to Brittany. All he knew was that, at the moment, he couldn't bear to stand by and watch her ruin another match he favored—and this, one they hadn't even discussed. He had to leave before his disappointment succumbed to curses and weeping.

"Ah, nay, m'dear. 'Tis merely that I'd forgotten an urgent business matter I was t' attend. Captain Tremaine —" He held out his hand to Bryce. "Your pardon for this abrupt departure, but I must be off. I thank ye again for yer services in this matter. I know my daughter will be in good hands."

"My pleasure, sir," said Bryce, shaking his hand.

"Daughter," Timothy continued, "mind what I've told ye." He went to kiss Brittany on the forehead, but was forestalled by the brim of her hat and settled for one cheek. Then, pausing a moment to look into the blue eyes that were so much like her mother's, "I love ye anyway, lass," he added quietly.

He turned quickly and made a brief farewell to Will, nodded in Tansy's direction and headed for the gangplank.

"Now I wonder what that was all about," mused Brittany, forgetting for the moment her concerns about Captain Tremaine.

Bryce shared her puzzlement for a moment, then quickly recovered. Throwing open the door to the cabin, he gestured for Brittany and Tansy to precede him.

Brittany looked briefly around the familiar cubicle, noting with satisfaction that all was apparently in order. The twin bunks had been made up with fresh linens, the small oak table that stood bolted to the floor gleamed from a recent polishing with beeswax, and the Turkey carpet underfoot had been freshly swept.

She watched Tansy set her valise before the built-in chest of drawers, along with the wicker hamper Brittany had bought the servant two days ago. Seeing this baggage reminded her of the chest they'd packed that morning.

"Captain," she said, turning to Bryce as he stood just inside the open doorway, "can you tell me if my other baggage has arrived yet? It was sent ahead with one of our grooms and should have been here already."

"It arrived just before you, Mistress," Bryce told her. "I've had it stored in the hold, safe and sound for you."

Brittany blinked, not sure she'd heard him right.

"I beg your pardon, Captain, but I thought I heard you say 'tis in the hold."

"So I did say, Mistress," Bryce replied with a bland smile. Behind him, he heard Will muffle a strangled sound.

Brittany couldn't believe her ears. Anyone with more than half a brain could figure out that personal baggage belonged in a passenger's cabin. Was the man half-witted?

"Excuse me, Captain," she said as pleasantly as she could. After all, if he wasn't quite right in the head, it certainly wouldn't do to stir him up. "I believe there's been some error. That ladies' chest belongs up here, in my cabin. 'Tis all the baggage I have."

Bryce gestured toward the floor where Tansy stood with the two minor pieces. "You have those," he said genially.

Brittany almost sputtered with incredulity. "Th-*those*, sir, contain a few books, some toilette articles, and my poor Tansy's few, unfortunate pieces of cloting—all she brought with her from her last—last employer, a fact I fully intend to rectify by ordering a new wardrobe made for her once we reach Sweet-briar. Sir, *those* do not contain my apparel!"

Bryce leaned lazily against the door jamb, his arms folded across his chest. "Tsk-tsk," he replied, "that does pose a problem."

"Problem!" Brittany almost wailed. "I see no problem. Kindly see that my chest is fetched up here at once!"

"I'm sorry," said Bryce, looking nothing of the sort, "but I'm afraid I can't do that."

She bristled. "And why not, pray tell?"

"'Tis a rule I have: No loose pieces of baggage large enough to cause injury, should they tumble about during a storm."

Brittany was beside herself with outrage. "Storm? *What* storm? We shall be navigating the Rappahannock, not the Atlantic! 'Tis a river, Captain—an inland waterway!"

"Bryce . . . call me Bryce," he replied. "After all, we are going to be traveling together in rather close quarters for a while and—"

"I'll call you a great deal more than that if you don't have my chest brought up here, you—you—" She held her arms rigidly at her sides, fists clenched, lest she be tempted to grab an object and hurl it at him.

"Person in charge?" he offered.

He had a grin on his face now, a lazy, mocking grin that infuriated her almost beyond reason. He had to be a madman of some sort, Brittany thought, to be saying the things he was, acting the way he did. Otherwise none of this made any sense! She decided to humor him.

"Ah, Cap—Bryce," she intoned as smoothly as she was able, "surely you can see how impossible it is for me to travel aboard ship without easy access to my clothing. Perhaps we can reach a compromise . . ."

"And as the person in charge," he continued, much as if she hadn't spoken, "I make the rules here." He unfolded his arms and took a step toward her; out of the corner of her eye, Brittany saw Tansy jump. "I therefore think it appropriate," he went on, "to inform you of what those rules are, especially with regard to passengers."

Brittany watched him take another step, closing the space between them, but she held her ground. The first rule in dealing with a madman, she intuited, was not to show any fear. Quelling the sinking feeling in the pit of her stomach, she looked him squarely in the face, although the act put her off a bit, for he was a great deal taller than she, and so close she could see the pale squint lines that radiated from the corners of his eyes, for they contrasted with the bronzed tan of the rest of his face.

"The first rule," said Bryce, "is that female passengers will remain in their cabin unless told otherwise by the captain. This is for your own protection. I've met the crew and they seem like a good lot, but men will be men, if you understand my meaning, and I'll not have you on deck unescorted."

"But Ca—er, Bryce," she countered, "I've known most of those men for years! They'd never do me any harm. Even Father allowed Melody and me—"

"You were likely a great deal younger then," said Bryce. "Little girls don't pose the—ah—temptation big ones do, so kindly do not go running about the open deck without me or Will Thatcher to escort you."

Tempted to fling at him that she'd only find herself "running" if he were behind her, Brittany made herself wait until she could hear more. His last statement had seemed remarkably lucid, and she was beginning to think he was less madman than martinet.

"Second," he went on, "passengers take their evening meals with me in the captain's cabin. Dinner is at eight. Please be prompt. If you are late, you will find the door locked and will have to wait until much later, when the cabin boy finishes serving me and can take you a tray in your own cabin."

"*Locked?*" she gasped. "Why, I've never heard of anything so—"

"Moreover," he continued calmly, "if you should have occasion to address me or any of the crew, you will do so courteously at all times. Order aboard the ship depends upon strict discipline and a certain amount of protocol. 'Twould be foolhardy to sail without it."

Brittany was so outraged she couldn't speak. How *dare* he lecture her on courtesy! Why, she'd held her own in the best drawing rooms in Virginia! It was *his* breach of manners to suggest that she required instruction!

"Now, as to the problem of your baggage, Brittany —I may call you Brittany, may I not? Ah, 'silence gives consent,' they say. Very well, we shall solve our problem this way: Once we are under way, I'll send Will to you, to escort your maid to the hold. Together, I'm sure they can retrieve sufficient garments from your chest to last you until we arrive. There, you see how easily that was done?"

His patronizing tone at the end of this disgusting monologue was the last straw for Brittany. Aware, in the back of her mind, that all her outbursts of temper had been deliberately staged thus far in her life, she now felt the genuine article come upon her.

Placing both hands—in fists—upon her hips hard enough to send the paniers beneath her petticoats swinging, she lashed out at him.

"Look here, you ignorant simpleton! I don't know how they treat women where you come from, but I didn't think I'd have to remind you that on *this* side of the Atlantic, well-bred Englishwomen are treated like *ladies*! I am well aware, sir, having sailed aboard my father's vessels many times, of the necessity of running a tight ship, but this is to be a two-day excursion down an American river—hardly an armed foray into unnavigated waters! Why, this ship's crew has made this journey so often, they could do it with their eyes closed, and for you to suggest that anything untoward would happen if I should so much as be late for *dinner*—ooh—"

Brittany was so incensed she could feel her entire body trembling. Lock her out, would he? What did he think her—a recalcitrant child? Or did he think she couldn't tell time? Did he think her backward?

"And that's another thing," she continued, her blue eyes flashing fire, "I am *never late*. Did you think that because I am a colonial, I would have no manners? Sir, you are the last one to be lecturing on courtesy. I require no instruction from *you*!"

"Really?" Bryce questioned. "And is your current manner of address intended to be a demonstration of how the well-bred colonial Englishwoman behaves?"

Well, he had her there. There was no getting away from it. What was happening to her? She'd never before flown into such a *genuine* full-blown rage. Why, all those trumped-up tirades with unwanted suitors had been a delightful sham. And yet, here, suddenly, she found herself resembling the creature she'd invented. But there was something about the man who stood before her which made her forget all the careful orchestration of her emotions and submit helplessly to the real thing—gone out of control. The realization was sobering.

"You, sir," she seethed quietly, "are no gentleman."

Bryce watched her strive to keep her fury in check and was filled with a moment's unbidden admiration. She was a rare beauty to begin with, but when all that feminine perfection was highlighted by the fire and spirit she displayed—even now, when her efforts to subdue it only succeeded in making her appear to smolder and simmer—he found her, as he'd told Will at the inn, magnificent.

He noted how her eyes had turned a smoky blue as she tried to control herself; he was aware of how her high breasts rose and fell when her chest heaved with indignation; he caught the coppery sheen of a curl that in her agitation had pulled loose from her formal coiffure, and he longed to touch it.

But then, as it always did these days, an inner voice reminded him that he was here on a deadly mission and could afford no distractions, and in the next moment he was all business.

"Gentlemen are bred by the company they keep," he told her pointedly. "Good day, Mistress." He turned and strode out, but before closing the door behind him, he added, "Remember, dinner is at eight."

"Ooh!" seethed Brittany, searching frantically about for an object to hurl after him. Finding it in the form of a letter opener on the small, built-in desk her father often used, she sent it smashing against the door. "Tory blackguard! Green eyed jackanapes!" she shouted. "'Twill be a cold day in hell before I choose to dine with you! Lock me out, would you, you—"

She paused, sensing movement beside her. Turning, she saw Tansy calmly going to retrieve the letter opener. "Oh, here, Tansy, let me get that. After all, 'twas I who threw it."

But the black woman already had it. She turned and handed it to Brittany, and there was a spark of mischief in her black eyes as she ventured, "Sho' wuz a good aim, Mistress. If'n de do' bin open, dat Tow-ree sho' would a had it!"

Brittany laughed, her anger quickly forgotten. "Tansy, do you even know what a Tory is?"

"No, ma'am, but if'n you calls him one, dass good 'nuff fo' me!"

"Well, a Tory," explained Brittany as she removed her bonnet before the small shaving mirror mounted on a stand nearby, "is a member of the political party in Britain that least favors change. Here in the colonies it includes those who strongly favor our, ah, subservience to the mother country—or to put it more simply, to King George."

Having doffed her bonnet, she turned to face the black woman. "There are a lot of people here—especially nowadays, with this new tea tax—who see the Tories as a rather backward-looking lot who would keep us 'upstart colonials' in our place...that is to say," she added thoughtfully, "to render us second class subjects."

"Hmm," mused Tansy, "Guess dat make us slav'ry folks *thuhd*- o' maybe even *fo'th*-class su'jeks."

Brittany grew solemn as she met Tansy's sad black eyes. "You're right, Tansy," she said quietly, "and 'tis an ugly thing, a shameful disgrace to the human condition. *I hate it!*"

Now was the time. She withdrew the papers that had been fairly burning a hole in her pocket ever since her father had handed them to her this morning. "Tansy, do you remember when I told you I intended to remedy my ignorance regarding slavery?"

The black woman nodded.

"Well, what I meant by that, though I didn't say so at the time, was that I wanted to learn more about that terrible institution so that I could set about doing all I could to fight it—at least in my own small way. And that begins right now. Here," she added, holding out the papers in her hand, "I want you to have these."

Tansy looked at her wide-eyed as she cautiously accepted the papers. "Wh-whut dese gots t' do wif me, Mistress?"

"Look at them," said Brittany, a soft, tentative smile on her face.

Tansy shook her head slowly as she stared at the official looking documents, then raised her head to look at her mistress. "Ah kin look at dem all de day long, Miz Britt'ny, an' it ain't gonna do me one bit o' good. Ah cain't read," she explained sadly.

Color flooded Brittany's face. "Ohh," she moaned, utterly ashamed. Of course, a slave would be illiterate! So were most white servants, and a great many simple farmers and tradesmen, to boot. How stupid and myopic of her to have forgotten that.

"Forgive me, Tansy," she said softly. "I should have realized and I didn't, yet that's a poor excuse. I'm truly sorry."

Tansy was again staring at the documents she held. "Whut dese be, Mistress?"

Brittany took a deep breath, then released it. "The top paper is the bill of sale Father received when he —he...when he purchased you," she stammered. She still found it difficult to use terms of commerce —buying and selling—when they applied to human beings. There was something sickening to her in the whole business.

Swallowing past the lump that had lodged in her throat, she went on. "The next paper is Father's transfer of ownership of—of you, to me." She shook her head in distaste and gestured to the third, and newest looking document.

"That paper is the most important. 'Tis a certificate of manumission." Seeing the bewildered look on Tansy's face, she hastened onward. "It declares that from this day forward, you are a free woman of color, or, in other words, no longer a slave. I'm giving it to you because I believe 'tis yours by right. I—"

"Mistress?" questioned the black woman, a look of stunned disbelief on her face. "Is you—oh, Lawd, don't be funnin' wif me!" Tansy raised her wide black eyes heavenward in a gesture of supplication. "Ah been a good Chrisshun, Lawd, so iffn ah didn't heah de Mistress right, dis be a cruel prank t' be playin' on me an'—"

"Tansy!" Brittany had to raise her voice over

Tansy's, which had begun to rise with the force of the emotions that shook her small frame. "Tansy, 'tis no prank! You heard me correctly. Those *are* your freedman's papers!"

A sob rent the air as Tansy fell to her knees before Brittany, the papers clutched to her bosom with both hands. "Oh, Lawd, Miz Britt'ny," she cried, tears streaming down her cheeks, "ah's so—so—oh, ah kin hahdly *stand* it! *Freedom!* Oh, God bless you, Miz Britt'ny! *G-God bless you!*" She began to sob uncontrollably now, burying her face in Brittany's skirts while she continued to clutch the papers with shaking hands.

Overcome with emotion herself, Brittany dropped to her knees and gently took hold of Tansy's heaving shoulders. "Tansy, stop. Oh, Tansy, please stop, darling. You must *stand up—please!* After today, you don't have to go on your knees to any human being, ever again!"

Gradually the sobbing diminished as the two women clung to each other for several long minutes, but Brittany's face was wet as Tansy's when at last they paused and, at the new freedwoman's request, joined in a prayer of thanks voiced in Tansy's humble words:

"Lawd, ah thanks you fo' dis freedom wid all mah heart. An' ah thanks you fo' Miz Britt'ny cuz she done brung it t' me after you put me in huh hands. Ah's gonna be grateful an'—an' a good Chrisshun fo'evah, Lawd. Amen."

"Well," Brittany laughed a bit tremulously as she rose, pulling Tansy to her feet, "that's the beginning, at least. Now, we've work to do."

"De . . . *beginnin'*?" Tansy eyed her questioningly.

"Indeed," said Brittany, smiling. "Freedom's the first step. The all-important one, to be sure, but now we must begin preparing you for the responsibility that comes with freedom."

"Re-resp'so—"

"Re-spon-si-bility," Brittany enunciated slowly. "It means taking charge of the thing that's in your power—yourself."

"Re-spon-si-bil-ity," Tansy repeated, then looked at her in anticipation.

"For example," said Brittany, "now that I no longer"—she shuddered—"own you . . . now that you own yourself, what should be done so that you can take care of yourself, Tansy?"

The black woman looked crestfallen. 'Ah . . . ah don' 'spect ah knows, Mistress."

Brittany laughed. "No, not 'Mistress,' Tansy. You don't have a mistress—or a master—any more."

"Oh." Tansy sounded glum.

"You'll just have to call me Brittany, silly."

Tansy sucked in her breath, shocked. "*Oh, no*, Miz Britt'ny! Black folks don't nevah call white folks by dere Chrisshun names. *Nevah!*"

"But you're free!" Brittany protested.

"But ah's still black." Tansy's expression grew adamant. "Ah only done seen one free person o' colah in mah whole life, an' he done call de ole massah, *mistah*, an' *suh*, an' de ole mistress, *Miz* Smif. Ah reckon ah bettah call you Miz Britt'ny!" If she'd appeared adamant before, Tansy's entire face denoted pure stubborness now, causing Brittany to laugh.

"Very well, then, have it your way. But, now, what about supporting yourself? Now that you're free, I have absolutely no hold on you, Tansy, but I'd consider it an honor if you chose to stay with me as an abigail—at least for a while—and, of course, I'll pay you a decent wage for it."

Tansy's eyes grew wide as some of the first implications of being a free woman began to settle in. In the first flush of joy at her new state, she'd given no thoughts to such things as work and supporting herself. It was a sobering notion, as Brittany had expected it would be, and it became just the first of many things the two women needed to explore.

The black woman gladly accepted Brittany's offer of employment—after all, where else would she go? —and then it became clear to both of them that she would need some instruction in sums or she'd never be able to manage the money she earned. Why, she'd never even so much as *touched* a coin of the realm before, let alone learned what its value was.

This, in turn, decided Brittany on a pursuit she'd been toying with ever since the difficult moment when Tansy'd reminded her she couldn't read. She was eventually going to teach the black woman not only sums, but letters as well. But even the initial idea—of learning sums—met with some frightened resistance on Tansy's part, for she'd heard terrible stories about the punishments doled out on plantations to her people for learning these things. But in the end, when Brittany explained how necessary education was to Tansy's survival—and swore to keep the lessons secret—Tansy reluctantly agreed to learn sums.

They spent the whole afternoon discussing the ramifications of Tansy's new freedom. The only interruption came when Will Thatcher arrived to escort the black woman to the hold to retrieve some of Brittany's clothes. And when both women, giggling, joyfully, explained to him that he was the first to learn of Tansy's manumission, now that it had been accomplished, the old salt congratulated her, then paused to regard Brittany with thoughtful eyes. There was more to this one than met the eye, he told himself as he left their cabin, and he made a mental note to discuss this revelation with Bryce.

As for the two women, a bond was formed that day on the Rappahannock that was to last their entire lives. It was a bond of friendship, and on the freedwoman's part, a lifelong devotion to the young woman who'd thought she deserved freedom, not as something that was hers to give, but as a right she saw as part of the condition of being human. But beyond these things, there was a bond that the two of them were only beginning to recognize. They were kindred souls, these two, each proud and fiercely aware of her need to be a free and independent spirit, no matter the status she'd been born to. Old Mammy Ruth had seen the spark in Tansy when she was a child, and had, perhaps rightfully, been afraid for her because of it; the Chambers family (and, indeed, all of Fredericksburg) had faced the flame as it burned brightly in the young white woman. And both women had been lonely most of their lives because of it. But now this was no longer the case; now they had each other, and the strength their kinship would give them; each was bound to flex her wings and grow under the other's encouraging eye. It was an impressive liaison, and their world would have done well to take note of it.

CHAPTER 6

"I TELL YOU, TANSY, THE MAN'S A MENACE to my sanity!" Brittany paced the length of the cabin, pivoted and paced back again, her petticoats creating a swishing sound as she moved. "He *knew* I'd choose to be late for dinner, so he deliberately sent the cabin boy to apprise me of the hour well in advance—to rob me of a satisfactory excuse!"

"Mo' dan dat," Tansy pointed out with sympathetic annoyance, "he done had dat chile mention 'bout how de chicken be *skinny* dis evenin'!"

"Aye," asserted Brittany, whirling about to face her friend in agitated indignation, "so as to suggest there'd be nothing left for me, save bread and water, if I took my meal here on a tray, later on!" She paused, taking a slow, steadying breath as if to control herself. "I am right on that score, am I not, Tansy? I'm not just imagining all this? He did tell young Harry to say—to imply—those things?"

"Sho' 'nuff, Miz Britt'ny." Tansy gave one last swipe to the pewter shoe buckle she'd been polishing, then placed the shoe beside its mate on the floor. "Ah heerd 'im wif mah own two eahs."

"All right. So I'm not inventing something out of whole cloth." Brittany pursed her lips in an attitude of concentration as she stared at the carpet for a moment, then glanced back at Tansy. "But *why*? Why would that—that *man*, a person I *barely know*, be doing all he can to make life difficult for me? What are his *reasons*?"

Tansy paused in the act of putting some of Brittany's undergarments into a dresser drawer. "Hmm. Miz Britt'ny, ah don't rightly know fo' sho', but . . ." She stopped, as if trying to sort out her thoughts. "'Membah when ah done went t' de hold wid dat Will gen'lemun?"

Brittany nodded.

"W-e-ell," mused Tansy, "dat baldy, he sho' talk a heap!"

"Oh . . . ?" Brittany's tone was anxious.

"An' Will say dat he an' de cap'n done heerd 'bout you an' yo' wicked tempah wid all 'dem suitors. Hee—hee—hee." Tansy giggled appreciatively, reflecting on the delight she always took in Brittany's brilliant ploy to discourage suitors.

"Now," continued Tansy, a cunning look in her eyes, "you know dere be some mens whut cain't stand t' see a lady wid de uppah hand. Dey jes gots t' try t' show dem dey's de boss."

Brittany slowly nodded, understanding lighting her eyes. "Tansy, you're right! As usual, I might add." She grinned at the smaller woman. "You know, you may not have been able to achieve any book-learning on that miserable plantation, but you certainly picked up a lot about human nature. Do you know how wise you are for your years?"

Tansy smiled ruefully. "Dat be part o' de slav'ry,

too, honeychile. Iff'n a slave don' learn, early on, how t' read de massah's mind, he be in a heap o' trouble. Take de ole missus, fo' 'zample. She be pow'rful moody, dat lady. An' in de beginnin', li'l Tansy don' know nuthin' 'bout dis, so's ah gits mah head box'd sumpfin' *awful*! Den, as time go by, ah learnt how she be crabby when she ain't slep' good de whole night, o' how she be fit t' kill when she find out de massah bin sleepin' wid dat no 'count yallah gal he done bought t' work in de pantry."

A look of pain crossed Brittany's face. Little by little, bit by bit, she'd gotten Tansy to open up about her life in slavery at the old plantation. All afternoon, as they'd talked and talked, the details had begun to emerge. It was almost as if, now that slavery was behind her, Tansy could at last bear to speak of it.

Suddenly Brittany realized what Tansy had just said. "Tansy," she said in horror, "do you mean to say that—that Algernon Smith *sleeps* with his—with his—" She choked, unable to finish.

Sadly, Tansy nodded. "Dere be a heap o' yallah babies on de Smif place." She flashed a rueful grin. "But ah done bin one o' de lucky ones, honeychile. De ole missus, she seen him pussyfootin' 'roun' me, so she stick me t' huh tighter 'n glue! Ah even slep' neahby—in huh dressin' room."

Horrified, Brittany had to ask. "But when she died . . . ?"

Tansy grinned. "De ole missus' sister come fum Chahlston, an' she be even *meanah* dan de ole missus. Massah, he don' dare mess wif me, cuz de ole missus done writ huh sister a lettah, an' dat sister wise t' him! She got me sold—*quick*!" The grin widened. "Lucky, huh?"

"Oh, Tansy!" cried Brittany, rushing forward to

hug her. "Ever so lucky—because then you came to us—to me!"

"Dass de biggest piece o' luck," grinned Tansy, then, suddenly all business, "now whut you gonna wear in yo' hair fo' dis Tow-ree cap'n dis evenin'?"

Brittany grinned back at her. "I'd *like* to wear a dagger—for the dear captain, that is—but, for my-self, let's see..." she mused, walking over to the small shelf where they'd arranged some toilette arti-cles: "How about this violet ribbon?"

The ribbon she chose matched, exactly, the shade of her silk gown and the stripes in the underskirt revealed by the open, inverted *V* of the gown's front. The gown was a new one, copied by her Richmond modiste from a fashion plate in *The Lady's Magazine*, a periodical the modiste had shipped from London several times a year. Of course, there'd been several French and other European fashion plates to choose from, but Brittany had opted for this English look for its greater simplicity.

Because she was on the tall side, she'd long ago decided to avoid the fussy little fripperies of dress that were the favorites of more petite women. Her sister Melody, for instance, with her pale blond, doll-like prettiness, could cover herself with elabo-rate bows and rosettes and not appear ridiculous—but not Brittany.

So it was with approval that she nodded at her reflection in the glass as Tansy threaded the simple violet ribbon through the red hair that was piled fashionably high, but without curlicues; for added adornment there was only a single long lock that draped gracefully over one shoulder. And she noted with satisfaction the simplicity of the ivory lace that accented the low, square décolletage; it was echoed discreetly by that which fell from the sleeves ending at her elbows, and the lace which could be glimpsed at the edges of her petticoat as she moved.

Her only jewelry was a single strand of perfectly matched pearls, inherited from her mother. Violet satin slippers adorned her feet. In her hand she would carry a lovely ivory and deep blue satin fan, a birthday gift from Melody. This she reached for now as she gave her reflection a last, assessing glance.

"Hmm," she mused, turning toward Tansy.

"Hmm, whut?" countered the black woman, recognizing the calculating look in the redhead's eyes.

"Hmm, I wish I had some powder, that's what!"

Tansy giggled, for she'd heard Bryce's remarks regarding Brittany's appearance. "De cap'n sho' would git upset 'bout dat, huh?"

Just then, there was a rap on their door. "Mistress Chambers? 'Tis Will Thatcher. I've come t' escort ye t' dinner."

Tansy rolled her eyes. "He sho' ain't takin' no chances, dat Tow-ree!"

"Well, neither am I," returned Brittany grimly as she slipped a lethal looking bodkin into the folds of her fan. "Coming, Mister Thatcher," she called. With a wink for Tansy's benefit, she walked to the door.

Moments later, Brittany found herself entering the captain's cabin on Will's arm; the door was drawn open by none other than Bryce Tremaine himself, and she had a few seconds to assess his appearance as he made her a low bow.

He was dressed quite formally, in a deep green satin coat with black satin knee britches, a white waistcoat with silver embroidery, and immaculate white silk hose. The buckles on his shoes looked to be silver. At his throat, and accentuating the bronzed tan of his face, was a snowy white cambric stock—or perhaps it was linen—Brittany couldn't be sure. She was far too busy assimilating the impression he made.

Again, there was about him a certain presence which made her a little afraid—at least for a split second, before she took hold of herself, refusing to be intimidated—especially since she now had his motives securely in mind.

But this didn't interfere with her initial impression of him: He moved like a panther, a big, sleek predator of the jungle whose very agility and swift, graceful motions belied his size. And those green eyes of his, as he raised his head to look directly at her— they, too, were the eyes of a cat; the eyes of a hunter, she thought wildly.

But then that look was gone, and he was smiling at her pleasantly as he took her hand and led her into the cabin.

"Welcome," he murmured, in smoothly articulated tones. "I see you made it on time, m'lady."

Brittany bristled, then forced a smile. "As you had no doubt I would." Her voice was at its civilized best.

"But of course. You're *never* late."

Was there mockery in his voice? Probably. "Unless I want to be," she replied airily as he led her toward a table whose drop leaves had been raised to accommodate the meal.

With a sidewise glance she caught Bryce's brows arching skeptically at her reply, but there wasn't time to ponder this; rising from their seats were two ship's officers she recognized; the *Louise's* first and second mates, Jonathan Grimsby and Hugh Milne, who had known her since she was a child.

"Ye're a full-blown beauty these days, lass," said Grimsby enthusiastically; he bowed over her hand. "Ye do yer father proud."

Milne, who was shy, merely smiled softly as he offered a polite greeting.

Brittany allowed Bryce to pull out a chair for her, and she found herself sitting to his right, with Will Thatcher on the other side of her. The two officers were across from her, but she suddenly noticed the places before the two seamen and Will were devoid of any tableware, save a trio of wine glasses.

Noting her discovery, Bryce explained. "Mister Grimsby and Mister Milne won't be staying for the meal. Neither will Mister Thatcher. They're joining us for a toast, but then they've duties to perform."

Brittany tensed. The execrable lout planned to dine *alone* with her here! It wasn't proper! It just wasn't *done*! She looked, panic-stricken, toward the other men for some help in the awkward situation, but all three seemed totally oblivious to it as they sat looking at her benevolently.

Then, seeing what he took to be her disappointment, Grimsby, whose favorite she'd been ever since she was a tiny moppet, grinned at her, obviously pleased. "Ah, 'tis heartwarmin' t' see ye'll be missin' our company, lass, and we'll be sorely missin' yours as well, won't we Hugh?"

Hugh nodded eagerly.

"But surely we'll be seein' ye t'morrow and the next day as ye take yer customary strolls about the top deck."

Brittany paused to glare at the man seated at the head of the table. "That remains to be seen, sir."

Bryce appeared to ignore her look as he lifted a decanter of wine and gestured toward her glass. "Mistress Chambers, does your father allow you to take wine?"

Brittany was indignant. "Sir, I turned one-and-twenty on my last birthday. I shall allow *myself* to have some wine. My father has nothing to do with it!" She could have added that Timothy had served her wine (a bit watered, it was true, but wine, nevertheless) at the table at home since she was sixteen, but she chose not to.

Bryce smiled. "On the contrary. Your father has everything to do with it. He is your legal guardian, is he not?" The decanter remained hovering above her glass.

She stiffened. "Captain, 'tis irrelevant. I have reached my majority."

Bryce's smile remained fixed; his voice took on the deliberately patient tones one might use with an obstreperous child. "Mistress Chambers, I fear 'tis my misfortune to have to disagree with you, but 'tis *entirely* relevant. The law, as it applies to His Majesty's subjects, grants certain rights of independence to *males* who have reached their majority, 'tis true, but in the case of His Majesty's *female* subjects, I fear this does not apply. A female remains under the rule of her father or male guardian until she weds. Thereafter, she—"

"Sir, are you saying you will not serve me a glass of wine without the—the written consent of my *father*?" There was no mistaking the outrage in Brittany's voice as she glared at him with open hostility.

Across from her, Grimsby and Milne bestowed anxious looks on each other, and Hugh fingered his wine glass nervously. Will cleared his throat and began to fiddle with a saltcellar.

Bryce seemed singularly unaffected. "Not at all," he told her. "A simple avowal of your father's policy will do. I have no reason not to take your word, now have I?"

It was all too much for Brittany. She'd come here this evening against her better judgment, sensing that his tactics boded her no good, but rather than create a scene her first day aboard ship she'd decided to ignore her instincts and try to be pleasant. But now here he was, proving her right not to have trusted him. He was bent on provoking her, and she was at last going to give him what he sought.

Pushing herself away from the table, she rose to her full height before thrusting her chin forward pugnaciously and gritting out between clenched teeth, "My word, sir? Aye, I'll give you my word! And several more before I finish!"

In her left hand she clenched her linen dinner napkin, her knuckles white as she struggled to keep it from shaking. "You, sir, are the most odious miscreant it has ever been my misfortune to meet! You undertake the duty of escorting me on what was to have been a pleasant river journey, then bait me with trifles aboard my father's own ship! You thrust and parry, then thrust again, and all with a smile on your face. Well, I am well aware that one may smile and smile and be the villain, captain!

"And don't think I don't know your reasons! The world is full of men like you, bent on dominating a woman for the sheer enjoyment of it!

"Well, this is one woman you'll not subdue so easily, Captain. This is one woman who fights back!" She threw her napkin on the table and turned for the door, only to find that Will and the two officers had beaten her to it.

"Er . . . good evenin', lass," Jonathan offered weakly, bowing hurriedly before disappearing through the door.

Hugh nodded at her and smiled nervously before he, too, disappeared into the darkness of the passageway outside.

Will gave her a smile that was apologetic before

glancing at the captain, receiving a nod from him and joining the others.

Brittany grabbed for the handle of the door Will shut in his wake, but was forestalled by a strong, masculine hand on her shoulder.

"I think not," said Bryce.

Whirling on him, Brittany made a sound midway between a sob and a hiss. "Don't touch me!" she spat, clutching her fan in her right fist.

Bryce took a backward step, offering a slow, elaborate bow. "As you wish, of course." The voice was mocking.

"What I wish is to be gone from your sight, you—you—"

"Tory?" he grinned. The grin was mocking.

"You—you've been eavesdropping!"

"Not really. 'Twas merely something Will picked up from your little abigail," he shrugged. The shrug, too, was mocking.

"You've set spies on me!" she accused.

The infuriating grin continued, unabated, his green eyes underscoring its message, and the eyes were mocking as well.

"I'm leaving!" she cried, turning for the door.

But he quickly placed himself between her and the portal. "You'll leave when I dismiss you."

"*When you dism*—ohh, I think not, captain." Clutching her fan with both hands now, she manipulated the bodkin out of it. The fan dropped to the floor and she thrust the sharp, pointed object menacingly toward his midsection.

She had never wielded a weapon in her life, but the bodkin, with its stiletto-like sharpness, gave her the feeling of wielding one now. "Out of my way, captain," she snarled.

The grin disappeared and Bryce's eyes glittered

dangerously. "Don't be foolish, little girl. You might hurt yourself."

With a rapid movement, he had her wrist before she could even think to move. Then, with a slight twist, he forced her fingers loose. The bodkin clattered to the floor.

"That's better," Bryce murmured. "I do so hate to dine under the threat of violence."

Brittany was close to sobbing with humiliation and rage. *"Dine!"*

"Why, yes, m'dear. You may recall we haven't eaten yet." He continued to hold her by the wrist and turned her toward the table.

"I have no intention of dining with you! I'd rather starve!"

"That well may be, but I've no intention of letting you. You'll recall I've undertaken the obligation of seeing to your safety and welfare."

"Does my safety and welfare including dining alone, in close quarters, with a man to whom I am not related, and whom I hardly know?"

He grinned. "Losing your courage, Brittany? Or is it simply bravado?"

Calmly, but firmly, he led her to her seat, and when he at last released her wrist, she glared at him, but, realizing that his very size put her at a disadvantage, she decided to sit.

At that moment there was a knock at the door.

"Enter," he said.

The door opened, and in walked Harry, the cabin boy, carrying a heavily laden tray.

"Set it down here, lad, and thank you, that'll be all," Bryce told him.

Harry did as he was told, gave Brittany a surreptitious glance from under lowered eyelashes, and left as quickly as he'd come.

As Bryce uncovered the food and set it in the center of the table, Brittany noticed bowls of savory rice and young, freshly picked, steamed green beans, the fluffy biscuits that were a specialty of Ben, the *Louise*'s cook, a corn pudding, and finally, not one, but *two* of the plumpest roast chickens she'd ever seen.

"A skinny chicken, was it?" she fumed, looking daggers at Bryce.

"Hmm?" he murmured as he began to carve one of the gigantic fowl.

"You told Harry there was merely one sorely emaciated chicken for dinner!"

"Oh? Did I? Well, 'tis fortunate I was mistaken." His nonchalance was maddening.

But as he served her generous helpings of the deliciously prepared foods and she caught their mouth-watering aromas, Brittany realized she was hungry. Luncheon had consisted of a couple of hastily downed hard-cooked eggs and a slice of bread, taken in her cabin as she and Tansy had unpacked and put away the clothing retrieved from the hold. It had been all she wanted at the time, but that was hours ago, and now she felt she could consume an entire chicken by herself. She promptly forgot about the irksome captain and began to eat, ignoring the fact that he filled her wineglass with water and his own with wine. Who cared about the damned wine, anyway? The food was delicious!

Bryce observed her as they dined, reluctantly admiring her ability to adapt to the circumstances he'd deliberately made difficult for her. She might be a hellion, but she was intelligent enough to know when to roll with the punches. This could make taming her far more difficult than he'd anticipated. He knew he ought to be disappointed; strangely enough, though, he was not. All his life he'd been easily bored by the simple, intrigued by the complex. And he was beginning to realize the complexity of the character embodied in the redheaded beauty before him.

And she *was* beautiful! He'd known dozens of beautiful women in his life. He'd spent time at court and had attracted the interest of beauties as mature as the duchess of Argyll (still handsome, though close to forty) and as young as the dazzling Mary Robinson. And he'd traveled on the continent, where he was hard put to affirm the superiority of French charmers over Italian, or vice versa; there'd been an abundance of feminine loveliness in both France and Italy, not to mention Spain.

But Brittany Chambers was in a class by herself. Offering a unique beauty that had much to do with her vibrant coloring, she outshone them all. Of course, he was well aware that the standards of the day gave preference to blondes, those pale, delicate creatures immortalized by English and continental poets, but he was of a mind to appreciate each woman as she was, weighing the total package against itself, so to speak. After all, beauty of face and form paled quickly if the wit were slow; beyond regularity of feature, there had to be intelligence, and he had to admit—at least since he'd encountered the lovely Mistress Chambers—there also had to be drama. Of course, it would remain to be seen whether the flashing eyes and mobile mouth of this exquisite creature would prove so overpowering as to spoil the total effect.

"Tell me, Brittany," he ventured while pausing to refill his wine glass, "what is the source of your given name? I mean, I am aware of the existence of Brittany, or Bretagne, as the French call it, and I even spent some time there a few years ago, but how did you come to be named for it, as I assume you were?"

With a flash of annoyance, Brittany watched him set the wine decanter down. Now that she'd eaten her fill and no longer suffered from hunger pangs, she would have enjoyed a few swallows of a good wine to "set" her digestion. With calculated slowness, she reached for the decanter as she answered him.

"My mother's people came from Brittany, Captain. She herself was born in St. Brieuc, but was sent across the Channel to Britain to be educated because the family was Protestant. Huguenots, even those who'd managed to retain their lands and wealth, did not find it easy to educate their offspring in Catholic France." She poured some wine into her glass, which still held about an inch of water.

"While mother was away at school, Louis XV managed to do what his great-grandfather had not: during a local anti-Protestant uprising, he stripped the family of its title and ancestral lands. My grandfather, a widower, fled to England to join his daughter—an only child, by the way, and the last of his line—but he caught a severe cold on the crossing and died within the month. My mother inherited what wealth he'd been able to bring out of the country with him—an abundance of concealed jewelry mainly—and finished her education under the protection of the Anglican nuns who taught her. She met my father at the home of a schoolmate when she was barely eighteen, married him shortly thereafter, and came with him to these colonies. She never saw Brittany again."

Holding his interested gaze with her own, Brittany raised her wine glass slowly to her lips and sipped.

"And because she loved the province that was her

homeland," Bryce added for her, "she named her firstborn for it."

"Exactly. And what of your name, Captain? Bryce . . . 'tis Gaelic is it not? What are its origins?"

Was she imagining it, or had his look turned dark at the question? She couldn't be sure, for his eyes quickly shuttered as he answered, "'Twas chosen by my mother, too." Then, as if anxious to change the subject, "What do you think of the burgundy? 'Tis far too robust a wine for fowl, I know, but the only white on board was a sauterne I rejected for being too young."

Brittany dimpled. "I was wondering if you'd choose to notice. 'Tis an excellent burgundy, I think, though watered as mine was, I am perhaps not in a position to judge it well."

"Well," he smiled, "then perhaps you should taste it unimpaired." With an easy motion, he refilled her empty glass.

"What?" she questioned archly. "Without a note from my father?"

The smile broadened. "Your taking wine mixed with water has already told me this was something that was established as a pattern at home. I am correct, am I not?"

Was there nothing he did not notice? His remarks concerning her person when they'd first met had been disconcerting enough, but now she was convinced that if there was anything those green eyes missed, it was quickly picked up by an all too discerning mind.

"You notice much, Captain," she told him, then raised her glass to her lips and took a sip.

"Bryce," he told her. "My name is Bryce."

It was an intimacy she didn't wish to accept, but he'd already managed to call her by her Christian name, and she felt she could hardly allow him the liberty without following suit.

Of course, to be honest, what really irked her was to be forced to follow his lead. She'd already determined that Bryce Tremaine was no ordinary merchant captain. For one thing, his manners were far too polished, his speech too precise and articulate for the position he held. Something told her there was more to the man than met the casual glance and this bore watching—and handling with care. And if he was to be carefully handled, the thing she could least afford was to let him gain control. She decided to test him.

"'Twas an excellent burgundy, Bryce," she stated, setting down her glass. "But now I fear I've taken more spirits than I intended and I need to take some air." She rose from her chair. "If you will excuse me..."

Bryce rose, too, and quickly moved to help her away from the table. "Of course. I'll escort you back."

"'Twill not be necessary, sir. I know the way to my cabin." She moved toward the door.

"I'm well aware of that," he said, reaching to open the door for her, "but if I'm not mistaken, you were planning a topside stroll before reaching it, were you not?"

Brittany sighed. He was going to be difficult after all. "Really, Bryce," she insisted, "can we not forget this nonsense regarding my being escorted? 'Twill prove ever so inconvenient, for one thing, and—"

"My apologies, Brittany, but no, we cannot. I have told you the rules and"—he ushered her out into the darkened passageway—"you will obey." A strong forearm linked hers. "Now, if you'll allow me...?"

Brittany's eyes flashed dangerously for a split second, but then she took the proferred arm and went along. For some reason—perhaps it was the wine—she decided now was not the time to defy him. And after all, *she* had decided to take the stroll. She hadn't had to ask his permission first, had she? It was a small victory, but it would have to do... for now.

Ah, but tomorrow! Tomorrow was another matter!

CHAPTER 7

BRITTANY AWOKE SUDDENLY IN THE SEMI-
darkness. Sitting upright in the bunk, she quickly
realized what had awakened her. The ship was rolling and pitching in a manner she'd never experienced while traveling on the river, and a loud clap of
thunder, followed by a flash of lightning, told her
why. They must have encountered one of those early
summer storms that frequently rolled in from the
Chesapeake, the kind she used to love to watch from
her bedchamber window as a child.

A low sound coming from nearby drew her attention.

"Ohh, ah's gonna die, fo' sho'," moaned Tansy as
she huddled in her bunk. "Ohh, dis be de end o' po'
Tansy!"

"Tansy, are you ill?" questioned Brittany anxiously.
She turned and set her bare feet on the rug, then
managed to rise and keep her balance when the floor
appeared to come up and meet her. As quickly as
she could, she crossed to Tansy's bunk.

"Oh, Miz Britt'ny, ah's gonna meet mah Maker,"

the black woman groaned, her fearful eyes illuminated by another flash of lightening.

"No, you're not, sweetheart," Brittany assured
her, placing a hand on the smaller woman's clammy
brow. "'Tis just a bout of the seasickness, though I
vow I've never heard of it striking on the river before. We must have hit *some squall*!"

Another anguished moan from Tansy sent her into
action. There was a pitcher of water and a bowl for
washing on a nearby stand. They were secured to its
top by a wooden frame, or fence of sorts, a device the
ship's carpenter had made years ago to keep the ce-
ramic objects from tumbling during inclement
weather. She managed to find a linen napkin, only
slightly soiled from yesterday's luncheon, and, wet-
ting it with water from the pitcher, she applied it to
Tansy's brow.

"You stay here and try to hold on," she told the
black woman. "I'm going to get something to help
settle your stomach . . . tea or brandy or some such."

A subdued moan was her only answer. Casting
Tansy a final, compassionate glance, she crossed to
the chest of drawers and managed to extricate a
dressing gown of midnight blue silk and don it before the ship lurched to starboard, throwing her
against the cabin door.

"Well, at least 'twas in the proper direction!" she
asserted to no one in particular as she clung to the
door's handle for support. Taking a fortifying breath,
she straightened, pushed the door open, and found
herself thrown into the passageway.

It was quite dark, the feeble light from the candles
in a pair of gimbaled lanterns bolted to the wall
doing little to illuminate her way, but as she reached
the companionway that would take her topside, the
hatch door above them swung open to reveal a sea-

man's legs and, behind them, a grayish cast of light
that told her it was daylight outside.

"Mister Runyon!" a familiar voice called. "Forget
your last order. I need you up here!"

"Aye, Cap'n!" said a voice that went with the legs
belonging to the seaman, who stood at the top of the
stairs.

Then the legs disappeared and the door slammed
shut, leaving her again in the near-darkness.

But a blast of cold, wet air, sent down into the
passageway while the door had been ajar hit her like
a shock wave, forcing Brittany to pull the thin dressing gown more tightly about her. With a look of chagrin, she glanced at her bare feet, then shrugged and
went for the stairs. After all, how cold could it be up
there? It was June, for heaven's sake, and Tansy
needed doctoring!

She soon found out how bad it could be. For one
thing, it took her the better part of a minute to force
the hatch door open, as the wind outside seemed to
do its utmost to keep her below. Then, the minute
she succeeded in pushing her way topside, she was
met by a sheet of driving rain and wind so fierce, it
robbed her of breath. Above her, the heavens
seemed to have opened up, making it all but impossible to distinguish the ship's rigging against the
dark, lowering sky.

The deck was awash with sluicing water, numbing
in its coldness as it poured over her bare feet and
caused her to lose her footing. Instinct made her
reach out for the nearest stable object. She gasped in
surprise when the object turned out to be human.

Very human, with a hard, well-muscled chest and
trim, masculine waist beneath the sopping wet captain's garb.

"What in the name of hell are *you* doing up here?"

Bryce demanded in a fury. "Are you mad as well as disobedient?"

"I—I—*Tansy!*" Brittany gasped, for the rain was so hard, it made speech close to impossible. "My—Tansy..." she persisted, "She's *ill!*"

Bryce muttered an indelicate oath. He was the sole reason she was standing upright, his arms supporting her about her waist and hips as she clung to his shirt and peered upward into his streaming face. "Mister Grimsby!" he shouted above the din of the storm. "Take charge here until I return."

He shifted his attention to her. "Idiot! I might have known you'd pull something like this the minute I had no chance to watch you!"

"But I only—"

"You're going below!" he shouted, then shifted his hold until he was able to drag her about the waist with one arm while, with the other, he reached for the hatch door.

A few seconds later he had her down the narrow stairs and was setting her on her feet in the passageway.

Brittany looked up into a face that was a mask of fury. "Look, Bryce," she said, though speech was still difficult—now because of chattering teeth, "I realize I—"

"Not another word, Mistress!" he ground out at her with jaws clenched. "'Tis bad enough I encounter a storm which wasn't supposed to happen on your damned colonial river, but now I find myself saddled with a willful brat who—"

"*Brat?*" Using both hands, Brittany pushed against his chest until she was free of him. The movement, coupled with the tossing of the ship, flung her wildly backward, but, fed by her anger, she managed to press against the wall of the passageway and remain upright.

"Brat!" she repeated, fixing him with a damning glare. "How dare you upbraid me and use me so, when I was merely doing what I could to—to run an errand of mercy! Tansy is *ill*, d' ye hear? And I'll venture where I must to summon aid for her. The woman needs help!"

As Bryce took in the figure she cut, confronting him there in the dim light, he was overtaken by a moment of speechless awareness.

Her long hair was plastered to her face and upper body, a dark, gleaming red with the dim candlelight reflecting off its wetness. The thin material of her sodden wrapper molded itself about her body like a second skin, rendering every curve and indentation visible. He was conscious of long, lithe legs . . . of gently rounded hips . . . and a waist so tiny, he knew he could span it with his hands. And gracing the chest which heaved with righteous indignation were a pair of breasts that were firmly upthrust, yet lush and full, their nipples erect from the cold and evident beneath the wet silk.

And suddenly he knew what he'd been suppressing ever since that moment at the inn when he'd first seen her. He wanted her, wanted her in a way he'd never wanted any woman before. She was fire and light and all things holy and unholy, it seemed—a promise of fire in a cauldron of seething female energy and will, and raw, elemental beauty that took all previous standards of loveliness and sent them tumbling to oblivion.

She seemed to derive life from the storm roiling above them, to take it and become one with it as she stood there challenging him with her eyes—they were deep indigo now—daring him to question her right to be there. Here was a woman to set a man's soul afire, he realized, a woman to answer all the helpless yearnings men had buried inside themselves over the ages.

Here was a woman who was dangerous.

With a silent click, his brain registered the threat she represented. He was on a vital mission, a duty to which he'd bound himself many long months ago with a vow that he would not rest until his mother's murderer—for that is how he saw it—the man who had betrayed and dishonored her, had been made to pay for his cruelty. He could afford no distractions.

And since the female before him represented a potential distraction, she was dangerous. Without another thought, he made the decision to set that danger aside.

"Mistress, you are indecent," he uttered in clipped syllables. "I suggest you return to your cabin and don suitable garb. In the meantime, I shall send Harry to you with such remedies as may be found for your servant. Good day." And with nary another glance, he whirled and headed back up the stairs.

Frozen into silence, Brittany watched him go. For one thing, the danger she'd faced during the frightening encounter on deck was only now registering a delayed shock; for another, she was belatedly recognizing the way he'd appeared as he looked at her in silence for several long seconds. She'd had enough experience with certain kinds of suitors to recognize lust when she saw it, and it was lust she'd seen in Bryce's eyes, that and something more which she was not prepared to analyze right now. And finally there was the insulting manner in which he'd just spoken to her. *Indecent!* Why, it was tantamount to saying she dressed this way apurpose and was in the habit of parading about for reasons of—of—

"*Bastard!*" she shouted at the top of her lungs. "*Devil incarnate! Miserable lout!*" The winds howling outside drowned out most of these epithets, but Brittany didn't care. She continued for a good minute more, hurling invectives at the man who'd long since disappeared from view.

At last she finished, feeling better inside for the release, but beginning to shiver on the outside from the cold, the drenching she'd suffered and, yes, her state of dishabille. With a final glare at the hatch door through which Bryce Tremaine had disappeared, she turned and made for her cabin.

"Mmm," said Tansy, "dat cook sho' know how t' fix a good possum!"

Brittany laughed, relieved to see her friend so well recovered. "'Tis a *posset*, Tansy, not a *possum*," she corrected gently, indicating the mixture of hot milk laced with rum that Tansy was sipping.

Tansy laughed too. "Uh-huh, well, posset o' possum, dis sho' done me up fine, Miz Britt'ny. Ah's feelin' like mah ole self agin."

They were sitting in their cabin in the late afternoon, a couple of hours after the captain and crew had found a suitable place to drop anchor so they could wait out the storm in safety. All that remained of the tempest now was a steadily falling rain, and once again they could feel movement as the sloop made her way along vastly calmer river currents.

"Well," declared Brittany, "no one could be gladder than I that you're well again . . . ah, except *you*, I suppose!"

They shared another moment of laughter.

"But, Tansy," Brittany continued, "I was just thinking, um, after that possum-posset business . . . um . . . what would you say if I were to start, ah, a bit of schooling to help you along with things like that, hmm?"

Tansy regarded her warily. "Things like whut?"

"Oh, things like choosing the correct word when you might want to know it, learning how to write it and read it, you know..." She smiled, but watched the black woman's face carefully...hopefully, for her reaction.

Tansy's eyes grew wide as understanding hit. "You means t' teach me *letters*?" she questioned in amazement.

"If you'd wish it." Brittany tried to keep her tone nonchalant, but underneath, her heart was beating with excitement. It was such a perfect next step, now that Tansy had her freedom. Not only was Tansy highly intelligent and full of a natural curiosity that would encourage learning, but an education would allow her to make use of that freedom. No one was truly free, Brittany reasoned, if he or she was illiterate.

"Mah wishin' ain't got all dat much t' do wif it," Tansy told her with a frown. "Dey's some massahs whut whups dere slaves fo' tryin' t'—"

"Tansy, Tansy!" Brittany exclaimed. "You're *not* a slave anymore, remember?"

But the black woman was still frowning. "It don't always matter t' some white folks, honeychile. T' dem, black is black, an' white is white, an' if you's de wrong colah, dey ain't gonna have no truck wif you havin' ideas dat puts you 'bove yo' place. Why, ah heerd 'bout some places passin' laws agin teachin' blacks dere letters!"

Sadly, Brittany nodded. She was beginning to understand how some narrow people could feel threatened by an educated black, slave or free.

Then, suddenly, she brightened. "But what if, just

as with your sums, we did it secretly?" she suggested. "I'm sure we could be careful." The blue eyes searched the black woman's face. "The important thing is, do *you* want it, Tansy? Are *you* willing to take the risk—although I think it won't be very great, considering the two highly intelligent female minds that will be working on this—but, tell me, *are you willing to take the chance?*"

There was a silence, punctuated only by the muffled snapping of canvas and the creaking of timber overhead, while Tansy considered. Then an ear-to-ear grin split her face. "Honeychile, 'pears t' me ah ain't de only one dat be takin' dat chance. Iffn you is willin' t' risk it, ah *gots* t' do de same. *Ah's gonna do it!*"

A yelp of delight broke from Brittany's throat as she threw herself at her friend. "Hooray!" she cried, wrapping Tansy in a fierce hug. "Hooray for you! Hooray for me! Hooray for a blow against ignorance!"

Laughing and hugging, the two women settled down to plan the campaign that blow would initiate.

Will Thatcher stifled a yawn as he surveyed the remnants of the meal he and Bryce had shared in the captain's cabin. They were bone-tired, as were most of the crew, from fighting the aberrant storm that had plagued them hours earlier. It was the main reason they'd elected to dine an hour earlier than usual, with most of the crew retiring early to their bunks and hammocks.

Thinking of this change in arrangements for the dinner hour, Will chuckled.

A questioning eyebrow from Bryce prompted an explanation.

"I wuz jest picturin' the expression on our 'ellion's face when ye sent me t' tell 'er there'd be no dinin' in the cap'n's cabin this evenin'." He chuckled again. "And the pretty speech she served up wi' it!

"''Ell will freeze o'er afore I sup wi' the likes of 'im!'" he mimicked in a farfetched falsetto. "'Tell *that* t' the blackguard, if ye dare! And if the meat 'r fowl 'e 'as sent t' us on a tray is anythin' less 'n *robust*,' she sez, ''e'll be 'earin' from me father about it!'"

More chuckling followed, and Bryce reluctantly joined in.

"Ah, I tell ye, lad, she's got a wicked temper, that 'un . . . but, say, wot o' yer plans t' tame the wench? I thought sure, by this evenin's meal, ye'd 'ave 'ad 'er wrapped about yer wee finger."

There was a pause as Bryce regarded the contents of his half-filled brandy snifter. Without removing his gaze from it, he replied. "I've decided to let the matter drop. I've better things to do than tame a colonial shrew."

Will was dumbfounded. "Let the matter drop?" he questioned, when he finally found his voice. "But I thought—"

"What you thought was based on a mistaken task I set myself. 'Twas a foolish notion, man, so let's forget it, shall we?"

"But, Cap'n, I—"

"Have you forgotten that we pursue a far more important objective on this voyage?" Bryce snapped. "That just a few more miles down this damnable river my mother's betrayer sits, fat and happy? We'll fix our sights on our true objective, Will, and there's an end to it!" He lifted the snifter and drained its contents in a single motion.

Will said nothing, but eyed him speculatively. It was unlike Bryce to speak to him that sharply. In fact, he couldn't recall the lad ever having done so before. What was troubling him?

He played the day's events over slowly in his head, at last focusing on an instance that had pricked his curiosity when it had occurred. The captain had just returned to the main deck during the height of the storm, having accomplished some task below. But instead of throwing himself immediately into the nautical activity on deck, as would have been natural, he'd stood for several seconds with both hands fastened on a ratline, staring off into the wetness with a brooding look about him. It had lasted only a moment, but the action was unusual enough for Will to mark it. Of course, it was quickly forgotten in the urgency of the demands his own job had made on him in the storm.

But now that he had time to think on it... hadn't Bryce ordered Harry to the women's cabin shortly thereafter? Aye, he had, the very next minute.

So the vixen had had something to do with that errand below—*and* with the captain's brooding. *And* with the shortness of his patience now, he'd wager!

Smiling to himself, Will considered the puzzle pieces he'd assembled and did some speculating. It was no secret that Bryce had admired the redhead from the outset—he'd even said so... magnificent, he'd called her. But that was before he'd come to know her somewhat. And now he was... what? Irritated by her? Troubled by something about her? Whatever it was, he'd never seen the man react in anything more than the mildest manner—good or bad—toward a woman before. Could it be the lovely hellion was beginning to get under his skin in some way? And he didn't like it?

To Will it was an intriguing prospect. "I've better things to do," the lad had said. Aye, like seek out and kill the man who sired him! It was a prospect that did not sit well with Will, no matter his resolution to be loyal to Bryce and help him achieve his aim.

Even an old salt like Will didn't take easily to the notion of patricide. Bryce's plan was to play about with the blackguard for a while and in some way force him into a duel. "A fair duel, strictly arranged, with seconds and an attending physician and the like," Bryce had said.

But Will knew better. Bryce Tremaine had been practicing with pistols for months now—ever since he'd learned Edmund Avery was still alive. Why, the lad could shoot the buttons off a waistcoat at twenty paces! And he was an expert swordsman—had been, ever since his public school days. Avery hadn't a chance. It would be out-and-out murder, and Bryce knew it.

And what if, by some fluke, things went awry and the older man found a lucky shot? What then? The lad could likely lose his own skin.

But what if something more fulfilling were to enter the captain's life? Something that distracted him permanently, enough to make him put aside his burning hatred—his quest for this terrible revenge. Could the redhead . . .

"Nay," muttered Will aloud as he shook his head regretfully. "'Twould never 'appen."

"What wouldn't happen?" Bryce asked him as he rose from his chair with a stretch and a yawn.

"Oh!" Will exclaimed, not having realized that he'd been thinking aloud. "Ah, I was merely thinkin', 'twould never 'appen that we'd be likely t' 'it such a squall agin." He too rose from his seat and headed for the door.

"We'd better not," scowled Bryce darkly. "I've had my fill of storms lately."

"Aye," nodded Will, suppressing a smile as he

opened the door. "Well, a pleasant night's sleep t'
ye, lad. Good night."

A muffled growl was the only response as Will
shut the door behind him and made his way to his
own sleeping quarters.

"'Tis a permanent distraction ye be needin', lad,"
he whispered to the darkness. "Aye, a distraction."

CHAPTER 8

BRYCE WATCHED JONATHAN GRIMSBY MAneuver the *Louise* gracefully around the sharp bend in the river, then nodded with satisfaction as, in the distance, a private dock came into view.

"There she be, sir," said the first mate with a grin, "the Wakefield plantation—or the northern edge of her. The rest of Sweetbriar stretches for miles beyond those trees."

"'Tis a large holding, then?" Bryce squinted against the bright sunlight that threatened his view of the distant stand of trees.

"Pretty large, as plantations around here go. Some sixteen thousand acres, give or take a few. But the interestin' thing be, very little of 'tis planted."

"Oh? And why is that?"

"Mistress Wakefield's fearsome rich, for one thing. Left a fortune by her late husband—family money, ye see. For another, the lady refuses t' own slaves. So she'll only plant what can be worked and harvested by hirelings or indentureds."

"Indentureds? But aren't they a bit like slaves? I mean—"

"Beggin' your pardon, sir, but there be a difference. Indentureds can work off their bondage. Slaves cannot."

Bryce nodded. "And since hirelings and indentureds are harder to come by than slaves around here, Mistress Wakefield allows a great deal of valuable acreage to lie fallow each year."

"Because of her principles, aye," said a familiar feminine voice behind him.

Bryce turned to behold Brittany, looking like something out of a Gainsborough painting as she stood facing him in the early summer sunshine.

She seemed to emerge out of the essence of the sunlight itself, dressed in a day gown of soft yellow silk with matching bonnet, gloves and parasol. Her hair beneath the fetching bonnet was once again stylishly coiffed, its coppery strands visible, but subdued into obedient twists and loops; the effect was civilized . . . and charming.

Equally charming were the deep dimples that formed as she smiled with—was it a hint of mischief he saw in those blue eyes?

"I do so admire a woman with principles, don't you, captain?" she questioned airily.

"Especially if those principles coincide with your own?" Bryce questioned, his eyes touching briefly on Tansy, who stood in animated conversation with Will on the deck below.

"Principle and the will to stand behind it are so rare," she said, "that I think I admire anyone who possesses them, but, aye, 'tis especially pleasing to find an individual with such tenets when they align with mine. I'd be a liar to say otherwise, and—"

"Ah, let me guess," he interrupted with a wicked grin. "You *never lie*."

Brittany knew from the challenging gleam in those green eyes that she'd been put on the receiving end of an improper double entendre, yet she was undecided what to do about it. Her immediate instinct was to slap his handsome, insolent face, but that would create a scene, and just as they were nearing Aunt Amelia's, too. Moreover, it would let on to Jonathan Grimsby, who was looking on with more interest than she would have cared for, that she comprehended Bryce's indelicate intent.

She finally decided to respond in the only way that would appear to be answering the innocent meaning while addressing the other as well.

"You are quite correct, captain," she said, smiling ever so sweetly. "*I never lie*."

Then, with a flounce of skirts and petticoats, she whirled and went to join Tansy and Will.

Bryce watched her go with wry humor lighting his eyes, for he suddenly realized he could not entirely cease his baiting of her, despite his gloomy resolutions of the night before. Whenever she was near, a kind of chemistry took over and he found himself helpless to resist a prod or two.

Ah, well, he thought, in just a short while he would deposit her at her aunt's and never lay eyes on the wench again. So, what the harm?

He was in excellent spirits this morning, something he attributed to the fact that his quarry was near and he would soon be about his mission. Avery's plantation was, he'd been told by Grimsby, just around the next bend of the river. He had to force himself to appear calm. Revenge would be his to taste, and very soon now . . . very soon. . . .

* * *

As Brittany approached Tansy and Will, she found the two in a heated exchange. The black woman stood, hands on hips, glaring up at the huge seaman who towered over her with a scowl on his face.

"An' ah 'spect t' see dat chest up heah in no time flat, undahstand? Miz Britt'ny ain't got no time t' waste lollygaggin' 'roun de dock, waitin' fo' her clothes!"

"And I told ye," growled Will as he thrust a massive forefinger at her in short, little jabs, "the cap'n already assigned the task t' 'Arry!"

"Harry!" exclaimed Tansy. "Dat skinny half-pint? Why it wouldn't take more 'n a sneeze t' blow him away! Dat chile ain't got de *strenf* t' tote dat chest, so you git down an' help him wid it, hear me? An' put yo' finger back where it belong!" she added, glaring murderously at the offending digit.

Brittany watched the two of them going at it and couldn't help chuckling. The little vignette, comprised of the pair as they faced each other, so incongruous in size, yet so earnest in their argument, tickled her sense of the absurd, and she had to struggle to keep from laughing aloud.

"Missy," Will was saying (as he slowly lowered his finger), "I doubt ye'd understand, but it so 'appens I be the first mate o' the cap'n's own ship, and a first mate—"

"Ah undahstands fine," Tansy angrily broke in. "You jes too high 'n mighty t'—"

"A-h-h, Tansy," said Brittany, "I seem to have caught my heel in the hem of my gown in back. Could you see about it? And Mister Thatcher, I fear I could not avoid overhearing your exchange just now, and, while I agree that helping the cabin boy fetch baggage does not coincide with the duties of your station, I am sure, sir, that as a *gentleman*, you would not be averse to assisting a lady to come by her clothes chest in time to disembark. Would you be so kind . . . sir?"

Will exchanged his scowl for a broad grin. "Certainly, Mistress. Anythin' fer a *lady*!" And with an elaborate bow, followed by a frown as he passed Tansy, he turned and headed below.

"Hmph," muttered Tansy as she threw him a final glare, then moved to examine Brittany's skirt.

"Oh, Tansy, thank you, but I find that won't be necessary after all," Brittany told her. "See? I seem to have freed it myself." She lifted her skirts slightly, producing a slim foot clad in a yellow kid slipper.

"Hmph," Tansy muttered again as she threw her a disbelieving glance. "Hmph!"

They left the sloop a short time later and were taken up the long drive to Sweetbriar's Big House, as it was called, by a grizzled old man driving an open landau. The pair of matched bays that pulled the carriage looked to Bryce to be excellent specimens of horseflesh and he remarked on it.

"Aye," said Brittany, "Uncle Tobias was a very successful horse breeder, and his sons have carried on with that interest since his death. And a good thing, too, for Aunt Amelia will have as little to do with horses as possible. She declares that anything which is that much larger than a man and possesses twice as many legs, yet half as much brain, is not to be trusted."

Bryce chuckled. "She sounds like a bit of a character."

"Oh, indeed! 'Tis one of the reasons I'm so fond of her—that, and the infinite number of kindnesses she's dealt me over the years."

Catching the wistful note in her tone, Bryce wondered about what it revealed. Was her childhood so devoid of kindnesses that she would find a singular adult who'd offered them so remarkable? He thought of his own youth and the wealth of kindness and affection showered on him by Olivia and William. What would he be like today, had all of that been missing or rare? Was this what accounted for her shrewishness? Yet Chambers had spoken of a once-sunny nature. . . .

Bryce shrugged mentally, endeavoring to clear his thoughts. Whatever she was, Brittany Chambers was no easy puzzle. Of that he was certain!

They were traveling down a long, winding drive that was flanked on both sides by a series of giant, evenly spaced oak trees. Beyond the trees lay acres of lush pasture, and grazing horses could be glimpsed here and there. Overhead, the sky was clear and blue with no traces of the storm that had troubled them yesterday, although occasionally, along the graveled drive, broken twigs and branches signaled that the tempest had passed over Sweetbriar, too.

"These sons of your aunt and uncle," said Bryce by way of making conversation, "they are grown, then?"

Brittany nodded. "Just barely, being a couple of years younger than I. So, of course they were still in the midst of their teen years when dear Uncle passed away five years ago."

"But I thought you said they took over the horse breeding for their father."

"Indeed, sir, and so they did!" Brittany laughed. "They're a plucky pair, those two, unwilling to allow a little youth to stop them, once their decision was made."

Bryce noted that her voice took on an affectionate

tone when she spoke of her aunt and cousins, and her expression became merry and cheerful. "You're fond of these cousins of yours, too, I gather."

"Of Toby and Tony? Oh, immensely! I count them among my dearest friends!" She didn't add that they had been perhaps the only friends she'd had as a lonely child growing up in her stepmother's household.

Anthony and Tobias Wakefield, Tony and Toby to all who knew them, were a pair of young rascals whose chief claim to virtue in Brittany's eyes lay in their total acceptance of her as an independent being. The three of them had spent a great deal of time together growing up, and the boys had willingly allowed her to join them in childhood pranks and antics ranging from salting the cook's sugar to skinny-dipping in a hidden stream.

The twins were characters in their own rights, Brittany thought to herself affectionately. She remembered the way each rarely spoke in complete sentences—of how, instead, one cousin usually began a statement, with the other picking up and finishing the thought. And they were quite a pair of dandies, those two. Why, even while working with their beloved horses, they always sported the nattiest attire—to the utter despair of their valet.

But above all, they were intensely loyal to those they loved and cared for. These two were the only ones (aside from Tansy, now) who were aware of the chicanery behind Brittany's shrewish stance with her suitors, and they would "expire and perish" before ever letting on. Indeed, when they'd recently visited Fredericksburg, they'd been the instigators of many of the rumors that flew about town regarding her temper.

Once again Bryce found himself wondering about

her. This time he was drawn to the subtle expressions that flitted across her face as she sat, quietly engaged in some private musings. They were pleasurable, whatever these thoughts were—that much was obvious. No doubt they had to do with those young male cousins of hers. Oddly enough, the thought annoyed him and he wondered why. Then, quickly brushing this last notion aside, he decided to satisfy his curiosity.

"Penny for your thoughts," he said.

"Oh, they're worth a great deal more than that, Captain!" she replied archly.

Bryce's eyebrows rose in mild surprise. "Well, in that case—"

"Now, would ye look at that!" exclaimed Will (who, along with Tansy, had been conspicuously silent on the ride thus far). "'Tis a bloomin' palace!"

What Will referred to was Sweetbriar's Big House, visible now as they rounded a bend in the drive. A huge, Georgian brick mansion with a pair of sprawling wings abutting its sides, it rested on a gentle hillside overlooking pastures that sloped down toward the river. Stately, and yet somehow welcoming, with its center gable and multiple chimneys covered with ivy, it could easily rival some of the grandest houses in England for size, grace and charm.

As the carriage approached the curve that began the sweeping circular drive in front, several figures emerged from the main entrance of the house. The shortest of them was a small, plump woman in a lavender day gown. Using her hand to shield her eyes from the sun, she scanned the drive in their direction, then began to wave enthusiastically.

"'Tis Aunt Amelia!" cried Brittany, waving back from beneath her parasol. "Oh, do hurry, driver!"

As the landau pulled to a stop, the little round

figure who was Aunt Amelia waddled happily down the pair of steps before the entrance and hurried toward the carriage. Only through the agility of youth did a pair of liveried footmen manage to arrive ahead of her and assist Brittany from the vehicle. Then, in a flurry of lavender and yellow, the two women embraced.

"Oh, Aunt, 'tis good to see you!" Brittany exclaimed with unabashed emotion.

"My dear, my dear," murmured the older woman, her niece's bear hug making speech difficult.

At last the two drew apart and stood for a moment, smiling at each other.

"You are quite the beauty, my dear," said Amelia, "even more so than when I saw you last. You favor your mother entirely, except for the Chambers hair." She briefly raised a pudgy hand to pat her own which, although liberally streaked with gray, still bore enough flame-colored strands to signal their kinship.

"Aunt Amelia," said Brittany, gesturing toward the three who had by now alighted from the carriage and were standing beside her, "I'd like you to meet my companions. First, meet Tansy. Not only is she my newest friend who happens to be my abigail as well, she is also a brand new free woman of color. Tansy, this is my aunt, Amelia Wakefield."

There was a moment of stunned silence as Brittany's obvious flaunting of polite protocol registered. She had elected to introduce this servant, a black woman and former slave, ahead of two white males who, moreover, were obviously dressed as gentlemen. It was a blatant breach of etiquette, one which might even be regarded as social suicide in some circles.

The first to break the silence was a tall, thin, sour-faced woman of about forty who stood on the steps behind Amelia. "Well, I *never*—"

"Aggie, that will be quite enough!" Amelia admonished. She smiled at Tansy. "Welcome to Sweetbriar, my dear, and know that you have my joyful wishes for your happiness on the occasion of your manumission."

She noted the traveling bags Tansy was carrying and gave the sour-faced woman a sharp glance. "This is my housekeeper, Mistress Murdock. She will show you where you can put your things and perhaps rest for a while. Aggie! Show the young lady to the blue room, please."

Agatha Murdock's face purpled for a brief moment, but then she nodded stiffly and gestured to a stupefied Tansy. "Follow me, please."

As the two women left, Brittany grinned at her aunt. "You and Aggie are still at it, I see."

"But of course, my dear. After twenty-three years, how could it be otherwise? But come, or have you completely rewritten the manners code? You must introduce—"

"Oh, dear!" exclaimed Brittany, sounding genuinely distressed. "I'm sorry." She glanced sheepishly at Bryce who, by now, had begun to gaze languidly about at the nearby scenery, and then at Will who stood next to him with a bemused look on his face.

"Aunt Amelia, this is Captain Bryce Tremaine and his friend, Mister Will Thatcher, who were kind enough to escort me to Sweetbriar on the *Louise*. Captain, Mister Thatcher, my aunt, Amelia Wakefield."

While Bryce bowed courteously over Amelia's hand, Will doffed the tricorn he'd been wearing to protect his pate from the Virginia sun.

"Well, gentlemen," said Amelia, "I am grateful to

you for bringing my niece to me in one piece, especially after yesterday's unsettling weather." She
glanced at the remaining servant standing on the
steps behind her, an elderly man with a florid complexion and a periwig of a somewhat old-fashioned
style. "Merriweather, you old scoundrel, what are
you standing about for? Show these gentlemen to
suitable chambers and then arrange for tea!"

As Merriweather bowed respectfully and left,
Bryce hurriedly remarked, "Your pardon, Mistress
Wakefield, but it won't be necessary to find us
chambers. Mister Thatcher and I have further business downriver—ah, for your brother, that is—and
we shan't be staying. I appreciate your—"

"Not staying? *Not staying!*" exclaimed Amelia.
"After an arduous river journey? *Nonsense!* Of
course, you're staying! I'll not *hear* of your *not* staying. My sense of hospitality will not hear of your not
staying!"

"But, madam—" Bryce began.

"Now, not another word, captain," said Amelia,
ushering all three of them before her like a mother
hen. "You're far too much the gentleman to argue
with a lady and—" she winked at Brittany—"far too
handsome to be allowed to sail off without offering
me your company for at least a day or two. My
brother's business can wait. He's far too rich, anyway, the old fool! Now there's an end to it! You're
staying. Come along, come along!"

Bryce looked imploringly and with some annoyance at Brittany as they were rushed along through
the handsome, porticoed entryway, but Brittany
merely rolled her eyes helplessly, as if to say, I told
you she was a character. Then he scowled at Will, as
if he should have been able to extricate them from

the situation, but the giant seaman only shrugged to indicate his own bewilderment.

Of the four who followed Merriweather's trail, only Amelia Wakefield had any positive thoughts about the invitation which had just been issued. In their minds, Bryce and, to a lesser extent, Will, had already been halfway back to the *Louise*, their mission beckoning. And Brittany had been close to tasting the expanded sense of freedom she'd enjoy once her Tory escort was out of the way. But the little woman who waddled ahead of them in the lavender dress was a force to be reckoned with, and either by experience or instinct, each of them knew it. The invitation would stand.

CHAPTER 9

"MORE TEA, CAPTAIN?" ASKED AMELIA Wakefield as she presided over an ornate silver tea service set atop a Queen Anne tea table.

They were in the formal drawing room of the Big House. Brittany sat beside her aunt on a settee upholstered in blue and cream striped satin. Facing them over the tea table, whose delicate button feet rested on an Aubusson carpet done in soft pastels, were Bryce and Will, seated in a pair of matching blue velvet wing chairs.

"Ah, no, thank you, madam," Bryce answered politely, "though 'twas a most excellent brew, I assure you."

"I am glad to hear you say so," Amelia told him, "but I must warn you, sir, it may well be the last time I shall be offering it here at Sweetbriar, if what I've been told is true." She raised her own dish of tea to her lips and sipped.

"Oh?" replied Bryce. "And what is it you've been told?"

Brittany set her fragile Sevres cup down on its

small, matching cup plate, having poured her tea into its dish to cool. "I believe I can answer that, Captain...if I may?" She glanced inquiringly at Amelia who, busy sipping her tea, nodded for Brittany to continue.

"The Burgesses—the Virginia House of Burgesses, that is—appointed, back in March, I believe, a Provincial Committee of Correspondence to keep us in touch with events in the other colonies, and—"

"I fail to see," Bryce interrupted impatiently (for patience had hardly been his strong suit once he realized the delay this stopover would cost him), "what that has to do with—"

"*Sir!*" huffed Brittany. "Kindly give me the *opportunity,* and I shall *tell* you!"

Amelia's eyebrows rose briefly as she detected the brittle air between the two. Her gaze swung to Will, whose look of quiet amusement puzzled her further. What had transpired between these young people on the journey downriver? And why did the handsome captain, with his perfect gentleman's manners and impeccable speech, seem to be more than the simple merchant shipowner he professed to be? (She knew something of the difference, having married above her station and having been painstakingly tutored in ladylike refinements by an adoring husband in the early years of their marriage.) With keen interest, she settled down to listen further to what the conversation between her guests might reveal.

"The Committee," Brittany was saying, "has recently learned that Virginia is not alone in its outrage over the tea tax, and word is going about that in order to protest its unfairness to us colonials, we might consider sending the East India Company's ships back to England still *fully laden* with *unpurchased tea!*" She smiled archly at Bryce. "'Twill turn us into chocolate drinkers, I daresay, but 'tis little enough sacrifice if His Majesty and the *Tories* take our message."

"I *say*! Well said! She's got that right!" said a masculine voice from the doorway.

All heads turned to behold a tall, slender young man wearing well-tailored riding clothes cut in the latest "English country" style. He sported a broad grin in an amiable face covered with freckles, but the most noticeable thing about him was the carrot red hair he wore unpowdered and tied in a fashionable bag at the nape of his neck. "Our dear Coz," he continued, "has ever been, ah—"

"—the best of wits when it comes to piecing things out in a parcel!" finished a second voice behind him, and a moment later the carrot-top was joined in the doorway by another redheaded youth, this one an exact copy of the first.

"*Toby! Tony!*" cried Brittany, as she sprang to her feet and rushed to greet them.

There was a flurry of enthusiastic hugs and kisses among the three. Amelia looked on with approval and Bryce and Will rose to their feet, open curiosity on their faces.

"I say! She's become a prime beauty, our Coz!" exclaimed the first twin, while holding Brittany at arm's length and running his eyes fondly over her. "Aye, prime! One of the first, ah—"

"—beauties of Virginia," his twin finished for him, while making Brittany an elaborate bow. "Or, better yet, one of the first beauties of, ah—"

"—the colonies!" his brother supplied.

"Aye, or mayhap, the entire kingd—"

"Boys, boys!" laughed Amelia, rising from the settee. "Enough of your prattle, now, or you'll turn her head."

"What? Our Coz? Never!" said one twin.

"Nay, never!" echoed the other.

"Well, then," Amelia chuckled, "we shall say you must cease because we have other guests." She faced Bryce and Will while beckoning her sons nearer. "Captain Tremaine, Mister Thatcher, my sons, Tobias and Anthony Wakefield, but you must call them Toby and Tony, as we all do, or I fear none hereabouts will know whom you mean."

The four men exchanged bows and greetings while Brittany looked on. She noted that of the four, only Will's formal movements appeared awkward and untried. Bryce Tremaine matched, and perhaps even surpassed, the grace and deportment of her cousins, who had been raised and schooled as gentlemen, as befitted the sons of a wealthy planter whose family traced back to William the Conqueror. And again she found herself wondering about Bryce's background.

Moreover, she'd begun to note a certain restlessness in him once they'd reached Sweetbriar. It was nothing overt, for the man exerted a masterful control over himself and, she supposed, of his emotions, most of the time; but on occasion, when she chanced a glimpse of him when he thought no one was watching, she'd observed a look here, a quickly stilled movement there, which hinted at impatience with the present situation, or perhaps an eagerness to be off and about other matters.

Oh well, she sniffed to herself, *perhaps the wretch is merely eager to rid himself of his charge of two days—me!* Trying this idea on for size, she found it fit, for wasn't she as eager to be rid of him? And yet it rankled, though through sheer perversity she refused to examine why.

"I say," Tony was saying as the four moved toward the tea table, "that was a regular ripper that tore through here yesterday, Captain. Did you, ah—"

"—run afoul of it?" queried his twin.

"Decidedly more afoul than I'd have wished," Bryce responded with a brief frown of annoyance.

Toby leaned forward and snapped up one of the little tea cakes on the tray, then made for the settee.

"Oh, no you don't!" cried his mother. "You may both snatch all the tea cakes you wish, but you may not avail yourselves of my drawing room furniture while you have the odor of the stables about you."

She stepped protectively in front of the settee looking for all the world, thought Brittany, like a puffed-up robin defending its nest.

Undaunted, the twins chuckled affectionately while Tony helped himself to two tea cakes.

"I say, Coz," said Toby, "'tis just as well, for we were wondering—"

"—as we walked into the house and heard you'd arrived," added Tony. . . .

"—if you'd care to go out to the stables with us—"

"—and see the new stallion we've purchased."

Will's head, as he watched these two begin and end sentences for each other, had begun to swing back and forth like a pendulum. "Er—my pardon, sirs," he said, "but do ye always, er—"

"Always!" grinned the twin closest to him.

"Without fail!" echoed the other.

"They've been going on like this for years," laughed Brittany, noting the bemusement on Will's face. "You'll grow used to it." She glanced at Amelia. "Aunt, would you mind if we dashed off to see—"

"Not at all, not at all," chirped Amelia. Her settee defended, she was the cheerful mother hen again. "By all means, go out to the stables and have a look at the beast. You, too, Captain," she urged. "And you, Mister Thatcher, or do you prefer ships to horses?"

Bryce chuckled. "He prefers ships to *anything,*

madam, but we've both an appreciation of good horseflesh."

"Then 'tis settled!" grinned Toby. He bent down to plant an affectionate kiss on his mother's cheek. "We shall see you later, Mama, and we promise—"

"—not to appear at your dinner table without having bathed and changed," supplied Tony, as he kissed her other cheek.

"See that you do not," Amelia told them with a merry twinkle in the gray eyes that were so similar to those of her two handsome sons.

The five made their way to the stable yard amidst a steady banter among the cousins, with the twins gayly teasing Brittany about her "courtship difficulties," and her giving them saucy replies in return.

"What, no husband clinging to your arm as yet, sweet Coz?" Toby taunted.

"*Dragging* me *by* the arm, you mean!" Brittany retorted.

"Egad!" Tony exclaimed in mock horror. "Methinks the lass is too . . . ah, *reticent*, too—"

"—*gentle* to catch a husband?" his brother finished with matching sarcasm.

"Better ungentle than undone!" Brittany snapped wickedly.

"*Brittany!* You *wound* us!" cried Toby, slapping his hand over his heart. "We speak of the noble state of matrimony, of—"

"—man and maid entering into a lifetime of eternal bliss!" his brother followed up.

"Spoken like two who could only know such eternal truths by having participated in them themselves!" Brittany's sarcasm echoed theirs, bite for bite, though her eyes twinkled with pleasure as she spoke.

Bryce witnessed their badinage with good humor

and a growing appreciation for the quickness of Brittany's wit. It was plain to see where she'd come by her facility with barbed retorts. Growing up in the company of these two wags couldn't have been easy, unless one learned to give as good as one got.

But what impressed him even more was the easy camaraderie shared by the three cousins and the definite sense of mutual respect among them. As an only child growing up on William's estate, he'd sometimes found himself missing the company of other children of his own age and station, and he couldn't help wondering now, as he observed these three together, what it would have been like if things had been otherwise with him.

To the side of the stable block was a large, fenced-in paddock, and this was where the twins led them. Suddenly, all five drew to a halt as the shrill trumpeting of a stallion cut the air.

"Well, there he is," said Tony proudly.

"All sixteen hands of him," added Toby.

Prancing across the far end of the enclosure was the most exciting piece of horseflesh Brittany had ever seen. He was coal black, and the satiny sheen of his coat reflected the sunlight as he moved. He had an elegant, finely chiseled head with a face that she noted, as he presented it in profile, was somewhat dished. Small, delicately shaped ears pricked forward as the stallion focused on a small group of mares in a pasture a few hundred yards away. Then, as Toby whistled to him, he turned his head, accentuating a neck that was beautifully arched and powerful.

With alert interest, he trotted toward them. His movements were graceful, yet the play of sunlight on the muscles rippling as he moved spoke mainly of power. In fact, power was everywhere a part of him. A deep, powerful chest told of an animal that would have staying power as well as strength when he ran distances; long, powerful legs denoted speed; and well-developed, massive hindquarters were the quintessence of power.

"My God," murmured Will, "wot an animal!"

"Where did you find him?" breathed Brittany.

But Bryce's comments were more specific as he stood, quietly assessing the noble animal. "I recognize the Arabian blood," he said carefully, "but the size of him..."

"Quite so," Toby noted approvingly. "He's out of an Arabian mare, and that accounts for the finely chiseled head and what, but the sire's the result of an experimental outcross...Irish racing stock, for one thing, and—"

"Oh, Toby," cried Brittany, "do tell us all about his breeding, but later! For now, tell me, is he broken to saddle? May I—oh, I've got to ride him. I've *got* to!"

Both twins laughed as Tony withdrew his pocket watch and flipped open the lid of the gold hunter case.

"You win," Tony said cheerfully to his twin. "And, yes, he's well broken," he added, for Brittany's benefit.

"Aye, I win," chuckled Toby. "'Twas less than three minutes!"

"Whatever are you two talking about?" Brittany demanded as she ceased petting the stallion's velvety nose and stood glaring at them, arms akimbo.

"A wager, of course," said Toby.

"Naturally," said Tony, "and Toby's won it."

"A wager," frowned their cousin. "What kind of a wager, pray tell?"

"Tony bet you'd be demanding to ride Saracen in under five minutes. I countered with less than three. As you can see," he added, happily holding out his hand for his brother's gold pieces, "I've won, and Tony—"

"—must pay," said his twin with mock glumness.

"Really, boys, whatever would Aunt Amelia say?" Brittany grinned, then resumed petting the stallion's nose. "*Saracen*," she crooned, "how beautiful he is! Now, when may I try him?"

"You may assure yourself that you may not," said a firm male voice behind her.

Brittany whirled about and locked eyes with Bryce. "What did you say?" she queried, her eyes narrowing to indigo slits.

Bryce cast an assessing eye over the stallion, then back at her. "As you may recall, I was charged by your father with the responsibility of seeing to your safety in his absence. As I see it, that includes preventing you from killing yourself on a mount that, no matter how well schooled, is far too powerful for a woman to manage. You will have to forego the opportunity, my dear."

Storm clouds gathered across Brittany's face in no uncertain warning. Recognizing the signs, the twins glanced at each other, perplexed, before backing away in unison. In a moment, each was leaning against the fence, his arms folded nonchalantly across his chest, eager curiosity on his face.

"You addlepated ignoramus!" Brittany cried. "How dare you presume to judge my equestrian skills without any demonstration or—or—evidence!"

"I do not require a demonstration," Bryce replied with maddening calm, "and, as for evidence, 'tis evident enough that an animal of this caliber is too formidable to be ridden sidesaddle."

"Ohh," fumed Brittany, "you are the most presumptuous—" She fought for self-control by clenching her hands into fists and forcing them down into her skirts. "How dare you presume to know what you do not!" she spat. "For your information, *Tory dunce*, I do not perform my serious riding on a side-saddle. I shall ride Saracen *astride!*"

Bryce's green eyes flickered with a brief look of surprise, but his voice betrayed no doubts as he continued in his well-modulated baritone. "Nevertheless, the stallion is too much horse for a woman. You are forbidden to ride him, Mistress."

"Forbid—" she choked. The man was an arrogant tyrant! She looked hopefully at her cousins, but their bemused faces gave her little encouragement. A glance at Will's carefully blank countenance promised less. Deliberately strangling her rage with a slow intake of breath, she exhaled slowly between clenched teeth before responding to her tormentor.

"My dear Captain Tremaine," she seethed, "I cannot think that you are presently in a position to forbid me anything. Your duty was to protect me from harm while escorting me to my aunt's and cousins' home. That journey has now been completed. You are no longer in charge."

"Am I not?" Bryce challenged with a mocking grin.

"No, you are not!" Brittany shouted as she stamped her foot in frustration. Beside her, the stallion flattened his ears and snorted. "And furthermore—"

Just then, the sound of cantering hooves intruded and a moment later, a liveried horseman approached from the drive beyond the stables.

"'Tis one of Edgehill's grooms," said Toby.

"Aye, 'tis Avery's livery, all right," Tony added, somewhat sourly.

At the mention of the name which was on his mind day and night now, Bryce cast his eyes avidly over the newcomer. The action was not missed by Brittany, and she was piqued by a moment's curiosity, but a second later she dismissed it; she'd had about all she could stomach of the Tory rogue for now, and all she wanted was to rid herself of his obnoxious company.

"Excuse me, gentlemen," she said. "I promised my abigail I'd meet her to discuss some things, and I'd almost forgotten." She threw the twins a bright smile, nodded cordially to Will and, carefully avoiding even a glance at Bryce, turned and headed for the Big House.

Will moved closer to Bryce while the twins walked over toward the mounted groom. "Careful, now, laddie," he murmured out of earshot of the threesome. "'Tis only 'is groom, and ye wouldn't wish t' appear uncommon 'asty." He gestured at the twins, now in quiet conversation with the horseman. "They'll be lettin' ye know 'is business soon enough."

Bryce nodded but kept his attention on the groom from Avery's plantation.

Moments later, the servant in red and gold livery turned his horse's head and trotted off in the direction from which he'd come. Toby and Tony (whom Bryce had finally learned to tell apart by way of the moles that appeared on Toby's right cheek and Tony's left) came strolling back toward the other two men.

"Well," said Toby with a measure of disgust, "it appears we shall have visitors on the morrow. Poor Mama! She'll—"

"—have to put up with that poor, ill-used wife of Avery's?" Tony queried. "What about *us*? *We'll* have to put up with *Avery*!"

"Aye," grumbled Toby. "*And* that rotten son of his, more than likely!"

"Ye're entertainin' guests ye've no likin' fer?" Will inquired cautiously.

"Oh, aye," asserted Tony, picking a speck of lint

off his sleeve. "'Tis a hellish thing, to be neighbored
so closely by a, ah—"

"—smooth, oily blackguard," supplied Toby.

"Ah, 'tis a pity," said Will, "t' be saddled wi' such.
A *good* neighbor kin be a boon t' country folk."

"Aye, well this one's a detriment," Toby told him.

"He goes about, lording it over one and all,"
added Tony, "as if he's better than all of us . . ."

"—when everyone knows he owes all he has to
his poor wife's dwindling fortune," said Toby.

"But worse than that," Tony interjected, "is the
way he treats his folk."

"His folk?" asked Will.

"Aye," said Tony disgustedly, "his slaves and
bondsmen. You saw the poor fellow that just left—
skin and bones, he was—"

"—and a lump purpling over his left eye," added
Toby.

"What you're saying then," said Bryce grimly, "is
that your neighbor starves and beats his servants."

It was the first time Bryce had spoken since the
groom's appearance, and both carrot-topped heads
swung in his direction, as if just realizing he was still
there.

"Aye, you've got that right," said Tony.

"And," whispered Toby, "some say he beats his
wife as well."

Bryce's mouth tightened into a hard line. Recognizing the dangerous glimmer in his eyes, and fearing Bryce might allow his emotions to give
something away, Will quickly searched for something to say.

"Er—I, ah, wonder that yer mum puts up wi' the
sod, 'er bein' so fine a lady and all."

"Oh, Mama doesn't tolerate Edmund Avery very
well at all," Tony told him, "but, ah—"

"—she's too much the lady to dismiss the rotter," finished Toby.

"And she feels sorry for Mistress Emily, his wife," Tony added.

"Poor drab that she is," commented his twin.

"Mama's not going to be very happy about their visit, I daresay," Toby told them.

"No, not very happy at all." Tony brushed some dust from his cuff and looked decidedly unhappy himself.

"Well," said Bryce, gazing off into the distance where the groom had ridden, "I believe Mistress Wakefield will require all the moral support she can come by tomorrow." He turned to look at Will and the twins. "And we gentlemen shall simply make a point of being here to give it to her."

"Well said!" exclaimed Toby, clapping him on the back.

"Good man!" said Tony, doing the same. "You're with us, then!"

"And I," Will told them.

"Capital!" Toby cried. "I knew I liked the two of you the moment I laid eyes on you!"

"And I," echoed Tony. "Now Mama has four champions against Avery. She'll like that. What say you, we go to our rooms and, ah—"

"—share a dram or two on it!" Toby suggested.

"Lead the way," said Bryce.

"Aye!" grinned Will.

And with the convivial rapport that comes to men with a common purpose, the four turned and headed up the path.

CHAPTER 10

THE FAINT LIGHT OF A GIBBOUS MOON SIL-
vered the leaves of the laurel and crepe myrtle that
lined the pathway to the stables as two slim figures,
one tall and one petite, made their way from the Big
House. It was late, well after the dinner hour, and
most of Sweetbriar's household was asleep. Only the
steady staccato of crickets and cicadas and the furtive
rustlings of other small nocturnal creatures per-
meated the silence; the pair of shadowed forms
made no sound as their slippered feet took them
over the brick path.

"Miz Britt'ny," whispered Tansy, "is—*are*—you
sho' you wants—*want*—t' do dis? Ah mean—"

"Shh!" her companion cut in, and in a softer tone,
"Aye, I'm sure. You know the only way I'm going to
get to ride that stallion is to start working on it now
—and in secret. That was our plan, wasn't it?"

The plan she referred to had been formulated after
dinner, when the two women had closeted themselves in Brittany's chamber; this was after she'd
learned that Bryce planned to stay at Sweetbriar for at

least a few more days and, more important, that he was still immovable on the issue of her riding Saracen.

"I'll just have to sneak a ride," she'd told Tansy. "Not that I prefer using stealth. It goes against the grain, but now that the Tory's staying on, who knows how long 'twill be before I can ride the black openly—and I'm *dying* to ride him, Tansy! I can barely wait!"

She'd decided her ride would probably be best taken in the early morning, before anyone was up and about, but she'd chosen to visit the black in the stables tonight in order to gauge his temperament better and perhaps to establish an acquaintance that would render the horse more amenable to accepting her as a rider, come dawn.

"Keep to the shadows and follow me," she whispered to Tansy now, "and when we reach that door, make nary a sound. The groom on night duty usually sleeps in the tack room at the other end, but we'll take no chances."

Tansy nodded and they resumed their stealthy pace. A couple of minutes later they found themselves inside the stables; having successfully opened the side door, they'd shut it behind them without a sound—for at Sweetbriar the buildings, like everything else, were kept in excellent repair, and so hinges and other movable metal hardware were oiled assiduously.

Once inside, Brittany looked around, her vision just barely aided by the moonlight which filtered in through a series of high windows left unshuttered at night to provide ventilation. She had heard that Saracen occupied the large box stall once belonging to her uncle's favorite saddle horse, so she pointed silently in its direction for Tansy's benefit, then motioned for the black woman to follow as she crept noiselessly along the stable's center aisle.

As they moved, a couple of horses stirred in their stalls; then a few snorts and other equine noises broke the silence, and Brittany gritted her teeth and muttered a silent prayer that they would not be discovered. But as they drew closer to Saracen's stall, it was not an equine sound that reached their ears, but one far more articulate—and human.

"'Tis a piece of luck, Avery's arriving here tomorrow," said a low male voice—*Bryce's voice*!

The two women looked at each other with startled recognition, then, in a single movement, crouched inside an unoccupied stall that neighbored the one from which the voice came.

"Aye," murmured a second voice they immediately recognized as Will's. "'E's played right into yer 'ands, ye might say. 'Twill give ye a good chance t' size 'im up—measure 'is mettle, so t' speak."

"Aye," said Bryce, "and then do what must be done."

"But, laddie, surely ye don't mean t' kill 'im 'ere, on Mistress Wakefield's land?" Will's voice rang with concern.

"Nay, the killing's not to be done here," Bryce reassured him. "I'd not do that to our kindly hostess."

At the mention of killing, Brittany and Tansy froze and stared at each other with looks of mutual horror.

"At *'is* place, then?" Will questioned.

"'Twould seem the most likely," Bryce answered, "since I'll have easy access by way of Timothy Chambers's cargo that awaits a fortuitously timed delivery."

"Aye," said Will, "but, laddie, I must ask ye one more time, no matter if ye bite off me 'ead . . . be ye *certain* ye wish t' do this deed?"

Bryce sighed, then rose from the bale of hay he'd been sitting on and began to pace the length of the horseless stall. He understood the reasons for Will's cautionary questioning. Killing was no easy thing. Oh, he'd killed men before, but only in self-defense or in fair combat. Well, this killing would come of fair combat, too—he'd see to that. But Edmund Avery must die. He'd sworn to it, on his mother's grave.

And so, almost like an old remembered litany, he patiently began to recite to Will his reasons for not veering from his course, pacing the stall as he did so.

Crouching in the next stall, Brittany and Tansy strained to hear what he was saying, but his voice was low, and the rustling of the straw as he paced seemed to obscure three out of every four words he spoke. Still, the two women cupped ears to the stall's thick wooden partition and tried to gather what they could.

"Edmund Avery raped and used my mother, then cold-bloodedly cast her aside when she was with child. And when she died bringing me into the world, my sire disowned all responsibility and fled to these shores to feed greedily on the heart of yet another helpless woman . . . self-satisfied . . . remorseless . . . and guilty as sin itself.

"Because of all these things, but mostly because of what he did to Beth Tremaine, this man will die, Will! For he killed my mother, killed her as surely as if he'd plunged a knife into her bosom. I spoke to Donald Tremaine the year before the smallpox took him and the others—my young uncles. He said, this humble grandfather of mine, that in the days before my mother died, 'twas as if the will to live had left her . . . Long before the actual night of her death, she'd given up on living . . . Edmund Avery had crushed her spirit . . . and her heart.

"The only thing I regret now is that it took so

many years for me to learn the truth—that the scum is still alive . . . that he's been sitting here in worldly splendor whilst I—"

"Now, yer lordship," interrupted Will, "ye cannot regret the *good* fortune wot befell ye followin' yer poor mum's death. 'Twas a saintly act, Avery's brother and sister takin' ye in and raisin' ye t' be the next heir. A marquis, ye'll be one day, and that be a fact!"

Brittany caught a good part of this last, and her eyes widened at it. Then she glanced at Tansy and gave a thoughtful nod. Some of the things she'd found perplexing about this so-called merchant captain were making more sense. Oh, but if only she'd been able to catch the whole tale! Ignoring the pain from her cramped muscles as she crouched in the darkness, she settled in to listen further.

"You are right about my own good fortune," Bryce was saying, "but I needn't remind you that 'twas my uncle, William Avery, and his sister, Olivia, who are responsible for that. Edmund Avery had no hand in it."

"Well," Will equivocated, "there's some would say that indirectly—"

"*Never!*" Bryce cried hotly. "The man's a villain without conscience, without a drop of merit in him! You heard what the twins said. He beats and starves his people . . . abuses even his *wife* . . ." He stopped and stared at the floor, running an agitated hand through his hair, then straightened and met Will's eyes. "Edmund Avery will die," he stated quietly.

"In a carefully arranged duel?" asked Will.

"In a fair fight, face to face," said Bryce grimly. "And before he dies, he will learn who it is that kills him—*and why!*"

Will sighed. "Well, then, laddie, I can see ye're set

on't, so I'll not be tryin' t' dissuade ye further. And ye'll be 'avin' me 'elp. Ye've me word on 't."

"Good man," murmured Bryce, clapping him on the shoulder. "And now I think 'tis time we were abed. We'll need our wits about us in the next few days."

Hearing this, Brittany signalled Tansy, and the two women just managed to duck into the shadows of the empty stall before the tall figures of Bryce and Will passed and headed down the aisle toward the door.

Only when she heard the door shut behind them did Brittany release the breath she'd been holding.

"Lord have mercy!" cried Tansy. *"Did you hear dat?* Dat ain't no cap'n! Dass a mar—a mar—"

"Marquis," finished Brittany, "or, rather, a future marquis."

"Whut dat be?" asked Tansy suspiciously.

"What would that be," Brittany corrected.

"Yas'm—ah mean, *yes ma'am*—what would dat— *that*—be?" she repeated, carefully striving for the proper sounds of the English she'd agreed to learn.

"That," said Brittany, rising to the popping sound of Tansy's knee joints straightening, "is the title of a highly placed lord."

"Hmph," muttered Tansy, "ah knowed—*knew*— dat Tow-ree be mo' dan he 'peared—um, *appeared*!"

Brittany nodded. "It seems we both smelled something amiss, Tans." She massaged the stiff muscles of her thighs and calves through the cotton of the gown she'd donned (without any petticoats underneath it to hamper her movements). "But little did I realize that what I'd sensed would amount to a plot to—to—"

"Kill somebody," Tansy supplied. "Who dis Av'ry be?"

"He's my aunt's neighbor. A planter downriver, and a very prominent man, I hear, although I can't recall ever meeting him. And 'twould seem he's also," she added as she moved toward Saracen's stall, "Bryce Tremaine's intended murder victim!"

"Who done somebody wrong!" said Tansy as she followed her to the large box stall.

"Apparently," said Brittany as she reached to pet the black stallion's soft nose.

Brittany's voice sounded nonchalant, but in reality her head was spinning with the implications of what they'd just overheard. Bryce Tremaine had actually contrived to set up this entire trip as part of a scheme to kill a man! And, not only that—the man was someone from his past.

What kind of a man *was* Bryce? *A very determined one*, came the answer. She stifled a shudder as she contemplated the ramifications of this. To think she'd broken bread with this man and shared close quarters with him . . . *argued* with him and— and *defied him*!

Brittany, old girl, she told herself, *one of these days you're going to reap more than you can handle with your impetuous ways! Bryce is nothing better than a murderer, a ruthless—*

Suddenly she stopped, giving the situation more careful thought. *Was* he really so terrible? She considered what she'd caught about Avery wronging someone . . . someone apparently close to Bryce. How would *she* have reacted, had it been someone close to *her* who'd been wronged?

The stallion nudged her hand with his nose, bringing her back to the present, but as she reached to pat him on the neck, she resolved to do some further thinking about Bryce Tremaine's partially revealed secret . . . some *very careful* thinking. . . .

Tansy stepped beside her, then drew sharply back as she caught sight of the large horse. *"He big!"* she esclaimed.

"Aye," grinned Brittany, "but as gentle as a kitten. See how he nuzzles my hand?" She reached into her pocket and withdrew a chunk of sugar she'd broken from a cone in the pantry, and the black accepted it from her flattened palm. "See? He's a lamb."

Tansy remained skeptical. "He a lamb fo' de sugar, but ya'll ain't—um, *you aren't*—on *top* o' dat hoss yet, Miz Britt'ny!"

Brittany's grin grew broader. "No, but I shall be, Tans, I shall be!"

"Tomorrah?"

"Tomorro*w*," corrected Brittany, then, "Ah . . . no, I think I'll wait another day. Tomorrow is when Avery comes to call, and I shall have enough on my mind as I observe what transpires between him and . . . his lordship!"

Tansy caught the crafty look in her eye and frowned. "Miz Britt'ny, whut trouble you hatchin' now?"

Brittany gave the stallion a final pat on the neck and turned to leave. "Oh," she murmured, linking arms with Tansy as they walked, "nothing in particular just yet . . . but give me time and I'll think of something. . . ."

Whispering conspiratorially together, the two made their way back to the house.

Edmund Avery inspected the cuff of the sleeve of his new powder blue coat after alighting from his carriage in front of the Wakefield's main entrance. His aristocratic features were arranged in impatient lines as he waited for a footman to hand down his wife, whose wide paniers encountered an obstruction in the carriage door's narrow opening. Beside him, their son, Richard, took a pinch of snuff and looked bored.

"Really, Mother," said Richard, "you must do

something about your wardrobe. There are narrower skirts available, I believe."

Joining them at last on the ground, Emily Avery held her tongue, but her mind held the response a less cowed and timid woman might have made: that it had been a long time since her husband had allowed her to make an expenditure for new clothes, and even if narrower silhouettes were coming into vogue, she would be the last creature on earth able to come by them.

Unfortunately, Edmund's pale blue eyes fastened on her features as she had these thoughts. "Disabuse yourself of any notions of self-pity, m'dear, for you know I do not take kindly to them. And, for God's sake, paste a smile on that pudding face of yours!" he hissed. "We are here to launch a courtship, not a funeral procession!"

Richard stifled a yawn. "I do hope the chit's comely. 'Tis the trouble with news garnered through the servants' grapevine. It rarely contains the details one would wish for, and I—"

"You'll court and wed the baggage, be she as plain as a flour sack!" Edmund cut in; then, in an unctuous tone of voice, "Ah, that is, if she's as rich an heiress as the gossip has it!"

Richard opened his mouth as if to reply, then shut it as the front door opened and Merriweather greeted them and led them inside.

A moment later they found themselves being welcomed by Amelia herself, inside the formal drawing room.

"Emily, dear, how good of you to come to call," said Amelia as she kissed the thin, pale-faced woman she'd known since the early days of her marriage, when Emily's first husband was still alive. Amelia tried not to think about the fact that it had been a prettier, more lively Emily she'd known then, but the comparison stuck glaringly in her mind as she turned to acknowledge the man she knew was the source of the changes in her friend. "Edmund," she nodded formally.

"Madam," Edmund intoned smoothly, as he bowed over her hand. Then, straightening, "I believe you must recognize our son, Richard, although the lad's grown considerably since last you saw him."

"Richard, of course," replied Amelia as she extended her hand to the tall, bewigged man who appeared to be a younger version of his father, except that the sire's eyes were pale blue while his were a clear, translucent yellow.

Their greetings completed, Amelia ushered her three guests toward the grouping of chairs about the tea table in the room's center. "And now, allow me to introduce you to my other guests," she said, indicating Brittany who sat on the settee, dressed in an afternoon gown of peach damask silk trimmed with simple ecru lace, and Bryce, who stood in front of one of the side chairs, wearing a bottle green, impeccably tailored, formal coat with buff colored knee breeches, tan waistcoat, and white stock and hose.

"I don't believe you've had the pleasure of meeting my brother's daughter from Fredericksburg. Mister and Mistress Avery, Mister Richard Avery, my niece, Mistress Brittany Chambers . . ."

As these introductions were completed, Brittany took the time to assess their visitors. Avery's wife was a plain, dowdy-looking woman with a timid smile and sad brown eyes, and Brittany found herself feeling instantly sorry for her; this feeling intensified as she watched the son, Richard, glare at Emily when her skirts, with their outdated, wide paniers, threatened to upset the tea table as she found her seat.

But it was Edmund Avery who dominated her thoughts in the next moment. Never had she seen anyone with such a cold, calculating aspect! Tall and domineeringly aristocratic in his bearing, he moved through the initial formalities like a well-oiled machine, but where this should have lent a commanding aspect to his presence, it instead had the effect of marking him as one to be regarded warily, perhaps even with suspicion.

This last impression was aided to no small degree by the look of his pale eyes, which she couldn't help thinking of in reptilian terms. She remembered seeing, in a book at home, some prints by a man named Hogarth; the artist had captured just such a look in the eyes of subjects he used to satirize the corrupt, nefarious elements of the seamier side of London life. Quelling a shudder of revulsion, she switched her attention to Bryce Tremaine.

The future marquis displayed perfect manners in greeting the newcomers, but the chiseled contours of his face revealed not a jot of emotion as he went through these formalities. Yet Brittany noticed he made a point of changing his seat to one which gave him an opportunity to study Edmund Avery in close profile while Edmund faced Amelia.

Observing the two men side by side for a moment, Brittany had an impulse to compare them, though she wasn't sure why. She soon found them as opposite as night and day. It wasn't that Edmund wasn't handsome; she supposed there were many who might find him so. But where Bryce's features were sculpted with elegant lines worthy of a Greek god, tempered with just enough of the look of the rogue to make them interesting, Edmund's were almost hawklike in appearance, with a high forehead and carved, aquiline nose.

And it wasn't that Bryce lacked an aristocratic look, either. But where Edmund's exuded haughtiness and self-imposed superiority, Bryce's came from a kind of inner self-possession that made itself felt in grace of movement and an inherently noble carriage.

Ending her comparison on this note, Brittany found herself surprised, at least concerning her assessment of Bryce, for she'd hardly evaluated him in such glowing terms before! *It must be the contrast with Avery,* she thought to herself quickly. *The man's a snake!*

She forced her attention back to the conversation at hand, which, following some pleasantries regarding the weather, moved to a discussion of Bryce's business on behalf of her father.

". . . so you see, Edmund, Captain Tremaine would have met you eventually, at any rate," Amelia was saying. "But my sons and I are most indebted to him for delivering dear Brittany, here, to Sweetbriar, safe and sound."

Edmund gave her a thin smile. "Ah, indeed, madam, and that reminds me . . . ah, your sons . . . where would they be today?"

Amelia bent more closely over the tea she'd been pouring to hide the look of amusement in her eyes as she thought of the twins' elaborately tailored new garb, which had caused a last-minute message to be sent by their valet, apologizing for the fact that they'd be late for tea. "Oh, I expect them shortly, sir. They sent their apologies, of course. It seems they've been detained by some . . . business matters . . . something to do with a newly arrived shipment of, ah, silks, I believe."

Bryce allowed himself a raised eyebrow at this explanation, for he'd received an identical missive from the poor, beleaguered valet, with the added assurance that the twins hadn't forgotten their pact to support Amelia and would be there soon.

Just then, a sound from the doorway turned all eyes in that direction.

"Why, here are Toby and Tony now!" exclaimed Brittany as the twins came into view. But as she spoke, her jaw fell agape.

Dressed to the teeth in the most foppishly elaborate afternoon attire, the twins posed in the doorway for a deliberately calculated moment, their faces frozen in an imitation of the stylish hauteur one might glimpse in the costume plates of a fashion book. Wearing identical white powdered wigs dressed high on their heads and prodigiously curled, they each sported an ornately embroidered coat so elegant, it might have been ordered by George III himself; these were identical in cut, but Toby's was of pale aquamarine silk while Tony's was pink. Also embroidered were their matching yellow satin waistcoats, these with figures of parrots and other exotic birds done in green silk thread. Their knee-breeches were also satin, Toby's in a light gray which had an amethyst cast, Tony's in powder blue. Snowy white stocks trimmed with what could only be termed fabulous frills of lace, and equally white silk hose dazzled the eye; jewels winked from the long rows of buttons on their triple-vented coats and from the enormous silver buckles on their shoes. And completing the picture, each twin held before him at arm's length, a gold-tipped walking stick whose gold head was encrusted with yet more jewels.

"Good heavens!" cried Brittany, her eyes alight with mischief, "'tis Louis XIV come back to life—*in duplicate!*"

"Only with the help of a modern tailor, I should

hope you mean," said Toby as he broke his pose and walked toward them with a grin.

"But thanks for the tip-off, Coz," echoed Tony behind him, "for now we know where we can send the bill—straight to, ah—"

"Versailles!" Toby finished for him, as he bent to kiss his mother's cheek.

Tony followed suit, and then, once the twins had greeted the others and seated themselves, the conversation resumed. But it soon became apparent to Brittany as the tea hour wore on that she had somehow become the sole object of Richard Avery's attentions.

The oily son of Edmund Avery (for that is how she categorized him) leaned embarrassingly close and peppered her with questions, some of them far more personal than she thought proper, considering that they'd just met. How was it that he'd not met her before, since this was hardly the first time she'd visited Sweetbriar, and her aunt and his family were close neighbors? How was it that such a comely young woman was yet unwed—or was she spoken for? No? Well then, what merits did she seek in a husband (for, certainly, all young women sought marriage and children as their ultimate fulfillment in life)? Her single state was due to the fact that she was merely being particular, wasn't it?

Brittany did her best to fend off these unwanted inquiries without giving him offense, as she'd have liked. They were both guests in Amelia's home, after all, and she loved and respected her aunt too much to cause a scene. But the restraint this involved cost her. This man with the nearly lidless yellow eyes made her uncomfortable. He reminded her of some slithery, predatory creature homing in on its prey, and it didn't take her long to realize who the prey was.

Moreover, young Avery wasn't the only one present

who focused his attention on her. Richard's father casually kept up a running conversation with both the twins and her aunt, but his pale eyes—so much like Richard's, except in color—slid continually in her direction, and she had the uncomfortable feeling she was being systematically scrutinized. She was reminded of a time once when, as a child, she'd encountered a peddler at a country fair, and the man had demonstrated the use of a glass which enlarged whatever was placed beneath it—in that instance, a small, wriggling insect held helplessly for inspection.

Suppressing a shudder, she longed for the tea hour to end. After all, she'd gotten what she'd come for. All of her doubts regarding the legitimacy of Bryce's mission of vengeance were dissipated as she came to grips with the nature of the man who'd wronged someone Bryce cared for. Every instinct in her told her that Edmund Avery was a corrupt, venal man; he would stop at nothing to gain his own corrupt ends, and his son was just like him.

Yes, gone were her questions regarding Bryce's right to hunt Avery down, whatever the reason, and in their place, unbidden, came a sudden fear that it was the Tory who was in danger. She glanced surreptitiously at Bryce. He remained seated in a position conducive to observing the man he'd come to kill, taking little part in the conversation, except for an occasional bit of small talk. His lean-muscled and fit body, evident even beneath the correct cut of his clothes, seemed to contradict its casual slouch in the chair; it reminded her yet again of the body of a great cat, poised to spring on its victim.

She dared another glance at Edmund who, at that moment, shifted his look to meet her gaze head-on. She froze, a frisson of fear coursing through her as she was again put in mind of a snake.

Damn! she thought, lowering her eyes and breaking the spell. *The man's not to be trusted, but 'tis not I who should worry! But Bryce—oh, I wonder if he knows what he's gotten himself into!*

At the same moment, the unwitting object of her concern was mustering his own concerns—for her. It hadn't escaped Bryce's attention that Brittany Chambers was drawing an uncommon amount of interest from both Avery men, and he wondered about this. Given men's natures, such interest would have bothered him little, for the redhead was a beauty. But he'd had ample time to verify his assessment of Edmund as a depraved, dangerous man; he was every inch the immoral piece of filth he'd imagined him to be all these years and the son (the only surprise) was cut of the same cloth.

So when he saw them focus on Brittany, all of his instincts for sensing danger came to the fore. These two were up to something regarding the Chambers wench, and he'd wager his last pound it boded ill for her. For some reason, he found this unsettling.

With a casual turn of his head, he cast a glance in the hellion's direction and smiled wryly; he realized there was nothing of the hellion about her now. Looking quite demure and breathtakingly lovely in the peach-colored gown which echoed the soft blush of her cheeks, Brittany was the very image of a lady. Lady Olivia herself couldn't have provided a more charming picture of decorum.

But what else was it he detected in her right now that seemed out of character? He watched her dart a sudden look at Edmund and then drop her eyes, and he had his answer. Brittany Chambers was *afraid*.

And then something happened to *him* which was out of character; unbidden, a great tide of protectiveness for the redhead washed over him. All of his instincts seemed to focus on the fact that, come what may, Edmund and that slimy son of his must not be allowed to touch this innocent!

The green eyes blinked as Bryce let this last thought register. But, yes, Brittany was an innocent, no matter what her public stance. Oh, she had a keen wit about her, and was uncommonly educated and well-read for a woman, but as far as raw life experience went, she was a babe in the woods—he would stake his life on it.

A smile played briefly about his lips as he savored this new assessment of her, but, as quickly as it came, he wiped it away. *Remember your mission!* he told himself. *You can ill afford distractions.*

Forcing himself to appear cool and detached, he took a sip of his tea. Yet somewhere in the back of his mind, the logic took hold that if in punishing Avery, he also had the opportunity to prevent him from inflicting further harm on a woman, and that woman happened to be Brittany Chambers, then he could scarcely shun such action. It was a satisfying thought, and, with an inward nod, Bryce took another sip of tea and settled down to continue his vigil.

CHAPTER 11

"I TELL YOU, TANSY, THE MAN GAVE ME THE chills!" Brittany hugged her thinly clad arms as if warding off an attack of cold. "You may be sure, given our June climate, 'twas not from the temperature!"

They were sitting on a bale of hay outside of Saracen's stall, having gained "permission" from Bryce (at Amelia's urging) to visit the stallion after dinner.

"You don't gotta—um, *don't have to*—convincify me, Miz Britt'ny! Ah spied dat pair o' rat-bait scoundrels from de upstairs window when dey—*they*—sashayed up t' de do'!"

"Door," corrected Brittany.

"Yes, ma'am, de—ah, *the door*. And ah saw they was up t' no good, straight away!"

"Well, you should have seen them close at hand, Tans. They were—they were—"

"Slopbuckets, right?"

"Right!" said Brittany, unable to conceal a grin at the colorful, but apt, epithet.

"But dat ain't—ah, *that isn't*—all of it, Miz Britt'ny—um, Brittany. Those two weasels didn't jes

—just—eye you over their tea cups and leave, did they?" Tansy eyed Brittany herself as she asked this, the look on her face suspicious.

Brittany sighed, mindlessly plucking at a piece of hay before answering. "Right again, Tans. I knew something was up when Edmund nudged his wife and she quickly asked to walk, in private, in the garden with Aunt Amelia before they all left." She sighed again, in exaggerated disgust.

"It seems Emily Avery has persuaded my aunt to give a ball here at Sweetbriar, in my honor. The apparent object is to introduce me to all the 'fine young people in the area.' "

"Oh, no!" cried Tansy. "And—don't tell me—Miz Wakefield done said yes!"

"Of course," said Brittany, further disgust lacing her tone. "And guess who's to be among the first invited?"

"Dat yallah-eyed lizard!" Tansy was indignant.

"Right again! Oh, Tans, 'twas all too obvious! Somehow the Averys learned of my visit—and marriageability—beforehand and conspired to have Richard court me. This ball is just a ruse to draw me out. I just know Richard and his father have no intentions of allowing anyone but that young snake to have a serious moment with me! I can feel it in my bones!"

Tansy frowned in sympathy, then all at once broke into a grin. "Miz Brittany, whut—*what*—you all so upset for? You knows how t' handle pesky suitors! You be prime for it!"

Brittany offered her a weak smile. "I know, but I was hoping 'twould not come to anything like my Fredericksburg antics here. At Sweetbriar I was hoping I could go about being *myself*! For one thing, Aunt Amelia doesn't deserve a scandal, and, for another, Richard Avery—and his father—are no mere country colonials. They're dangerous!"

"Hmm," murmured Tansy, "but didn't you say dat—*that*—Tow-ree plans t' take that cargo t' their place tomorrow?"

"Aye, but—"

"Well," Tansy interjected with a crafty look, "maybe you won't have no Averys t' worry 'bout afterward."

"Ohh," breathed Brittany, "I hadn't thought of *that*!"

"And dat—*that*—Tow-ree better watch his step!"

"Exactly what just crossed my mind, Tans." Brittany rose from the hay bale and drove her hands deep into the pockets of the work apron Amelia had thrust at her, "to protect your gown from the smelly beast, dear," as she was leaving the house. In his stall, Saracen nickered to her, and she withdrew a hand to run it absently along his neck.

"You know, Tansy, I've been thinking . . ."

"Oh-oh, here it come," muttered the black woman.

"Bryce might be letting himself in for more than he bargained for, pursuing Avery." Brittany began to pace back and forth before the stall, both hands in her pockets again.

"For one thing, there's not one Avery, but two," she continued, "and for another, those two snakes have a large staff at their beck and call."

"So . . . ?" prompted her friend.

Brittany whirled and faced her, an earnest expression lighting her face. "Tansy, we've got to stop him!"

"We . . . ?"

"Oh . . . well, *I* must, then, but I fear I'll need your help."

"Uh-huh," muttered Tansy, wearing her I-was-expecting-this expression.

"Look, Tansy, I've really given this some thought, and—well, we just cannot allow Captain Tremaine to endanger himself in such a manner. Someone has to talk him out of it, or—"

"Ah thought you was—*were*—put out with the man, Miz Brittany. So, how come you all of a sudden so fired up t' help 'im?"

Brittany paused, reflecting on this. Evidence of conflicting emotions flitted across her expressive face as she wrestled to find an answer. At length, she met Tansy's gaze. "Tansy, the truth is I have a hard time abiding the man. He's egotistical, autocratic, and thoroughly overbearing, but that shouldn't mean we ought to let the Averys have him!"

Tansy rose from the bale of hay, keeping a wary eye on Saracen, who was calmly munching on some hay of his own. "'Pears t' me that Tow-ree can take care of himself."

"Maybe so, but let's say he does kill Edmund Avery without harm coming to himself. Do you suppose Richard—or any number of others, for that matter—would let the matter rest there? Do you not suppose the constables would be summoned to seek out and punish Avery's killer?" Brittany shook her head, as if to clear her thoughts. "Tans, I may not be able to stand the man, but I've no wish to see him hang for murder!"

Tansy sighed. "All right. Ah agree, but what can two gals like us do?"

"*Women,*" said Brittany.

"Huh?"

"Women, Tans—we're *women*, not girls, and let us not ever forget that!"

Tansy grinned. No one had ever referred to her as

anything but a "gal"—or girl—before. But Brittany had called her a woman, and she *meant* it. And, Lord, didn't that feel good, somehow! Just as a large part of whatever happened in her life felt good these days.

Suddenly the black woman was filled with a sense of overwhelming joy at being blessed by the good Lord she believed in, for giving her this woman as a friend. And she knew in that moment that she would stand by Brittany Chambers through thick or thin (no matter how hairbrained her shemes, she added realistically) for the rest of their lives. She'd never had cause to be loyal to anything or anyone before, and she savored the new sensation, knowing it spoke of her friendship with this white-skinned woman as nothing else could.

"All right," she said, still grinning, "what can two womens like us do—or, t' put it more plainly, what you want *me* t' do?"

Brittany grinned back and gave her a quick hug. "Thanks, Tans," she murmured with feeling. "Now, listen carefully..."

Edmund Avery watched the elderly black groom lead his white gelding into the stable yard. Running a critical eye over the horse, he took an angry stride forward and struck the old man viciously across the head.

"I told you to fetch the Spanish saddle!" he snarled, raising his hand again. Beside him the gelding snorted and reared its head with alarm, its eyes rolling fearfully in their sockets.

The old man cringed and covered his head with both arms. "Yassah, massa, yassah," he whimpered. "Ah's gonna do it, massa! Don' hit me agin, please, massa!"

Behind his father, Richard Avery stifled a yawn. "Really, Father, can you not ride English today? This old good-for-nothing's so slow and lazy, he'll be a year if you send him back to change the tack, and I did so wish a longish ride before dinner."

Edmund glared at the groom for a long moment before dismissing him with a curt gesture. The old man moved his arthritic joints as quickly as he was able, and scurried out of sight.

Edmund jerked the gelding's reins cruelly downward. "Stand still, you stupid creature!" he commanded. "'Tis high time you knew your master's touch!"

Withdrawing a riding whip from where he'd inserted it in his boot, Edmund held it before the frightened animal in a meaningful gesture, then succeeded in leading him to the mounting block a couple of yards away.

Moments later, both Averys were cantering down a pebbled lane leading from the stables toward an open field. With Edmund leading, they switched to a gallop and cut across the field, then rode its length before jumping a low hedge at the far end.

"Hessian took that rather well," called Richard as he slowed and reached down to pat his Austrian stallion's neck. "I think his leg's well healed. What say you we try a stouter hedge?"

Edmund circled the gelding in a wide arc, bringing him to a stop as he signalled for his son to do the same. "I'd wait a while before attempting it," he said. "That stallion—"

"Oh, come, Father!" Richard jeered. "The horse is ready. I know he is. He—"

"You damned fool!" Edmund shouted. "You cannot be sure of that! And what if he isn't? That horse cost two thousand pounds, and he's not even paid for yet!"

Richard gave him a sullen look.

"And cease looking at me thusly! He wouldn't have taken lame in the first place if you hadn't pressed him when he was tired, the moment he arrived last month!"

Richard's sullen look remained in place, but he held the stallion to a walk as Edmund signaled they should follow a path into some nearby woods.

"Moreover," Edmund told him as they entered the shade beneath the trees, "I agreed to this ride not for the pleasure you seem so bent upon seeking, but because I wished a word with you in private—away from prying ears and eyes."

Curiosity overcame sullenness, and Richard reined in closer to his father's mount.

"I've done some checking on the Chambers chit, and 'twould appear the rumors are accurate. She's heiress to a handsome fortune left by her late mother. Moreover, there are even noble bloodlines involved, though the titles were lost . . . French Huguenots and all that."

"Well, now," grinned Richard, "that settles it, then. She's a plum ripe for the picking. I need only to—"

"Hold a moment!" Edmund commanded. "There's more, and none of it good. It seems the beauteous Mistress Chambers is an independent bitch who's bent on remaining unwed. You will recall that Barker, our erstwhile overseer, was in Fredericksburg last month, and while he was awaiting that damned stallion's unloading at the docks, he heard a few tales told about Brittany Chambers." Edmund swatted angrily at a fly buzzing about his tricorn.

"Well?" Richard urged impatiently. "What did they say?"

"They told of how Timothy Chambers's brat has had dozens, nay, *scores*, of eligible suitors and has managed to trounce them all soundly, driving each one away by means of a wicked temper. 'The Chambers Hellion,' they call her."

Richard frowned. "I've often heard redheads are a temperamental lot . . . that they make poor wives. . . ."

Edmund made a gesture of annoyance. "It matters not to me—nor should it to you. If you should succeed in wedding the chit—and I say *if!*—you'll have little problem making her wear the yoke—I'll see to that.

"But the problem arises in the matter of pursuing and catching the bitch. . . . Tell me, how did you feel it went yesterday?"

Richard considered his thwarted attempts at drawing the redhead out. He was twenty-eight years old and had had scores of successes with women over the years. In fact, he regarded himself as something of a lady-killer, priding himself on his prowess with the so-called fairer sex. So it didn't sit well with him that the heiress had shown little more than polite interest in his initial advances, though he was less than eager to admit this. With only the briefest of glances at his father, he offered him an indifferent shrug.

"I thought so," said Edmund.

Richard was immediately defensive. "Well, she could hardly be properly courted at a tea in her aunt's drawing room!"

"Save your excuses for your gambling and whoring cronies!" snapped Edmund. "You're speaking to *me*—your father, remember?"

Richard shifted his weight in the saddle but said nothing.

"Now, then," continued Edmund, "as to my plans. The fact is, Richard, that you *must* wed the Chambers heiress. There are no two ways about it.

Our family's future depends on it. In fact, I am *ordering* you to pull it off!"

"Yes, but how—"

"Silence! Hear me out. You will begin by following all the usual procedures in such matters . . . flowers, sonnets to her eyebrows . . . whatever. But if these should fail—and by the night of the ball I had your mother instigate, we should know for sure—'tis only a fortnight hence—I want you to put my secondary plan into effect."

"Which is . . . ?" Richard's yellow eyes narrowed with expectant interest.

The pale blue eyes coldly met his gaze. "You will unhesitatingly compromise the chit. Do so in such a manner that her reputation will be in shreds unless she marries you." Edmund allowed himself a thin smile. "Do I make myself clear?"

Richard's smile matched his father's, then rearranged itself into a leering grin. "Perfectly clear," he said.

"Good," said Edmund. "Now, let's have ourselves some dinner."

Turning their horses' heads, they trotted toward home.

"Damn!" Brittany muttered under her breath as she strove to conceal herself beneath some wet canvas the *Louise*'s crew had left in the longboat the ship carried. It had been raining lightly since before dawn, when she'd made her way to the sloop in secret. At the time, she'd been glad of the weather, finding it aided her stealth; indeed, she'd spied no one about or on deck when she arrived. But now the drizzle had given way to a drenching downpour, thoroughly soaking the cape she'd donned for protection, as well as every stitch she wore beneath it.

Her plan to stow away on the sloop had been successful thus far, but she hadn't bargained on all this
rain. It was hard to tell, with the dark thunderclouds
roiling overhead, but she guessed it must be close to
dawn, the time she'd overheard Bryce tell her
cousins he planned to board the *Louise* and set sail
for Avery's plantation. All she had to do was await
his arrival, and then the sailing, and—

"Ah-choo!" The sneeze shook her slender frame,
and she swore an unladylike oath she'd heard her
father's sailors use. *What a fine fix this is!* she thought
dismally. *You stow away to save that Tory's life, only to
lose your own—to the ague!* Morosely, she drew her
sodden cape more tightly about her and tried to concentrate on what had gone well so far.

She'd succeeded in escaping the Big House undetected, leaving Tansy in her chamber to proclaim to
her aunt and the rest of the household that she was
feeling under the weather and had asked not to be
disturbed. The seed had been planted earlier, last
evening at dinner, when she feigned a spell of the
vapors and retired early to her chamber. Now Tansy
had only to play her part—and Brittany had no
doubt she would—and she'd have an excuse for
being missing for a while.

It only remained for her to stay concealed until
they were well downriver and she could confront
Bryce about his secret and endeavor to talk him out
of this killing. She realized Will Thatcher, a man he
seemed to be close to, had already tried this, but she
also knew that Will lacked what she called her "desperation maneuver": the threat to expose to one and
all what she knew about Tremaine if he couldn't be
otherwise persuaded.

As calmly as she could, she tried to envision his
reaction to this. He would be furious, of course—but

then, she'd seen him furious before. And she'd weathered it. On the other hand, disobeying him to appear topside during a storm was a far cry from threatening to foil his plan for some sort of terrible revenge that seemed to be his sole reason for being here in the colonies.

Clenching her teeth in an attempt to prevent their chattering as the cold began to pervade her entire body, Brittany went over the facts she'd been able to glean from that half-audible conversation in the stables. At some time in the past, Edmund Avery had wronged someone very near and dear to Bryce Tremaine. And for that transgression, Bryce was bent on killing Avery. Moreover, Bryce was not a simple merchant captain, but an English nobleman in disguise—the heir of a marquis. But marquis of what? She still didn't know his full title. Nor had she been able to learn who the loved one was who'd been wronged—or in what way. After they'd returned to the Big House that night, Tansy had told her that she thought she'd caught something in his muffled words to indicate that Avery had killed the person in question, but she wasn't sure. They had also deduced that the deed prompting Bryce's vengeance had to have taken place a long time ago; a few casual inquiries of Aunt Amelia had turned up the information that Avery hadn't traveled much— certainly not across the Atlantic—in all the years they'd been neighbors. Indeed, Aunt Amelia had surmised it was likely the man hadn't been to England since he'd left it and wed Emily some thirty years ago!

Stifling another sneeze, Brittany puzzled over this. Bryce Tremaine didn't appear much older than thirty himself. How, then, did a deed most likely committed at or before the time of his birth come to involve him so heavily? Finding this difficult to piece out, she tried another approach.

Perhaps the nasty business hadn't taken place in England thirty or more years ago. Perhaps it had taken place here, at a much later date, and had implications far-reaching enough to stretch across the Atlantic and touch Tremaine, even in England. The other possibility she hadn't considered before was that this wasn't Tremaine's first trip to the colonies. He could have visited these shores before, perhaps with this loved one (a woman? a wife, perhaps?) and Avery had done what he'd done at that time. But then, how would that explain Bryce's waiting until this trip to—

"Ahoy! Who goes there?"

Brittany froze as the voice of the sailor on watch rang out.

"'Tis Captain Tremaine, Hurley. I've Mister Thatcher with me. We'll come aboard."

"Aye, Cap'n! The plank's down, as ye instructed . . ."

As she listened to the sailor's response, Brittany gave a brief prayer of thanks that the plank had been in place. What if it had been hoisted when she'd arrived? She'd never thought of that! Suddenly she began to wonder if there wasn't a lot more she hadn't thought out in this impetuous plan of hers.

All at once, the sounds of Will's and Bryce's boots came tramping across the deck so close to her, she could feel the vibrations. What, after all, had she gotten herself into? She ought to be back at her aunt's Big House, snugly tucked into a warm four-poster. Sitting here soaking wet and shivering under a hunk of canvas in a longboat was *insane!* What if—

Suddenly recognizing the panicky turn her thoughts were taking, Brittany bit sharply down on her lower lip, causing just enough pain to jar her into a state of control. *Enough of panic!* she told herself. *You've made your move. Now all that remains is to bide your time and follow it through.*

With a grimly renewed sense of purpose, she settled down to wait. . . .

CHAPTER 12

SOUNDS OF MOVEMENT IN THE RIGGING and the creaking of timbers met Brittany's ears, telling her the *Louise* was getting underway. Mate's cry brought seaman's response, canvas snapped, greedily catching the heightened breezes of dawn, and, yes, she could feel movement. They had cast off. Now all she had to do was—

"Ah-choo!" The sneeze claimed her before she was able to think about stifling it.

"Wot wuz *that*?" came a voice that was all too near, "'Arry, are ye catchin' cold?"

"Nay, sir!" answered the cabin boy. "'Twarn't *me* sneezed, Mister Thatcher!"

"Well, then, 'oo . . . ?"

There was a shuffle of booted feet, and all at once daylight yawned above Brittany as she felt the concealing canvas snatched away. And gaping downward at her in total astonishment were Will and Harry.

"Well, well, and wot 'ave we 'ere?" Will's voice rang with the smug sarcasm of discovery.

"M-mistress Chambers!" young Harry stammered.

"What does it look like you have here?" Brittany snapped, directing her response to Will. "A stowaway, of course!" She did her best to voice a confidence she didn't feel, having decided beforehand that the moment called for it.

Will blinked, momentarily taken in by her bravado. Then a grin of amusement split his weathered features. *Oh, but the captain is going to love this!* he thought. He suddenly realized things had been all too dull since they'd docked at Sweetbriar, and the chief reason was the reduced frequency of the clashes he'd come to expect between Bryce and the redhead; he'd actually *missed* their explosive battle of wills! Well, there'd be fireworks anew now!

His grin widening with this thought, Will made Brittany an elaborate bow, much as if they were in some fine drawing room, instead of on a ship's deck with the rain pouring down on them.

"If ye please t' be followin' me, Mistress, I'll be takin' ye t' the cap'n now." He extended a hand to help her out of the longboat.

Brittany suddenly found herself greatful for his help, for her limbs were numb from the cold and dampness, not to mention the cramped position she'd assumed under the canvas. With a helpless groan, she unbent her contorted legs, then nearly screamed with the pain that shot through her lower torso as she made it shakily to her feet.

Seeing her distress, Will's grin vanished. "'Ere, now, ye're blue wi' cold!" he exclaimed sympathetically. "'Ow long wuz ye under there, anyways, Mistress?" Then, seeing she was in no condition to answer, he bent and swept her up into his arms.

Shivering violently now, Brittany weakly tried to murmur a protest, but Will ignored it.

"'Arry," he ordered, "fetch some towels and a spare blanket 'r two and bring 'em t' the cap'n's cabin. 'Urry!" Then he turned and headed for Bryce's cabin himself, his burden held effortlessly in huge arms.

Bryce was in the process of changing out of the wet clothes he'd worn to the ship. Comfortable in a full-sleeved cambric shirt he wore open at the throat, minus any stock or cravat, he tucked it into a pair of buckskin breeches he'd purchased from a frontiers-man-peddler near the dock in Fredericksburg. Pleased with the fit of the breeches—they were close-fitting, but not so snug as to hamper his move-ments—he tugged on first one black tallboot and then the other, grunting his satisfaction that they were still dry inside.

He was just settling down at his desk with a mug of hot chocolate the cook had sent up when, without warning, the cabin door flew open and Will barged in carrying a large, dripping bundle.

"Beggin' yer pardon, Cap'n," said Will, "but I fig-gered ye wouldn't mind . . ."

"What in hell—"

Bryce got no further as he recognized the long, wet, red curls that could only belong to one person. Dumbstruck, he watched Will set her carefully on her feet.

She presented a picture he would remember for days afterward as she stood shakily before him on the rug. Wet, mahogany-colored curls lay plastered about her face and upper body, which was covered by a long, sodden, black cape which clung to her slender frame from neck to toe. Her blue eyes were huge in her face as she gazed at him in what he guessed was a weak attempt at a mutinous defiance, but which succeeded only in making her appear like a half-drowned kitten ready to spit, and he was on the verge of telling her so when he noticed the unnaturally white pallor of her skin and a tinge of blue about her lips.

"*Christ!*" he swore. "Will, what—"

"Stowaway, Cap'n."

Swearing mightily under his breath, Bryce went into action. Reaching for the flask of brandy he kept near his desk, he dumped a generous portion of its contents into the remainder of his chocolate and carried the mug over to Brittany, thrusting it to her lips.

"Drink!" he ordered, then barked over his shoulder to Will. "Go below and have some water heated in the galley. Then find Harry and—oh... Harry! Good lad. Leave those towels and blankets here and go with Mister Thatcher and help him fetch that brass tub from the hold. Hurry now! There's a lad."

Brittany held a measure of the adulterated chocolate in her mouth and closed her eyes as she listened to this, then, hearing the door shut behind Will and Harry, decided she had no choice but to swallow. A second later her eyes flew open and she fell into a paroxysm of coughing.

Bryce waited for this to abate, then raised the mug again.

"No!" she gasped, averting her head.

"Drink!" he commanded.

"I won't! 'Tis *vile!*"

Muttering an oath, Bryce brought his free hand to the back of her head, and turned it until she was forced to contemplate the mug again. "Drink!" he repeated.

Brittany gave him a look that was lethal, but when the green eyes failed to do so much as blink, let alone indicate he'd back down, she sighed and quietly obeyed.

"That's better," Bryce murmured. He glanced at the wet cape. A moment later he was tearing it from her body and Brittany, even though she felt a welcome warmth suffusing her insides from the brandy she'd downed was far too weak to offer more than token resistance.

The cape fell in a sodden heap on the rug.

"*What the*—" Bryce couldn't credit his eyes. The chit was wearing . . .

"T-Tony's old c-cast-offs," Brittany explained through chattering teeth when she caught Bryce's shocked, questioning look. Then, as he continued to gape at the wet, clinging breeches and shirt she wore, "Or m-maybe th-they're T-Toby's," she amended. "I d-didn't ask."

Another oath broke from Bryce's mouth. With an angry jerk, he turned to the chair where Harry had dumped a stack of towels and a pair of folded blankets.

"Here," he muttered gruffly, shaking out a blanket and wrapping it firmly about her. He paused for a second, then grabbed a towel and threw it over her head before bending to scoop her up in his arms. Two long strides brought him to the big bed built into the corner of the cabin. Blanket, towel and all, he deposited her on its mattress.

"Mmph," Brittany muttered as the towel fell across her face. She struggled to dislodge it, but the blanket-cocoon held her arms at her sides.

"Here," said Bryce impatiently. He grabbed the towel and manipulated it about her head until it was fashioned into something vaguely resembling a turban. Then, glancing down at her face, he saw a pair of mutinous blue eyes focused on him.

The combination of brandy, blanket and brisk handling had worked to dispel the chill seizing Brittany, and she was feeling herself again; but that self didn't take kindly to what she regarded as Bryce's high-handed behavior, and she was about to tell him so when a knock sounded at the door.

"Come in!" called Bryce.

The door swung open, and into the cabin paraded Will and Harry carrying what Brittany recognized as the big brass bathtub Timothy Chambers kept aboard for his personal use. Behind them trooped three seamen carrying buckets of steaming water.

"Excellent," pronounced Bryce. "Just set it over there." He directed Will and Harry toward a spot near his desk, and when they'd deposited the tub, he gestured to the other three, and the next few minutes were consumed with splashing noises as six large buckets of water were dumped into the brass receptacle.

Then, as quickly as they'd come, the five disappeared, leaving Brittany alone again with Bryce.

"Well," he said, approaching the bed, "let's get this over with." He bent forward and began unwrapping the blanket before Brittany realized what was happening. As the damp folds of the blanket fell aside, he placed his hands about her waist and hauled her off the bed, then set her on her feet in front of him.

"Let's get what over with?" queried Brittany, frowning.

"I should think that would be perfectly clear." He made a mockingly elaborate gesture toward the tub.

"Certainly not!" she told him, but the final word was muffled as the misbehaving towel again slipped downward, covering her face.

Bryce heaved an impatient sigh, picked up the for-

ward edge of the towel and raised it to peer into her
face. "Certainly—yes!" he told her. "Five men have
just taken considerable time and trouble to set up
that bath—*six*, if you count the cook who heated the
water—and *you* are going to *use* it!"

Brittany tore the wet towel from her head and
glared at him. "I am not in the habit of taking baths
in the quarters of unmarried gentlemen, Bryce Tremaine, so you can just forget it. Besides, I—I'm feeling quite warmed and—and altogether myself now,
so I'll thank you to—"

She paused, warned by the look on his face. He
was standing just a couple of feet from her—so
close, she could see the tiny white squint lines radiating from the corners of his eyes, contrasting with
the bronzed tan of the rest of his face. Towering
above her, he stood with legs spread and fists
planted angrily on his hips, while his green eyes
gave her a look that dared her to continue. Yet it was
not that look alone which arrested her actions.
Something...nameless—it was a feeling she
couldn't quite put her finger on—seized her as she
regarded him with his open shirt, tight breeches and
wide-legged stance.

She didn't know it, but this was the first time in
her life she'd come face to face with blatant, raw,
masculinity. She only knew that the potency he exuded was overwhelming, even frightening, and she
felt helpless in its presence.

Inside, her heart seemed to be pumping hard
enough to leap out of her chest, and the palms of her
hands, icy only moments before, were sweaty and
damp. There was also a strange tightening at the
base of her belly, and her knees felt as if they'd
buckle if she took a single step.

"Are you getting into that bath willingly, or do I

have to carry you into it?" Bryce's words were spoken quietly, but the challenge in his green eyes spoke volumes.

"Sure—surely you don't mean—I mean..." But suddenly Brittany wasn't sure what he meant. Did he intend to be *present* while she—*Unthinkable!* her mind cried out, and then, all at once, she found her tongue. "If you're so concerned about the time and effort that tub involved, Bryce Tremaine, I suggest you take the bath yourself."

Bryce was nearing the end of his patience. Not only had she yet to explain her uninvited presence aboard a ship that was less than an hour away from delivering him to his quarry, but she had clearly endangered her health in coming here. Why, a short while ago she'd arrived looking blue with cold! How dare she interrupt his life thus!

"*Damnit!*" he growled. "I've had enough!" With an abrupt movement he reached out and grabbed her by the shoulders. Spinning her about, he held her by the waist from behind and began to remove her wet shirt. Buttons flew in several directions as he ignored their intricacies; in seconds the shirt fell to the rug, leaving her in a damp shift and wetly clinging breeches.

Brittany's gasp as he began the disrobing gave way to a voiceless terror when she realized he meant to do the unthinkable. At last accepting the reality, she opened her mouth to scream, but a strong hand clamped over it.

"I wouldn't do that if I were you," he bit out. "Sound the alarm, and the entire crew will be here in minutes, but I hardly think your reputation will survive the scene they discover!"

Recognizing the truth in this, she slumped against

him in defeat, and he removed his hand from her mouth.

But as he turned her about to face him, Brittany recovered her wits enough to think about forcing a compromise.

"I-I'll strike a bargain with you, Bryce. Leave the cabin, and I'll take the bath. After all, 'tis the only way to protect my reputation anyway. 'Twould soon be common knowledge on this ship, should you remain while Mistress Chambers bathed . . . and, of course, many of the men are quite loyal to my father. . . . 'Twould safeguard *your* reputation, too, you see. My father can be quite—"

Her argument had begun to sound plausible to Bryce, something he could easily agree to, but when she mentioned her father, it suddenly took on the connotations of a threat, and that, given everything else he'd already put up with, was more than he could abide.

"Threaten me, will you?" he ground out from between clenched jaws. He went back into action, this time with a vengeance, peeling her breeches from her body, ignoring her furious struggles as he stripped her of all but the shift, whose wet folds wrinkled about her upper thighs.

Brittany fought him valiantly, but he was far too strong for her, and in a few moments she found herself, shift and all, plunged bodily into the tub's steaming warmth.

"*Ahhh!*" she cried. "'Tis *hot!*"

Mocking laughter met her ears as Bryce, again assuming that spread-legged stance, voiced his amusement at her expense. "'Twould seem to be the general idea, Mistress!" he taunted.

This was finally too much for Brittany. He'd gone too far! Angrily pushing a dripping mass of hair out of her face, she snarled back at him, "I'll see you pay for this—*your lordship!*"

The laughter ceased and he eyed her with a cautious frown. "What was that?" he queried, in a voice grown deceptively soft.

Brittany hadn't meant to approach him on his secret in such a way. She'd meant to wait until he calmed down after her presence on ship became known, and then to try to reason with him, quietly. But the arrogant Tory hadn't behaved as she'd expected and—oh, well, a cat let out of the bag was a cat well gone!

"I *said*," she pronounced tartly, "that you'll *pay*, your lordship.... Ah, '*tis* the manner in which one addresses the heir of a *marquis*, is 't not?"

Bryce's expression suggested a thunderbolt as her words sank in, and then he was on her in seconds, hauling her from the water, standing her before him as water cascaded down her body and puddled at their feet.

"You'll explain yourself, Mistress," he thundered, "and *now!*"

Brittany beheld the emerald anger in his eyes and nearly shrank from it before forcing herself to remember that, with her knowledge of his secret, she likely held the upper hand. "I know all about your secret mission, Bryce. 'Twas my reason for coming here—to talk you out of—of killing Edmund Avery!"

Bryce's hands fell away from her shoulders, where he'd been holding her, and she heard him suck in his breath. He stepped back a pace and ran a distracted hand through his hair, letting out his breath slowly. Then, casting his glance about, he reached for one of the large towels Harry had left and tossed it to her.

"Cover yourself, Mistress," he told her, "and then— *we talk!*"

Silently, Brittany obeyed, hurriedly doing a little towel-drying in the process. At length, she stood before him swathed in the long towel which was wrapped saronglike about her slender frame.

Bryce slung one hip on the edge of his desk and eyed her thoughtfully. "Exactly how much do you know," he began, "and how did you learn it?"

"I was in the stables the other evening when you were discussing this—this plan of vengeance with Will Thatcher. Oh, you must believe that I never meant to eavesdrop! 'Tis not my habit! I—"

Bryce cut her off with a curt gesture that signaled it made little difference to him, then nodded for her to continue.

"We—Tansy and I—heard only parts of your conversation..." At the flicker of anger she read in his eyes, she hastily added, "Oh, never worry about Tansy! She's closemouthed as they come and won't say a word—I *swear* it!" She watched his face carefully for a reaction.

"Go on," he said.

"We only learned that you were bent on killing Avery because he'd once wronged someone... someone you knew—*whom*, we weren't able to hear. Beyond that," she shrugged, "we learned nothing, ah, save that you're a marquis's heir, and even then, we failed to learn your full title—or that of the marquis, for that matter."

There was a silence, broken only by the ticking of the ship's clock on the shelf above his desk, as Bryce studied her face for several long seconds.

"What else?" he questioned at last.

"'Tis all we learned," she replied simply.

Under ordinary circumstances he would have believed her, but these were not ordinary circumstances. He'd risen before dawn to be about the mission that had consumed most of his energies for months; he'd walked to the ship in wet, miserable weather; and *then* once he was aboard, he'd found his objective thwarted by the untimely, unasked-for presence of this hellion! No, these were not ordinary circumstances at all, and *she* was to blame!

"You're lying!" he accused hotly.

"No!" Brittany hadn't expected to be accused of deceit, and her own anger rose in response. "'Tis all we learned, you Tory schemer!"

"Tory schemer, is it?" he countered. "And what kind of a schemer does it take to be listening to a man's private conversation, sneakily hidden behind walls?"

"Sneakily?!" she cried. "Why, you wretched—" She drew back an arm to strike him, but never got that far, as he leapt up and forestalled the action by seizing both her wrists and pinning them to her sides.

"*Bastard!*" she cried, struggling against his grasp, but this seemed to enflame him further. Moving his hands to her shoulders, he gave her a violent shake that was intended to bring her under control, but only succeeded in loosening the towel, which dropped unceremoniously to the floor.

Shocked by his actions and suddenly chilled by the cool air on her damp body, Brittany gave an involuntary shudder, accompanied by a half-audible whimper of protest. Then her eyes locked with his.

Bryce was acutely aware he hadn't intended anything to go this far. Heaven knew, he had more important things on his mind right now than challenging this spitfire. But as he looked into her wide-eyed face, he was also acutely aware of her as a woman. He knew he could lose himself in the deep blue liquid of her eyes, knew, as he focused on the lush, ripe mouth which trembled ever so slightly, that he could grow helpless under its spell if he didn't tear his eyes away. And yet his eyes refused to obey his instincts, lowering only to take in the coral-tipped swell of her breasts as they pushed against the thin, wet material of her chemise, and then Bryce knew he was totally undone.

With a groan, he lowered his head and covered her mouth with his, drawing her to him in a hard embrace.

Brittany caught his intent a split second before he moved, and all her instincts were to fight him, but as she felt his mouth descend on hers, felt the heat of his body envelop her, she succumbed to an explosion of sensation such as she'd never before experienced. Hot flames seemed to lick at her belly as it met his masculine hardness, reminding her of those moments earlier when she'd felt frightened and overwhelmed by him.

And then there was his mouth, which had quit the punishing hardness of its initial contact and was plying her lips with a far gentler persuasion now. Moving his warm lips over her own with mesmerizing thoroughness, he worked hers apart to let his tongue slip between. Then he slid it along their opening, teasing her senses . . . sending her reeling . . .

Dimly, she became aware of his hands gliding over her thinly clad torso, and the heat inside her grew. She felt his mouth slide to the sensitive point below her ear at the same moment that one of his hands came around to cup a breast. When he brushed his thumb across its hardening peak, Brittany gasped; an intense curling sensation gripped the place below her belly, and a heartbeat later she felt a gathering of moisture at the juncture of her thighs.

With a moan, she curled her arms about his neck, wanting him closer, wanting . . .

"Brittany . . ." Her name on Bryce's lips blew hot breath into her ear, and a shivering ecstasy claimed her. "Brittany . . . oh, sweet, sweet lady," he murmured, his thumb continuing its devastating work, "forgive me, sweet . . . I know you're an innocent, know I must stop, and—"

"No!" Was that her own voice she heard? "No, Bryce, don't stop . . . not now . . . not . . . *ever*!" In some deep, nether region of her brain, Brittany knew what she'd said was wrong, knew it branded her shameless . . . wanton, but her conscious thoughts were too filled with the things he was doing to her body, too consumed with the white-hot, candent fire that blazed wildly through her limbs, too lost in his nearness to care. . . .

But Bryce heard her words. With a swift movement, he encircled her small waist with his hands and set her away from him to look into her eyes. Meeting his searching gaze were two lambent midnight pools of blue, and he felt he could drown in them. Then his gaze fell to her parted lips . . .

"Please . . ." she whispered.

With a groan, he swept her up into his arms and carried her to the bed, all the while murmuring her name as he nuzzled her throat, her ear, her hair, which was damp and smelled faintly of flowers. Once there, he laid her carefully on its covers, then knelt beside her for a moment. Gently, his fingers lacing into the hair at either side of her head, he took her face between his hands.

"Brittany . . . ?" he questioned softly. "Brittany, are you *sure*?"

But Brittany was long past coherent speech. It was as if a stranger had invaded her body, robbing her of reason, of thought itself. She thought only with her senses now, and all of them were screaming for his touch, for a continuation of the joy that was still coursing hotly through her body.

In helpless abandon, she raised both arms to him.

And with a harsh cry, Bryce obliged her, dropping to cover her pulsing form with his own. Again, his mouth covered hers, his tongue seeking—and gaining—instant admission. There it glided along her teeth before meeting the quick, hesitant dart of her own. Tongue meeting tongue, they tasted each other and found sweetness, and Brittany only wanted more.

And more he gave her, caressing her body with knowing hands, finding its curves and hollows, making it throb with longing. Again, he found her breast, and then the other, and when the damp cotton of her shift proved too chaste a barrier, he tore at its lacings until the twin orbs spilled free.

Then she felt his mouth leave hers and descend until it covered one coral peak while with his fingers he teased the aching bud of the other. At this, Brittany's breath quickened, then broke from her parted lips in a whimper of need, and she began to twist and writhe beneath him, seeking . . . seeking . . .

Bryce knew what she sought, but bit back harshly on his own raging desires to take his time with her, wanting to make it good for her, knowing he must if her pleasure was to outweigh the pain . . .

And when he considered the pain she'd feel and was again reminded that she was an untried virgin, he made a last, desperate attempt to check their passion, but Brittany would have none of it.

"Take me, Bryce!" she cried urgently. "Oh, Bryce, take me now!"

The effort to stop had already cost him enormously. But Bryce was now the recipient of her hands as they began coursing over his body in untutored, yet effective, exploration. He rasped her name with a surge of renewed passion and heeded her cry.

In moments, he stripped the shirt from his body, tore off his boots and breeches and rejoined his body to hers. Then his hands and lips lit a devastating trail of fire that led him to her lower body.

While his lips pressed hot kisses to her belly and thighs, well below the shift that was now wrapped about her waist, he stroked the triangle of mahogany curls at their joining with skillful fingers. He heard her moan deep in her throat, and smiled. Soon... soon she'd have her wish...

But first he had to ease the way for it, and with this thought in mind, he grazed the swelling bud that throbbed above her nether opening, once... twice... then again, and heard her cry out her need. Then he felt her hands in his hair while her body thrashed beneath him and she parted her thighs, trying to tell him of that need where words had failed.

And still he took his time, forcing himself to go slowly, making himself place her needs before his own. With infinite care, he ran a finger downward from the bud he'd been stroking, feeling with increased pleasure how slippery she'd grown. Then, ever so gently, he slid it into the aperture.

A rush of sucked-in breath met his ears, followed by a sound that was half plea, half sob. Raising his head, he moved it toward her own, while all the while his adroit finger moved within her, plying her softness, working to stretch her tightness, making her ready...

Brittany saw his face hover over hers for an instant before closing her eyes to the sweet torture he was working below. "Bryce..." she heard herself murmur, "oh, Bryce..."

"Aye, sweetheart," he whispered urgently, "that's it... you're almost ready now..."

And then she felt his mouth join hers in a kiss that was unbelievably sweet, sucking the honey from her core, devastating her with its pliant care. His fingers stroked a final heated caress before leaving her lower body to come again to her aching breasts. These he teased with masterful strokes before sweeping both hands to her waist, and then her hips, positioning her for his possession.

She felt him shift his weight, felt the touch of his masculine hardness against her inner thighs, while his voice at her ear gave rasping, yet clear, instructions.

"Relax, darling, aye, that's it... now open to me ... no, don't rush it, sweet... slowly... aye..."

But Brittany felt he must be trying to drive her mad with this slowness, and suddenly she knew she couldn't wait a moment longer. With a sudden instinctive thrust of her hips, she met his probing manhood, felt it begin to enter, and pushed it home.

All at once a sharp, tearing pain sluiced through the place, where, seconds ago, only pleasureful longing had driven all else from her mind. With a cry, she arched her back, hoping to separate herself from its source, but only succeeding in driving him deeper within her.

"Bryce—no!" she cried, panic lacing her voice.

Instantly, Bryce stilled his movements, then with a slight turn of his head, he whispered at her ear,

"Brittany . . . ? Sweetheart, tell me, are you . . . have I hurt you? Look at me, sweet."

But just as she was about to tell him, Brittany realized the pain was gone. Incredulous, she opened her eyes to find his green-eyed gaze intently on her.

"Ohh, Bryce," she breathed, "it *did* hurt . . . a . . . moment ago. . . . But now—*but now*—"

A wide grin crossed his face before Bryce closed his eyes and again gave himself up to his passion. "Aye, little one," he murmured softly, "but now you can *fly!*"

With slow strokes at first, and then a rapidly building rhythm, he began his ride, urging her on with his voice, his hands, his entire body, in the age-old cadence of male meeting female. Like a master musician playing the instrument he loved, he made her respond until she was again mindless with passion, and all the while Brittany met his thrusts joyously, giving as well as she got, driving him mad with her eagerness, her ready responses.

Upward they climbed, soaring dizzily to a vast height neither had known before—she in her innocence, he in his heretofore shallower ventures—until at last they approached the final summit and he felt her shudder beneath him a split second before that quintessential convulsing overcame him, and he joined her there as one.

Time passed, Brittany knew it did, but as to how much, she could merely guess. She only knew that it was a long while before she was able to think, or to contemplate speaking. Slowly, she became aware of Bryce's breathing against her hair, of the still-rapid thudding of his heart—or was it hers?—as he continued to hold her against him.

Bryce, too, was taking a long time to regain his senses. Slowly, bit by bit, the moments they'd just shared filtered into his rational mind. *My God!* he thought. *She'd been . . . wonderful!* He'd never tasted a woman like her before . . . such fire! Such *passion!* And, to think, she was a virgin, an untutored—

And all at once, the enormity of what he'd done struck him. He'd taken an inexperienced innocent, a woman he'd promised to protect and—

Like a sledgehammer blow to his midsection, he felt the guilt hit him. She was the kind of girl he'd sworn all his life to avoid. Hadn't his mother been such an innocent before Edmund Avery's rape? Consumed with remorse, he drew back and made himself face her.

Brittany felt his withdrawal and opened her eyes to look at him. "Bryce . . . ?" She whispered his name, then blushed deeply as their eyes met.

The apology he'd intended died on his lips as Bryce beheld her face. It was more beautiful than he'd ever seen it. As the lantern light flickered over its delicately chiseled contours, he ran his eyes over every inch of it, mesmerized by the exquisite loveliness there . . . the full, curving lips, cherry-red now and faintly bruised from his kisses . . . the straight, perfect nose . . . the high cheekbones and flawless skin . . . and those eyes! Hauntingly beautiful, they were a limpid midnight blue, a color he knew came from the satisfaction she'd experienced in their lovemaking . . .

"Brittany . . ." he murmured, then reached to take her lips in a gentle kiss that communicated all the tenderness she made him feel in that moment.

Brittany returned the kiss with equal feeling, letting it say what words could not. She was still consumed with thoughts of the passion they'd shared, of the overwhelming intimacy of it all, and she was content to let him lead the way, to control the moment until she could gather her wits and put it into perspective.

But when at last they broke apart, she thought she detected a slight stiffening in his mien. Puzzled, she opened her eyes. His head above her was as dark and handsome as ever. A brush of ebony curls fell over his forehead, giving him a boyish look that was at odds with the strong, masculine planes of his face, and her heart skipped a beat at the mere sight of him.

But then she looked into his eyes and beheld something that hadn't been there a moment before. Why, he looked almost . . . angry!

"Bryce?" she questioned, searching his face.

"Brittany, I know the words sound empty, but . . ." He ran a hand through his tousled curls as he voiced a disquieting sigh. ". . . but I cannot tell you how sorry I am that this has happened. I—"

"Sorry?!" She tumbled from his embrace and bolted to a sitting position on the bed. "Sorry? Why should you be sorry if I am not? 'Twas I who had something to lose, and—"

"And that is exactly my point!" he cut in. "You were a virgin, and I had no right to—"

"You had every right!" she fumed. "'Twas I who urged it, so that *gave* you the right!"

But Bryce was shaking his head. "That, my dear, is hogwash! You were too much the innocent to make any such decision, whilst I—" He laughed bitterly to himself. "I long ago promised myself that —" With an angry gesture, he cut himself off, then swung his legs over the side of the bed and began searching for his clothes.

Brittany caught the anguish in those final words and sensed there was something important in what he was not telling her. Kneeling behind him on the bed, she put a gently restraining hand on his shoulder.

"Long ago you promised yourself what?" she asked softly, and when his shoulder stiffened and there was no response, she decided to probe again. Tentatively, carefully, sensing his long-nurtured habit of being a private person, she put forth her question.

"Bryce . . . why are you seeking to kill Edmund Avery?"

Bryce rose and turned to face her. And what he saw nearly took his breath away. She was, oh, so lovely, kneeling there in the lamplight with her long hair swirling about her in delightful disarray. With her dramatic coloring and nubile, exquisitely shaped body, she reminded him of some pagan goddess. And again her eyes held him, intensely focused now, framed by a thick mahogany sweep of lashes and beckoning with impossible blue depths . . . and as he felt himself again getting lost in them, he almost told her . . . almost . . .

But in the end, there was the guilt—and a fear of intimacy, too, growing in a small way out of the determination he had made in childhood, not to allow his heart to lead him into the kind of plight his mother's had.

With a curt shake of his head, he bent to retrieve his clothes and began to draw them on rapidly. While he dressed, his voice assumed a businesslike tone.

"Crawl under those covers and pretend to be asleep, Brittany. I'm going on deck and giving the order to turn about. I'll tell them you've been sleeping and are too chilled to remain aboard, that I've been nursing you and, although I think you'll recover, we must return you to Sweetbriar.

"With luck, we'll save your reputation—and mine—" he added wryly. "I'll send Harry to you in a while with some of his clothes. . . . They might even prove a better fit than your cousins'." He finished dressing and turned for the door.

"Bryce, wait!" Brittany held out a hand as if to stop him, and he turned to look of her. "What . . . what about Avery?"

He sighed. "That, my dear Mistress Stowaway, will have to wait." And without waiting for a response, he turned and left the cabin.

CHAPTER 13

BRITTANY SAT MUTELY STARING OUT THE window of her chamber. Outside, the southern sun shone brightly on the lawns and fields of Sweetbriar, erasing all traces of the rain which had fallen earlier, and the earth had a newly washed look to it. The grass in the distant pastures was lush and green, birds chirped in the branches of the big magnolia tree by the garden gate, and the air was perfumed with the heady scent of honeysuckle.

But, caught as she was in the tangle of thoughts that had plagued her ever since she'd left the ship, Brittany was immune to the early summer grandeur beyond the window. Somewhere downstairs, she knew, Tansy was fixing a pot of herbal tea to bring up to her. She vaguely recalled their mutual relief that she'd been returned to the Big House without anyone in the household having been aware she'd been gone. But her mind's inner workings were thrust on the events which had occurred on the *Louise* a few hours before.

What had she done? She'd given herself to a man

whose cool demeanor in the ensuing hours, when he'd seen her home, told her he was quite unaffected by the whole business, and yet, somehow, she'd allowed herself to be more than a little moved by the intimate moments they'd shared. In fact, to be honest, what had happened had shaken her to the core. And she was self-aware enough to realize that it wasn't the obvious—the loss of her innocence—that was at the root of her distress. Far from it. In fact, the singularly heartening thing in the whole incident was that the choice had been *hers; she* had made the decision to lose her virginity to Bryce Tremaine, and she alone would bear the responsibility for it.

But, as she reminded herself for the umpteenth time, that was not the problem. The problem was that she'd thought, at the time, that she could subsequently walk away from that intimate scene and remain untouched by it, *fool that she was!*

What was wrong with her? She'd spent months being the most courted female in three counties. Dozens—nay, *scores* of men had plied their charms for her benefit, and she'd remained securely unaffected, as distant as ice in January. And yet, here she was, after just a few moments in his arms, totally besieged by remembrances of Bryce Tremaine, of how his lips had burned on hers, of how his arms had made her yearn as they held her, of how his eyes had looked deeply into hers and made her giddy, of how his skillful hands had made her hot with—

"*Enough!*" she shouted, clapping her hands over her ears to shut out the damning thoughts. But she wished she could shut out the anger as well. Anger at herself. For allowing a moment's pleasure to threaten her independence. For forgetting to concentrate on her campaign to remain self-reliant . . . on her steady string of refusals to wed, no matter how handsome the man, or how attractive his "prospects," on the cleverly wrought image of herself as a shrewish hellion. . . .

Well, my girl, a lot of good that did you, she berated herself. *The moment a pair of devilish green eyes looked your way, you—*

"Miz Britt'ny?" Tansy's voice at the door cut across her thoughts. "Miz Britt'ny, you still in there? Ah got mah hands on some biscuits, an' dere's—*there's*—hot tea, but this door 'pears t' be—ah! Here we is—*are!*" The door swung open and Tansy entered, wearing a satisfied grin and carrying a tray laden with goodies.

"Somebody better tell that Merriweather t' oil the latch on—Miz Britt—?" Tansy hurriedly shut the door, then set the tray down and rushed toward Brittany. "Honeychile, what's wrong? *Why you been cryin'?*"

But a wretched sob was her only answer as Brittany threw herself into the smaller woman's outstretched arms.

"Now, now, baby," Tansy soothed, "don't cry. Whatever it is, it can't be all dat bad—ah mean, *that* bad! Now you just tell Tansy all about it, honeychile. We'll make it better, you'll see . . ."

And so, with sobs and hiccoughs punctuating every line, Brittany spilled out her story to her friend. Sparing very few details, except those of the most intimate nature, she chronicled for Tansy her disastrous trip on the *Louise* and the fate she'd met in Bryce Tremaine's arms. More importantly, she told of her self-directed anger, ending with a bitter denunciation of her own weakness in the matter.

But Tansy wasn't about to let her get away with such self-reproach. After fetching Brittany a handkerchief to dry her eyes, the smaller woman poured her a cup of tea and handed her a biscuit, then sat beside her on the bed and waited. She watched Brittany sip the steaming brew, then, satisfied that the tears were subsiding, took a deep breath and launched her attack.

"Miz Britt'ny—ah means Brittany—" She returned the small smile Brittany gave at her self-correction. "There's no way ah'm goin' t' listen t' you doin' this t' yourself. Honeychile, you ain't—*haven't*—done anything wrong! You just got caught up in the natural, that's all."

"Th-the *natural*?"

"Uh-huh. That Tow-ree's powerful good lookin', right?"

Brittany hesitated, then sighed and nodded.

"And it be natural for a good lookin' man t' 'tract a young, healthy woman—and you is a *young, healthy woman*, woman! It be plumb natural for you t' be—"

"But Tansy, you don't un—"

"Ah understand perfectly. What was *un*natural was for you t' think you could hide from something like dat—*that*—for so long. Baby-lamb, *that's* what ain't natural! You wrappin' yourself up in all those 'don't touch' wrappin's. It ain't healthy!"

"*Isn't* healthy," Brittany corrected with a watery smile.

"Right!" grinned Tansy. "So, along come this 'knock-me-dead-on-de-head' Tow-ree, and—" She snapped her fingers. "*Mah* only wonder is how come it didn't happen *sooner*. It sho *sure*—was bound t' happen *sometime*!"

Brittany laughed, partly at the staunch expression on Tansy's face, partly because it felt so good to hear someone with common sense shed some light on what had begun to seem overwhelming. But a second later Brittany was serious again, caught up in the details of her dilemma.

"But, Tans, what do I do now?"

"Do what you've always done," came the sensible reply. "Get on wif—*with*—the business of livin'! Your aunt's downstairs this very minute, plannin' a fancy ball in your honor, and ah been hard put t' keep her from sashayin' up here t' inquire 'bout your health."

"Oh, but—"

"Now, ah know you ain't—*haven't*—been keen on goin' along with her on it, but right now ah'd say all the fussin' that comes with gettin' ready for a ball is just what you need t' take your mind off, um . . . other things . . ."

Brittany met Tansy's pointed gaze over the rim of her dish of tea and was again reminded that the black woman was wise beyond her years. She was reminded, too, of the harsh life in slavery that had brought her that wisdom, and the thought humbled her. If Tansy could bear those hardships and come out a better person for them, then who was she to wallow here in self-pity over a brief misstep? It was a sobering thought, and with it, Brittany suddenly vowed to take a lesson of her own—from Tansy.

"Tans," she said, setting her tea down abruptly, "you're right. Now, where do I start?"

Tansy heard the strength return to Brittany's voice and grinned. "You start by lettin' me do up your hair and climbin' into one of them—*those*—gowns hangin' in that"—she gestured with a thumb over her shoulder at a large piece of furniture in the corner—"that war-road over there."

"*Wardrobe*," Brittany corrected with a giggle. She was struck by the notion that, given the ammunition such a closet contained, to provide the average woman with the weapons of fashion to launch against poor, unsuspecting males, Tansy's term might be the more apt.

But moments later, as she sat before the guest chamber's Queen Anne dressing table and allowed her friend to dress her hair, Brittany's face again turned somber.

"Miz Brittany, what you puzzlin' 'bout?" Tansy asked.

Meeting her dark eyes in the mirror above the table, Brittany sighed. "You know, Tans, I never did get him to tell me the exact nature of his cause for revenge . . . or who it was that Avery wronged . . ."

"Hmph," muttered the smaller woman, "that Tow-ree's good at sittin' on a heap of secrets!"

Brittany nodded, but slowly, so as not to dislodge the pins Tansy was working into her hair. "And the only concession I was able to wring from him was that he not attempt anything toward Avery immediately. 'Twas on the trip back from the *Louise*, and I'm lucky to have gotten him to agree to that much. . . . Oh, Tansy, I don't think I've ever seen anyone that —that *cold with anger!*"

Tansy met her eyes in the mirror again for a moment and nodded, then gave a short shrug. "Most mens—*men*—don't like it when their plans get upset—and by a *woman?*" She shook her head. "Mm-mm, no, they don't like that *at all!*" She inserted the final hairpin in the cluster of coppery curls she'd fashioned at the crown of Brittany's head, then stepped back to assess her handiwork. "Hmm, not bad . . . not bad at all . . ."

"*Not bad?*" Brittany grinned. "Why 'tis positively *stunning*, Tans! I vow, there's magic in your hands!" She turned her head from side to side, admiring the enchanting coiffure her friend had created.

"Stunnin' enough t' get a stubborn Tow-ree t' see reason?" Tansy questioned slyly.

Brittany blanched, then whirled about to look at her. "Oh, Tans, I hadn't thought ... that is ... oh, sweet Lord, how am I ever going to *face him*?!"

But the black woman just nodded sagely, fixing her with a knowing look. "Oh, you'll do it, Miz Brittany," she told her in a tone filled with conviction, "you'll *do* it."

Will Thatcher drew thoughtfully on a long-stemmed clay pipe as he sat in the small sitting room between his guest chamber and Bryce's. Across from him, Bryce sat at a kneehole desk and penned a letter with brisk, sure strokes. Will knew the message was to be delivered on horseback to the Avery plantation by the liveried groom waiting downstairs, just as he was aware that its contents conveyed an apology for their delay in delivering the *Louise*'s cargo "owing to a small problem with Chambers's sloop," but it was none of these things that prompted the seaman's inner musings as he observed his friend.

No, he was satisfied that Bryce's anger at the delay had long since cooled, and he'd even gotten the young lord to view the delay in a positive light. Bryce now saw it, as Will had, as an opportunity to practice his patience, to contribute to the control he would need if he was to carry off his mission successfully.

But what still had Will puzzled was the younger man's less obvious mood since they'd left the sloop. To everyone they'd met since abandoning this morning's trip, Bryce Tremaine appeared thoroughly at ease with himself, casual about the delay and ready to take tea in the drawing room in a short while. . . .

But Will knew him better. Underneath that calm

facade, he knew the lad was agitated about something. He could tell it by the way the green eyes darkened and grew pensive when he thought no one was looking... by the way he clenched and unclenched his fingers when they weren't busy... by the way a barely noticeable tic disturbed the taut plane beneath one cheekbone whenever Brittany Chambers's name was mentioned....

That was it, of course. The Chambers wench. Something had happened between the two of them aboard ship, something... important.

That much decided, Will leaned back in the Windsor armchair and savored his pipe for a long moment, watching the blue smoke travel upward in lazy rings above his head. Slowly, taking his time, he let the facts sort themselves out in his mind.

For one thing, he wasn't buying that tale about Bryce spending all that time alone with her because he was tending her health. And he was willing to bet all the others on the *Louise* weren't buying it either— except maybe young Harry, of course. But the crew were a decent lot, loyal as family to the lass, and he knew they'd grown to respect the captain in the short time they'd worked under him; he doubted there'd be any repercussions from that quarter.

But if those two had gotten to know each other so much better, what had gone wrong? He'd have sworn, from all the earlier cannon fire between them, they'd have hit it off just fine, once they cleared away the smoke and were able to see each other's good points. Hell, that redheaded firecracker was just made for a man like Bryce! And she needed strong hands like his to steer the proper course for her, too!

But something *had* gone wrong; that much was plain. And so now, instead of providing a healthy diversion for him, she was proving to be just the opposite—a worrisome distraction from his dangerous purpose. Damn! It was just—

"I'll be taking this downstairs now, Will." Bryce rose from the desk, the sanded and sealed letter in hand. "Ah, you did ask the groom to—"

"'E's waitin' below fer ye, lad." Will meant to go back to his pipe and let his troublesome thoughts rest, but suddenly his keen eyes caught sight of what looked suspiciously like a pair of *tiny teeth marks!* They were on the side of Bryce's neck, visible now because, the room being hot and stuffy, Bryce had removed his stock when he sat down to write the letter.

"Er—um . . . laddie, I suspect ye may wish t' don yer stock afore ye go down," he said awkwardly.

Bryce paused, then heaved an impatient sigh. "I suppose you're right, though I hardly think Mistress Wakefield would be offended if I appeared without it." He grabbed the discarded garment from the top of the desk and took it to a small mirror on the nearest wall.

"On the other hand," he continued with a wry grin, "that housekeeper of hers is the type to faint dead away at the sight of . . ." As he caught sight of himself in the mirror, Bryce's tone lost all color. ". . . something improper . . ."

Will watched him touch disbelieving fingers to the telltale marks, then stiffen as he continued to stare at his reflection.

"Ah . . . laddie . . ." the bigger man began cautiously, "ye ken I be the sort wot never likes t' interfere, but—"

"Then don't!" came the clipped retort.

Will's eyebrows rose at this, then quickly lowered into place, but not before Bryce caught the gesture in

the mirror as he worked furiously to replace the concealing piece of apparel.

Pivoting to face him, Bryce was a study in barely
leashed fury. "Not a word of this to anyone, Will, I
swear, or—"

"Laddie, laddie, 'tis *me*, Will Thatcher, ye be talkin' t', remember? *O' course* I won't be blabberin' tales
about!" He set down the pipe, which had grown
cold, and attempted a nonchalant pose in the chair.
"Why, I wouldn't even be talkin' t' *yerself* about . . .
anythin' . . ." A briefly arched eyebrow suggested a
hint of shrewdness. ". . . Ah, unless ye wuz t' be
wantin' me t', o' course . . ."

For several seconds Bryce debated accepting the
invitation; his instincts told him it might be a relief to
share the conflicting emotions which had been be-
setting him since leaving the *Louise*. Just who in hell
was Brittany Chambers, to be intruding on his life
this way? After all, she was just a woman, wasn't
she? And just barely emerged as such, from the
status of maiden!

But it was the nature of that emergence, and his
own hand in it, that was so disturbing. Why, she'd
surrendered her virginity to him with no compunc-
tions—and even less regret!

Then why did he carry such guilt? He should
never have heeded her; she could hardly have been
expected to know what she was doing—it had been
in the heat of passion that she'd begged him to—

But that was the crux of it. It was a passion *he'd*
ignited, randy fool that he was. And he had a mission to accomplish, *damn it*!

And now he was bombarded in his mind by
images of that passion . . . and his guilt. Ah, if only
he could unload some of these feelings, talk to

someone. . . . To Will . . . ? After all, Will had proved
to be a helpful confidant in the past. . . . Perhaps . . .

But at the last moment, he couldn't do it. The
emotions were too new and too raw. So he opted for
a partial explanation, one he hoped would satisfy his
all too perceptive friend.

"She knows about it, Will," he said wearily. "At
least, the part relating to Avery."

"'Ellfire! *She doesn't!* But 'ow—"

"She and that little abigail of hers, they overheard
us talking in the stables the other day." Bryce ran a
hand distractedly through his dark curls. "I wish—"

"But, lad, this changes everything! I never knew a
female wot could keep 'er mouth shut—let alone *two*
o' them!"

Bryce's face was grim as he again picked up the
letter to Avery. "This changes *nothing*, Will. Suffice it
to say I've adequate reasons to believe those two will
keep silent, and we continue as planned, do you
hear? *We continue as planned!*"

And with a parting look of pure resolution, he
whirled and left the room.

Amelia Wakefield's face was a study in concern as
she peered up at her niece. "Are you quite sure
you're feeling better, my dear? 'Twas a long time to
be abed with the vapors."

"I am fit as a fiddle, Aunt," Brittany told her with
a gaiety she didn't quite feel. She glanced at Tansy
beside her. "Thanks to Tansy's tender ministrations,
I assure you I am quite myself again."

"Well . . ." Amelia murmured, eyeing her apprais-
ingly, "I suppose I—oh, what *is* it, Aggie?"

Brittany smiled to herself as she watched her normally even-tempered aunt react in her predictably ir-

ritable fashion to Agatha, who tiptoed up behind her and tapped her shoulder.

They were like day and night, those two, and many a newcomer to their situation wondered how the relationship had lasted as long as it had. The mistress of Sweetbriar, with her unbridled cheer and zest for living, her unorthodox ideas on social niceties, and a penchant for thumbing her nose at institutions she couldn't abide (slavery and its cruelties being the foremost of these), was the last person in the world one would expect to retain a housekeeper as narrow, prudish, and rigid as Aggie. Why, Aunt Amelia had once whispered to Brittany that Aggie bathed in her *shift*! (Because, of course, Amelia had once unabashedly spied on her—"just to verify the rumors circulating among my staff, my dear"!)

But those who lived at Sweetbriar soon noticed what the newcomers could not: that an underlying bond existed between the two women, a bond that went back to the day Agatha met Amelia when she was installed as a new bride at Sweetbriar. While Amelia's husband tutored her in the arts of being a member of the landed gentry, it was Aggie who had patiently, day after day, helped her to practice what Tobias taught. And it had been Aggie, and not some unknown midwife, who'd been at her bedside for hours, the night the twins were born. And then there was the winter Aggie had taken deathly ill, and Amelia herself had nursed her faithfully for months until she recovered. And not everyone knew of the fire that broke out in the summer kitchen and was fought by these two, laboring side by side until—

"The invitations to the ball await your signature, madam." Agatha's crisp announcement cut neatly across Brittany's reverie.

"Oh, for heaven's sake, Aggie, is that all? For if ·

'tis, it hardly warrants an interruption when I am discoursing with my favorite niece!" Amelia fairly bristled as she glared her displeasure at the house-keeper.

"No, madam," Agatha sniffed, "'tis not all. There awaits in the kitchen a young woman who says she is a seamstress."

"Ah, splendid!" cried Amelia, clapping a pair of pudgy hands together in glee. Then she scowled. "Whatever is she doing in the kitchen?"

"I thought it best to have her wait there, madam, inasmuch as I was unacquainted with her person, and she arrived without warning, bearing no letters of ref—"

"Letters of reference are not needed," Amelia interrupted loftily, "since she comes directly from Mount Vernon. Mistress Washington herself was kind enough to recommend her—and send her—to me!"

"She looks, ah, rather dusty and worn to me, madam," Agatha warned.

"And so should *you* look, had you traveled straight from Mount Vernon!" Amelia returned testily. "Now, what are you standing around gaping for? Show her to the chamber off the sewing room—at once!"

Aggie's thin lips tightened into a reproving narrow line, but she nodded and turned to do Amelia's bidding.

"And put some pepper into it!" Amelia called after her. "That young woman's got to make us each a new ball gown and sew Tansy a wardrobe, to boot!"

As soon as Agatha disappeared, Amelia seemed to calm visibly. "There, there, my dear," she said, patting Tansy's shoulder, "we shall have you properly clothed in no time."

"But Aunt," said Brittany, "I know I told you we needed new clothes for Tansy, but how were you able so quickly to—"

"Oh, no, no, my dear!" Amelia laughed. "I daresay the Washingtons are effective people, but even they couldn't have gotten a seamstress here in two days' time! No, you see, Martha and I had already arranged for this paragon with needle and thread—weeks ago. But the timing could not have been better, don't you think?"

"Timing? Timing for what?" came a young male voice from the doorway.

"And when, and where?" followed a second.

"Tony! Toby!" Brittany exclaimed.

"Hello, my darlings," said Amelia, thrusting her cheek out for their kisses.

Tansy remained silent as she eyed their matching finch-yellow coats with a fixed wonderment that culminated in a rolling of her eyes.

"I say," said Toby, glancing at the bare tea table in the center of the room, "are we late or—"

"—early . . . for tea?" Tony finished.

"Good Heavens," Amelia exclaimed, "I'd forgotten all about tea!" She glanced at the face of the mahogany tall case clock in the far corner of the room, then back at her niece. "Well, Brittany, there's no help for it but to ask you to pour for me . . . ah, would you mind, my dear?"

"No, of course not, Aunt, but—"

"Splendid, splendid! On my way to the sewing room, I shall send Merriweather around with the tray." She placed a motherly arm around Tansy's waist and began moving her toward the door. "Come, my dear. You'll have your first fitting whilst I sit by and work on my invitations. And I've had Aggie take out some lovely bolts of cloth I saved from the last shipment my brother was fortunate enough to fetch from France. There's a lovely coral and cream stripe, and . . ."

In typical Aunt Amelia fashion, she ushered a bemused Tansy out of the room while her sons and niece looked on.

"Well," said Brittany when they'd gone, "I suppose we'd better—"

"Your pardon, Mistress Chambers, sirs," said Merriweather from the doorway, "Mister Richard Avery awaits without. Shall I show him in?"

Brittany froze, then glanced at her cousins, distress plainly evident in her eyes.

Toby and Tony caught this, then gave each other a knowing look.

"Show him in, Merriweather," Tony said, "and, ah—"

"—then you may bring the tea," added Toby, but not before placing a calming hand on Brittany's arm.

The butler nodded respectfully, then bowed out of the room, leaving Brittany to stare helplessly at her cousins.

"Not to fret, Coz," said Tony cheerfully. "We'll handle the rounder."

"Aye," said Toby, "we were even expecting him. 'Twas merely a question of, ah—"

"—how soon he'd show up," Tony finished.

Show up for what? Brittany was about to ask them, but was forestalled by Merriweather's voice.

"Mister Richard Avery," the butler announced.

Richard entered, took in the three of them for a second as they stood facing him, then smiled as he came toward Brittany.

She assessed his appearance in the moment before he bowed ceremoniously over her hand. He wore a deep lavender afternoon coat over a silver-embroidered, blue waistcoat, with gray breeches meeting well-polished black riding boots. Hatless, he had on a powdered periwig, and in his hand he still carried his riding crop.

"Mistress Chambers, how fortunate I am to find you in," he told her as she withdrew her hand from his with a haste he could hardly ignore. He gave her cousins a perfunctory nod. "Gentlemen."

Brittany found it impossible to tear her gaze away from his riding crop. Somehow, in his hands the item was distinctly unnerving, and she found herself commenting on it.

"Good day, Mister Avery . . . ah, you really might have left your crop with one of the footmen, you know."

Richard glanced down at the whip, then laughed as he began to flex it between both hands. "Oh, yes, but you see, I was hoping I might persuade you to go riding with me, my dear Mistress Chambers." The yellow eyes met hers in an unmistakable look of invitation.

"I see . . ." Brittany groped for a means of refusing. "But—"

"I fear 'twill be quite impossible, Avery," Tony cut in. "You see, we were, ah—"

"—just about to enjoy some tea, ah, herbal tea, that is," Toby told him as he signalled to Merriweather standing at the doorway with the tea tray. "Join us, won't you?" he added, making it sound quite obviously like an afterthought as he took Brittany's arm and guided her toward the tea table.

"Yes, if you like," Tony said casually while taking her other arm.

A few seconds later, Brittany found herself safely sandwiched between the twins on her aunt's sofa, leaving Richard no choice but to find himself a singu-

lar seat across from them. It had all happened so
fast, Richard had had no chance to maneuver, and
the look on his face showed his displeasure. She
smiled a grateful smile to first one twin, and then the
other, as Merriweather set the tea service in place.

Brittany then proceeded to pour their tea as her
cousins engaged Richard in small talk about crops
and the weather. Several times when Richard would
have changed the direction of the conversation by
aiming a remark her way, either one twin or the
other immediately jumped in with yet another tidbit
about this year's foaling problems or a question
about the falling price of indigo in the market.

And through it all, Brittany could see Richard
growing angrier. It showed by the way the lobes of
his ears turned from white, to pink, to a bright,
angry red beneath his wig, and she was glad for the
stalwart presence of the twins on either side of her,
aware, without knowing why, that to be alone in the
presence of an irate Richard Avery was something
devoutly to be avoided. His yellow eyes slid continually back from their barely polite attendance on her
cousins, to roam over her person as she sat pouring
the tea. They studied her in unblinking detail, taking
in her coiffure, her face and, above all, and all too
keenly, the square-cut décolletage of her gold silk afternoon gown.

It was during one of these ungentlemanly forays
toward her neckline that Toby, on whom Richard's
too-bold behavior had not been lost, decided he'd
had enough. "See here, Avery," he said, interrupting
one of Tony's deliberately tedious monologues on
the price of grain, "why don't we repair to the
stables to have a look at the stallion we plan to put to
the blooded gray mare, ah—what's her name,
Tony?"

"Gray Gambit!" Tony exclaimed. "Aye, 'twould be only right, Avery, that *you* see the bloodlines we plan to add to hers!"

Brittany almost shrank from the look of hostility in Richard's eyes, though it was clearly aimed at the twins. But what she couldn't know was that her cousins had just conspired to bring about that hostility to goad Richard into leaving the drawing room—and her company.

Aware of their cousin's dislike for Richard, these two were clearly bent on keeping him at a safe distance from her. Moreover, they loathed Richard themselves, but they were not above playing whist with him on the occasions they ran into him at certain establishments in Fredericksburg and "taking him to the laundry" at such times; the twins had done their Grand Tour the year before, and skill at gambling was something they'd picked up while abroad, "among other gentlemanly accomplishments."

And what Brittany also couldn't know was that Gray Gambit was the most recent in a string of gambling losses for Avery, the twins having won the mare from him in a "gentlemanly game" at the Rising Sun Tavern. Of course, had she known, she might have wondered at their audacity in provoking Richard with their current suggestion, even if it was for her benefit. Richard Avery, she could have told them, was not the sort of man who tolerated having salt rubbed into his wounds!

"Capital idea!" Tony was saying as he and Toby rose to escort their guest to the stables. "Neither of us knows her bloodlines as well as you, old boy, so you might as well have a say in our breeding plans."

"Aye," Toby chimed in as they reached the doorway, "after all, who knows but what you might recoup one of these days and, ah—"

"—get her back again, eh?" finished his brother as he delivered a jocular nudge to Avery's ribs with a well-aimed elbow.

Brittany watched Richard's frame stiffen at their running commentary, saw his features go rigid with some unnamed fury, and realized there was a game being played out here by her cousins, a game to which she was not privy. At least, she thought, now was not the time to question it, but as Richard's hostile form disappeared from view, she made a mental note to query the twins about it later—and to warn them. Richard Avery was not a person one should choose to make an enemy!

She heard the outside door close after them and had just a moment to glance at the unfinished servings of herbal tea cooling in their saucers when a deep voice hailed her from the doorway.

"Are we too late fer tea?" asked Will Thatcher as he peered into the drawing room. "Eh . . . ? All alone, Mistress Chambers? Thought we 'eard several voices down 'ere a moment ago."

Brittany knew she ought to be responding to the big man's questions, but her thoughts were entirely consumed by the tall figure that joined him as he entered the room.

Bryce had never looked more handsome as he strode toward her with those fluid, graceful movements she knew so well by now. Bareheaded, he wore his casually curling hair in a fashionable queue at the nape of his neck, tied there by a narrow black ribbon. A deep green coat fit his wide-shouldered frame perfectly, and she immediately became aware of how the color accentuated the green of his eyes. A snowy white stock contrasted startlingly with the deep bronze of his face. It also served to draw the eye to the white of his form-fitting breeches which, along with a pair of shiny mahogany tallboots, encased his long, muscular legs in a manner that brought instant heat to her cheeks; she needed no reminder of the strength of his thighs or of the equally apparent maleness outlined adjacent to them in those breeches right now!

"Will asked where the others went, Brittany," he reminded her as he drew near the sofa.

A delicious shiver rippled along her spine at the sound of his voice, its deep timbre instantly recalling for her those moments when she'd heard it murmuring passionately suggestive endearments as he'd made love to her—*Dear God—had it only been this morning?*

She felt a hotter blush invade her face as she struggled to dismiss these unsettling recollections and answer him. *But what was it he had asked?*

"Brittany . . . where is your aunt?" Bryce's insistent voice cut through her helpless thoughts with a greater intensity.

She blinked and met his eyes, totally unprepared for the amusement playing in their green depths.

"I . . . ah, Aunt Amelia went upstairs," she managed to get out.

"And . . . ?" he prompted, a hint of a smile playing about his mouth as the green eyes continued to hold her gaze.

She heard Will clear his throat, and this at last served to spur her into action. Rising from her seat, she took a deep breath and pasted what she hoped would appear to be a nonchalant smile on her face.

"Oh, I'm so sorry, gentlemen. I've . . . taken on a bit of a headache, you see. Er . . . 'twas the reason Aunt Amelia and the twins left me here whilst they attended to business. But you can find my aunt upstairs, if you wish. She's working on the invitations to this ball she seems so bent on having for me. Of course, I'll be glad to pour you some tea in her stead. But perhaps you'd care to see Toby and Tony. You'll find them in the stables. They decided to go out . . ."

Bryce listened with an indulgent ear to the rapid, flustered chatter which was so totally uncharacteristic of her, for he'd readily guessed its source. *So she was the cool sophisticate, well above all that maidenly demureness, was she?* he thought, then almost laughed at the strange sense of delight this realization brought him. In fact, there was a great deal about her he was finding delightful right now, from the light sprinkling of freckles across the bridge of her pert nose—why hadn't he noticed them before?—to the delicate blushes that kept suffusing her cheeks. And had there ever been a blue as blue as her eyes?

His gaze dropped to the pale coral of her lips and he was just savoring a memory of how they'd tasted when something she said brought him up short.

"What did you say?" he cut in.

Brittany paused, then repeated the phrase she'd just uttered. "I said when Mister Avery turned up, Toby and To—"

"Avery? *Edmund* Avery?" Bryce questioned.

"Why, no—'twas Richard, his son."

"That yellow-eyed—!" Will exclaimed.

"Aye, the same," Brittany confirmed. "As I was saying, my cousins took him out to the stables just now, and—"

"Now?" queried Bryce. "You mean they're still out there?"

"'Twould seem so, inasmuch as they just left," said Brittany. "I think—but wait! Where are you going?"

Will threw her an apologetic look as he bounded after Bryce, who was halfway out the door. "Beggin' yer pardon, Mistress," he called over his shoulder. "Ah, we've decided t' let ye nurse yer 'eadache in peace. Be seein' ye later—at supper!"

And with these hastily uttered words, he disappeared out the door after Bryce, leaving her alone with her thoughts—and a dozen unanswered questions!

"Well," she said aloud to herself in the suddenly quiet room, "all the more reason to find some way of getting his lordship to confess the rest of his secrets. This Avery business is getting out of hand!"

Picking up her skirts, Brittany hurried out of the room. It was time to find Tansy and plan some strategy!

CHAPTER 14

DAYS PASSED WHILE THE INHABITANTS OF Sweetbriar played a waiting game. For Bryce and Will, it was a frustrating wait; news had come (by way of Richard Avery the afternoon of his visit) that Edmund was away on a business venture up north and wouldn't return for a fortnight. For Brittany and Tansy, not to mention Amelia and her household, it was a countdown to the night of the ball.

And a busy countdown it was! Beautiful gowns were sewn by the remarkable seamstress from Mount Vernon, while acceptances to Amelia's invitations poured in; every nook and cranny of the Big House was put to mop and broom by the legion of maids and footmen that labored from sunup to sunset under Agatha's eagle eye; and a plethora of mouthwatering aromas began to waft their way throughout the house from the summer kitchen, where the cook and her army of helpers seemed to labor day and night.

Finally the evening of the ball arrived, and with it, a flaring of the guest of honor's temper—for real.

"But how *could* she have done it, Tansy?" Brittany fumed. "And without even a word to me!"

"You know the answer to that one," the black woman pointed out patiently as she put the finishing touches to Brittany's coiffure. "If she had told you first, you'd have told her not to do it."

"Bloody right!" Brittany exclaimed to the dark face in the mirror. "Imagine my shock at learning—from one of the kitchen maids, no less—that Aunt Amelia had deliberately let it be known that my mother was a French aristocrat! She knows how I loathe trading on that business."

She pivoted about on the small bench in front of the dressing table and met Tansy's eyes directly. "But what I had the most difficulty believing was that *she'd* be the one to *do* it! Aunt Amelia herself has never been one to indulge in the snobbery all this class business breeds. . . . Ohh, *how could she?*"

"She could . . . and she *did* . . ." reasoned Tansy, "because she thought she was bein' helpful, ah imagine . . . probably just wanted to make your ball a big success. Ah wouldn't be blamin' her too much, honeychile. All that motherin' just got the best of her."

Hearing the calm logic, Brittany felt herself begin to relax. It was just like Tansy to relieve what was likely a case of last-minute jitters on her part. Heaven knew, Aunt Amelia had never once incited her to anger before now.

Glancing at her reflection in the mirror, a wave of shame hit her. About her slim neck rested the most exquisite diamond and sapphire necklace she'd ever seen. It was her aunt's, and Amelia had sent it to her chamber this morning with a note that said, "Wear these jewels tonight, my dear. I wish to see them on you, for they'll be yours one day, as I have no daughters to leave them to." These were hardly the words of someone who wished her anything but happiness. Yes, the more she thought about it, especially now that she'd heard Tansy's soothing words, she realized she was likely brewing a tempest in a teapot.

"I think you're right—as usual, Tans," she smiled.

"Good," came the satisfied response, "now let's get that ball gown on you."

Brittany rose and crossed to the wardrobe, where Tansy had hung the gown that had been completed only the day before. Of a deep sapphire blue silk, it was calculated to echo the blue of her eyes, and she knew the gems about her neck would heighten that effect.

Minutes later, as Brittany stood in front of the pier glass in her dressing room, she also knew that Martha Washington's little seamstress was a gem of another sort. Not even the modiste in Richmond was up to the fashionable excellence that had been created for Brittany in the sewing chamber upstairs.

The sapphire silk hugged her minuscule waist (made even tinier—an impossible eighteen inches—by the tightly laced corset Amelia had insisted she wear) and formed a deep *V* at the base of the bodice, while the deep square décolletage above was edged with only the narrowest trim of dove gray silk ruching, which made the generous swells of her breasts quite visible. (There had been considerable debate in the sewing chamber over the propriety of the décolletage, with Aggie insisting that such a low neckline was too immodest for a young, unmarried woman, and Amelia insisting that she would have her niece wear only what was the height of fashion. And, of course, Amelia had won.)

Now, as Brittany stood fighting the blush which

rose to her cheeks at the sight of this display, she wasn't certain that Aggie hadn't been right. But, thank heaven for the necklace! A display in itself, it served to distract from the other to some degree.

Her eyes dropped to the voluminous skirts that fell to the floor in shimmering folds. The inverted *V* that revealed the gown's dove gray silk underskirt was bordered by four-inch-wide panels of the same gray, echoing the ruching of her neckline and the pale gray silk that fell from the narrow sleeves ending at her elbows. The panels were exquisitely embroidered with dozens of blue silk roses and forget-me-nots, as was the eighteen-inch-wide panel of gray silk that bordered the hem of the underskirt. The embroidery alone, Amelia had told her, had taken six months to be applied by a local embroidery wizard after the silk had arrived from France.

"The fabric fairly begged for her skills," Aunt Amelia had said the day they'd begun designing the gown, when she'd shown Brittany and the seamstress the bolt of decorated silk, "and now I know I was right to have it done, for your coloring fairly begs that you have it. Wear it with joy, my dear!"

Tansy set out a pair of dove gray satin slippers and signalled for Brittany to step into them. When she had, the hemline was raised a bare half-inch off the floor, allowing the skirts to swing gracefully with the movements of her paniers.

"Hmm," murmured Tansy as they viewed the total effect together, "'pears—ah mean, *it appears*—to me you need something in your hair . . ."

They both eyed the intricate coiffure she'd created. Elaborate without being fussy, it consisted of an elegant cluster of curls at the crown of the head, and a yard-long swirling hank of the red tresses that was allowed to fall down her back from the center of this cluster. The hair about her face was drawn smoothly back, however, framing its chiseled beauty with simple grace.

"Aha!" exclaimed the black woman victoriously as she pounced on a vase of freshly picked flowers on a side table. Plucking one of the waxy blossoms, she had Brittany bend low while she deftly secured the flower beside the cluster of curls.

"Ah don't know what kind of flowers these be, Miz Britt," she said, grinning, "but they sure do smell nice!"

"Uncle Tobias was an amateur horticulturist," said Brittany, nodding her agreement to the blossom's placement, "and he never made a trip—abroad, or wherever—without bringing back some exotic *flora*. On one of his trips he made the acquaintance of a Dr. Alexander Garden, who had a similar interest. The good doctor gave him some specimens of the evergreen shrub these grow on, and Uncle promptly presented them to Aunt for her birthday when he returned. She's been growing these gardenias ever since."

"From Garden's garden, huh?" Tansy grinned.

"Mmm," murmured Brittany as she gazed speculatively at the remaining flowers in the vase. "Aha!" she exclaimed, echoing Tansy.

A twig snapped as she broke off the largest of the blossoms and, with a smug smile, inserted it into the cleavage above her gown's daring neckline.

"There!" she pronounced with satisfaction. "Now I can help greet the guests."

The guests began arriving in great numbers shortly after she reached the entrance to the enormous upstairs ballroom where her aunt and cousins waited. Amelia looked fetching and youthful in a gown of lavender damask silk, and Brittany told her as much, but her cousins' attire robbed her of speech.

Similarly dressed in gold-embroidered dress coats of parrot green satin, the Wakefield men sported purple silk waistcoats, also embroidered in gold, with patterns of exotic fish swimming amid even more exotic seaweed. Their knee-breeches were also made of the eye-stopping green, meeting snowy white silk hose which covered their calves and echoed the elaborate white lace of their stocks. A row of gleaming gold buttons ran down the front of each coat, and their high-heeled shoes had huge gold buckles. Finally, topping off this showy set of double images were two of the most prodigiously curled and powdered formal wigs Brittany had ever seen.

Toby gestured with an ebony-handled walking stick, the only item of his ensemble that differed from his brother's, whose was done in ivory. "Well, Coz, you're dazzling as ever, but, ahem . . . what d' ye think?" He turned slowly before her, stopping to give her a carefully held profile.

"Aye," Tony chimed in, imitating his twin, "what's the verdict?"

"I . . . why, ah . . ."

Amelia caught her distress and smiled knowingly. "Come now, darlings, I just know she feels as I do, that your tailor has simply, ah, outdone himself!"

The twins beamed at both women, but in the next second, they were listening to Merriweather's careful announcement of the names of the first guests. Brittany endured the rigors of their small receiving line with practiced grace, having been through similar procedures before, under Timothy's roof. She smiled and nodded and smiled again, demurely lowering her eyes each time she was introduced to an eligible male from the area—their eligibility being something her aunt was quick to point out to her discreetly in every instance.

There was planter Jonas Ridgeway, a widower with six children, who stuttered and smelled of garlic; there was Captain Sprague, of His Majesty's Regiment which was stationed in Fredericksburg—quite, quite handsome in a blond, mustached way, but terribly shy; there was Squire Denton, on holiday from Dorset, visiting his colonial cousins—a foot shorter than Brittany and a good ten stone heavier; and she could hardly overlook the fabulously wealthy Geoffrey Burlingame, a distant cousin of planter Fielding Lewis (whose wife, Betty, was George Washington's sister). Mister Burlingame was quite tall and distinguished looking—and eighty if he was a day!

Besides these, among the "eligible" men Brittany counted three Thomases, four Williams, two Johns, and three Richards, of which the last to arrive was Avery. He came with his mother, explaining that Edmund had been expected home by now, but had somehow been detained.

Brittany's heart went out to Emily Avery, who wore a faded, drooping gown so hopelessly out of fashion it looked like a costume piece. And when Brittany beheld it beside the obviously new, expensively tailored formal attire worn by her son, she felt her dislike of Richard mushroom.

"I am looking forward to sharing a dance with you, Mistress Chambers," Richard was saying as he lingered over her hand a bit too long. "Be so kind as to save me one, m'dear."

Brittany felt herself cringe as the yellow eyes ran over her with indelicate interest. Managing to nod cordially to him, and with a vast sense of relief, she felt him release her hand.

But in the next moment, all thoughts of the younger Avery flew from her mind as she heard Merriweather announce: "Captain Bryce Tremaine."

She'd seen very little of Bryce in the past week or so, as she'd been totally preoccupied with helping Amelia—not to mention getting ready for the ball herself—while Bryce and Will, for reasons she could only guess at, had taken to spending most of their time aboard the *Louise*. Even at mealtimes they'd failed to cross paths; most of hers were spent hurriedly sharing a tray with Amelia and Tansy in the sewing chamber.

Now, as she viewed his tall, broad-shouldered form approaching, she could only wonder at how so many days had been consumed with thinking of other things.

He was devastatingly handsome in a brandy-colored formal coat and breeches that were simply yet expertly tailored in the latest English mode. His ivory satin waistcoat was tastefully embroidered with bronze thread, and the white silk of his formal hose covered well-muscled calves. He apparently eschewed the wearing of wigs, she thought, for he again wore his own dark hair, unpowdered and queued at the nape of his neck.

She watched him greet the twins and then bow over Amelia's hand, and was struck by the thought that he must have been spending a great deal of time in the sun. His face was of an even deeper golden bronze than before, as were the strong, long-fingered hands she found herself staring at as he released her aunt's fingers.

And in the next moment she was looking up into those mesmerizing green eyes with the tiny laugh lines radiating from the corners. Then he smiled, his male dimples cutting a pair of slashing grooves on either side of his mouth, his teeth a dazzling white against his tanned face.

"Brittany..." he murmured as he took her hand (why was it trembling?), "you're the loveliest creature on God's earth tonight..." His warm lips grazed her fingers; she let her gaze rest on his shiny black curls and felt a tremor along her spine. Then he straightened and his eyes were meeting hers again.

"A dance..." he said, "...save me one." Then he moved away, disappearing into the crowd that thronged the dance floor.

Toby and Tony watched this, saw the speechless wonder on their cousin's face as her eyes followed Bryce out of sight, and exchanged knowing looks over their mother's head.

"So that's the way of things..." murmured Tony with a slow nod.

Toby's nod echoed his as Amelia looked curiously from one son to the other.

"What's the way of which things?" she queried.

"Oh...nothing, Mama," Tony smiled, "ah, 'tis merely, ah—"

"—the minuet they're playing," finished Toby as he gestured at the musicians playing in the small balcony above the ballroom. "'Tis a lovely piece." He took his mother's arm. "Will you do me the honor, madam? I simply cannot resist such a ravishing redhead a moment longer!"

Amelia made a sound that was close to a giggle and allowed him to lead her out, all questions forgotten.

Meanwhile, his brother had taken Brittany's hand. "Fair Coz," he smiled, "may I...?"

Brittany at last shook off the daze that had claimed her at Bryce's appearance and smiled gratefully up at her cousin. "Sir, 'twould be a pleasure," she told him, and she allowed him to lead her onto the floor.

The evening began to pass quickly for Brittany after that. The music alternated between stately minuets and lively reels; champagne flowed freely, borne by liveried footmen in crystal glasses on silver trays; and everywhere one looked, the cream of Virginia tidewater society moved in a kaleidoscope of brightly colored silks and satins, punctuated with many-hued jewels that winked their opulence beneath the hundreds of candles in the huge, multitiered chandelier above their heads.

She found herself dancing almost every dance, besieged by the very thing she'd sworn to hate—unmarried gentlemen who were eager to become suitors (if their requests to come calling were any indication, and she knew they were). But somehow, tonight she didn't find herself minding such attention. Time enough later, she told herself, to be sending them away disappointed; tonight was hers, a wonderful fairy tale of an evening arranged by an aunt who loved her and had spared no energy or expense to lavish all this attention on her (even if it was for the wrong reasons), and Brittany would be the last person to rob her of the pleasure it brought.

Of course, there were moments when she was sorely tempted. William and Thomas Whitaker, a pair of unwed brothers thrust toward her by a shove of their eager mother's hand, attempted to speak to her in halting *French*! It wasn't too hard to guess the source of *their* interest—or their mother's, and she was tempted to concoct a tale that *her* mother's lineage wasn't all that noble, as it descended from one of Louis XIII's whores—but she stopped herself at the last minute.

There was one point in the evening, however, when she found her high spirits threatened. It happened during a lull in the dancing, when the musicians stopped to partake of some refreshments Amelia sent up to them. She stood at the side of the room talking to Captain Sprague (or trying to—the poor man was so painfully shy, all she could pry out of him were monosyllabic answers to her questions!). As she spoke and sipped sparingly from a glass of champagne the captain had brought her, she caught sight of a dark head of queued hair across the room. Bryce's head and shoulders were all that was visible to her as he stood surrounded by a bevy of young female guests. There were the Lee girls; and that beautiful brunette stepsister of Aunt Amelia's solicitor; a tiny blonde who reminded her of Melody; and three or four others whose names escaped her at the moment—and they were all gazing up at Bryce with rapt expressions on their faces. She stiffened as she saw him bend to hear something the petite blonde whispered in his ear and then laugh delightedly while giving her a playful tap on the nose. And when a coy, dark-eyed look from behind the brunette's fan made him grin and wink at her, Brittany found herself gritting her teeth.

What was wrong with her? She felt like a schoolgirl disappointed in her first crush, but the sudden ache in her chest was something she was not ready to acknowledge, and she downed the remaining bubbly liquid in her glass and turned quickly to Captain Sprague, forcing a smile to her lips.

"Dear Captain, I seem to be quite out of champagne. Would you be so kind . . . ?"

Sprague flushed slightly, then took the proffered

glass and made her a gallant bow. "Certainly, Mistress," he mumbled, then turned to seek out a passing footman.

She was vaguely aware that the music had resumed as she again found her gaze straying to the tall, popular figure across the room when an all too familiar male voice intruded.

"I believe I'll have this dance," said Richard Avery; yellow eyes skimmed over her from top to toe.

Brittany noticed his words were slightly slurred and she had every intention of refusing; a sober Richard would have been enough to generate this intention, and a Richard under the influence of too much champagne made it imperative! But then, out of the corner of her eye she caught a glimpse of Bryce leading the petite blonde onto the floor, and in the next instant she found herself accepting Richard.

"You look ravishing tonight, m'dear," Richard told her as the measured bars of the minuet brought them within speaking range.

And judging from the look in your eyes, I'd wager you're thinking you'd like to be the one to ravish me! thought Brittany as she managed a demure nod.

The steps of the dance separated them, and a glance to her right took in a tall figure in brandy-colored coat and breeches. But Bryce was not smiling now as his gaze rested not on his partner, but on hers; Richard was swaying slightly, and his feet missed a step in the dance.

But in the next moment he recovered, and she found herself meeting the yellow eyes as they raked over her.

"You have made your company exsheedingly scarsh in reshent daysh, Mistress," he complained when they were in speaking range.

"I . . . have been busy," she told him, wrinkling her

nose in distaste at the alcoholic smell of his breath. *Good Heavens!* she thought. *He's been imbibing spirits more substantial than champagne!* She recalled the twins mentioning that a gaming room had been set up in one of the downstairs chambers where "gentlemen might refresh themselves," and guessed Richard had gone there to drink and gamble at some point during the evening.

The dance's intricate steps saved her from having to respond further to his complaint, and she found herself using their separation to look about her. Across the line of dancers she saw Toby in smiling conversation with one of the Lee girls and then spotted Tony dancing with the beautiful brunette who'd been flirting with Bryce. And standing on the sidelines, looking forlorn, was Captain Sprague holding two glasses of champagne.

A few more steps brought Richard near again, and he was frowning at her. "Busy or nay, Mistress, I mean to shee more of you," he told her as the minuet wore down to a conclusion.

They completed the final bow and curtsy, and Richard was about to take her arm when Tony's voice cut in.

"You look hot and thirsty, Coz, and so am I after all this footwork. Come, let's take a glass and get some air." With a peremptory nod at Avery, he ushered her off toward the door that led to the stairs.

"Oh, Tony," she told him with a grateful look, "thank heaven you rescued me. I don't think I could have stood another minute of that—that—"

"Say no more, Coz," he interrupted, taking a pair of glasses from a passing tray. "Toby and I have no more liking for the Averys than you or Mama. We've seen the lay of the land and we'll protect you."

They'd reached the top of the stairway leading to

the gardens, and Brittany paused, placing a hand on Tony's arm.

"My thanks," she said, "but you needn't accompany me further." She nodded at the glass of champagne he held out to her. "Take that to, ah, Mistress Calvert.... Wasn't that her name...?" She smiled archly at him.

He smiled back. "She is rather stunning, don't you think?"

Remembering the beautiful brunette's coy looks, Brittany nodded, but cautioned, "Those dark eyes behind her fan will devastate you if you don't take some care."

Tony winked at her. "Exactly so." He turned back to the ballroom before pausing to look at her over his shoulder. "Ah... you'll be all right by yourself?"

"Of course I shall, silly," she returned as she began down the stairs. "'Tis a lovely evening and I intend to enjoy the gardens. Enjoy your Mistress Calvert, dear Coz!"

She made her way down the stairs and entered the gardens through the French doors below.

It was a balmy evening, the heavy air redolent with the scent of honeysuckle and roses. From unseen corners came the steady staccato of crickets chirping their ode to summer. The only other sound was a dog's barking in the distance as she made her way along a graveled path between privet hedges whose tiny leaves were silvered by the moonlight filtering through the branches of several giant oaks.

Then the orchestra upstairs struck up a lively reel and the sounds were so clear, it was almost as if the garden had been turned into a second ballroom. Finding a bench at the place where the path divided and circled a small, manmade fish pond, she sat down to listen, her slippered foot tapping lightly to the beat of the music.

Minutes passed with Brittany content to remain there, enjoying the moonlight and the scented air as reel gave way to minuet and then another reel, and finally a minuet again.

She was so engrossed by the tinkling baroque chords that she didn't hear anything until the sound of a foot slipping on the gravel alerted her.

"Ah, there you are, you vixen!" Richard Avery crowed triumphantly while his big form loomed over her. "Thought I'd find you alone when I shaw those coushins 'fyours both upshtairsh."

Brittany stiffened, then scrambled to her feet. "Richard, you're *drunk*. Please leave me. I cannot—"

"Drunk, am I? Aye... mayhap," he told her. He staggered toward her. "But not too drunk t' cap— *hic*—capture a proud redheaded... vixen!" He lurched forward and grabbed her about the shoulders, pulling her to him in a fumbling embrace.

Brittany struggled against him, but even in his inebriated state, Richard was too strong for her. She opened her mouth to scream, but his large, wet mouth covered hers before she could draw enough breath. Then she felt one of his hands come up to grab her breast, and a tide of loathing washed over her.

But in the next instant she felt herself freed as she caught a flash of purple in the moonlight.

"Blackguard!" Tony's voice cut across the sounds of the orchestra.

"Swine!" Toby growled as he joined his brother in pulling Richard off her.

Richard launched a string of expletives while trying to tear himself free of the twins, each of whom had him by an arm.

"Here now," said Tony, "that must cease! 'Tis no way to be talking—"

"—in front of a lady," added Toby.

Richard continued to swear and struggle, but they held him fast, and when Toby wrenched one of his arms behind him with a painful twist, he grunted and at last grew still.

"That," said Toby, slightly out of breath, "is better . . . much better. Now, sir, you will apologize—"

"—to the lady," Tony finished with a threatening look, "and then we shall allow you to be on your way. . ."

". . . home, that is," Toby added.

Richard cast a sullen, heavy-lidded look at first one twin, then the other. There was a moment of silence, and finally he glanced at Brittany, mumbling, "Your pardon, Mistress." All traces of drunkedness were gone from his voice.

Brittany gave him a stiff nod, eyes lowered as she stared at the ground where the moonlight picked up the crushed, brown-tinged petals of the gardenia that had been tucked in her bodice.

Her cousins released Avery with cautious movements, their muscles tensed for action. He muttered an angry, incoherent sound, turned, and stalked down the path toward the stables.

"Are you all right, Coz?" Toby inquired when he'd gone.

"A-aye, I think so," said Brittany shakily.

"That no-good rotter. . ." Tony fumed as he placed a comforting arm about her shoulders.

"Should have known he'd try something like that," said Toby. "He's desperate enough," he added, looking at his twin.

"Aye," murmured Tony.

"Wh-what do you mean?" Brittany queried.

Her cousins led her back to the bench and sat down with her, one on either side.

"Look, Brittany," said Toby, "we think there are a few facts you should know about Richard Avery."

"Aye," said Tony, "and that father of his."

With their protective presence about her, Brittany began to feel less shaken by what, at one frightening moment, she had felt would end in nothing less than rape, and she allowed her curiosity to take over. "What *about* the Averys?"

"They think they're rather clever," Tony began, "but, ah—"

"—neither of them is as clever as they'd have people think," said Toby.

"Aye," his brother continued, "we've learned, dear Coz, that the Averys are deeply in debt . . ."

"*In debt?*" Brittany was incredulous as she thought of the fine, expensively tailored clothes the Avery men wore, the blooded horses they rode, the grand carriage that took them about in style . . . but then her mind seized on an image of poor Emily Avery's moth-eaten gown, and she nodded. "Go on."

"They're in debt because of poor estate management, for one thing," said Toby.

"And Richard's penchant for heavy gaming, for another," Tony told her.

"With heavy losses," Toby added.

"From a shameful lack of skill," said his twin with a regretful shake of the head.

"Oh . . . I see," Brittany said sagely, "and you two have been in a position to—"

"—relieve him of some of his, ah—"

"—fortune."

She looked from one twin to the other and saw the furthest thing from remorse on their faces. In fact, they looked rather like two satisfied cats who'd eaten their fill of a big, nasty canary.

"I see," she repeated.

"And it occurred to us this evening," said Tony.

"—as we took Avery for yet some more of his coin at the gaming tables inside," added Toby.

"—and heard him plying others with questions about the fortune that was left you,"

"—that the man is desperate for an heiress,"

"—to shore up the dwindling family assets," Tony finished.

"Good Heavens!" Brittany exclaimed. "You don't mean that—that is—oh, I can't believe it! You think he meant to compromise me into—into—"

Just then there was the sound of gravel crunching underfoot, and a second later, Tansy ran up to them, breathless and agitated.

"Miz Britt, Miz Britt, is you all right? Ah jes done seen dat Av'ry snake hightailin' it outta here, an' he wuz a-cussin' an' a-fumin', an' *mumblin' yo' name* sumpfin', awful, an—"

"Hold on, hold on, Mistress Tansy," Toby broke in. "She's fine, really she is, ah—"

"—now that she's with us," Tony added.

Tansy drew herself up short and peered at the three of them. "Guess ah kin see dat," she said, "but dat Av'ry—"

"You were right to worry, Tans," Brittany sighed. "He did try to—to harm me, but . . ." Her words trailed off as she gestured at the twins.

"Well, God bless you gen'lemuns," Tansy declared, still taking care to use her slave patois in front of the twins. "Miz Britt'ny sho is lucky t' have you t' call on!"

"That I am," echoed Brittany as she gave her cousins a grateful smile.

"Well, ah sho be glad o' dat," Tansy asserted, "but, still, dat Av'ry..."

Then Tansy told them some of the things *she'd* been hearing about the Averys by way of the servants' grapevine. It was said Edmund Avery was little better than an animal at home, brutally mistreating his slaves and his stock (refraining only if there was an unusually extensive amount of money tied up in them), and even abusing his wife —and word was that Richard was cut of the same cloth.

She told them of the "whuppin' tree" behind the disgracefully dilapidated row of Avery slave cabins where every Friday night, a slave was arbitrarily singled out and taken to be whipped, whether there was a reason or not, as part of the Avery method of "keeping them in line." She confirmed what the twins had already heard about the poor food rations that half starved every slave on their plantation. She chronicled a shameful lack of medical attention and nursing care that led to two out of every three slave babies being born dead—and all too often, the mothers along with them. And she told of the fear that ruled the lives of slaves and animals alike on Avery land.

"*Dear God...*" whispered Brittany when she had finished, "*those men are monsters...*" Her voice trailed off, then choked on a sob as she gave way to the powerful emotions Tansy's tale had called forth. She looked up and saw Tansy's sorrowful face through a blur of tears, and reached out to her friend.

Tansy glanced briefly at the compassionate faces of the twins, then moved forward to take Brittany in her arms, where her friend sobbed uncontrollably for several long minutes.

At last the tears subsided, and Brittany drew back

but continued to hold Tansy's hand as she turned a tear-stained face to her cousins. "There—there must be something we can *do*!" she cried.

Sadly, Tony shook his head. "The pity of it is, we can't."

"'Tis all perfectly legal," Toby added grimly. "Slaves as well as livestock are the lawful property of their masters, who may treat them as they wish."

"Fortunately," Tony continued, "in the large majority of cases, the slavemaster's sense of protecting the value of his property, if not his compassion, keeps things from going this far..."

"...but the Averys," said Toby with a quiet fury Brittany had never heard him evince before, "are too stupid or too venal—or both—to do even *that*! Oh, Edmund's been known to caution that blackguard we just trounced to take care with his prize horse-flesh on occasion..."

"...but half the time he's off somewhere, making one of his notoriously bad market deals," Tony told her, "leaving his wastrel son Richard to run things for him. They're a bad lot, those two."

Brittany's thoughts turned at this to Bryce and his mission of revenge. She'd guessed at the evil nature of his quarry from the vehemence with which the Englishman had spoken of his purpose, but there'd always been a niggling little suspicion regarding his motives. Now, however, in light of what she'd just seen and heard, there wasn't a shred of doubt in her mind as to the veracity of Bryce's claims; Edmund Avery was a brute who was capable of any evil, and his son along with him. As her tears dried, she found herself praying for Tremaine's quick rendering of the justice he sought.

"Well," said Toby, patting her hand as it released

Tansy's, "you seem to be feeling better . . . ah, shall
we escort you to your chamber, or—"

"—take you back upstairs?" Tony finished for him.
"Mama's likely to be missing us at this point, and—"

"Oh," said Brittany, "why don't you two go back
up and reassure her, then? No need to upset her
with what occurred out here, of course. And I'll just
stay here a bit longer and—"

"Yes, but—"

"Really, Tony," she told him, "I shall be all right
. . . truly. . . . After all, Richard's gone now, thanks to
you two, isn't he?"

"Well, if you really think—"

"I do," she told them with a smile. "I . . . simply
need a few moments by myself . . . out here in the
garden. . . . 'Tis so soothing, you see . . ."

"Very well then," said Toby, rising, "but, ah—"

"—don't be long," Tony told her as he also stood.

Both cousins bent simultaneously to place an affectionate kiss on her cheeks, one on either side.
Then they turned, patted Tansy gently on her
shoulder, and headed for the house.

"They're a decent pair, those two," said Tansy,
once they'd gone.

"Aye," Brittany murmured with a sigh, "one
couldn't wish for better. Aunt Amelia—"

"Oh—oh," muttered Tansy, "speaking of your
aunt, ah just remembered—ah'm supposed to fetch
her a spring of mint from the garden. Some old lady
wants it for her hot water."

"Hot water?"

"Uh-huh," Tansy grinned as she headed for the
herb garden, "because your aunt told her she
couldn't have real tea—said she'd be unpatriotic unless she drank the mint tea the rest of us here at
Sweetbriar been drinkin'—ah—*have been drinking!*"

She paused to bestow a concerned look on Brittany. "Um . . . you'll be all right . . . ?"

"I shall be fine, as I told the twins," Brittany smiled. "Now, for heaven's sake, run along. We wouldn't want to be the cause of an old lady's lack of patriotism!"

Tansy disappeared down the path, leaving her alone with her thoughts and the moonlight. She'd told the truth when she said she was feeling better. Certainly she was well past the fright Richard Avery had given her. But her thoughts kept returning to Bryce Tremaine and his quest, for they were spurred on by what she'd learned of the Averys tonight. And with these thoughts, she found herself more curious than ever as to the details of what had happened between Bryce and Edmund Avery at some time in the past. What could have happened? Or, rather, what had Avery done? He was so much older than Bryce . . .

"What? All alone out here?" asked a deep male voice. "Oddly solitary behavior for a guest of honor, don't you think?"

She'd once heard an old wives' tale about conjuring up a person on certain moonlit nights, and in that moment Brittany was ready to believe it as Bryce strode into view.

"Oh! *Bryce* . . . you . . . startled me." She took in his tall, impeccably dressed form as he stood there, the moonlight silvering his dark hair and throwing the strongly hewn planes and angles of his face into stark relief. Feeling, for some reason, at a disadvantage by sitting while he stood, she quickly rose from the bench.

"I didn't mean to, m'lady . . . ah, or am I not supposed to use the title? I mean, it having to do with confiscated lands, not to mention coming down matrilineally and all that . . ."

Brittany blushed at his reference to her background before focusing on the sarcasm in his voice and rising to it. "At least I have good *cause* to drop *my* titles, m'lord!"

"*Touché!*" He gave her a mocking bow.

But she was not in the mood to exchange barbed witticisms with him after all that had happened tonight. "Let be, Bryce," she told him wearily. "I . . . haven't the heart to fence with you this evening."

Bryce caught the brief look of distress that crossed her features and frowned, then stepped closer and ran his eyes carefully over her face. "What is it? What's wrong, Brittany?"

"Oh, 'tis nothing. I just—"

"Bloody hell it is!" he growled. "Something's happened, and recently, too, by the looks of you." He took her chin gently with his fingers and tilted it upward, forcing her to look at him. "Now tell me what it is."

Brittany looked up into his face with its demanding expression and resolute green eyes and sighed. "Aye, I'll tell you . . ."

She recapitulated the events of a half hour earlier, sparing few details and therefore failing to spare herself; she finished retelling Tansy's account of Avery brutality by lapsing into a wrenching sob.

Bryce heard her out in complete silence, his mouth forming a grim line that told of barely leashed, simmering anger, but when he caught the sob and saw tears coursing down her cheeks, his emotions took a different turn.

With a sure, strong movement, he drew her into his arms and held her there while she continued to sob softly.

"Shh, little one, don't cry. 'Tis over, and you're safe—thank God!"

The soft sobbing continued for a brief time before she managed to get out, in a watery voice against his chest, "Oh, Bryce . . . I th-thought I'd cried enough . . . cr-cried it all ou-out in Tansy's arms when she— when she told us . . . oh Bryce, those poor people! I *hurt* for them, I *do!*"

Bryce went very still. He'd thought she was weeping from the shock of Avery's near-rape. But it seemed this woman who always had the ability to surprise him had done it again. She cried not for selfish reasons, but for the plight of *others*! Would she never cease to amaze him?

And yet his own reaction to her account of the attack on her person had been nothing short of rage. How dare that slimy whelp of Avery's touch her! Even now, he felt if Richard were anywhere within reach, he'd kill him.

He felt a strange, yet all-consuming, possessiveness overtake him as he held her, and his arms tightened fiercely about her slender frame. Richard Avery would pay for what he'd done tonight, he swore it —aye, the son along with the father!

Brittany felt him stiffen and pulled back to look up into his face. "Bryce . . . ? What is it? What—"

"Avery. . ." she heard him murmur from between clenched jaws. "The very name sickens me!"

That it was his name too, and the name of the kindly uncle who'd adopted and reared him, didn't seem to matter; all he associated with it now lay in the persons of the two men he would destroy.

Brittany saw the cold anger in his eyes, and a frisson of fear ran through her. Yes, after what she'd learned tonight, she wanted the Averys stopped, but what if Bryce had underestimated them? If nothing else, she'd learned the Averys were desperate men. Perhaps she ought to apprise Bryce of that desperation as a means of forewarning him. Would he appreciate her warnings? She decided to try.

"Bryce...I think there's something else you should know about the Averys..."

He released her but kept his eyes on her face. "Go on...."

"My cousins say they're deeply in debt...bad husbandry and gambling, largely.... 'Twas likely behind Richard's attempt to—to compromise me tonight. The twins say he's in need of an heiress, and I'm—"

"The hell, you say!" Bryce's anger was back in full force. The very thought of Avery touching her was anathema to him, and when he imagined her wed to the scum—yoked to him for life, his to do with as he chose, like that poor, miserable creature Edmund had married, he felt a blind, red rage sweep him.

Brittany saw the emotion seize him and knew instinctively she had to divert it, for his sake. "Bryce, no!" she cried, reaching out to him. She felt if she could just touch him, she had a chance of quelling that terrible anger before it consumed him. "I *loathe* the Averys! You cannot think I would fall prey to such a scheme!"

Bryce heard her words, felt her fingertips brush his chest and sensed a return to sanity. The fury left him and he found himself staring down at her face, so hauntingly lovely in the moonlight as she gazed up at him with wide, beseeching eyes.

Then the raw emotions coursing through him took a different turn. With a groan, he pulled her into his arms.

Brittany uttered a sharp cry and threw her arms about his neck, accepting with a fierce need the onslaught of his mouth as it covered hers. She welcomed the heat of him, meeting his hunger with her own, born of the long days and nights without him when, she now realized, she'd moved about like an automaton, branded by the memory of his touch and craving it again.

They clung together in an embrace that was almost savage in its intensity, mouths crisscrossing hungrily, wanting more, each of them feeling there could never be enough. Bryce's hands coursed intimately over her body, touching the remembered curves and hollows...urgent, insistent, and when Brittany's hands began to do the same, he felt he could go mad with longing.

"Brittany..." he cried hoarsely, "oh, God, I've wanted you..." His hands found the ripe curve of her breast, felt the hardened peak through the thin silk of her bodice. "Wanted this..." he murmured against her ear as his thumb brushed the eager bud.

Brittany felt her limbs turn to water, felt the liquid heat between her thighs; her knees buckled just as she felt him pull her to him with a hand beneath her buttocks, ignoring the restrictions of paniers, petticoats, and stays.

"Bryce..." she moaned, and his name was a plea on her lips. "Oh, Bryce...you make me ache for you..."

Bryce raised his head to look into her eyes and saw in them a hunger which echoed his own. His need was a swollen, insistent throbbing against her belly and his senses cried out for him to find a way to take her—now.

But at that moment the orchestra upstairs, which had been playing softly, struck up the jolting chords of a brisk reel, and a shaft of reason intruded, reminding him of where they were and how unthinkable it would be to take her here.

With a slow, deliberate intake of breath, he made

his hands go to her waist and gently set her away from him. Closing his eyes, he released his breath, which came out unsteadily as he reassumed control over his passions.

Brittany, too, had heard the musical intrusion; with shaky limbs she felt the ground beneath her feet again and the cool night air on her heated face. Slowly, as her eyes traveled to his face, she became aware that they were both still breathing hard.

Bryce opened his eyes and met her gaze, then almost wished he hadn't. Her eyes were deep, smoky blue and heavy-lidded with unfulfilled passion. The response they struck in his own barely controlled state was almost more than he could resist.

But somehow he did. Smiling ruefully down at her, he took his hand and let his knuckles graze her cheek. "Ah, Brittany..." he whispered, "if this were but another time and place..."

"Aye," she murmured, feeling a smile tremble on her lips, "or if only we were not who we are...I, a woman bent on keeping her independence, and you, a man sworn to a desperate mission..."

The green eyes darkened at this as he was reminded of what had transpired earlier. "Stay away from the Averys, Brittany! Naught but ill can come of it. They are poison, and I cannot bear to think of—"

"Becalm yourself, Bryce! I know full well what they are.... Or do I?" She gave him a searching look. "What happened between you and Edmund Avery, Bryce?"

He grew silent as he considered her question. He really had no reason not to tell her...she knew so much already.... And it was clear, based upon her silence of the past fortnight, that she could be trusted to keep his secret.... Yet, aside from his aunt and uncle in England, and Will, of course, he'd never shared the secret of his past with anyone, and he wondered why her request should give him such cause for deliberation now.

But in the next instant, he was saved from having to answer as Tansy's voice cut across the strains of the orchestra.

"Miz Britt'ny, Miz Britt'ny, is you out here? Miz 'Melia done been lookin' fo' you, Miz Britt'ny!"

With a wry smile, Bryce gestured with his head in the direction of Tansy's voice. Then he leaned down and kissed her softly on the cheek. "Stay away from the Averys," he ordered in a gruff whisper, then touched his fingers gently to her lips, gave her a regretful smile, and disappeared into the darkness.

A second later Tansy came running up to her, all hints of the slave patois gone from her speech when she realized Brittany was alone. "Are you still out here by yourself, Miz Brittany? I'd think you'd have gotten lonely by now. Are you all right?"

Brittany gave her a slow smile. "No, Tans," she said, "I've . . . not been lonely . . . and as for how I am . . ." She touched her fingers to her lips which still bore the remembered touch of Bryce's ". . . that remains to be seen . . ."

CHAPTER 15

"HERE'S ANOTHER ONE," SAID TANSY, AS she handed Brittany a letter from the pile of mail a footman had just brought in.

"Drat! That makes six, not counting this disgustingly long missive from Althea. And four arrived yesterday, and *five* the day before! I wonder if this one's another out-and-out proposal or just a request to come courting."

"Well, you could always open it and see," Tansy drawled idly, "but they all amount to the same thing. . . . Seems like anything that showed up at the ball wearin' breeches is hearin' weddin' bells, Miz Britt."

An unladylike snort of disgust was her only response as Brittany threw the unopened letter on the pile accumulating atop the writing table.

"Ain't—*aren't*—you goin' t' open it?"

Brittany heaved a sigh. "I don't need to, Tans. It bears the Burlingame seal and is written in a decidedly masculine hand." She peered dubiously at the envelope atop the pile for a second. "Why, even the crosses on his *T*s look lovesick! Oh, Tans, what am I going to do?"

Tansy nodded sagely. "You'll think of somethin'. After all, you never had any problems in Fredericksburg."

"But that's just it. I am not *in* Fredericksburg! I am at Sweetbriar, home of a dear aunt I wouldn't offend for the world!" Brittany rose from the chair in front of the writing table and began to pace.

"Why, just yesterday I began to pen my regrets to each of those panting Romeos, contents as follows: 'Dear Sir—I am dreadfully sorry, but I cannot marry you, for I have the *pox*!'"

She cast a wicked grin at Tansy, who'd begun to chuckle, but a second later her features drooped in despair. "But, of course, I didn't go through with it. Aunt Amelia would never be able to show her face hereabouts again."

"Nor you, neither," Tansy grinned.

"Little I care," she grumbled.

"Well," said Tansy, glancing at the mantel clock, "Ah'd better take the rest of the folks their mail." She headed for the door. "But, honeychile, you'll think of somethin', once you put that *superior woman's brain* t' work on it. Meantime, try t' relax. That Captain Sprague isn't comin' callin' till the afternoon."

"Don't remind me!" Brittany growled. When the door had closed behind the black woman, Brittany resumed her pacing. She was beginning to feel as caged in as she'd felt at home—*here, at Sweetbriar,* where she'd always enjoyed such wonderful freedom! It almost made her wish she hadn't come.

But a pause before the writing table where she glanced at Althea's lengthily penned lecture made her wince. No, Sweetbriar was infinitely preferable, no matter what unsettling events had transpired here.

At this, her thoughts went to what was even more unsettling than all those cursed suitors . . . Bryce.

She'd neither seen nor heard from him since the ball three nights ago. Word had come, through her cousins, that he was again spending time on the *Louise*, and since she'd also heard, through her aunt, that Edmund Avery was further detained on business—this time in Fredericksburg—she didn't worry that Bryce was off doing the thing that was beginning to trouble her sleep these days: exacting his awful revenge.

She still hoped she might talk him out of anything dangerous. . . . A vague plan of sorts had even begun to form in her mind . . . but how was she to talk to him when she didn't even see him?

She stopped her pacing at this, and chuckled softly. Now that was a fine turnabout! Only a short while ago, she'd been chafing at his overbearing presence, and now here she was, wishing she'd run into him!

Idiot, she told herself, *you ought to be glad he isn't around to—*

All at once she began to assess her situation with new eyes. *Dolt!* she accused, *you don't know an opportunity when it stares you in the face!*

Moments later, when Tansy returned to the chamber with a pot of mint tea, Brittany breezed past her, wearing a concealing cloak even though the day was warm.

"Enjoy the brew yourself, darling," she grinned, "and make some excuses for me if you need to. I . . ." she added wickedly as she swept the cloak open for a second to let the black woman glimpse her breeches, "am on my way to a rendezvous—with Saracen!"

Bryce waved his thanks to the twins and cantered away from Sweetbriar's dock on the sleek blooded chestnut they'd brought him from their stables. At first he'd declined their generous offer—the horse was one of their finest mounts—not wanting to be too far away from the ship should word arrive, from one of the footmen he'd paid to alert him, that Avery had returned.

But the day was perfect for a ride: warm, with a cooling breeze from the river, and the few clouds in the blue sky overhead were puffy, white, and innocuous. And Will, who'd remained behind to play some whist with the twins, had promised to send for him, should the critical message arrive.

And all the tedious, nerve-wracking waiting had begun to wear on him. What was Avery doing, anyway? The twins had told him they thought Edmund had a credit problem and had gone to make arrangements with some Northern bankers, but if that were so, he must be having trouble securing the credit— he'd been away so long.

Of course, if this were true, it verified what Brittany had told him of Avery's indebtedness, and— Brittany . . . her name tripped the chords of his mind like a familiar song. . . . God, but she was something . . . something wild and sweet and untamed, like the coast of the land she was named for . . . all spirit, and full of a zest for life, the way he could remember being before his terrible quest began eating him up inside, driving him, making him shut out all but this obsession that had become his sole focus.

With an abrupt shake of the head, he dismissed these familiar musings and turned the chestnut's head away from the path he'd been following, to cut across an open meadow to his left. Enough of his mission for now! The day was glorious and the purpose of this ride was to relax and enjoy it!

He gave the horse his head and rode at a full gallop until he reached a low hedge at the far end of the meadow. Preparing for the jump, he leaned forward over the withers, felt the chestnut's muscles gather, and a moment later they were on the other side.

But as he came out of the jump and slowed to a sedate canter, he lifted his gaze and suddenly pulled to a halt, not wanting to credit his eyes with what they saw.

There, racing across a second meadow, was the twins' black stallion, and on his back—astride—was the only person in the world with hair like that— *Brittany*! Coppery curls flying loose behind her like a banner, she crouched low over the black's withers, and—

My God! he choked. *She's riding bareback!*

In the next second he was spurring his horse to a full gallop, his jaws clenched in anger as he focused on the flying pair up ahead. *Damned little fool!* he swore, but silently, for he doubted she'd hear him if he called to her from such a distance—or that she'd heed him if she did!

Brittany felt the wind in her face, felt Saracen's big muscles bunch and stretch beneath her and thought this must be what heaven was like. Never had a ride felt this good. The stallion was everything she'd ever dreamed of in a mount, and the minute she got back, she was going to pester the twins into selling him to her. She thought she stood a chance of it if she promised to allow them to use him in their breeding program.

She was so intent on her ride, on the exhilarating

sound of the big hooves thundering on the ground beneath them, that she missed the first clap of thunder overhead. Crouching tightly over the massive withers, she even missed the suddenly ominous darkening of the sky.

But Bryce saw it all as he rode furiously to close the gap between them. He saw the storm clouds sweep suddenly in from the east, saw the stallion swerve and rear at the second crash of thunder, saw, with a sick feeling in his gut, the copper-haired rider twist and fall to the ground, then lie there still as death while the black bolted away in terror.

Seconds later he was reining the chestnut to an abrupt halt a few yards from Brittany's crumpled body. His breath caught on the lump of fear in his throat as he swiftly dismounted. Later he would thank himself for having the presence of mind to keep hold of his horse's reins, but for now, all his thoughts were bent on the still figure on the ground.

Kneeling beside her, he pressed an ear to her chest while around him the wind picked up with a frightening intensity and the sky grew steadily blacker. He released the breath he hadn't been aware he was holding when the *thump-thump* of an erratic heartbeat told him she was still alive.

Drawing back, he ran his eyes over her, wondering if there were any broken bones. Her face was chalk white, apparent even in the decreasing light, and suddenly his blood froze as he noticed a fine trickle of red ooze from between her lips. But in the next second his fear gave way to a measure of relief as his gently probing fingers revealed the blood was from a cut on her lower lip and not from the internal injuries he'd feared.

A deafening crash of thunder resounded, and then the first huge drops of rain began to fall as Bryce slipped the chestnut's reins to his elbow and carefully ran his hands over Brittany's body, checking for broken bones. But he was oblivious to the downpour that quickly soaked both of them, to the frightened shriek of his horse at the bolt of lightning that split the heavens overhead, to all but the helpless woman before him, as his eyes followed his hands in their painstaking assessment.

Then, just as he reached her slender calves, he thought he felt a movement. Jerking his head up, he scanned her face, and—*yes*! She was moving her lips!

"Brittany!" he cried, raising his voice over the fury of the storm, "Brittany, can you hear me?" He bent his head anxiously over her face, noticing for the first time that it was wet with rain.

He saw her eyelids flutter, then struggle to remain open; he bent to place his ear to her lips.

"H-hurts . . ." she whispered in a thready voice he could barely make out, "m-my head . . . hurts . . ."

Then, as she turned her head, he saw it—a wet, red stream being washed by the rain out of the hair at the back of her head, into the sodden ground.

A head injury, he thought, trying to keep his mind from panic, remembering that head wounds were often bloodier than others, but not necessarily more dangerous, and she was conscious . . . lucid, thank God . . .

"Brittany, can you open your eyes? . . . Look at me, sweetheart . . . talk to me . . ."

He watched the eyelids flutter again, then found her eyes on him as she squinted against the rain.

"Can you tell me where else it hurts?" he questioned. "Can you move anything?"

Her eyes closed, and he saw her wince as she

began to move her shoulders and brace her arms in an effort to sit up.

"Brittany, don't—" he warned, but she ignored this, her mouth drawn into a grim line as she pushed herself into a sitting position.

"I—I'm all of a piece, I th-think," she told him, trying to force a light tone into her voice, but failing.

"Are you *sure*?" he shouted over the howling wind. "Can you move your legs?"

She started to nod, but the movement brought forth a groan. Then, as Bryce supported her back and shoulders, she managed to raise both knees.

It was all the signal he needed. With a quick movement, he scooped his arm under her knees and drew her to his chest, then rose carefully, his powerful thighs bearing the brunt of their combined weight, until he was standing with her clutched protectively in his arms.

The chestnut sidestepped nervously as Bryce approached, but then settled at a few soothing words, allowing him to transfer Brittany to the horse's withers in sidesaddle fashion.

Brittany was fully conscious now and, despite the throbbing pain in her head, managed to brace herself against the horse's powerful neck, allowing Bryce to free his hands, loop the reins back over the horse's head, and mount.

Once astride, he encircled Brittany with his arms, gathered up the reins, and urged the horse forward, bending his own head against the driving force of the rain as he turned toward the river, knowing they were closer to the *Louise* than to the Big House.

Thunder boomed overhead while jagged streaks of lightning split the sky, and the wind set up a shrieking din as the storm built toward a fever pitch. The chestnut tried valiantly to forge ahead, but the wind was against them, and his movement was painfully slow.

Bryce realized now that, because of the wind's direction, it might take them longer to reach the ship than the Big House and, after a moment's deliberation, turned the chestnut's head in the opposite direction, toward the stables.

Brittany accurately assessed his purpose and placed a hand on his shoulder to gain his attention. "Over there, in those trees," she shouted, the action bringing a grimace of pain to her features, ". . . overseer's cabin . . . sh-shelter . . ."

Bryce nodded and moved them toward the clump of woods at the far end of the meadow, hoping he wasn't heading for the next place where the everpresent lightning would strike.

Minutes later, while thunder cracked and rumbled fiercely overhead, they reached what looked like a deserted cabin of some kind. The clearing it stood in was overgrown with weeds and vines, two of its four shutters hung half off their hinges at crazy angles, and the door banged loudly in the wind.

"I—I guess 'tis not in use these days," Brittany stammered. "'Twas lived in t-two years ago when last I s-saw it."

Bryce nodded, glad for the open shed at one side of the structure, where he was able to shelter the twins' horse. But he was reluctant to take Brittany into the cabin first and then come back to see to the chestnut, afraid to leave her alone until he knew better what her condition was.

"Brittany, can you stand here by yourself for a few minutes?" He indicated the sturdily built side wall of the stable shed.

"A-aye, I think s-so."

Lowering her carefully to the straw-strewn

ground, he helped her move to the wall and lean against it. Then, using some fairly clean straw he found in a corner, he rubbed the chestnut down after unsaddling him, while Brittany leaned weakly against the wall and watched.

Then he was carrying her out into the rain again, but moments later they were sheltered inside the ramshackle cabin, and Bryce slammed the door behind them with a booted heel.

Darkness settled over them with the shutting of the door; the cabin's two windows were caked with grime, and there was little light outside as it was, because of the storm.

"Brittany," Bryce said as his eyes adjusted to the all but nonexistent light, "I'm going to set you down again, whilst I find a way to light a fire. Do you think you can manage if you lean against the door?"

Brittany heard the quietly delivered words, felt the measured calm of his heartbeat against her side as he held her, and felt infinitely better than she had in all the frightening moments since she had regained consciousness. "A-aye," she told him, her lips beginning to tremble in the cabin's cool interior from the chill to her drenched body.

Setting her carefully on her feet, Bryce moved toward the stone fireplace he'd spied occupying one wall when they first entered. A flash of lightning illuminated things enough to verify this, as well as a surprising supply of stacked firewood beside it. Working quickly with a rusty tinderbox he located, he soon had a decent fire going.

Turning toward the door where he'd left her, he was momentarily taken aback when he saw no one there.

"Where—?"

Then his glance found the cannonball-posted rope

bed across the room—and Brittany, huddled and shivering, in the center of it.

Murmuring an unintelligible oath, he quickly crossed to the bed. *Can you not stay put for five minutes?* hovered on his lips, but when he saw the distress on her face, the trembling of her body, and the blood that ran from her head into the dusty old coverlet, he said nothing, but gathered the coverlet about her, then pulled her into his arms.

"I-I'm all r-right," she protested, "j-just—"

"Shh," he ordered, and carried her, coverlet and all, over to the fire.

Minutes passed while radically opposing emotions warred within him as he held her: anger at her for disobeying him to the extent that she would put her life in jeopardy fought alternately with relief that she didn't appear to be badly hurt, and worry that he was wrong, and she was.

Finally he noticed that she'd stopped shivering, and when he glanced down at her face as it rested against his shoulder, he saw she'd fallen asleep.

CHAPTER 16

BRITTANY DRIFTED SLOWLY TOWARD CONsciousness, the warm, lambent cocoon that cradled her so delicious, she was in no apparent hurry. In fact, her bed felt so snug and cozy this morning, she...

Her eyes opened, and the rough-hewn beams in the ceiling overhead told her she was not in her canopied bed at home, nor even in the one at Sweet—

Suddenly it all came back to her: Saracen, the storm, and, yes, Bryce, taking her to safety in the old overseer's—*Good God*!

Her eyes widened in horror as she realized she was stark naked beneath the coverlet. Then two and two easily added up to four as she determined that the only person who could have undressed her was *Bryce*.

Flicking her embarrassed gaze about the cabin's single room, she was relieved not to find him there, though his boots drying by the fire told her he hadn't gone far. *But where are my clothes?* she asked herself. She raised herself up on her elbows to get a better look around. There was a fire burning merrily on the hearth, and rain was still pelting the windows, but her thoughts remained focused on her embarrassment. It wasn't, she told herself with a blush, as if he hadn't seen her unclothed body before, but there was something disturbing about his having seen it while she was unconscious, not to mention that *he* had done the disrobing!

With a small moan, Brittany sank back onto the pillow, just as the door swung open.

"Ah," said Bryce, "you're awake."

She watched him discard the large homespun flour sack he'd used as protection against the rain and walk toward her.

"How do you feel?"

Was that concern she read in the green eyes that were more often aloof, mocking, or angry when he looked at her?

"I . . ." She paused, realizing she hadn't paid any attention to her state of health since awakening. ". . . um, there's a tenderness about the back of my head, but other than that—why, I feel quite well, thank you." Acutely aware of her nakedness beneath the coverlet, she averted her eyes as she spoke. *Where were her clothes?*

"You were lucky. You apparently struck your head on a stone when you fell, but it seems all you suffered was some minor swelling and a small cut. It could have been much worse," he added with a castigating look.

"Aye . . . lucky . . ." she murmured, raising her fingers to the tender spot beneath her hair. The movement pulled the coverlet from beneath her chin, where she'd tucked it, and she was again reminded of her state of undress. Glancing upward, she beheld his steady, green-eyed gaze and felt the heat rise to her cheeks.

"Ah, what of Saracen?" she asked, needing a distraction.

"Unharmed, by the looks of him, and probably well ensconced in his stall by now. Of course, when he returned riderless, someone probably sent out a search party to look for you, or will, as soon as the storm eases." He paused. "—Or... does anyone know 'twas you who took him?"

"I—I managed to slip out unseen... the entire staff at the stables was involved with a—a difficult breeding taking place in one of the paddocks and..." She shrugged, letting her words trail off as she realized, by the hardening of his eyes, that he was probably thinking of her stealth in the act of disobeying him.

Moreover, she felt at a distinct disadvantage with him now. While she cowered nude under the coverlet, wondering where her clothes were, he towered above her beside the bed, arms akimbo and spread-legged, his tight riding breeches hugging his muscular thighs like a second skin, his full-sleeved white shirt half open at the chest, exposing more than she needed to see of the crisp, dark chest hair she remembered well, his raven hair falling negligently over his forehead while, all the while, the green eyes bored into her.

"Brittany," he began in the chastening tone she'd been expecting, "do you have any idea of how recklessly you behaved? Not only did you endanger your own life by riding that stallion, but the stallion's as well. And bareback!" He paused and ran a hand through his hair in agitation. "My God, what were you thinking?"

A muscle twitched in the lean plane beneath his

cheekbone as he leaned forward, bracing his hands on the mattress beside her; his eyes were riveted to hers. "—or were you even *thinking* at all?"

"I—"

"And underlying those blunders is something more critical I haven't yet touched upon: *Disobedience!* I distinctly forbade you to ride that animal, and —young lady, *look* at me while I'm speaking to you!"

While trying to appear contrite as she tuned out the lecture (something she'd had years of experience doing under Althea's strict rule), Brittany had been surreptitiously scanning the room from beneath lowered lashes, looking for her clothes. But now his raised voice claimed her attention, and she raised her gaze to his.

Ohh, she thought, *he's very angry!*

"You little fool!" he continued scathingly. "You could have been *killed* out there—you very nearly *were*! Of all the stupid . . ."

Until now, Brittany had been prepared to endure a certain amount of lecturing with good grace—or at least a penitent demeanor—after all, he had rescued her, perhaps even saved her life. But hearing herself called a *fool*, and then *stupid*—why, 'twas indecent! It transcended the bounds of civilized lecturing!

Fuming, she pushed herself up into a sitting position and glared at him. "Listen to me, you insolent Tory, I may be independent, aye, and perhaps even a bit headstrong, and—"

"Headstrong . . . a *bit*?!"

"Aye, and I said *perhaps*!" she snapped. "And these things are troublesome faults in a female in our society, I realize," she continued with dripping irony, "but I am not, nor have I ever been, a *fool*! How dare you call . . ."

Her words died as she saw Bryce's gaze drop, the

look on his face alter, and in the next instant she knew why.

The coverlet had slipped to her waist, and her downward glance brought fiery heat to her cheeks.

With a small, anguished moan, she snatched the edge of the coverlet, but it was too late.

Bryce's hands shot out to still hers, even as she felt his knee lower the mattress beside her.

Jerking her head up, she met his gaze, which was intense and hot with desire.

"No," she breathed, shaking her head as if to deny the message she read there, for the last thing she wanted was to share a bed with him now. She'd been passionate with anger—not desire. If she succumbed to him now, it would be just that—succumbing . . . giving in . . . allowing him to—

But she got no further in her split second of piecing this out, for his head swooped down and his mouth slashed across hers as he joined her on the mattress, pushing her back onto the pillow, taking her hands and pinning them to the bed on either side of her head, claiming her with his superior strength.

Brittany fought him as much as she was able, twisting her head in an effort to dislodge his mouth, struggling to free her hands, but it was no good. Because just as quickly as his mouth had descended on hers, the kiss changed direction, softening now and plying her lips with an exquisite tenderness that was her undoing.

With a soft moan, Brittany ceased her struggles and parted her lips, allowing his gently probing tongue entrance.

Bryce growled deep in his throat as he released her wrists and moved to his side, gathering her even closer, his tongue playing havoc with her senses as it slipped between her lips, retreated and then, oh so sensually reentered her mouth, grazing the edges of her teeth, touching her own tongue, tasting her, savoring the sweetness he found there.

When she felt his tongue rim the edges of her parted lips and deliciously probe the corners, Brittany uttered another soft moan and threw her arms about his neck as she began to kiss him back, hesitantly exploring with small, quick darts of her tongue at first, then meeting his in a series of bolder thrusts that told him of her growing hunger.

Bryce's hands began to move, one cupping the side of her head, fingers threading through the heavy mass of coppery curls, the other sliding from her back to her midriff and then on to a bared breast, cupping it too, before fingering the sensitive peak and sending a jolt of intense pleasure straight to the dampening core between her thighs.

At this, Brittany arched against him, driving her fingers into the hair at the nape of his neck and crying out softly against the mouth that continued to move against hers.

A soft laugh broke from his throat as he raised his head to gaze into her half-closed eyes, but his fingers, and then his thumb, continued their devastation on her nipple as he murmured, "Easy, now, sweet . . . not so fast . . . this time I'm going to make it perfect for you . . . promise . . ."

And then Brittany lost all track of words as his mouth replaced his fingers on her aching nipple, which had grown ever so hard and pointed, making it easy for him to suck and nibble; at the same time, his hand moved to her other breast, the fingers circling tantalizingly before a deft thumb brushed the tip until it, too, thrust impudently upward, into a hard, swollen bud.

By now the heated sensations in the moist, secret place between her thighs had begun to radiate outward; creeping upward to her flat belly, and then her stomach, and downward to the very tips of her toes, they set her limbs trembling with pleasure and need.

"Bryce!" she cried, lacing her fingers through his dark hair as his head hovered over her throbbing breasts, "Bryce, for God's sake—"

But her only answer was his hand moving to the soft spot above her triangle of deep red curls and the mound they covered, pressing knowingly on it while his mouth continued its assault on her nipples as Bryce took his time with her, making her twist and squirm in mindless delight, working to bring her to the brink.

Somewhere amidst this heady assault to her senses he'd managed to shed his clothes, for all at once she realized that the big male body that covered hers was also nude. But the flicker of rational thinking she devoted to this was fleeting, for in the next instant all she was cognizant of was the butterfly-light strokes of his fingers as they drifted over her hips and then her thighs, urging them gently apart with the whisper touch of implicit promises, promises of a thousand delights to come . . .

But when his lips began to trace a trail of exquisitely sensual kisses across her abdomen, and lower, to where his hand again pressed so devastatingly, she had to stop him: for his hands to touch her there was one thing, *but for his mouth*—

Bryce laughed, catching her protesting hands in his on either side of her slender hips, but as he would have placed an unerring kiss just above her nether opening, she cried out to him:

"Bryce! I *beg* you—no!"

He raised his head to look at her and, smiling,

gave a slow nod. "All right, sweetheart," he murmured, reminding himself she was barely past losing her virginity. "We'll have it your way...this time..."

And his fingers took up the direction his mouth had sought, finding the pulsing bud nestled among the tight curls, making it throb, making—

All at once Brittany forgot her shyness; welcoming this intimacy, she arched her hips upward, seeking to intensify the pleasure.

"Bryce!" she cried. "Oh, I...oh, Bryce, oh, don't —*don't stop*! I—"

And then she felt it, a wildly careening whirlwind of sensation radiating from that apex, outward to every nerve and fiber of her, convulsing her in its sweet intensity, making her cry out with the pleasure of it.

But even then, Bryce didn't stop; he parted her thighs with his hand as he moved his head up to take her mouth in a drugging kiss that only heightened what she was feeling; his fingers found the creamy wetness of her core and one entered gently, slipping between the folds of quivering flesh, stroking her to completion while she arched and bucked against him in a frenzy.

And then, just when she thought it was over and she was beginning to wonder where he would find his own pleasure, he withdrew his hand, braced himself on the mattress, and drove into her, his manhood so big and hard, it made her gasp.

"Brittany," he rasped, burying his face into the hair at her neck, "Britt—oh, God, Britt, you're so lovely...so...damned...beautiful...I can't wait ...any longer..."

And with each roughly whispered cadence, he thrust, then withdrew, though ever so slowly, then thrust again, harder and harder, until she caught his rhythm and, incredible though it seemed, found her longing building anew. Like a raging fire gone out of control, she was meeting him, stroke for stroke, in the primeval movement of man and woman, moving with him, riding toward the crest, until, at last, in one shimmering, soul-wrenching wave, they found the climax they sought, wordlessly, mindless, and together.

The rain outside beat a steady tattoo on the small panes of the cabin windows, but inside all was silence, except for the occasional pop and crackle of the fire as Brittany at last realized she could no longer hear the wild thumping of her heart while Bryce held her close in the aftermath of their lovemaking. How long it had been since they'd reached those incredible heights together, she had no idea; she was only now beginning to become truly aware of where they were and what time of day it was.

Slowly she became aware of the textured whorls of his chest hair against her cheek as he held her, felt his big, muscular leg thrust possessively across hers, heard the even rhythm of his breathing as it feathered the wisps of hair at her forehead. Opening her eyes, she tilted her head backward, curious to see if Bryce was awake.

A brief movement of cheek muscle and the deeply slashed groove of a dimple gave her the answer.

"You're grinning," she accused, with only a touch of petulance.

"Aye, madam, that I am." He shifted until he was braced on an elbow and looking down at her. The look in his green eyes was knowing and sensual, and the grin widened.

For some reason, Brittany found herself blushing furiously, and she quickly lowered her eyes.

A deep chuckle rumbled from his chest and he took his free hand and caught her chin, tipping it upward to force her to look at him. "You should never be embarrassed by the things we've just shared, Brittany, though, I vow, you blush as prettily as you do . . . oh, lots of other things, darling."

Unbidden, a flush of pleasure coursed through her at the endearment, and she threw him an abashed smile. "Y-you're still grinning," she said.

"Aye," he answered again, "and you're smiling. 'Tis a pleasant means of communicating with each other, don't you think?"

Watching his lazy grin and losing herself in the deep green, heavy-lidded sensuality of his gaze, Brittany thought him the handsomest, most devastating male she'd ever encountered, and the thought made her forget her shyness of moments before; grinning now herself, she boldly ventured a reply: "'Tis a wonderful means of communicating, sir, though I can cite a better . . . lately tried."

Bryce burst out with a delighted laugh. "Saucy wench!" he chided, tapping a playful finger on her nose.

Brittany's laughter joined his, and they went on for several seconds this way, but at last the laughter died down, leaving a weighted silence as their eyes met and the seconds ticked by.

A low moan from Bryce was all Brittany heard before their mouths met hungrily, each devouring the other in the throes of full-blown passion.

There was no slow pace this time, for each was caught up in an instant and fully realized craving for the other so fierce and intense that the only answer for it was the wild, heated joining of their bodies, which followed without preamble.

They came together with a frenzied need that

Bryce, in all his years of experience with women, had never known before. All he knew, as he took her there amid the tangled coverlet which already smelled headily of them, was that somehow he could not get enough of her. She had a natural, unconscious sensuality that drove him mad with wanting her, and he reveled in it.

As for Brittany, she knew somewhere in her nether brain, that she was not behaving wisely, that, in surrendering to him so mindlessly, she was jeopardizing the hard-won independence she treasured, but, somehow, when Bryce Tremaine so much as looked at her with desire, let alone touched her, she was helpless in his presence.

A long while later—a very long while—Bryce looked down at her flushed, enchanting face framed by a tangle of wild red curls and caught her rapt gaze. "Ah, sweet hellion," he murmured, stroking a delicate cheekbone with the backs of his fingers, "perhaps I ought to stay close to the *Louise*. God knows, I don't seem to have any control when you're near me. I fear you've bewitched me, little one."

Brittany's eyes darkened and she looked away while unconsciously biting her lower lip. *Bewitched*, she thought with a bitter ache, *aye, but 'tis I who am bewitched . . . bewitched by a mysterious stranger into surrendering myself . . . giving up my very will when he is near . . .*

Giving herself a mental shake, she made herself smile and, meeting his eyes again, said, "Nay, Tory, I'm no witch—merely a humble colonial who prays she hasn't acted too unwisely."

Bryce caught her troubled look before it changed, and puzzled over it, but decided to let it pass, for he sensed himself on unsure ground concerning the closeness that seemed to be growing between them. Instead, he decided to address something else he'd heard her say.

"'Tis time, my lovely colonial, to disabuse you of a notion you've been carrying about." He spoke casually, giving no indication of haste or concern as he traced the perfect contours of her nose, and then her mouth, with the tip of his forefinger.

Brittany fell in with his unhurried manner. "Oh? And what would that be, pray tell?" she inquired as she played with the dark whorls of hair on his chest.

"Why, the notion that I am a Tory," he told her lazily, bending to kiss the tip of her nose, and then, oh so sweetly, her lips. "I was raised by the father whom I left behind in England to be a liberal-minded Whig, and I've been one all my life."

"Whaat?" Brittany raised herself up on an elbow and stared at him. "B-but then why did you allow me to—to go on thinking that—that—"

"Because it seemed to give you such pleasure to think the worst of me, because it vexed you, and I found you magnificent when you were angry, because I somehow couldn't help myself when—"

"Bryce Tremaine, do you mean to tell me that—"

A thorough kiss silenced her before he breathed, "Aye, hellion, guilty as charged."

Forestalled in her burst of temper, Brittany's thoughts took a different turn. Sitting up beside him on the bed, her legs folded gracefully to one side, she met his eyes and questioned quietly, "Bryce, who is this father you speak of who raised you thus?"

He sighed and gave her a long, level look before answering. "Aye, 'tis time you knew the full story, I think." He sat up, propping himself against one of the cannonball posts, then bent one knee and rested an arm on it as he looked at her.

"My full name is Bryce Tremaine Avery," he began.

Brittany's eyes went wide when he dropped the final name, but she held her tongue, sensing the importance of letting him speak uninterrupted.

"*Lord* Bryce Tremaine Avery, if you will," he continued, "the adopted son and heir of Lord William Avery, the marquis of Clarendon—and the natural, bastard son of his younger brother, Lord *Edmund* Avery."

Brittany gasped, but otherwise remained silent, intent now on his every word.

"I was born thirty years ago in a poor tenant's cottage in Somerset, seat of Lord William's holdings. My mother, Beth Tremaine, was the only daughter of a humble crofter who was a widower with four other children as well. She died giving me life, but not before confessing to my adopted father, the marquis, and to his sister, Lady Olivia Avery, something my mother's peasant family already knew: that she'd been raped and used by Lord William's younger brother, Edmund, and then abandoned by him when he learned she was with child.

"I was reared by William and Olivia Avery with all the privilege wealth and title can afford. I was also made aware of my humble origins at an early age, but I learned only six months ago that my sire, Lord William's morally bankrupt younger brother, was *not dead*, as I'd been led to believe all my life.

"In a moment of crisis, when we feared Lord William was dying, my aunt informed me that Edmund was still very much alive, living here in the colonies."

Bryce ran a hand distractedly through his hair and gazed off, as if into the distance.

"Apparently Edmund came here shortly after being confronted by William and Olivia with the tragedy of my mother. They openly accused him of raping and impregnating her, then leaving her to die bearing his son." Bryce heaved a sigh of disgust and looked at Brittany.

"Edmund flatly refused to be held accountable for the deed, informing them he was wedding a rich colonial widow he'd met in London and going abroad to live in luxury on her Virginia plantation. Indeed, he'd callously boasted, 'twas the lure of the widow and her fat purse that prompted him to desert my mother with nary a backward glance—'after all, she was nothing more than a peasant slut, now, wasn't she?'" he mimicked.

Brittany watched the green eyes grow brittle and hard as emeralds when he paused after these words, and her heart ached for him, for the pain he must be feeling.

At last he continued in a weary voice. "Thoroughly ashamed of their brother's immoral, conscienceless behavior, William and Olivia resolved to dismiss Edmund from their lives, giving out to all they knew that he was dead—lost at sea. But my adopted father's regret-filled ravings during a feverish delirium late last year prompted my aunt to tell me the truth. She never guessed her brother, now approaching sixty (and a widower with no natural offspring, by the way), would recover, much less that I would seek revenge on the man who shamed my mother, and whom I hold responsible for her death.

"I knew Lord William's tenderness of heart would never countenance such notions of revenge, so I devised a scheme whereby I'd track Edmund down and end his miserable life without William or Olivia knowing.

"My adopted father being a Whig—" He smiled briefly at Brittany. "—That is, having sympathetic leanings toward your aggrieved American colonies, I offered to take a ship and sail to America to survey the political situation here and send word to him of what I learned regarding the unrest that was fomenting. Lord William would have loved to come and see for himself, but he was still recovering from his illness and too weak to undertake such a journey, so he readily agreed to my going.

"The rest of the story, I guess you know. I enlisted the help of Will Thatcher, who was the only person who knew of my intent—until you and Tansy, that is—and . . ." He gave a brief, expansive gesture. ". . . Here we are."

There was silence in the room as Brittany digested what he'd told her. Foremost in her thoughts was the sense that he'd taken an enormous step in sharing these intimate details of his past with her. It increased, many times over, the growing sense of closeness between them, and she didn't take lightly the fact that he must be aware of this too.

Oh, how her heart went out to him, and to Beth Tremaine, the woman who'd been his mother. Dear God, no wonder he'd sometimes resembled a man obsessed. Edmund Avery was *slime*. Her mind tripped rapidly over the details of the last few weeks, fitting them into the rest of his tale. She'd known without a doubt that Edmund Avery deserved punishment—his very nature spoke of it, and she'd therefore long since ceased doubting the veracity of Bryce's claim for justice—but now that she knew the truth about why he sought his revenge, she found

herself deeply stirred and wholeheartedly committed
to his cause. That Edmund Avery, a wealthy member
of the nobility, had wronged one of the helpless poor
and downtrodden was reason enough for this com-
mitment; that the wronged person had been a
woman ensured it.

Reaching out her hand to touch his she said, in a
voice brimming with compassion, "Bryce . . . tell me
what I can do to help."

He looked up at her, a hint of surprise shading his
impassive features. "You . . . ?"

A frown of annoyance creased her brow. "Yes,
I—*a mere female*—how can I help you punish that
wretched excuse for a man whom you had the misfortune to have sire you? There, has my poor female
brain made itself clear?"

Bryce laughed, despite the solemnity of the subject. "You know, hellion, it never fails. The moment I
see your eyes begin to turn that dark, stormy blue,
I'm drawn in. There's no one lovelier than you when
you're irked."

"Bryce, be serious! Edmund Avery is a vicious animal and he needs to be stopped, and . . ." There was
a pause as she pressed her lips together, her eyes
narrowing in thought. ". . . And I think I have an
idea," she finished quietly.

She'd actually been toying with the germ of a notion for several days, ever since the night of the ball,
but suddenly, in the wake of Bryce's tale, it had come
to her fully formed. Before now, she'd been torn between the desire to see Avery get what she'd sensed
he had coming to him and the growing fear that
Bryce might come to harm in carrying out his plans.
Bryce's need to see justice done was very real, but
did it have to be carried out in a bloodbath? Wouldn't
cunning serve just as well?

Bryce was looking at her as if she hadn't spoken. "I'll take care of Avery," he said calmly . . . perhaps too calmly.

"Bryce, please, I have an idea. If—"

"Forget it, Brittany." He swung his legs off the bed and bent to retrieve his breeches. "You have no business involving yourself in this. Moreover, what kind of a man do you think I am, allowing a woman to endanger—"

"But 'tis just my point! I have a plan that avoids bloodshed!"

He gave her a scathing look before resuming the fastening of his breeches. "Then I'm doubly uninterested."

"Bryce, for God's sake, will you forego *this insane bloodlust*?"

"Why should I?" he bit out.

"Because there are other—more effective ways to skin a snake!"

Perhaps it was because of the apt metaphor she used (he, too, had thought there was a reptilian quality about Avery), or perhaps it was the way she knelt there on the bed, spitting and hissing at him in all her naked loveliness, totally unconscious of how provocative she appeared, that he decided to listen to her—not to act on what he heard, he reminded himself, but at least to give an ear.

"Very well, hellion," he said as he headed for the pair of boots drying by the fire, "you have my attention for about five minutes." He glanced out the window. "The rain appears to have stopped, and I want to get you home before someone discovers us here and I really do have your father to answer to."

She shot him a deprecating look, annoyed that he should be thinking of what she regarded as trivia compared to what they were discussing, but in the next second she put it past her, eager to tell him her plan.

"Bryce . . . why would you need to kill Avery when there might be a more satisfactory means of destroying him?"

He paused in the act of tucking his shirt into his breeches and looked at her. "How satisfactory?"

Warming to her subject, Brittany slid off the bed, snatching the coverlet and wrapping it around her as she hit the floor. "Perhaps there's a sweeter means of wreaking revenge on Avery." She walked toward Bryce. "With the way the man craves wealth, would it not be fitting to achieve his . . . total financial destruction?"

Intrigued, Bryce nodded for her to continue, though his manner was reserved; he'd lived with the idea of Avery's death for too long to discard it readily.

Propping her hip against a battered pine table, Brittany launched into her plan.

"As you know, Richard Avery hopes to wed me—or should I say, to wed my fortune? Suppose I were to encourage Richard's courtship . . . 'twould lull both Avery men into a false sense of financial security, would it not?"

Bryce frowned, but waited for her to continue.

"In the meantime, you and whomever you wished to enlist to help could work to lure Edmund into a business venture that would ultimately overextend him. I'm sure we could purchase a vast load of some commodity in Fredericksburg and then offer it to Edmund at such a low price, he'd be a fool not to commit, and—"

"We?" Bryce questioned archly.

"Oh . . . well, I only meant that you must be willing to gamble a large sum here, to come by the commodity in sufficient size to attract your quarry, and if funds are a problem for you on this side of the Atlantic, or whatever, I think I can manage to free some of my funds. Father's been more than accommodating in allowing me access to—"

"Then what?" came the terse interruption.

She paused, on the verge of a pout at his manner. "Avery's payment date must be arranged so that he loses everything if he defaults by a certain time. The time will be made to appear safe to him, say, a date that occurs a week after he thinks Richard and I will be wed.

"But, of course," she smiled, "there will be no wedding. I shall find a way to break with Richard at the last minute, and both Averys will be *ruined*!"

Bryce was silent as he considered the plan. He had to admit he found it attractive. In short, he found it nothing less than brilliant and daring.

But there was the rub; it was *too* daring. He could not allow Brittany to risk so much. What if something went awry? Just the thought of Richard, that unctuous lizard, laying a proprietary hand on the woman before him made his blood freeze.

"I'm sorry, Brittany, but I cannot allow you to put yourself in such danger."

"*Danger?*"

"Aye, danger! What if Edmund or Richard—or both—were to become so enraged at your refusal to wed that they harmed you?"

"Bah!" she scoffed. "'Tis nonsense. They wouldn't *dare*!"

He stepped closer to her and held her gaze. "Wouldn't they? Those two are treacherous at best. If cornered, they could well become the animals they resemble. No, Brittany, I cannot allow you to involve yourself in so dangerous a scheme, though I thank you for the offer. 'Twas most courageous."

"But, Bryce—"

"I say nay, and there's an end to it!" He stalked to the door, tossing his words over his shoulder at her, "I'm going to see to the horse. When I return, I hope to see you dressed." He opened the door, admitting a flood of rain-washed, late afternoon sunlight.

He added before closing the door after him, "You'll find your clothes neatly folded... in the warming oven... oh, and Brittany?"

"Aye?"

"If I ever catch you wearing breeches again, I'll turn you over my knee and spank that shapely bottom so thoroughly, you'll find it difficult to sit for a week!"

CHAPTER 17

WILL THATCHER IGNORED THE RAIN THAT pelted his chest and shoulders, gathered along the brim of his tricorn to funnel between the breaks, and otherwise inundated his massive form, as he strode purposefully toward the Big House. Let the twins figure out why that black devil stallion of theirs returned to the stables minus a rider or a saddle, he thought. His problem had to do with locating Bryce, now that word had come that Avery was back.

For more than two hours he'd searched the fields and meadows near where the *Louise* was docked, with no sign of Bryce; he'd then gone to Sweetbriar's stables, on the off chance that his friend had ridden there to shelter the borrowed chestnut when the storm broke, but no chestnut and no Bryce—only that damned riderless black.

The stable help had been in an uproar when he got there, wondering who could have taken the stallion out unseen, but Will had handed the reins of his own borrowed mount to a stable lad, turned on his heel, and headed straight for the Big House. *He*

knew who'd been secretly trying out the black devil,
late at night, when she thought no one was about;
he'd traipsed to the stables late one night in search of
a pipe he'd left behind and spied Brittany Chambers
atop the stallion, putting him through his paces—
bareback—in the moonlight. At the time he'd just
grinned, keeping to the shadows as he watched her
astride the big horse, bold as a blue jay as she'd
walked, trotted, and cantered him about the paddock. He'd known, of course, of Bryce's orders regarding the hellion and that stallion, known that she
was defying him with her secret midnight antics, but
he decided to keep her secret to himself, admiring
her spunk, as well as the obvious skill she displayed
in the saddle.

But now, he thought, he might well have to reveal
her little secret. Now, if Mistress Chambers wasn't in
the Big House it could well mean she was in trouble,
for a riderless mount returning home usually signi-
fied that the rider had been thrown, or in some other
nasty way had lost his seat . . . or *her* seat, he corrected. And if some such disaster had happened,
he'd have to sound the alarm. She could well be
lying out there in the rain somewhere, injured or—

Will hastened his pace, a worried frown creasing
his brow.

A few moments later he was listening to the butler
tell him that Mistress Chambers was resting in her
chamber upstairs and that her abigail had left "ex-
plicit instructions" that she was "not to be disturbed."

Unsure of why this news didn't bring the relief
he'd expected, Will thanked Merriweather and
turned back toward the stables. The wench might be
safe, but he still had to find Bryce. At least the chest-

nut hadn't returned riderless, for that would mean that Bryce—

Suddenly Will paused, unsure of what sixth sense moved him, and glanced up at the corner, past the tall magnolia tree in front of the window he knew belonged to the redhead's bedchamber. There, peering down at him with an unmistakably worried face, was the little black woman, Tansy. Something was amiss.

Not knowing why, but certain of the feeling in his gut, Will turned back toward the house, but this time instead of heading for the main entrance, he made for one of the back entrances reserved for the help.

It took him several more minutes than he'd have liked, but he eventually found his way to the second floor via a servants' stairwell, and then along the hallway until he reached the door he sought. Pausing for only a second, he raised his fist and knocked.

"Aye?" Tansy's voice.

"Ah, 'tis Will Thatcher, miss. I'd be 'avin' a word wi' yer mistress."

A pause, and then, "She sleepin'. Come back later ...*sir*." Did he imagine it, or did her voice seem strained?

"I be awful sorry, Miss Tansy, but I fear ye'll 'ave t' be wakin' 'er. Cap'n Tremaine wants t' speak wi'—"

The door opened, and an annoyed black face peered up at him. "Ah said, de lady ain't awake! Now, why cain't you understan' dat? Go 'way, an' come back later when Miz Britt'ny's had her rest!"

She'd have shut the door in his face, but Will managed to insert a booted foot before she got the chance. "Sorry, but this be important and cannot wait. Now, do ye awaken yer mistress, or do I?"

Black eyes glared at him for a moment, and then the petite form wedged its way through the narrow opening, after which Tansy shut the door behind her and stood, nose to chest with him in the hallway.

"*You* ain't wakin' *nobody*," she announced angrily, underscoring each syllable with a small black forefinger that poked menacingly at his midsection. "An' who let you up here, anyway? Look at dat mess you's drippin' on Miz 'Melia's fine rug! Git yo' wet carcass outa here, man, 'fo' ah fetches ol' Merriwig!"

Will would have smiled at her colorful speech, had not the situation been so urgent. Removing his sodden tricorn so as to appear more respectable, he decided to try again.

"Now, see here, girl, I—"

"Don' yo' '*girl*' me, baldy! A propah gen'lemun don't come sashayin' up t' a lady's bedchambah dis way! *Git!*" She glared up at him, her flashing black eyes daring him to refuse, and for a moment Will was hard put to remember which was the hellion, mistress or fire-spitting maid.

Undaunted, he decided to take a different approach. "Ye seem t' be awful pressed t' keep me away from 'ere, miss. Ye wouldn't be '*idin*' somethin', would ye?"

The startled look in the black eyes was fleeting, but it was enough to tell him what he wanted to know. "See 'ere, woman, I ken all about—"

"Hmph! Least 'tain't '*girl*' no mo'!"

Will had had about all he was going to take. The redhead was probably out there in the storm somewhere, needing help, while this one continued with the charade they'd concocted. It was time to deal in truths.

"As I wuz sayin'," he said archly, bending down to glare at her, eyeball-to-eyeball, "I be aware o' yer mistress's secret rides on that 'orse, and ye kin stop yer pretendin' wi' me! Trouble is, the 'orse jest come back t' the stables, minus 'is rider, and if she—"

Just then, there came a loud clatter from inside the bedchamber. Will and Tansy gaped at each other for a split second, then, almost as one person, turned on the door and pushed it open.

There, standing across the room in front of an open window, stood Brittany, wearing breeches, muddy boots, and an old wet flour sack about her shoulders like a cape.

"Oh-oh," muttered Tansy.

"Now 'oo's messin' up the rug?" Will couldn't help jeering as he covertly breathed a sigh of relief that the hellion was safe.

"Come on in, you two," Brittany muttered sheepishly, as she plucked a magnolia leaf out of her damp hair. "I fear I don't climb trees as stealthily as I used to."

"Lord Almighty!" breathed Tansy. "What happened? Are you all right? Will, here, said that horse just showed up at the stables alone, and I thought—"

She stopped and looked up at Will, who was staring at her peculiarly. *Good Lord! In her excitement, she'd dropped her patois!*

"Ye've the tongue of a bloomin' duchess!" Will exclaimed, wonder lighting his eyes as they roamed Tansy's form and came to rest on her abashed face.

"Now, Mister Thatcher," said Brittany as she bent to remove a sodden boot, "you must swear never to reveal that to anyone." She gave a tug and uttered a soft grunt as the boot came off, then went to work on the other. "You see, I've been, um, tutoring Tansy in a few things, and 'twould never do to let people around here learn of it. They'd—" She broke off with a grunt as she succeeded in removing the second boot.

"—do somethin' 'orrible to 'er if they 'eard," Will finished for her, his voice serious. "Aye, I'll be keepin' yer secret. Wild 'orses couldn't drag it out o' me."

Tansy's face softened, and she offered a grateful smile. "My thanks, Mister Thatcher."

"Will," he said. ". . . Call me Will."

"Aye . . . Will, then," Tansy murmured. She took a step forward, then paused, eyeing him curiously. "What do you know of laws against educating my people, Will?"

Will looked mildly uncomfortable for a moment as he appeared to ponder her question. "Well, fer one thing, the laws be o' two sorts: the written and the *un*written, and, if ye wuz t' ask me, 'tis the unwritten ones wot be the worst."

"Mm," nodded Tansy, her eyes never leaving his as she absently handed Brittany a towel to dry her hair. "But how do you know so much about this?"

Again, a disquieted look passed across the big man's face, but he answered her without pausing. "In the islands where I 'ail from, there be every bit as much a class system as 'ere—maybe more. No one grows up there wi'out learnin' the ins and outs."

Tansy nodded, then scanned his face. She still wasn't satisfied with his answer. There'd been a look in his eyes when he'd spoken of keeping her secret a few moments ago, a certain tone in his voice . . . "Aye, but—"

"Ah, I think it be time I wuz leavin', ladies," Will cut in. "I've solved the riddle o' the riderless black and, don't fear, I'll figger out somethin' t' tell 'em about it, down at the stables, but I still 'aven't found Cap'n Tremaine, so I'd best be—"

"Oh," said Brittany, "you needn't worry about

Captain Tremaine, Will. I...ah, happened to run into him...on my way back from...ah, where Saracen and I parted company...he was taking the chestnut mount he was riding over to the *Louise* for some reason. I believe you'll find him back at the ship."

Will hid a smile as he saw her color with the obvious tale she'd concocted, but he made no comment. *So the two of them weathered out the storm together somewhere, did they? Well, so much the better. With Avery back, Bryce is going to be hot to move, and mayhap the hellion could yet prove to be the right kind of distraction!*

"I thank ye, Mistress," was all he said as he executed a bow before each of them. Then he made for the door and left.

Will was right in predicting Bryce's eagerness to act when he learned of Avery's return, but once again, it seemed the fates had other things in mind for the Englishman. The following day, word came to the Big House that a fever had broken out aboard the *Louise*; young Harry, the cabin boy, and Will Thatcher were stricken. Not knowing if it would spread any farther, but fearing the worst, Bryce ordered all hands off the ship, arranging with the twins to quarter the crew in one of their barns. Then, despite the Wakefields' pleas to let them send for a physician, he vowed to nurse Harry and Will himself. He sent a note to the Big House, saying, "no damned leech is going to bleed them dry—and *dead*—as long as I'm captain of this ship!" And so, promising only to leave notes on their progress for a footman to pick up at the dock, Bryce settled down to care for his patients.

* * *

Bryce stood beside the bed in Timothy Chambers's cabin and watched the sweat pour off Will's brow. Closing his eyes, he murmured a prayer of thanks that the fever had finally broken.

It had been a hellish couple of days and nights, he reminded himself, running a hand over his face and the stubble of beard that gave testament to the fact that he'd neither shaved nor slept during the bedside vigil he'd kept for the past forty-eight hours.

A groan from Will caught his attention and he bent anxiously over the bed. "Will? . . . Will, can you hear me?"

The first mate mumbled something incoherent, then went silent, but his even breathing told Bryce there was nothing to be alarmed about. Reaching for one of the clean pieces of toweling he'd stacked on the bedside stand, Bryce dipped this into the pan of cold water next to it, wrung it out, and blotted Will's brow.

"Rest quietly, my friend," he told the sleeping giant, "you're on the mend—*thank God*."

A crash from another part of the ship drew his attention.

"Harry!" Moving quickly, despite his weariness, Bryce ran for the captain's cabin.

He'd put the boy there himself, after discovering him in the passageway outside the galley, collapsed and delirious with fever. That had been a few hours after Will had taken sick. Harry had been the first to have his fever break, and he'd been well on the way to recovery this morning. What was amiss now?

Tearing ajar the door to his cabin, Bryce beheld a shaken and trembling Harry clinging weakly to the edge of the big bed as he stared at the shards of a broken water pitcher on the floor.

The boy raised his head and leveled huge, worried

eyes at Bryce. "I—I didn't mean t' break it Cap'n," he began.

"Harry, lad, 'tis nothing worth troubling yourself over." Bryce strode toward him and gently pushed him back on the pillows. "What is important is that you rest until you're well again."

"But—but, the pitcher..."

"'Twas an old one and sorely in need of replacing." Bryce smiled. "On the other hand, a top-rate cabin lad like you is irreplaceable, so you set your mind on recovery, and damn the blasted pitcher, d'ye hear?"

Harry offered him a weak smile. "A-aye, sir."

"Good lad!" He rumpled the boy's curls affectionately, then moved across the cabin to the shaving stand where a second pitcher rested. Pouring some water from it into a pewter mug, he returned to the bed and raised it carefully to Harry's lips. "Here, lad, drink as much as you can. You'll be needing it to replace what the fever baked out of you."

Harry accepted the drink gratefully. When he was done, he raised tired eyes to his captain and smiled, then fell almost immediately into a deep, restful sleep.

Bryce cleaned up the remains of the broken pitcher, then pulled up a chair to watch the boy, for while he was bone-weary himself, he didn't want to close his eyes until he was sure Harry and Will were totally out of danger; in the back of his mind lay the memory of another time a fever had raged—and he'd been helpless to do anything about it...

He was ten years old, and the look on Aunt Olivia's face as she came out of his grandfather's cottage made him want to run somewhere and hide—so no one could ever reach him to tell him the terrible news he'd already heard too many times that week.

First, there'd been the twins... those laughing young uncles of his who, along with Ben, the eldest, had taught him to fish and to swim and how to select the right kind of flat pebble to send skipping across the surface of the pond, who'd let him have his own puppy from the litter whelped by their hound...

Dead, they were, on Sunday night, despite Aunt Olivia's ministrations... dead, both of them—Jamie first, with Johnny following an hour later... dead ... of the smallpox.

And then the two middle lads had followed... young Donald with the voice of an angel, so promising in his talent that William had convinced the vicar to allow him to sing in the boys' choir, even though he was a mere crofter's son... and then Tom, the one they said looked so much like Beth—and like himself... Tom, who'd been so quick of mind, William had sent him to sit in on Bryce's lessons with his tutors... dead now, both of them, their young bodies lying under freshly dug mounds beside the twins'... and Beth's.

But even then the hand of death had not been satisfied... reaching out yet again, only the day before it had claimed the life of Ben, the eldest of his mother's brothers... Ben, who'd loved horses so much, William had given him a job at his stables where he'd risen from stable lad to head groom... dear, wonderful Ben, who'd put Bryce on his first pony and patiently taught him to ride, who'd taken the time to tell him stories of his mother when she was alive... gone with the others, victims of the fever, that brought the rash, that brought... death.

And now Aunt Olivia was wrapping her arms about him and weeping, weeping for the humble grandfather he'd loved, who'd just closed his eyes for the last time. 'Twas so strange, he remembered thinking, that the old man should have been the last, preceded by his five sons, all vigorous and in the bloom of youth... 'twas as if he made himself last until all hope for them was gone, and only then allowed himself to surrender his aging body to the rapacious disease...

"Bryce! Bryce, where be ye, lad?"

Pushing himself out of the chair, Bryce swept the lingering ghosts from his mind and answered Will's call. "Hold on, man, I'm coming!"

He entered Timothy's cabin to find Will half out of bed and swearing to himself.

"Will, for God's sake, get back in that bed!"

The big man paused in a sitting position at the edge of the bed and looked at him. His swarthy skin was ashen and sweat ran down the sides of his face from his temples. He attempted a grin, but succeeded in forming only a half smile.

"Ye ken, lad," he murmured weakly, "that might not be such a bad idea. Trouble be, I...cannot... quite...manage it..."

Rushing across the cabin to catch him as he slumped forward, Bryce managed to push him back onto the mattress before he fell.

"Damnit, man," he muttered, "don't you know how sick you've been?" He straightened Will's legs and pulled the blanket back over him. "I don't want to see you move from here until..."

But Will was fast asleep.

Feeling Will's brow, Bryce ascertained that his temperature was normal. He bent his head to Will's chest and determined his breathing was steady. Heaving a sigh of relief, he wrung out another cloth and carefully wiped away the accumulated perspiration, noting briefly that along with a fair length of beard, the hair on Will's head had begun to grow in.

Satisfied at last that his friend was resting comfortably, he straightened and looked about the cabin, wondering when it had grown so hot in there.

He reached up to massage the cramped muscles at the back of his neck, trying to focus on what he'd do next. But why did his arms feel so heavy?

Turning, he made for the door, only to find the distance between him and it suddenly huge, and in the next instant he found himself staggering on legs that threatened to buckle, while at the same time his head began to pound.

His whole body felt as if it were on fire as he reached the door. Then, as he struggled to open it, he was seized with chills that caused an uncontrollable quaking.

Damn, he swore silently, at last recognizing the signs. The act of opening the door left him weak and trembling, but he forced himself to put one foot in front of the other as he staggered toward the companionway.

Must reach the dock, he told himself... *must leave ... message ... no good ... no good to Will and Harry ... this way ... must get ... help ...*

Tansy thanked the footman for delivering the note, and turned to go upstairs and find Brittany's aunt, since she could now read enough to see it was addressed "MRS. WAKEFIELD." Of course, it helped that the sender had used block letters, even if they were rather poorly drawn... shaky looking, really...

A grin crossed her face as she stared at the simply folded piece of parchment. It being unsealed, no one would be the wiser if she were to sneak a peek for the purpose of testing her reading skills...

Glancing about to be sure no one was watching, she paused at the base of the servants' stairs, unfolded the note and read:

**WILL, HARRY MENDING, BUT I AM
ILL—PLEASE SEND HELP—*NO LEECH!*
B. TREMAINE**

"Lord have mercy!" Tansy exclaimed. Hastily refolding the parchment, she flew up the stairs in search of her hostess.

Several minutes later, when a search of numerous upstairs chambers still hadn't produced Mistress Wakefield, and she was wondering where to look next, she saw Agatha Murdock emerge from her chamber at the end of the hall.

Tansy ran up to her, bobbed what she hoped would be an appropriate curtsy for the straightlaced housekeeper, and asked her if she knew Mistress Wakefield's whereabouts.

"She is out for the afternoon, having been invited for tea at Edgehill Manor," came the prim reply.

"Oh," said Tansy, clutching the note tightly against her skirts as she pondered what to do next. With Brittany's aunt absent from the household, she supposed Merriweather was in charge, and after him, this old crone, but Merriweather was nowhere about, and she had serious misgivings about entrusting the captain's message to this one. If only Miz Brittany weren't busy down in the drawing room, attempting to disillusion one of those pesky suitors . . .

"What is that you have in your hand, miss?" Agatha suddenly queried.

Drat! The old crone had eyes like an eagle! Oh, well, too late for anything else now. "Um, dis note done come fo' Miz Wakefield, ma'am." Tansy handed it to Agatha.

"Very well," said the housekeeper, taking the note and sliding it into her apron pocket. "I shall see that she receives it as soon as she returns."

Oh, no, thought Tansy, *now how do I let her know it's urgent without letting on that I read it?*

"Well," said Agatha, peering imperiously down her long, thin nose at the black woman, "what are you standing about for? I'm certain you have some chores that need tending to, miss. As Mistress Brittany's abigail—"

"Did I hear my name mentioned?" asked a feminine voice at the opposite end of the hallway.

"Miz Britt'ny!" *Praise the Lord!* Tansy added to herself as Brittany made her way toward them.

"Oh, Mistress Murdock," said Brittany, "you're just the person I was looking for. It seems I'm ever so clumsy today. I fear I just spilled a pot of chocolate all over poor Mister Melrose's lap. Merriweather's with him now, but he asks that you come at once—says you know just the thing for removing chocolate stains from a gentleman's, ah..." Brittany paused, managing to hide the mischievous sparkle in her eyes from Agatha, if not from Tansy. "Ah, at any rate, Merriweather asked that I remove myself from the room, given the nature of the accident, you see..." She finished by giving the housekeeper a helpless shrug.

"Oh, dear!" exclaimed Agatha as she hurried toward the stairs. "Oh, poor Melrose...oh, how *could* you have been so clumsy..."

When she had gone, Tansy eyed her friend archly. "A pot of chocolate, hmm? Miz Britt, you ain't been clumsy a day in your life!"

"*Haven't*," Brittany corrected with a giggle. "*Haven't*, not *ain't*—"

"Never you mind my grammar right now, Miz Britt! Did you, or did you not, deliberately—"

"I did," Brittany grinned, then burst into a peal of laughter. "Oh, Tansy, you should have *seen* him! I had all I could do not to burst out laughing then and there. Oh, the expression on his face, as he tore his eyes away from my bosom—where they'd been fastened from the moment he came—and gaped down at the mess I made on his lap! Oh, I wish you'd been there! He looked so *funny!*"

Picturing the scene, Tansy began to laugh too, but a moment later she sobered, recalling the note from Bryce. Quickly, she explained what it had said as well as why Agatha had it.

"Good God," said Brittany, "we've got to do something!"

"*We?*" Tansy asked suspiciously.

"Aye," came the reply as Brittany grabbed Tansy's arm and urged her toward Amelia's chamber. "I believe I recall where Aunt Amelia keeps her medicinals. Come on, hurry!"

"But why us?" the black woman protested. "Why can't we fetch old Merriwig or that old biddie who just left?"

"What, and have them send for a leech? You read what the captain wrote!"

"We could tell your cousins!" Tansy had been a party to more than a few of Brittany's escapades by now, and she wanted no part of sneaking off to participate in something she felt should be left in more capable hands.

"They're busy with a foaling, last I heard, and, besides, they'd likely know less about nursing a fever than we do. I often helped my stepmother tend servants who were down with—ahh, here we are!"

Brittany grabbed the basket of bandages, various herbs, and medicinals that Amelia, like any other mistress of a large plantation, kept on hand for ministering to those in her charge.

"Here," she said, thrusting it at a reluctant Tansy, after which she picked up a stack of neatly folded towels from the linen press where she'd located the basket. "Now, let's hurry! There's no telling how sick he is."

A half hour later, the two women thanked the groom they'd bribed into taking them to the *Louise*, promising to be ready when he returned for them in a couple of hours. They watched him jingle the coins he added to his pocket and drive off; then they hastened aboard.

Reaching the captain's cabin first, they found Harry sleeping peacefully; cool to the touch, he appeared well on the way toward recovery.

Their next stop was at the cabin they'd shared on the way downriver, where Will lay, dwarfing the bed Tansy had once slept in. The big man awakened with a snort at the sound of the door rattling the contents of the basket Tansy carried as she brushed past it.

"Eh?" Will squinted sleepily at them in the cabin's dim light.

"We've come to see how you're faring, Mister Thatcher," Brittany explained. *But where was Bryce?*

"Oh, ah, I be on the mend, ladies," Will yawned, "on the mend."

"I'm glad to hear it, sir." Brittany placed her hand on his brow, noting with relief that it, too, was cool, then questioned in as casual a voice as she could summon, "Do you happen to know where Captain Tremaine is?"

Will's gaze had shifted to take in the petite figure of the black woman beside the door. She looked like a vision, standing there in what had to be a new frock, fashioned as it was out of a cheerful peach-colored fabric, instead of the drab servants' gray he'd always seen on her before. In fact, he'd never seen her looking lovelier . . . almost angelic, and he wondered for a moment if he hadn't died of the cursed fever and gone to heaven—not that it was a destination he'd ever expected to reach.

"Mister Thatcher! I *asked* if you know where the captain is!" Brittany tried not to appear unduly alarmed, given the fact that Will was still far from recovered and therefore in need of rest and freedom from worry, but the fact was, she was anxious about Bryce and wished to tend him as soon as possible.

"The cap'n . . . ?" Will asked dazedly. "No . . . can't say I do . . ."

Noticing the way he stared at Tansy as he spoke, Brittany made a brief gesture that indicated to the black woman that she should see to Will while Brittany left to find Bryce.

A few moments later she found him. Entering the first mate's cabin she heard a moan, and as her eyes adjusted to the dim light, she spied Bryce tossing fitfully on the narrow bunk there.

She called his name as she advanced toward the bunk, but there was no reply. Touching his arm, she almost recoiled from the heat it gave off; he was burning with fever!

Back in the cabin Will occupied, Tansy wrung out a towel she'd dipped in a basin of water and stepped toward the bed.

Will eyed her warily. "Wot—?"

"'Tis only a wet towel, man, so relax." Tansy began wiping his brow with sure, gentle strokes.

"Mmm," Will murmured, "a man could get used t' bein' nursed back t' 'ealth, 'e could!"

"Hmph! It appears to me you're well on the road to recovery already, Mister Thatcher."

"Would ye just listen t' the King's English she's spoutin'!" he marveled. "Ye've learnt yer lessons well, lass."

Tansy paused in the act of applying the cloth to the big man's neck and looked him in the eye. "And why should that be any kind of surprise? Women have brains in their heads, too, you know!"

"Now, woman, don't be gettin' yer dander up wi' me! I've always thought women t' be as smart as men—maybe smarter . . . and black women, maybe smarter even yet," he added cryptically.

Tansy ceased her ministrations and gave him an assessing look. "You seem to know a good deal about black women, Mister Thatcher."

Will looked uncomfortable for a long moment, then suddenly gave her a wide grin. "'Ere, now, ain't I said fer ye t' call me Will?"

But Tansy ignored this as her mind sorted out some questions and clues it had stored regarding the swarthy giant. She ran her eyes carefully over him, from shoulder to crown, as she pondered the clues, letting her gaze come to rest finally on the new growth of hair covering the head that used to be shaved clean. *His hair*—it wasn't straight or even softly waved, as the captain's was. It was a soft, downy black and tightly curled—kinky, in fact—*like her own!*

"Will Thatcher," she accused softly, "you're *black*, aren't you?"

Will's dark eyes shuttered for a moment, but then he raised them to meet hers. "'Alf black," he said quietly. "Me mum wuz a black woman . . . she be the reason, I guess, I ken so much o'—o' black women."

Tansy nodded slowly. "Ah knew there was something . . . Ah just wasn't sure what." She picked up the cloth again and began to apply it to his massive shoulders, which were all that showed above the blanket of the giant torso.

"Ye're a clever lass, Tansy, me sweet. I could see that from the minute I laid eyes on ye." He raised an eyebrow when she pushed the blanket down to reach his chest with the wet cloth, but continued speaking. "But ye've blossomed in the time ye've been a free woman . . . grown int' yer own, ye might say."

She nodded. "Freedom does dat—*that*—for a person, ah guess."

Will smiled at her self-corrected diction, but the smile turned to a minor look of horror when she began to lower the blanket further.

"'Ere, now, woman, that'll do!" he gasped. "Ain't ye bin taught some *modesty*?"

She shot him a reproving look, then sighed with a note of exasperation. "Ah nursed a few men in mah time, Coffee Man. Modesty's got nothing to do with it!" But she set aside the wet cloth.

"Coffee Man?"

"Uh, huh," she grinned. "You're the color of a cup of rich coffee with a good dollop of cream. Now, turn over and I'll do your back."

"Mmph," Will groused, but he complied.

Picking up the wet cloth again, Tansy queried, "Your mama—where is she now?"

"Dead," came the reply. "She died when I wuz seven."

"That's curious. *Mah* mama died when *Ah* was

seven . . . but mah mama was a slave, Coffee Man, and ah'd wager yours wasn't, was she?"

"Ye'd win that wager, lass, but 'ow—"

"Oh, something about the way you carry yourself. . . . Ah figure 'twern't no slave woman taught you t' walk tall like a man."

Will turned on his side to look at her with amazement. "Tansy, lass," he said softly, a slow grin spreading across his face and lighting his features, "'tis a sorry shame I didn't meet ye when I wuz ten years younger."

Tansy seemed to be studying the wet cloth she held in her hand for a moment, then raised solemn dark eyes to meet his. "Ten years don't mean nothin'," she said, her low voice falling consciously back into a rich patois, "de point be, whut you gonna do 'bout *now*?"

CHAPTER 18

BRITTANY DIPPED THE TOWEL IN THE basin, wrung it out for what felt like the hundredth time in the past hour and applied it to Bryce's brow. It had grown quite warm in the cabin, whose close confines failed to catch the cooling river breezes, and she could feel the perspiration gather on her own brow as she worked. Silently damning the conventions that stuffed females into corsets and stifled them under layers of petticoats, she swiped at the dampened curls that stuck to her forehead with a forearm and went on to blot Bryce's temples and neck.

While she worked, Bryce tossed and turned restlessly on the narrow bunk, much as he had ever since she arrived. Occasionally he would mutter something incoherent, but most of the time only his erratic breathing and the intermittent sounds of water sloshing in the basin broke the silence.

She wished she knew how long it had been since he'd taken ill, figuring it might help her gauge the hour when she could expect the fever to break; she made herself believe that the fever would break, of course, taking heart from the fact that such had been the case with Harry and Will. She didn't let herself think that it might not.

More time passed, and she was just considering what to do about the groom who would be returning for her and Tansy when, suddenly, she saw Bryce twist and stiffen. "Grandfather!" he cried.

Grandfather? It was the first intelligible sound he'd uttered. Her mind switched to the conversation they'd had in the overseer's cabin, when he'd mentioned . . . no, that wasn't his grandfather; it was his uncle—the one who adopted—

"Grandfather," Bryce murmured, this time less urgently. "Tell me about her, Grandfather. . . . Tell me . . . oh, aye . . . green eyes just like mine, aye, and—Why did she have to die, Grandfather, *why?* . . . What's that you say? *Alive?* The stinking vermin *lives?* The colonies . . . aye, the colonies—must go . . . find him . . . kill the bloody . . . aye, Will, magnificent . . . a   woman   to   make   a   man   dream of—*No!*—mustn't let—mustn't allow her to . . . must remember my purpose . . . Avery . . . forget her . . . think of Avery . . . *must get Avery . . .*"

The words drifted away into an unintelligible murmur as Bryce was seized by a particularly fierce bout of restiveness, arms thrashing, legs kicking bedclothes onto the floor.

Alarmed by these increasingly fierce movements, and afraid he might fall off the bunk and injure himself, Brittany tried to calm him with soothing words, but it was clear he couldn't hear her. When he arched his back with a particularly violent motion, she threw herself across his chest in an attempt to subdue him, then held on fiercely to the mattress as he heaved and bucked, nearly throwing her to the floor.

"Bryce! Bryce, for God's sake—you've got to be still!"

She had no idea whether he heard her, or if it was mere coincidence, but all at once he calmed, abruptly falling back onto the mattress and lying quiet. Pushing herself into a standing position, she realized she was breathing hard, and she felt a trickle of perspiration run down her spine beneath her clothing.

Heaving a sigh, she was about to reach for the basin when she heard noises up on deck. A glance at her patient told her he was still unconscious and resting quietly, although she knew from the absence of any heavy perspiration on him, that the fever still hadn't broken.

There it was again. Voices. She decided to chance leaving Bryce alone for a moment and investigate, but first she took the thin blanket that partially covered him and tucked it tightly about him and under the mattress on both sides to form a confining wrap she hoped would keep him in the bunk, should he start to thrash again.

Moments later, she stepped out onto the *Louise*'s main deck, just in time to see Agatha Murdock cross the gangplank, with a somber-suited gentleman behind her.

"Mistress Murdock! What— what are you doing here?"

Agatha ran a disapproving eye over her, taking in the sweat-stained day gown and her disheveled hair, which had come loose from its pins when she tried to wrestle Bryce to the bed. "I might well ask the same of you, Mistress Brittany," she replied stiffly.

"I . . . Tansy and I came to see what we could do for Mister Thatcher and the captain."

"What, just the pair of you without a suitable escort? 'Tis indecent, mistress, and well you know it!"

Brittany dismissed the accusation with an impatient gesture and turned to the dark-suited stranger. "And who are you, sir?"

"I am Doctor Arbuthnot," the man replied. "I was tending Mistress Avery at Edgehill when Mistress Wakefield received word of her guest's illness. Mistress Murdock has brought me to tend the man. Where is he, please?"

Brittany threw a condemning glance at the black bag he carried, then met Agatha's eyes with a look of accusation. "You read the message the captain sent, I presume?"

Agatha's gaze wavered. "Well, I...yes...yes I did."

"Then you're aware that Captain Tremaine specifically ordered that no physician was to be sent for!"

Her tone was angry, even caustic, and Agatha blinked a moment before responding. "That may be, but your aunt has directed me to—"

"My aunt likely never saw the captain's message herself—isn't that so?"

"I...well..."

"So, in truth, we have you to thank for Doctor Arbuthnot's presence."

Silence.

"I thought so." Brittany turned toward the physician. "I'm sorry, doctor, but I'm afraid you've come for naught. You'll have to leave."

"Now see here, young woman—"

Brittany ignored the indignant man and turned back to Agatha. "Turn around and go back to Sweetbriar, and take him with you."

"I—how dare you!" Agatha bristled. "I take no

orders from you, Brittany Chambers, and your aunt—"

"My aunt will understand, once I've explained. Now, if you will excuse me, I have a patient to look after."

She turned to go back to Bryce, missing the exchange of looks between Agatha and the doctor. Then, a second later, she felt herself being taken by the shoulders and moved out of the way as the pair she'd confronted charged by.

"Stand aside, young woman!" Arbuthnot ordered. "I came to see a man down with the fever, and see him I shall!"

He rushed past her, bag in hand, while Agatha followed with a triumphant look on her face.

Brittany watched them go in silence for a moment, too stunned by their behavior to move. In her mind she fixed on Bryce's words in the note: "No leeches!" Somehow, without knowing why, she understood the urgency of that plea. Perhaps it had to do with the time she was ill, when she was about eleven, and Althea had sent for a so-called physician—or leech, as he was more often termed, because of the "cure" he employed. The man had opened his little casket and reached in for one of the disgusting, wriggling little creatures, intending to fasten it to her chest "to draw out the bad blood." But she had screamed and screamed at the sight of it, screamed so long and so loudly that Timothy had heard her downstairs and come running up to her chamber and then—thank God!—succumbed to her hysterical pleas to send the leech away, despite Althea's urgings to the contrary. *God!* Even now, her skin crawled to think on it!

Bryce Tremaine would have no leech.

Springing into action, she ran for the cabin where

she'd left Will and Tansy, reaching it half out of breath, a few seconds later.

"Will!" she cried, "Have you a—ah, here we are!"

Tansy sprang up from the side of Will's bunk, where she'd been sitting, and watched Brittany grab the pistol lying on a nearby stand.

"Miz Britt, what on earth—?"

"'Ere, now," cried Will, "ye cannot—lass, are ye daft? That be a loaded—"

"No time to explain now," called Brittany as she ran for the door, "but don't worry," she lied, "I know how to use it!"

Bryce felt himself drifting toward consciousness, then slipping back again, but the dim sound of voices in the room pulled at him. His eyelids felt heavy, as if they'd been weighted, but he forced them open in time to see—

"*No!*"

His cry was terrible, and the sound of it so jarred Arbuthnot, he dropped the casket he held, spilling a half dozen slimy, wormlike creatures on the blanket over Bryce's abdomen.

"Get them *away*! *Away, I say!*" Bryce pushed himself weakly to his elbows, which trembled under the strain. "For God's sake," he screamed, "get them off me!"

"He's out of his mind with the fever," said Agatha. "Ignore him."

"Young man," said Arbuthnot, nervously scooping the leeches back into their container, "you must know I only wish to—"

"Stand back!" said a firm female voice from the doorway.

The physician and Agatha whirled about simultaneously to behold Brittany standing with a pistol pointed at them. It was cocked and ready to fire.

Agatha gasped.

"Get out, both of you, and take those disgusting vermin with you."

"Y-young woman," Arbuthnot began.

"Out—*now*!"

The somber-suited man needed no further encouragement. With a shaky hand, he thrust the container of leeches into his bag, grabbed the bag by the handle and stepped cautiously toward the door, his eyes never leaving the leveled pistol. Agatha trembled in his wake, her lips compressed in a tight line.

Brittany stepped into the cabin to let them pass, but never lowered the hand that held the weapon until they were out of sight. Then, hearing their rapid footsteps up on deck, she called a final admonition after them.

"Send me and my patient no more unbidden aid! If you do, 'twill be at his or her peril!"

There was the sound of swiftly running feet on the gangplank, and then nothing else that she could make out; slowly exhaling the breath she'd been holding, Brittany lowered the weapon, noting only then that the hand that held it was trembling.

She set the pistol on a nearby stand and glanced anxiously toward the bed. Bryce was lying on his side, facing her, and his green eyes were wide open, taking her in with a look of wonder.

"Hellion..." he rasped, "you were...magnificent..." Then his eyes closed, but she thought she detected a slight upturn at the corners of his mouth as his head sank back onto the pillow.

But suddenly Brittany was too engrossed in something else to ponder his words. With a leaping heart, she saw that rivulets of sweat had begun to pour down his face and neck. The *fever*—it had broken!

Grinning, she stepped toward the bunk and laid a hand on his forehead. Sure enough—it was damp, and cool to her touch.

She breathed a prayer of thanks and had just begun to wipe his brow with the all too familiar wet cloth when a noise in the passageway intruded.

A moment later a pair of carrot-topped heads peered through the aperture.

"I say, Coz, ah—"

"—what's this about you and a pistol?"

"Toby! Tony!" Brittany sprang up from her seat at the side of the bunk, her glad smile telling them how much she welcomed their presence. Then she burst into tears.

The ship's lantern hung, suspended in its gimbaled bracket, over the table where the three cousins sat deep in conversation. It was late—nearly midnight —and they were the only ones awake on the *Louise*. Bryce was resting comfortably, as he had been for most of the afternoon and evening, now that the fever had gone. The same was true of Will and Harry, although the boy and the big man were a lot farther along on the road to recovery, and had joined them and Tansy in the dining room for a light supper. Tansy, acting strangely quiet, had retired soon after supper, stopping only to see that her patient— Will—was safely abed for the night.

"So 'tis settled, then." Brittany spoke in hushed tones as she gazed at her cousins. "Tony is to push the Averys' ruin through gambling with Richard while you, Toby, are to use what funds we can free to set up the commodity deal with Edmund. We're agreed?"

"Aye," nodded Toby, "I'll send your letter to Uncle Timothy in the morning. But are you sure he'll free your funds?"

Brittany laughed. "When he believes they're to be a first installment on my dowry? He'll be so overjoyed at the idea of seeing me wed, he'll tell my bankers to forward the moon, if I ask it! No problem from that corner."

"Hmm, perhaps not," said Tony, "but what if he and Aunt Althea decide to come downriver to investigate first?—check Avery out, that sort of thing. Your father's no fool, and I wouldn't blame him if he—"

"What? After all these years of my avoiding wedlock?" Brittany giggled. "He'll be so anxious, he'll do anything to keep me from changing my mind. Let's see ... all I need do is mention something about ... ah, I have it! First, to ease any fatherly concerns, we'll include a letter from the two of you, stating what a fine prospect you know Richard to be ..."

"Oh, bother!" groaned Toby.

"Oh, hell!" muttered Tony, "You know we shan't enjoy lying to—"

"Then," Brittany went on, blithely ignoring both of them, "I'll add a paragraph about how I shall be coveting these days alone with my intended—um, properly chaperoned, of course—unwilling to share him with the intrusive attentions of Althea and Melody. I'll hint that I fear Melody's beauty will detract from my own ... ah, charms. That'll get him!"

"I daresay, 'twill!" Tony exclaimed. "He'll be so afraid of Melody's turning Avery's head to the point of switching his affections to the daughter he'll have no problem marrying off—"

"—and *from* the daughter he cannot afford to chance seeing jilted," added Toby, "that—"

"—he'll do exactly as I ask," Brittany grinned. "Now, what about the choice of a proper commodity to tempt Edmund? Toby? Any ideas?"

"It awaits my contacting our factor in Fredericksburg, of course, but I'm sure something can be found. Indigo's out.... 'Tis way down, but tobacco, perhaps, or—"

"Wait," said Brittany. "I have an even better idea. Since your factor's in Fredericksburg, why don't you *go* there? That way you can talk to Father in person when you *deliver* my letter, and I'm sure the commodity business will be speeded up as well. What do you say?"

Toby groaned. "I knew we were getting in deep water the moment we let this little minx inveigle us—"

"Inveigle?" Brittany cried. "Why, wasn't it the two of you who cried of my honor when—"

Another groan cut her off. "Peace!" exclaimed Toby. "You're right, of course. We'll go to Fredericksburg."

"No, only you will go," corrected his twin. "I shall remain here to—"

"I know, I know," moaned Toby, "to play whist with Richard. Er, are you sure you wouldn't rather let me do the gambling? I took him for a bundle last time."

His brother grinned. "'Tis exactly why I shall have a go at him now. 'Tis my turn. Fair's fair! Besides," he added. "'twill hardly be all play. Someone has to look after Sweetbriar."

"And protect me from a betrothed who wouldn't be above trying to exercise some 'prenuptial rights'!" Brittany put in.

"Good Heavens!" cried Toby.

"He *wouldn't*!" exclaimed his twin.

"He *would!*" Toby decided.

"You're right!" said his brother.

"I'm glad we got that settled," Brittany told them, "so we're agreed. Toby goes, Tony gambles, and I..." She shuddered. "...become engaged to Avery."

The three looked at each other for a moment, then reached out with their right hands to place them in a pile, one upon the other. It was a carryover from pacts made in childhood, implying *"a pledge to the death,"* but as Brittany watched her slender hand being sandwiched between her cousins' she shivered, hoping the term was not a portent of things to come.

CHAPTER 19

DAYS PASSED, AND SLOWLY THE OCCU-
pants of what Brittany called "our hospital ship" re-
cuperated from their bouts with the fever. But
Brittany herself was no longer among those nursing
the patients there; her aunt had received a highly
charged, colorful description of the incident she
termed "that nasty pistol business" from Agatha
and, Brittany's explanations notwithstanding, Amelia forbade her niece to remain at "the scene of your
hoydenish behavior." Instead, Tansy was put in
charge of an efficient crew of housemaids-turned-
nursemaids while her mistress remained confined to
the Big House.

Of course, in the long run this suited Brittany just
fine, for she was able to pursue her plan of encouraging Richard Avery's courtship without Bryce being
any the wiser. And if there were moments when her
conscience troubled her for going against Bryce's
wishes, she promptly swept these misgivings aside,
telling herself she was only acting in his best interests; the Averys' destruction would be effected with-

out bloodshed. In the end, Bryce was bound to thank her ... wasn't he?

In the Big House, too, she could freely meet with Tony to learn how the business they called "Operation Whist" was proceeding, while they both awaited word from Toby in Fredericksburg.

As for Bryce, he chafed under the confining bed rest, seeing it as yet another in the long line of obstacles fate seemed determined to set in his path. Fortunately, he was able to voice his frustrations in the ear of a patient Will Chambers, and this he did, daily and heatedly, when the two shared a private meal in his cabin.

But then one evening, a little over a week after Bryce had taken ill, Will brought him, along with their supper tray, a piece of news that made his concerns about delays pale in comparison.

"She's *what*?"

"Announced 'er engagement t' wed Richard Avery," Will repeated calmly to the question roared at him.

Green eyes glittered dangerously as Bryce's tone fell to the level of his mate's. "Will, get me my clothes."

Will complied, then sat back to watch as Bryce donned them with a series of abrupt, angry movements.

"When?" Bryce queried as he tucked a white, full-sleeved cambric shirt into his buckskin breeches.

"This arfternoon, accordin' t' Tansy."

"A full, formal announcement with family approval—the works?" The question was bitten out as Bryce jerked on a pair of tall riding boots.

"'Twas 'er aunt wot called ev'ryone t' the drawin' room so's the 'ellion could tell 'em."

"Christ!" Bryce swore as he buckled a wide belt

about his lean hips. "And to think I actually congratulated myself on getting the little fool to listen to reason!" He charged toward the door. "Well, more the fool I, but never again," he added as he entered the companionway. "Never again!"

Brittany sat before her dressing table and allowed Lucy, Amelia's personal ladies' maid, who'd been temporarily assigned to her in Tansy's absence, to brush her hair. At first she'd protested Lucy's attendance, saying she was perfectly capable of dressing and undressing herself, but Aunt Amelia, it seemed, was on a campaign to see her cured of her "wilder ways," and would have none of it. Apparently a letter had arrived from her father several days before, wherein he told how he'd caught wind of an "outrageous rumor" going about Fredericksburg to the effect that his daughter had been seen wielding a pistol in a situation "so extreme it tests credibility." The fact that the same letter had mentioned that Althea had a new physician, and that additional word had come that Arbuthnot had removed to Fredericksburg to practice was, in Brittany's mind, telling.

"That will be all, Lucy, and thank you," Brittany told the plump little servant.

"Oh, but, mistress, I've yet t' lay out yer night rail, and ye're only wearin' the wrapper ye donned after yer bath, and—"

"I shall be fine," Brittany smiled. "You've worked very hard today, and I'd like you to get some rest. A night rail's not a difficult thing to don by oneself, now, is't?"

The maid gave her a shy, appreciative smile. "Oh, thank ye, mistress, thank ye." She bobbed a curtsy and withdrew, promising to attend Brittany "bright and early in the morn."

When the door had closed behind her, Brittany heaved a sigh of relief. Then, in the next second, she moved like a whirlwind, running for the highboy and withdrawing the boy's breeches and shirt she'd carefully hidden there.

It had been an emotionally exhausting couple of days, what with the engagement announcement and, far worse, having to endure Richard's attempts at pawing her person whenever they chanced to be alone for a few moments. She remembered with acute distaste the feel of his hard, dry hands on her arms as he drew her to him for the one "engagement kiss" she'd allowed him, and then recalled with nausea the sensation of his thin lips covering hers. God willing, she would never have to endure that again —*never*!

Drawing her cousin's tight cast-off breeches over her slim hips, she willed herself to forget the humiliating, yellow-eyed gaze of her "intended," his reptilian eyes raking her form day after day as their courtship proceeded. In a few minutes, she'd be on her way to the stables where Saracen waited.

At times during the past week, she knew it was only the promise of her secret nightly rides on the stallion that allowed her to endure each trying day— to endure Richard. Today had been no exception.

And with difficulty, she worked at blotting out the expression on her aunt's face when she and Richard had come with their announcement . . . the shock and disappointment she'd read there. Oh, how she wished she had been able to confide in Amelia regarding her secret plans! She'd even suggested it to the twins, but they'd immediately refused, pointing out that their mother had such an honorable, open nature that asking her to be part of a conspiracy would be like asking a lamb to masquerade as a wolf; she was quite incapable of it.

Oh, well, just a few more days of this deception, if Toby's letters were accurate, and she could go back to being her old self. The thought brought a smile to her lips as she bent to pull on her riding boots, and she was so absorbed in this that she failed to catch a movement of the draperies at the open window—a movement too great to be caused by the slight breeze that blew from the river.

Suddenly she felt herself gripped about the middle by an iron arm and drawn upward, her back slammed against a rock hard male body while, in the same instant, a strong hand clamped across her mouth. Panic seized her, and she began to twist and kick while, with both hands, she sought futilely to dislodge the hand that gagged her.

Then, just as she caught a faint whiff of the sandalwood scent of the soap he used, she heard Bryce's voice, grating and harsh.

"Becalm yourself, you sneaking little bitch, or, by God, I'll make you wish you had!"

Incensed by his tone as much as the words he used, Brittany ignored the warning and succeeded in driving an elbow into the side of his rib cage.

Bryce grunted, then, with lightning speed, shifted his hold on her so that her arms were pinned to her sides. This necessitated removing his hand from her mouth, but as she opened it to scream, he bit out a warning.

"Don't try it! Any sound you make will bring the household down around us, and I don't think you'd like the implications of the scene they'll find."

"M-meaning what?" she dared, but she kept her voice low.

"Meaning," he said silkily, "that I'll be sure to tell them that this isn't the first time we've trysted like this . . . that we've been lovers for weeks."

"'Twould be your word against mine!" Her challenge was sheer bravado, for she was feeling anything but confident right now. For one thing, though she'd anticipated his anger in the face of what she'd done, she'd been quite unprepared to face him this soon; her defenses were down, and the fury emanating from him, though tightly held in check, was frightening.

"I hardly think so, my dear," he replied in a nasty, insinuating tone. "I've only to point out the unsuitable apparel you're wearing—at a time when a *decent* woman would be abed in *nightclothes*. Whom do you think they'll believe?"

Sensing that all the fight had gone out of her with this threat, he set her down and, taking her by the shoulders, whirled her about to face him.

Brittany forced herself to meet his menacing gaze, but remained silent as he ran his eyes over her with insolent slowness.

"Going riding, my dear?" he purred. Then, "By God, your apparel renders you a double sneak! I distinctly recall warning you against wearing breeches."

Regaining some of her courage now that he'd released her, Brittany considered throwing caution to the winds and calling his bluff with a scream that would, indeed, bring the house down, but he must have read the look in her eyes; caustically, he grated a warning:

"Go ahead, yell your head off, for it suddenly occurs to me that nothing would pleasure me more than to tell them of the 'riding' we had in mind tonight."

Suddenly, he reached out and grabbed hold of the

front of her shirt as well as the shift she wore beneath it and, with a violent motion, yanked downward. There was a tearing noise, and then the sound of Brittany's disbelieving intake of breath as her breasts spilled free, their pale fullness and darker, coral peaks mortifyingly evident in the generous light coming from a nearby candelabra.

Bryce laughed, but it was a laugh with no humor in it, and a superior grin crossed his face as he continued. "I'll tell them how I've ridden *you*, my dear hellion—ridden you hard and thoroughly, until you cried out your pleasure beneath my—"

"*Don't!*" The word came out in a desperate whisper, for she now knew his anger was such that this was no bluff. Her cheeks burned with shame at the images he'd conjured, as well as the physical exposure she tried to cover by crossing her hands over her chest, and she bowed her head in defeat. "You've won," she murmured miserably. "What is it you want of me?"

Snide laughter met her ears as she felt herself hoisted like an ignominious sack of potatoes and slung over his shoulder.

"I think I'll let you worry about my intentions for a while," he told her as he moved to the open window. "Suffice it to say I've no intention of letting you off too quickly—or easily!"

In the time that followed, while he dragged her out the window and down the tree she herself had often used for secret escapes, then onto a waiting horse— Good God, he'd appropriated Saracen!—Brittany willed herself not to cry or to act in any way that would shame her further. Over and over, she kept telling herself that he was a gentleman, a proper, civilized Englishman, and future member of the peerage, and that she had nothing to fear from him. He was angry—that was all, and since it was she who had provoked that anger, she would take her medicine, which could hardly be all that bad, once he calmed down and his anger faded . . . *if* it faded . . .

They rode for some time, both in utter silence, Brittany slung, face down, over Saracen's withers. She noted a change in terrain, from pasture to field to woods, where the stallion picked his way carefully between trees and over fallen limbs.

At last Bryce drew the black to a halt; he dismounted, and when he'd hauled her off, she saw he'd taken them to the deserted overseer's cabin they'd shared—she tried not to recall how intimately—during the storm.

"Inside," he ordered. "I'll join you as soon as I've settled the horse." The words were bitten out.

So he was still angry. *Well*, she thought, *in a few more moments, I'll know what he plans to do with me. At least the waiting's over.* Mustering what courage she had left, Brittany drew her torn shirt together with one hand, squared her shoulders and, head held high, entered the cabin.

Bryce watched her go with a twinge of admiration, despite the anger that renewed itself every time he thought of her duplicity, thought of her holding hands with Richard Avery, accepting his kisses, his —*damn*! It did not bear thinking on!

Leaving the cabin door ajar to admit the moonlight that filtered through the trees and into the clearing, Brittany was able to locate a tinderbox and a pair of half-burned tallow candles, and she'd just succeeded in lighting them when Bryce stalked through the door. With a calm she didn't feel, she watched him kick it shut behind him. Hugging her arms across her chest to conceal what he'd so savagely exposed, she waited.

Seeing her standing there with candlelight spilling over her touseled mane of fiery hair, her delicately chiseled cheekbones looking like sculpted alabaster in the soft glow, Bryce thought her wildly, impossibly beautiful, and he almost relented—almost.

But a downward glance caught the tight-fitting breeches she'd donned—donned deliberately, against his wishes, and his ire flamed anew.

She caught the renewed glitter in his eyes and her resolve to remain silent vanished. "Wh-what are you going to d-do with me?" she questioned, damning the apprehension in her voice.

He grinned wickedly, enjoying her discomfort. "Why, that should be obvious, my dear . . . at least, for your first infraction—wearing such indelicate garb." He came slowly toward her, his pantherlike movements menacing.

Before she had a chance to back away, his arm snaked out and caught her about the waist, then lifted her against his hip while he cast about, searching for something.

Spying it, he dragged her toward a sturdy looking, armless country chair, sat and hauled her, face down, across his lap.

"If you'd listened carefully when I warned you— here, in this very room—you'd remember what I promised, if you disobeyed me!"

And as her brain recalled with dismay his threat of a spanking, Brittany felt the first stinging assault on her helpless posterior.

But in the next second, dismay became anger— that he should treat her so . . . like a—like a naughty child! It was too much.

"Bryce, no!" she cried out, as a second resounding

wallop made her squirming buttocks sting even more. "You cannot treat me thus! *Ow!* I—I am a woman grown, not a *child*! Oh, please, can you not find a more fitting—an adult punishment? I promise to bear—*Ow!* Bryce! 'Tis a bullying thing to do!"

Bryce paused, spanking hand held aloft, as he considered her words. Perhaps she was right. God knew, he'd never struck a woman before.

Suddenly he seized on her phrase *adult punishment*, and a satisfied grin creased his features. "Aye, m'lady," he drawled, lowering his hand slowly, "an adult punishment 'twill be!"

With a rapid movement, he jerked her to her feet, then rose and pinioned her two wrists together before transferring them to his one hand.

Her eyes widened fearfully as she felt her arms wrenched forward and upward.

Then, with his free hand, he finished the work he'd begun on her shirt and shift, tearing them totally apart. And before she could do more than blink in horror, he unfastened her breeches and was pulling them down about her knees.

Brittany grew redfaced as she stood before him, exposed from chest to knee while he ran his eyes slowly, insolently, over her nakedness.

In the next second she recovered enough to shriek at him an obscenity she'd heard from her father's sailors, but he only laughed as he was again in motion, positioning himself once more on the chair and forcing her to the same helpless posture across his lap.

Brittany was a study in outrage. He—he meant to administer a spanking after all—only this time to her *exposed derriere*! Kicking and shrieking all the vile words she knew—which were not very many, she

unhappily realized—she let him know what she
thought of him.

"Tsk-tsk," he told her, "don't you think 'tis about
time you learned to act like a lady—even if you cannot succeed in *being* one?"

"Bastard!" she cried. "Miscreant pig in a dung
heap!"

More laughter answered her, but as she braced
herself for the onslaught of his punishing hand, a
curious thing happened. Instead of the assault she
expected, his hand came down upon her buttocks
with utter gentleness—why, she would even have
called it a *caress*. And that was only the beginning.

With a sensual slowness, he traced a path down
the backs of her thighs, and then up again, grazing
the crevice between them while, with his other
hand, he found her bare breasts, cupping their fullness, teasing the nipples until they hardened and
peaked in wanton impudence.

Brittany felt a jolt of pleasure sluice through her,
homing its way to her woman's core, and she
groaned. So this was what he saw as fitting adult
punishment! Oh, the beast, that he could do this to
her on the heels of what had gone before! Too late,
she wished for the promised spanking. That, she
could have borne—but *this*!

"Bryce, *no*! I—" But a devastating probe between
her thighs, just below the buttocks, made her words
collapse into a moan, and Bryce echoed it with soft
laughter.

"Does this satisfy your request, my sweet? Is this
adult enough for you?" His voice was honey-smooth
and soft as summer rain, teasing her senses, even as
his deft fingers teased her betraying body.

She tried to resist, clamping her thighs tightly together and pushing away the fingers that pulled

lightly at an aching nipple, but to no avail. Soft laughter again met her ears as strong, masculine fingers found the swollen bud above her nether opening and slid across it, then back again, and again, her own wetness aiding their course.

In the next second a spasm of delight shook her, and she gave a small cry as she felt her body succumb.

"That's it, sweetheart," he told her. "Cry out your pleasure so I may know your... punishment is complete."

Dimly, between the devastating strokes which rendered her mindless, Brittany realized that while his words spoke of her punishment, all anger had gone from his voice. Gone was the tight, furious tone of the abductor; as well, the insinuating sarcasm of moments before.

Bryce, too, was aware of the change in him, but he was powerless to stop it. He'd truly meant to punish her with this clever (he'd thought) change of tactic, but the game, once begun, had caught him up in it: the seducer had become the seduced.

She was so damned beautiful, her exquisite body a temptation beyond telling. All thoughts of chastisement fled as he felt himself going rock hard.

He gazed with sensuous, heavy-lidded eyes at the rounded perfection of her back and derriere, at the pair of dimpled indentations where they joined; he saw the gleam of candlelight on her tangled mane of copper hair; he caught the perfumed scent of her skin as she moved beneath his hands, and he was lost.

With a groan, he turned her over and drew her into an embrace, burying his face in her hair. Violets ... *she smelled of violets* ...

And in the next second he was lifting her in his

arms, carrying her to the bed they'd shared before. There, loath to release her for even the time it took to set her down, he stood holding her, while his eyes found and locked with hers.

Brittany read the desire in the green depths of his gaze, and it fired the furnace in her that was already building to a crescendo. Her earlier resentment wasn't even a memory as she spoke his name: "Bryce...oh, Bryce..."

He felt himself drowning in the deep blue midnight pools of her eyes as he answered her in a ragged whisper: "I know, love...I know..." And then he lowered his mouth. And kissed her.

It was a soul-wrenching kiss, beginning sweet and lambent in its gentleness, then slowly, ever so slowly, building to something more. His mobile lips moved over hers with an increasing urgency, now a temptation, now a promise, then a demand, and when her own parted to accept his questing tongue, she moaned, deep in her throat, then met it with the tip of hers. He deepened the kiss, feeling her arms tighten about his neck as she sought to meet his need, and he was on fire. But his was a fire that was only beginning to flame.

They broke asunder at last, each breathless with the heady exchange, each longing for more. With a quick movement, he laid her gently on the bed, then knelt on the mattress beside her, running his eyes hotly over her body, then feasting on the exquisite beauty of her face. His eyes held hers as he slowly, sensuously, removed her clothing, making the very act a celebration of the intimacy they shared.

Brittany felt his palms graze the hardened peaks of her breasts as he swept aside the torn fragments of her shirt and shift and knew a quicksilver dart of sweetness at her center; she felt the caress of his

skilled hands along her calves as he removed her
boots and went giddy with renewed longing; she felt
him slide the rumpled twist of her breeches down
along the same path and gasped as he followed with
a shower of unbelievably arousing kisses along the
soles and arches of her feet. She felt his tongue slip
between her toes, then stay to lick and probe, and
suddenly a burst of liquid fire spread between her
thighs, where they joined, and she knew she could
lie passive no longer.

"Bryce!" she cried, reaching out to him with trembling arms. "Oh, Bryce, I cannot wait! Oh, please,
my darling, *take me*. I want you so!"

Bryce heard her words, and the endearment
seemed to enflame him. With a rapid movement, he
joined her on the bed, covering her trembling body
with his own, running his hands over her heated
flesh, exulting in the soft whimpers of pleasure she
uttered. His mouth covered hers in a demanding
kiss, then slid to her ear.

"Sweet hellion," he rasped, "you know how I
want you . . . dear God, how I want you! You're *mine*,
do you hear? Mine, and I'll share you with no one!"

"Oh, aye!" she cried. "Only, take me, Bryce. Make
me . . . *make* me yours!" Then her hand reached for
the pulsing hardness beneath his breeches, finding
the shaft of him through the cloth, stroking, loving the feel of him . . . the maleness of him.

With a harsh cry, he clasped her buttocks and
drew her to him, truly letting her feel his need.

But Brittany was beyond this, his clothed embrace
driving her mad. With a rapid, graceful twist, she
moved to kneel beside him on the mattress. Her
hands went to his shirt, which she almost tore from
him in her haste. Belt, boots, and breeches quickly
followed, until she sat devouring him with greedy

eyes; he was so beautifully male ... powerful of arm
and shoulder ... broad-chested ... lean of hip. She
ran her eyes over his flat, muscular abdomen and
long, powerful thighs, then allowed herself at last to
focus on his proud masculine shaft, her sharp intake
of breath at the huge size of him provoking a low
rumble of delighted laughter from Bryce.

But in the next second his look went serious as he
found her eyes ... held them ...

Seconds ticked by and then, with a mutual, wordless cry, they fell into each other's arms. Kiss followed kiss, their mouths slanting and crisscrossing
until there was no breath for more.

Then Brittany felt the pulsing hardness of him
probe the juncture of her thighs, which she instantly
parted, welcoming what she knew was the only
thing that could answer the frenzied longing at her
core. She saw him brace himself on his elbows and
rise above her, saw the handsome planes of his face
carved with desire, then felt his thrust below.

"Aye!" she cried, "Aye!" arching up to meet him,
feeling his swollen maleness deep inside of her, and
still she yearned, and he gave what she craved, his
own need blotting out all save the feel of her sweet
body beneath his, her cries of pleasure, the way she
took him to a place he'd never been before.

Then, when each thought the pleasure-pain could
be borne no longer, they found each other in a
sweet, soaring burst of oneness. Wave after wave of
pleasure rocked them, lifting them high above the
earth, the moon and stars at their feet, the universe
at their center.

Minutes passed, seconds ... years, for all that Brittany could tell, before she began to sense again the
touch of their sweat-slicked bodies as Bryce held her
close in his arms. Slowly, she became aware of the

still rapid beating of his heart where her head rested against his chest. She felt the rhythm of their breathing begin to slow, then a languid, steady return to time and place.

Bryce was as silent as she. Shaken by the enormity of the passion they'd shared, sated as he'd never been in his life, he gave himself up to the moment, willing himself unconscious of anything, save the woman in his arms.

At long last, Brittany felt a movement and, turning her head, she looked up to find him leaning on one elbow and smiling enigmatically at her.

"Tell me why you smile," she said, a shy smile lighting her own features.

His look grew thoughtful as he reached out to trace the line of one of her winged eyebrows with his fingers, then run his forefinger lightly down the straight line of her perfectly chiseled nose.

"I smile because I find myself more at ease than I've been in months and wonder why that should be, considering that the cause is something I never intended and swore not to pursue."

Brittany thought back to the day on the *Louise*, when she'd heard his feverish ramblings and wondered at their meaning, but had then promptly forgotten about them in the heat of ensuing events. What was it he'd murmured? Something about a "magnificent" woman . . . and then "mustn't allow her to—" To what? "Must remember my purpose . . . Avery," he'd said.

"You wished to avoid me because you thought I'd distract you from Avery," she told him.

Bryce raised a surprised eyebrow, then withdrew the hand that had been playing with a lock of hair that curled over her breast and frowned. "Aye," he said tightly, "and now it seems, instead of providing a distraction, you've enmeshed yourself deeply in the whole affair!"

He took her chin in his hand and raised it, making sure he had her full attention. "Brittany, how *could* you have done it?"

She saw the renewed anger in his eyes and felt a stab of regret at the loss of the mood they'd shared. "I—I was desperate to—to prevent the bloodbath I feared was coming." She didn't add that she was chiefly afraid of losing him to the violence, that he'd aroused a host of powerful emotions in her, emotions she wasn't ready to name just yet, but which made her realize she couldn't bear seeing him dead.

"And so you went ahead and effected the engagement to young Avery—*Avery*, for Christ's sake!"

He pulled away to sit upright, his arms braced on the mattress in front of her. "The very name is anathema to me! And when I think of what this engagement—false or no—entails . . . of that slithering reptile feeling he has the right to put his hands on you, to—Sweet Christ, I cannot allow it! And I shall not, by God! You'll break with him—at once!"

Brittany pushed herself to a sitting position and looked him in the eye. "'Tis too late. What reason would I give him?"

"The same you'd have used when your scheme was carried out." The green eyes narrowed. "Or is that something you haven't bothered to figure out yet?"

"Well, I—"

"I thought so. Well, you'd better think of something, and soon!" He swung his legs over the side of the bed and stood, then turned to look down at her. "Tell him—tell him you've become enamored of another."

"But, who—"

"It matters not!" He leaned forward, bracing his hands on the mattress. "By God, we'll think of something, even if I have to wed you myself!"

A surge of joy shot through her at this, instantly coupled with confusion at the emotion. To cover her response, she scrambled off the bed and began to reach for her clothing.

She felt her heartbeat increase as she pondered her reaction. What could it mean? But even as she asked herself the question, she knew the answer. She'd fallen in love with him. With Bryce Tremaine Avery, this high-handed, often arrogant Englishman who gave no indication whatsoever that he might love her back—or, worse, who was the last man she'd choose as a husband, a husband who might allow her the freedom and independence she craved. She almost laughed at the irony of it.

But in the next second, as she stared ruefully at the torn shift she held in her hands, she felt tears threaten. Willing them away, she focused on the problem at hand: how to persuade Bryce to allow her plan to remain in place.

"I—I thought you were fearful of Avery's anger toward me when I broke with him. Would you now invite it all the sooner?"

He gave an impatient gesture, then placed his hands on his hips and turned aside, ostensibly contemplating a board in the floor, though the truth was that he needed to look somewhere, anywhere, but at her. She stood near him holding her torn shift, but still fully unclothed, and the sight of her lithe, graceful body with all its perfected curves was enough to drive reason from his mind. Incredible as it seemed, after the explosive lovemaking they'd shared, with its aftermath of total repletion, he felt he could take her again—nay, not *take* her—*join with her*, forgetting the world.

Forcing a stoicism he could not feel, he kept his eyes on the floor and answered her. "'Twould have been most dangerous when he found himself penniless in the bargain, with his family's entire fortune gambled away, but this early on, the danger will be far less, and—"

"'Tis not so early on!"

He raised his head and looked at her. A moment of silence. Then, in a low, dangerous voice, "No. Don't say it. If you're implying what I think you are . . ."

She clutched the fragments of her shift closely to her and swallowed past the lump in her throat. "I—I fear I am, Bryce. Even now, Toby is completing arrangements with his factor in Fredericksburg while he awaits Edmund Avery's response on a tobacco deal so fat, 'twould tempt an angel out of heaven, and Tony holds a small fortune in notes from Richard . . . lost at whist," she added with a small shrug and a half smile that pleaded his understanding.

He groaned, running his hand through his hair. She'd involved her cousins as well! But he couldn't even summon up the anger she deserved. He was past all that, for what good would it do? Now, instead, he had to deal with another emotion—the fear that lodged in his gut when he thought of the danger she'd placed herself in.

He quickly denied the enormity of the emotion, telling himself it was no more than he would feel for anyone who'd so jeopardized herself, for she'd become important to him in ways he wasn't able to deal with yet, and he was not ready to acknowledge that.

"I see," he said at last. "The die's cast." A heavy sigh as he contemplated her apprehensive face. "We're in for it now. Sit down." He gestured toward the bed.

She complied, sitting rigidly on the edge of the mattress while he moved to sit beside her.

He saw her shiver while she nervously twisted the ragged shift with her fingers.

"Here, give me that thing," he said, grabbing the garment and casting it aside. Then he pulled the old coverlet from the bed and wrapped it snugly about her. "Better?"

She nodded, then looked at him with expectant eyes that were two huge pools in her face.

"Don't look so glum," he smiled. "You've gotten what you wanted, you little vixen, so now let's contemplate our moves from here."

Surprised at his warmth, she gave him a brilliant smile, and Bryce felt something twist and wrench his midsection. That smile . . . she could tempt heaven with it!

Clearing his throat, he began questioning her on the details of the twins' activities, and then hers; he made her promise to allow him to protect her, telling her that when she broke with Richard, he would spirit her off to her father's, or if that did not seem far enough, to England, to his family's estate. He finished with a final admonition: "The one thing I shan't tolerate is your being left alone with Richard. I'll see you protected from his slimy person, if I have to tie you to your bed! Is that understood?"

Brittany found herself unaccountably warmed all over by this high-handed possessiveness, and she answered with a grin. "Aye, my lord, but are you sure 'tis *my* bed you have in mind?"

The green eyes caught the mischief in hers and

glowed with an emerald light. "You little minx, I ought to—"

"Ought to what, my lord?" she laughed.

He shook her shoulders with playful roughness, then paused, sliding his hands upward to take her face between them, and his look grew serious. "Ought to do this," he breathed, and lowered his mouth to hers.

And the magic was between them again, claiming them, making them a world unto themselves. And it was a long time before he took her back to the Big House . . . a long, long time . . .

CHAPTER 20

IN MID-JULY, SEVERAL DAYS AFTER BRYCE agreed to adhere to Brittany's scheme, word came from Toby that Edmund had accepted the twins' terms on the tobacco transaction. He would be responsible for what he'd signed for on July thirty-first; his son's marriage to Brittany Chambers was scheduled for the thirtieth.

Bryce was for having Brittany break with Richard as soon as they learned this, or, in his words, "now that the snake is trapped in his hole and ready to be scotched," but a second letter from Toby informed them that a last minute snag threatened their plans: Timothy Chambers, at Althea's instigation, had decided to free only half of the dower funds Brittany requested and, because the twins were unable to make up the difference from their own money without alerting their mother, the deal was in jeopardy. Fortunately, Bryce himself had enough, in the form of gold coins safely hidden aboard the *Lady Beth*, to enable them to pay for the huge quantity of tobacco with which they'd lured Edmund. It only awaited someone to go to the ship to pick it up.

Because Bryce refused to leave Brittany unprotected, Will was sent to Fredericksburg, and Brittany, Bryce, and Toby settled down once again to wait.

But it was not that there wasn't a great deal going on at Sweetbriar in the meantime. Word came that Emily Avery was dying, and Amelia made daily trips to Edgehill "to do what I can." She also suggested that, in view of his mother's condition, Richard should postpone the wedding but, as certain others had anticipated, Richard and Edmund would have none of this, agreeing only, at Amelia's angry urging, to keep the ceremony small and simple.

Then, too, there was what Brittany came to regard as Tansy's "odd behavior." The little freedwoman seemed, in some ways, to be happier than she'd yet seen her, going about with a twinkle in her bright, black eyes, humming to herself as she worked. But she also disappeared for long hours at a stretch, during her free time, and when she returned from these forays, she was mysteriously silent about where she'd been. Moreover, she took to spending far more time before the looking glass than had been her wont, and here Brittany observed her doing everything from making strange faces at her reflection to trying out new hairstyles, which ran from the outrageous to the demure.

But then one day, just before Will left for Fredericksburg, the pieces of this puzzle fell into place. It began in the morning. Brittany came from the breakfast room into the kitchen to search for a piece of sugar cone for Saracen when she heard Tansy's voice. Glancing across the kitchen, she saw her friend standing at the back door, talking to one of the sailors from the *Lady Beth*. In the man's outthrust hand was a bouquet of wildflowers.

"Hmph!" muttered Tansy. "You call dat a boo-kay? Look at dem scrawny li'l weeds!"

"B-but ma'am—" the seaman stammered.

"Don't you *'but ma'am' me*! An' how come he done sent you? Ain't dat big jackass *man* 'nuff t' trot dem weeds up here hisself?"

"M-mister Thatcher is b-busy makin' ready fer a trip upriver, miss, and 'e bade me take these t' ye with 'is c-compliments. Please, miss, won't ye take 'em?"

"Hmph!" she huffed, snatching the flowers abruptly. "Ah'll take 'em, but next time, tell 'im he better git hisself sumpfin' biggah! Ah likes mah presents *big*!"

"Y-yes, miss!" said the unfortunate messenger, before backing away from the door as it closed in his face.

Not wishing to be thought to be eavesdropping, Brittany moved silently back into the corridor, but not before overhearing Tansy's final words: "Hmph! Dey sho' is puny!"

Then, shortly after noon, Brittany chanced to be in the garden when she heard voices coming from the other side of a tall hedge.

"You call dat a *cake*?" Tansy's voice.

And then the stammering response. "'E—'E 'ad the cook bake it 'specially fer ye, m-miss—in the galley!" It was the voice of the same unfortunate seaman who'd delivered the flowers.

"Ah seen bigger cakes at a chillun's tea party! Ah could swallah dis in *one bite*! An' how come he done sent *you* agin?"

"'E's awful b—"

"Ah knows, ah knows! He *busy*. Well, mister, you

tell 'im t' fetch sumpfin big 'nuff up here, an' ah'll take a look at it! *Big*, hear? Now, *scoot*! Ah be busy mahself!"

There was the sound of steps fading down the gravel path, and then—

"Hee, hee, hee! Dat Coffee Man's got a lot t' learn when it comes t' courtin'!"

A few moments later, Tansy appeared from around the end of the hedge. She eyed Brittany, who'd scurried to the far end of the garden and appeared to be deeply involved in examining a gardenia bush. Then, out of the corner of her eye, Brittany saw her smile mysteriously to herself, and she heard her hum a lively tune as she disappeared into the house.

Finally, later the same day, just as Brittany and Amelia were coming down the stairs following a visit to the sewing chamber where the seamstress was altering one of Brittany's old gowns for her "wedding," they saw Merriweather peering, aghast, at the open doorway.

"Ah, just a moment, sir," said the butler. "I'll call her."

Amelia paused halfway down the staircase and motioned for Brittany to do the same, just as Tansy came strutting across the foyer.

"Will Thatcher, it be 'bout time you showed up *yourself*! An' how come—*Lord have mercy*!"

"Tansy, me love, 'ere's me final *offer* o' the day."

Will stepped into the foyer with a wide grin on his face, and beside him, on a leash, was the biggest dog Brittany had ever seen. He was tall enough to reach even Will's waist, and more than a dog, resembled a small pony in size. His grizzled coat was rough and shaggy, and he had a long, noble looking head with a thatch of hair which looked like a beard along the underjaw. The inordinate length of his houndlike body finished in a long, gently curving tail which began to wag furiously as soon as he spied Tansy.

"Is this big enough fer ye, lass?" Will questioned.

"Wh-what is it?" Tansy managed to ask.

"A dog, o' course! Didn't I 'ear ye say ye've always wanted a dog o' yer very own?"

Dumbly, Tansy nodded.

"And 'aven't ye been tellin' poor Jocko that me courtin' gifts oughta be bigger?"

Courting gifts! Realization struck, and Brittany looked at her aunt. But the older woman merely grinned as she signaled with a finger to her lips for both of them to remain quiet.

"'Is name's O'Leary, and I 'ave 'im from a ship wot passed us on the river. Seems O'Leary's mistress died and 'e wuz passed on t' the son, but the son wuz sellin' 'im cuz 'e says O'Leary 'ole-'eartedly prefers *women*! 'E's Irish—a wolf-'ound, and 'e's only a pup, so—"

"*A pup!* You call dat a—"

But at that moment O'Leary came closer and licked Tansy's fingers, and when she bent to look, he stretched his long neck and licked her gently on the cheek.

A helpless grin split the black woman's features, and with one hand stroking O'Leary's head and a twinkle in her eyes for Will, she moved through the door.

"Come on, Coffee Man," she crooned, "let's see dis *black* Irishman strut his stuff!"

When they had gone, Brittany stared at her aunt for a long moment. "*Will and Tansy?*"

Amelia chuckled as they continued down the stairs. "It's been going on for weeks, apparently."

"Weeks? But why haven't I—"

"None of us have been made privy, exactly, my dear. I only stumbled on it when I saw them out walking and holding hands on one of my trips back from Edgehill Manor. They were so engrossed, they never saw me!"

Brittany laughed, then suddenly grew quiet, and a small frown knitted her brow. "But Aunt Amelia," she began thoughtfully, "Tansy's a black woman, and Will—"

"—is a black man—or half black, which, in these parts, serves as the same thing."

Brittany's brows rose with surprise. "But how did you—"

"By marching straight up to that nice Mister Thatcher and asking him, my dear. You see, I, too, feared for what might happen to young love if the unenlightened around here got wind of those two. 'The course of true love never did run smooth,' the bard tells us, and I felt those two certainly didn't need the extra complications."

She laughed. "Did you see the new cap Mister Thatcher was sporting? Well, he's wearing it now, but in just a few more days, he tells me, there will be an unveiling."

"Unveiling?"

"Aye. He'll remove it to reveal his new head of nappy, black hair, grown in, at Tansy's suggestion, to show the world he's of her race! Bright, that young woman is . . . keen as a newly honed blade!"

In the time spent awaiting Will and Toby's return from Fredericksburg, one factor remained distastefully unchanged for Brittany: Richard's unwelcome visits. One afternoon, as she stood watching Tansy cavort with O'Leary on the front lawn, Brittany saw Richard's by then all too familiar gelding trotting up the drive. She was slightly alarmed at his unannounced arrival—Tony was in the stables with a sick horse and Bryce, with whom she'd had luncheon, had been summoned back to the ship to settle a quarrel. Brittany was without male protection, and she stiffened as Richard drew nearer.

Suddenly she saw O'Leary dart across the drive, not too far ahead of the bay gelding. A second later, Tansy ran after him. It was obvious that Tansy was intent on their game and hadn't even noticed Richard's approach. As she cut across the bay's path, the horse reared, forcing Richard into a hasty maneuver to control it.

Brittany's sharp intake of breath at her fear for Tansy's near-miss gave way to a sigh as she beheld her friend unharmed. But in the next few seconds her fear returned—and then became outrage.

"You stupid black bitch!" screamed Richard as he raised his riding crop over his head. "I'll teach you to spook my mount!"

And as Brittany watched in horror, he brought the crop viciously down on Tansy's shoulder. The small woman staggered under the blow, and Brittany screamed as the crop was raised again.

"N-o-o-o!" cried Brittany as she ran forward, murder in her eyes, but then, in the next moment, she saw a great blur of black fur leap mightily, unbelievably, high into the air, straight at Avery's hand.

"Aargh!" Richard screamed as the whip was seized and torn out of his hand by O'Leary. "My hand! That cur bit my hand!"

Brittany watched O'Leary shake his head furiously, the whip clenched between his great jaws, while she ran to Tansy.

"Tansy, oh my poor Tansy!" She curled her arm

around the black woman's back, carefully avoiding the injured shoulder. "How is it? Is it bad?"

"How *dare* you ask her that?" snarled Richard. "Release that piece of black trash at once—*at once, I say!* 'Tis *I*, your fiancé, you should concern yourself with! Brittany, *I'm speaking to you!*"

Slowly, Brittany turned her head to look at him, and Richard grew silent as in her eyes he read accusation . . . and pure venom.

By God, the bitch needs taming! he thought. *And I'm going to enjoy doing it—every long, drawn-out minute of it. We'll see how proud and arrogant she is when she's tasted the lash!*

He thought of the iron ring he'd had fastened to the wall of his bedchamber, about six feet from the floor. To this he tied the wrists of certain recalcitrant female slaves, the new ones he'd purchased because they were young and slightly plump—juicy, he liked to think of them, with small, upthrust breasts and well-rounded buttocks. And when he'd shackled them so they faced the wall—stripped naked, of course—he would apply "corrective discipline" with his riding crop . . . he found it a particularly apt tool, for, afterwards, he would mount them and . . .

His eyes slid over Brittany. *Only a few more days . . .*

He dismounted and moved menacingly toward the women, but in the next second, O'Leary placed his huge body between them and Richard. There was a crunch, and the mangled riding crop dropped from the great jaws; then, as a livid Richard would have advanced further, bared fangs and an ominous rumbling in O'Leary's throat held him in check.

"I suggest you get back on your horse and leave, Richard." Brittany's voice trembled with controlled fury. "You see, we've begun training him to attack . . . for our protection, of course, but I'm afraid we haven't yet gotten around to teaching him to desist. Calling him off simply isn't possible."

Richard eyed her skeptically, suspecting the lie, but another threatening growl from the dog made him decide not to put it to the test. Murmuring a vile oath, he backed up, then turned and quickly mounted.

Turning the gelding's head toward home, he gazed for several seconds at the threesome with eyes that were narrow yellow slits, then delivered his parting shot: "Get rid of him. I'll tolerate no such savage animal on my estate. I warn you, get rid of him, or I'll shoot him down like the vicious cur he is!"

As they watched him ride away, Brittany shivered, then suddenly clutched her middle and was instantly sick on the ground.

"Miz Britt! Oh, Miz Britt, are you—"

"'Tis nothing, Tans," she gasped, "o-only a fitting gesture to mark Avery's departure." She wiped her mouth with the back of her hand, then took a cleansing breath before reaching to bestow a couple of pats of praise on O'Leary's withers. "How's your shoulder?"

"It's been better."

"Aye, well we'd best get you into the house to tend it." She took Tansy's arm and turned, then drew to a halt, a slow, satisfied grin spreading across her face.

"You know, Tans, we may just come to thank Richard Avery for this little exercise."

"*Thank* him?"

"Aye, for, you see, he's just provided me with the excuse I'll use to break with him, and 'twill satisfy Aunt Amelia as well, which is something I've been worried about. I'll tell him I cannot wed a man who beats women. And I'll no longer have to worry about making my excuse sound believable, for when I inform him, 'twill have the ring of truth to it—the utter truth!"

The next morning Tansy came bursting into Brittany's chamber with the news that Will and Toby were back. The trap was set!

Brittany sat up in bed, a smile on her face at the announcement, but it quickly gave way to a look of distress.

"Miz Britt, what's amiss?"

"*Oh, God,*" moaned Brittany, raising her hand to her mouth. She managed to throw back the covers and swing her legs over the side of the bed.

"Miz Britt, what is it? You're white as a sheet!"

A groan came in response as Brittany hit the floor and raced for the washstand. Reaching it, she bent her head over the basin and retched violently for a good minute.

Tansy came and put her arm about Brittany's shoulders. "That's it, just take a couple of deep breaths... easy now..."

After a couple more minutes, the spasms passed, and Tansy helped her to a chair. Slowly, Brittany raised her head and they looked at each other for several long seconds.

"I'm pregnant, Tans." It was said matter-of-factly, but the blue eyes held a hint of sadness.

"You don't know that for sure."

She toyed with the handkerchief Tansy had handed her to wipe her mouth. "No, but this makes the fourth morning this week—and then there was yesterday."

Tansy went to the washstand, poured some water

from a pitcher into a glass and handed it to her. "There have to be other signs," she said.

"I'm also over a month late."

"That's one of them," the black woman said resignedly. "How do you feel?"

"About the babe?"

"Well, that, too, but how's your stomach?"

"Just fine, now. It always passes."

"And about...?"

Brittany sighed. "I don't know. I'm in shock, I imagine... but I've always loved children...'tis— 'tis just that I never expected to have any, you see, because I never planned to wed." She gave a small, brittle laugh. "Of course, as it turns out, I'm having the one without the other. Lord, how the fates must be laughing at me and all my grandiose plans!"

Tansy didn't laugh. She stood eyeing her solemnly for a moment. "You could always *get* married."

Brittany choked on the water she'd been sipping. "You—you cannot mean I ought to go through with—"

"Ah *mean* to the Tory!"

Brittany blinked, no less aghast.

"He *is* the father, isn't he?"

"Yes, but—*no*! 'Tis out of the question. And he's not a Tory after all, by the way."

"Why?"

"Why isn't he a Tory?"

"No, why is it out of the question?"

"Because... because he doesn't love me and I don't love him."

"Yes, you do." The words were spoken ever so softly, and yet they held the sound of utter conviction.

Seconds ticked by as the two women stared at each other.

"You're right," Brittany whispered.

Sagely, the black woman nodded. "Your eyes rarely leave him when the two of you are in the same room . . . and every time you've been with him lately, you've spent the rest of the day smiling and humming." She smiled. "Besides, ah ought to know. It takes a woman in love to know one."

"Aye, but in your case, your man loves you back. With me . . ." She couldn't finish. Ever since the night in the cabin, she'd been fighting her feelings, trying to deny they existed. For one thing, they threatened her hard-sought independence, but— and this was far more difficult to bear—she also knew they were not returned by Bryce. Oh, he'd murmured little love words and endearments to her in the heat of passion, but that was all. There was nothing of the growing sense of caring she knew she was feeling, the sense that she would love him all her life, wanting to grow old with him, to have his children—

Suddenly she felt the hot sting of tears, and a sob erupted. "Oh, Tansy," she cried, "what am I going to do? *What am I going to do?*"

The smaller woman came and wrapped her arms around her heaving shoulders, "Don't cry, honeychile," she soothed. "There's got to be a good way through this for you, *and we's gonna find it!*"

CHAPTER 21

BRYCE STOOD ON THE QUARTERDECK AND felt the *Louise* slip into the current, then check and swing about, bending to the mastery of the wind that filled her sails to take them back upriver. Tersely, he snapped out the orders that were taken by Will, then passed on to the second mate, and further, filtering out in all the necessary directions that would keep them moving and on course. It was growing dark, and they would need the knowledge he'd stored in his log on the downriver trip to help them navigate, for there were clouds passing over the moon that had just appeared, and he feared he would gain little visual assistance from that source as he sought to keep the sloop from wandering too close to the shore and running aground.

It was with mixed feelings that he'd chosen to sail at sunset. Of course, there was the advantage of having the wind that picked up at that hour, but sailing at night on a river he and Will barely knew could have proved foolhardy; he'd done it only because the rest of the crew knew the Rappahannock like the backs of their hands—that, and the need for stealth.

He'd gotten the news of Toby's and Will's arrival—and their success—at almost the same moment he'd learned of Brittany's and Tansy's ugly encounter with Richard. And it was only seeing the normally cool Will Thatcher flying into a red rage when he'd examined Tansy's lacerated, swollen shoulder that had forced Bryce to control his own fury at the incident and not set out after Avery immediately and kill him on the spot.

It had taken both himself and the twins to hold Will down, subduing him until the worst heat of his anger passed and he was at least rational again. And it was then that Bryce had decided to leave as soon as the sloop could be made ready, and at night. That Avery was capable of taking his revenge on a woman, he had no doubt; the darkness that would cover their leaving would be extra protection for Brittany, and right now he knew she would need all the protection he could give her.

He'd been worried about leaving the Wakefields behind, fearing the Averys' talons capable of reaching out toward any and all they suspected of contributing to their destruction, but both Amelia and her sons had refused his offer of safe passage to Fredericksburg—or beyond. Of course, Brittany's aunt was still unaware of the plot that had brought the Averys' ruin; she'd merely concurred wholeheartedly when she learned of his brutalization of Tansy that a break with Richard was necessary.

The twins, on the other hand, had no illusions about the danger they all might face, and they'd urged their mother to sail with Bryce, but to no avail. *"Leave Sweetbriar?"* she'd exclaimed. "But whatever for? 'Tis my home, and, what with the harvest coming, I am sorely needed here!"

Toby and Tony had toyed with the idea of confessing all to her, but in the end, decided against it, reasoning that her innocence could well be her best protection—that, and their own fierce resolution to protect her, as well as Sweetbriar and themselves. Fear that the Averys were capable of launching an attack on their plantation had been their first reason for remaining behind themselves, despite Brittany's pleas that they leave. When their mother dug her heels in, they took steps to guard her, themselves, and Sweetbriar; right now, pistols (they had a fancier's collection of more than thirty of the dueling variety), gaming guns, and even knives were being passed out to the bondsmen and freedmen who worked at Sweetbriar. And the staff had been trained, long ago, to use them, for they were not so far removed from the wilderness that the danger of Indian attack was nil.

In one respect, Bryce longed to join them. It would give him the chance to meet the Averys face to face at the hour of their destruction. In fact, it went against every fiber of his being to sneak away in the night like this, rather than meet his enemy head-on. He thought of the years spent longing for some way to bring Edmund back to life, that he might wreak a fitting revenge; he thought of the moment he'd believed his prayers had been answered, when he'd learned the miscreant lived; he thought of the months and weeks of anticipation as he'd tracked his quarry and pinned him down; and he knew a frustration so deep, it almost paralyzed him.

But in the next second he caught in his mind's eye a vision of Brittany, helpless under Richard Avery's yellow-eyed perusal, and the frustration left him, melting away with such ease, it took him by surprise. Then his gaze drifted, as if led by some unseen hand, in the direction of the lower deck, where a slim silhouette pressed against the rail.

Brittany...

She wore a plain cotton gown, donned without petticoats or paniers, and her long, heavy hair was drawn simply back with a narrow ribbon at the nape of her neck. But even in this unadorned state, she evinced a grace and beauty that mesmerized him.

For several long minutes he gazed at her darkened form, unable to let go. What was it about her that riveted his attention whenever she was near? That captured and held him, even when he would have dismissed her with his mind, knowing he could ill afford the luxury of a distraction from what had been an all-consuming purpose? She was only a woman, after all, no matter how beautiful...

But in the next instant he knew that it was not just her beauty that drew him—or, rather, that it was the inner beauty he'd come to know as he began to learn who and what she was. She had a spirit that was fiercely alive—oh, not just the fiery temper that caused her to be dubbed "hellion," but a way of taking charge of life, of seizing it by the horns and wringing the most out of it—a rare thing in one so young, and in a *woman*...

Smiling, he shook his head, caught up in the wonder of it.

And then there was her intelligence. The very course they embarked on now had been set by her ...engineered by her fine mind. He knew most men eschewed a woman if she even hinted at intellectual accomplishment; in the past, he'd even assumed that he was among them. Wit was about all he'd expected of females before, but now, strangely enough, he found he relished both the wit and the keen ability to reason that this woman possessed, taking delight in it . . . *respecting it* . . .

As he respected—and admired—her courage. He knew women who would have fainted at the suggestion they play the part she'd chosen in this endeavor, aye, and a great many men who'd have walked the other way—but Brittany Chambers? Ha! 'Twas meat for her hungry spirit!

He frowned suddenly, thinking that most of the traits he'd listed were those taken to be masculine virtues. This gave him pause for a moment, but . . . no, there was nothing he could define as remotely unfeminine about her. It was all a matter of what convention dictated; he recalled reading histories of earlier cultures and other peoples, wherein women played a far more substantial role in society . . . the early Greeks, for instance, and the mysterious Celts.

And all at once he wondered if, some day in the future, his own civilization might grow to embrace women like Brittany Chambers as the norm, rather than the exception. . . . What would it be like, that world?

He glanced around him at the vast shores of the Virginia wilderness slipping by, at the freedom their bounty implied, evident even now, under the shadows of nightfall. If it were ever to happen, it would begin here, he knew. There was something about this untamed land that birthed a freer spirit, that dared to question the old ways and suggest there might be something better.

Embroiled as he'd been in his private quest, he'd still been unable to ignore the signs of things already itching for change . . . the rumblings beneath the surface, coming from faraway places like Boston and Philadelphia, as well as those nearby, like Williamsburg, here in Virginia. Of course, he hoped it wouldn't come to any further open conflagration— there'd already been enough violence in an incident Brittany termed "the Boston Massacre" and something called the Battle of Golden Hill a few years before. But names like Patrick Henry and Samuel Adams were on everyone's lips, and while their sentiments had been thought too radical by most colonials just a few years ago, now they were being taken seriously by a growing majority.

He smiled as he thought of the letter he would be writing to Lord William tonight. Gathering such facts for his adopted father had been merely a cover for his true purpose here, but as he became involved in it, he realized he'd developed his own fascination with colonial America—and, he thought, as his glance caught sight of the slim figure moving away from the rail, with some of its inhabitants, too.

They docked in Fredericksburg without mishap, and after young Harry was sent to the Chambers home to apprise Brittany's family of her return, Bryce sent word to the crew of the *Lady Beth* that he and Will were back and would be coming aboard shortly. Once all the baggage had been brought up and unloaded on the dock, he joined Brittany and Tansy on the main deck, saying he would see them safely into the carriage Brittany knew Timothy would be sending ("Father will be far too busy at this time of day on a Friday to fetch me himself") before he left for his own ship.

"But, you'll . . . be coming over to our home later, won't you?" asked Brittany, hating herself for asking. She knew he still had business with her father —in the midst of everything else that had occurred this week, Bryce had at last managed to send Timothy's cargo to Edmund at Edgehill (and to collect his promissory note of payment by August first)—but little had been said between them on the trip upriver, and nothing regarding seeing each other after she was home. Lying on her bunk last night, her hand pressed over her still-flat abdomen as she thought of the child she carried, she'd been beset by all kinds of troubling thoughts. Once she was safely within the bosom of her family, would Bryce decide he'd done his part and simply take off for England? Will, she knew from Tansy, was going to look into the possibilities of settling here, for he'd been a ship's carpenter at one time and knew he could earn a living "as a landlubber—so long as I be near the sea," but Bryce had powerful ties to the Mother Country, responsibilities. He would inherit an important place in the peerage one day, and could hardly be expected to—

Abruptly dismissing her unsettling thoughts, she flashed Bryce a brilliant smile to cover what she feared her face may have begun to reveal.

Bryce caught his breath at the beauty of her face in the sunlight . . . her smile. . . . Had it always had this effect on him? Robbing him of breath and speech, making him want to catch her up in his arms and take her to a private place where he would make sweet, slow, and very thorough love to her and never stop?

Forcing the impulse aside, he returned the smile.

"Once I've ascertained all is well on the *Lady Beth*, I'll locate your father and settle our business. Then, if you feel he'll be amenable to my extracting a dinner invitation out of him, I'll see you this evening."

Brittany looked doubtful. "He won't be very happy with the news that I've broken my engagement." She sighed. "And that reminds me—just how much are we going to tell him about—about—"

"Leave it to me," he said quietly, and she thought she heard a note of protectiveness in his voice.

"But I'll be seeing him first—and Althea!—God, there are going to be questions! I don't—"

A sun-bronzed hand shot out and caught her gently, but firmly, by the chin.

"Brittany," he said softly, "I said I'll handle it." He smiled, sensing the concern in the blue eyes. "But for your own part, why don't you tell them as much as we've told Amelia? After all, you carry a letter from your aunt to that effect, do you not?"

Smiling, she nodded.

"Good. Then, once I've spoken to your father and gauged him more carefully, I'll decide whether he needs further enlightening. In the meantime," he grinned, "why don't you concentrate on preparing your stepmother for a last minute dinner guest?"

As it turned out, Althea not only invited Bryce for dinner, but on hearing he had no immediate plans for leaving the colonies, she also insisted he remain as their houseguest. And that evening, just before Bryce arrived for dinner, Brittany learned her stepmother's true motives for encouraging the presence of the Englishman.

Brittany had just finished dressing after a long, leisurely bath, during which she'd managed to shut out Timothy's look of bitter disappointment at her news of the broken engagement; instead of fixing her mind on that, she'd fastened on the memory of his conciliatory hug as she'd left his study—and the lecture that had occurred there. Coming downstairs to see if there was anything she might do to help Althea, she heard a strident female voice coming from the drawing room, whose double doors were partially ajar.

"I tell you, husband, this break with the young man, practically on the eve of their wedding, is the final straw! Face it, your elder daughter is never going to wed, and this proves it. She'll play these games for years, finally winding up quite on the shelf, and my poor Melody along with her." At the mention of Melody, Althea's voice rose to a tearful whine, prompting a quick response from Timothy.

"Now, madam, ye cannot know that for cer—"

"Oh, aye!" came the tearful response. "She's a willful, selfish child who thinks only of herself, whilst our sweet Melody—oh, I cannot *bear* it—*I cannot!*"

"Come, now, m'dear," said her husband, "ye must look t' the positive. Why, I take it as a sign of encouragement that Brittany became engaged at all! She's never come that far before. I prefer t' think that if she was able t' see herself as the bride of one man, then there is hope another may be found who will suit. We can hardly blame her for breakin' with this Avery. Why, Amelia—"

"Amelia, Amelia! Why should we take her words to heart? She's always spoiled that girl terribly, and, what's more, she can afford to be lax in such concerns. *She* has only *sons* to worry after!"

Brittany turned from the door, preparing to withdraw. She'd heard it all before, and she was sick of it. She only wished that Althea would win in this ongoing battle. Then she could relax and watch the frantic courtship rituals pass to Melody. But Father would never—

Suddenly she halted, as Althea's next words riveted her to the floor.

"Well I intend to have this lord's son for Melody, d' ye hear?"

"Shh!" replied Timothy. "We're not t' let on we know that about the man. 'Twas merely by chance I discovered that discarded letter he'd begun t' his father when I inspected the *Louise*."

"Aye," came the triumphant reply, "the one with their family coat of arms embossed on 't! Well, I say 'twas fate led you to spy it sticking to the bottom of that rubbish bin. And fate, with a little coaxing from us, will deliver him up to Melody."

"But, madam, Brittany is—"

"Naysay me not, sir! Brittany is on the shelf by her own choosing. If this aristocrat had been meant for her, why did nothing develop between them? Nay, I say. She's had her chance. Now I shall see Melody have hers, whether your shrewish hellion is wed or not!"

A knock at the front door and the sound of Preston's approach sent Brittany scurrying across the hall into the music room, but not before catching sight of her half sister floating down the staircase. Melody was a vision in pink silk, her dainty blond loveliness the epitome of what the fashion of the time considered beautiful in a female. Barely five feet tall, she had hair the color of palest spun gold, accompanied by a translucent, porcelain complexion that had never seen direct sunlight—and china blue eyes. Her tiny, slightly retroussé nose was perfect for her angelic face and was complemented by soft, rose petal lips and a gently rounded chin.

When she was vexed, a barely perceptible, petulant and childlike pout formed, but most of the time Melody maintained an expression that said butter wouldn't melt in her mouth. And then there was her voice. Gentle and softened to perfection by the developing accent of their region, it was the reason she was called Melody and not the Millicent she'd been christened with . . .

Just at that moment, Brittany heard her sibling's mellifluous voice as it rose in greeting: "Why, you must be Captain Tremaine. I'm Melody Chambers, and I know it's naughty of me, for we haven't been properly introduced, but I just had to come down and meet you as soon as I heard you arrive!"

Inclined toward a nausea that was not from morning sickness, Brittany quietly shut the door and turned away, catching only a few words of Bryce's deep baritone, which sounded utterly charmed. Suddenly she found herself without interest in the evening that was to follow, though she'd been looking forward to it all day. She looked down at the rich cinnamon folds of the gown she'd donned with such care and stifled a mirthless laugh, once again seeing herself as a helpless plaything of the gods, at the mercy of their capricious whims.

How ironic that she should have spent weeks and months wishing Melody could replace her as the recipient of her suitors' visits, only to have the transformation take place now, when the visitor was the man she'd fallen in love with! And she knew all of her father's protests couldn't save her now, for Bryce was the sort of man who took what he wanted and wouldn't let some silly rule about the elder daughter marrying first stand in his way. Once charmed by Melody, he—

Wait a minute! she thought, stopping herself abruptly. *What's gotten into you? You've all but signed, sealed, and delivered Melody up to him in a pretty package! Since when have you given anything up without a fight?*

But, a darker voice within her whispered, *what if he*

should want Melody? He's certainly made no promises to you.

"Aye," she said aloud to herself in a low voice, "no promises . . . no declarations of anything, save passion." She took a deep breath and released it slowly . . . unsteadily. "Well, we'll just have to wait and see which way the wind blows, won't we?" Clenching her fists to will away her trembling, she prepared to join her family and their guest.

"Some more wine, Captain Tremaine?"

Brittany watched Bryce look into Melody's eyes and smile at the sweetly intoned question, then nod his assent. She watched as her sister poured the deep red liquid into his glass while Bryce murmured something into Melody's delicate, shell pink ear, causing the petite blonde to blush and lower her eyes, only to raise them a second later as she met his lazy gaze.

Torn between sobbing out loud at the deep pain that sliced through her, and the urge to dump the contents of the soup tureen over both their heads, Brittany forced a neutral expression on her face and took a sip of her own watered wine.

Serving him wine, indeed! The two footmen who hovered about the dining table had been personally trained by Althea to make sure no Chambers dinner guest wanted for anything during the course of a meal. Since when had Melody learned to play the coquette? But a glance at Althea, smugly presiding over the feast from her end of the table, gave Brittany her answer. Seething anew at this, she almost missed the polite question from the man seated next to her.

"I—I beg your pardon, sir?" she stammered.

Colonel Mark Edwards smiled and repeated his inquiry, asking how she'd enjoyed her recent trip downriver. Brittany attempted to concentrate on his words and form a coherent response, while inwardly she boiled with rage. A colonel in one of His Majesty's regiments stationed nearby, Edwards was a surprise dinner guest, invited by Althea without anyone's prior knowledge. His extreme good looks and charming manner (unexpected in light of Althea's previous history regarding eligible men she'd thrust her way) did nothing to soften Brittany's outrage at this obvious attempt on Althea's part to thrust a barrier between Bryce and herself—a barrier that would ensure that his attentions would be confined to Melody all evening.

It had begun in the drawing room before dinner, with Althea somehow managing to maneuver Bryce into sitting beside her daughter on a small sofa meant for two; this left the colonel no option but to take the only vacant seat nearby—beside Brittany on the matching sofa across from Bryce and Melody, while Althea and Timothy looked smilingly on at the cozy little arrangement from single chairs on either side.

Then, when Preston announced dinner, Brittany was forced to watch in mute outrage as Melody clung to Bryce's arm in a manner that ensured his being her escort.

But that wasn't the half of it—oh, no! There had followed a series of coy looks and fluttered eyelashes, of dimpled smiles and cloyingly sweet murmurs on Melody's part, all directed toward Bryce as he sat beside her during the meal, and all fashioned to make the man on the receiving end of them feel he was the only person in the world, indeed, that he *was* her whole world!

But what was worse—what cut more deeply than

she could have imagined—was that Bryce was soaking it all up like a damnable sponge: a fickle, betraying, contemptible male sponge! Why, after the initial introductions had been made, with captain and colonel carefully taking each other's measure, Bryce had barely looked at her all evening!

Well, she thought as she felt the hurt being replaced by simmering anger, two could play at this game! Steadying her resolve, she cast a sidelong glance at Colonel Edwards. Almost as tall as Bryce, he sat in her stepmother's Chinese Chippendale side chair with an easy, erect bearing that came from years of military training. His level, honey-colored brows and blue-green eyes bespoke blond coloring, although his hair was hidden by a white powdered campaign wig. And although she normally disliked wigs on men, she had to admit that the colonel's merely accentuated his handsome features, for it was well-styled and fit perfectly. Straight, even features, including a nose that was slightly aquiline and a strong chin, gave him an undeniably attractive aspect, as did the virile physique that was enhanced by the crisp red uniform he wore.

Aye, she thought to herself as she flashed a brilliant smile at the man, *you'll do*.

"Tell me, Colonel Edwards," she said in a sweetly lilting voice she hoped was loud enough for Bryce to hear, "what does a man like you like to do with his free time when in Fredericksburg?"

"My dear Mistress Chambers," the colonel said, grinning, "why, anything you'd care to suggest... anything at all..."

It was late when the dinner party broke up, and later still when a restless Brittany paced her room, unable to sleep. Attributing her state to the oppressive heat of the sultry August night, she paused to shed her shoes, stockings and petticoats, but left the thin cinnamon silk gown in place as she prepared to go down to the kitchen in search of a cool drink. She knew a crock of lemonade was always taken from the springhouse by Cook just before the family retired on hot summer nights, for Timothy often rose before dawn to work on his ledgers and required a glassful of the tart beverage while he labored.

Tiptoeing out of her chamber, she shut the door behind her noiselessly and padded down the hallway on bare feet. A floorboard squeaked beneath the narrow Turkey rug, and she halted, straining to hear if it had awakened anyone. The faintly audible sound of snoring came from behind the closed door of the master bedchamber on her right, and nothing but silence came from the left as she studied briefly, through narrowed eyes, the door to the guest chamber where Bryce slept.

Ha! she exclaimed silently to herself. *He's likely sleeping like a rock, exhausted from all the effort his attentions to Melody cost him!*

Barely stifling an unladylike snort, she resumed her pace, reaching the end of the hallway and creeping quietly downstairs.

A few moments later she was in the kitchen, finding her way half by memory, half by the silvery stream of moonlight that filtered through the windows Mistress Henley kept spotlessly clean. Spying the stoneware jug that held the lemonade, she moved toward the huge hearth which dominated the west wall, intent on one of the pewter mugs which hung on hooks from the vast lintel beam.

About to reach for a mug, she thought she heard a faint sound behind her; she began to turn around when, all at once, she felt a firm hand clamp across her mouth. A well-muscled arm curved about her waist and slammed her back against its owner, whose big body evinced a rock hard, muscular wall of flesh.

"Looking for something, sweet?" Bryce's smooth inquiry, spoken softly above her ear, threatened with a menace lying just beneath the surface. "Or perhaps 'twas some*one*," he continued in an insinuating tone, "someone you were planning to meet at this hour when you erroneously believed everyone asleep, hmm?"

Brittany struggled furiously, clawing with both hands against his iron grip, even though she knew it would be useless; he'd held her thus once before. But as she recalled those circumstances and what they'd led to, she redoubled her efforts to free herself; she wanted no part of Bryce Tremaine tonight— no, not now, not *ever*! He was a shallow, faithless trifler—a callous brute, and even if he was the father of the child she carried, she meant to be rid of him— for good!

With a strength born of her anger, she managed to jerk and twist her head to one side, freeing her jaws long enough to gain access to the hand that covered them. She bit down—hard.

Stifling a yell, Bryce swore violently under his breath as he broke her hold and repositioned his hand. He'd had about all he was going to take from her tonight!

First, he'd arrived for dinner full of eager anticipation at seeing her again—she'd crowded his thoughts all day—only to find she'd begged her stepmother to invite a second *male* dinner guest ("a man she's long admired from afar," Althea Chambers had whispered to him before Brittany joined them in the drawing room).

Then she'd foisted him off on her beautiful but empty-headed little sister while pairing off with that —that uniformed peacock, right beneath his nose!

And then—*then* he'd had to endure little Melody's vapid sighs and—God, if he heard one more giggle, he'd go mad!—while this heartless, inconstant bitch proceeded to mock everything they'd shared these past weeks by sidling coyly up to Edwards. *Christ!* She'd played the flirt like the part was made for her!

Well, he had a remedy for such behavior. Bending his head to hers, which he held tautly against his shoulder, he grated out a message in a rough whisper.

"I'm going to release you in a moment, and when I do, you're going to stand docilely still and not make a sound. Because if you do, I promise you, I'll tear your clothing off your body and leave you here to face your family stark naked whilst I make a timely exit. And I wouldn't second-guess me if I were you. I think you know me well enough by now to realize I'm quite capable of doing what I threaten. Am I understood?"

There was a brief pause; she nodded.

"Wise ... very wise," Bryce murmured as he let her go; he watched her spin around to face him.

"You bastard!" she hissed.

"Your epithet happens to be accurate, but unfortunate, my dear, for you see, I do not take kindly to having my mother's misfortune so crudely bandied about by a bitch the likes of you."

There was a flash of cinnamon silk in the moonlight as her arm shot out and she struck him hard across the face.

Her other arm drew back with similar intent, but Bryce caught it and, with an angry jerk, twisted it behind her back as he moved around her. Then he grabbed the hand that had struck him and pulled it behind her as well, pinioning her two wrists together near the base of her spine.

By now Brittany was hissing and spitting like a wild thing, dimly aware of the need to avoid making any sounds loud enough to awaken the household, but consumed with a rage that was almost past all reason. With a twist of her torso, she slammed her hip against him, and a grunt of pain from Bryce told her she'd struck a vulnerable spot.

"That does it!" he grated out in a furious half-whisper. "I warned you . . ."

With his free hand, he reached around in front of her and tore the front of her gown downward; the sound of ripping silk split the air.

She gasped, only then recalling his threat.

"What, shocked, my dear?" His tone was mocking. "But I really don't see why. A wanton should find it easy to bare her wares!"

She felt another movement of his hand at her breasts and then a tug, followed by a rip that sent her shift the way of the cinnamon silk. She looked down in horror as her breasts spilled free, and heard his low laughter behind her.

Humiliated beyond reckoning, she felt the sting of tears assault her eyes.

"Why?" she questioned with a voice that broke on a sob. "Why are you *doing* this?"

Bryce's hand came up to cup one bared breast and then the other, but his touch was strangely gentle as he found the peak and teased it into an erect bud while his mouth moved to the creamy skin of her neck.

"Because I have a need to demonstrate something you seemed to have forgotten tonight, Brittany," he told her between the devastating kisses he pressed to the sensitive area beneath her ear. "You're mine, do you hear? *Mine*, and I'll share you with *no one*!"

Hope flickered, then died as she recalled the events of the evening. His precious ego was bruised at her attention to the colonel, but what of *his* toward Melody? Was she supposed to let him *own her* while he chased the first skirt that crossed his path? Hell would freeze over first!

"You have no claim on me!" she bit out.

"Oh, no?" His anger was back, evident in the way his body stiffened against her.

With a quick movement, he released her wrists, only to pull them up over her head and pin them against the brick wall of the fireplace with an iron hand.

"No!" she exclaimed, endeavoring to push him away from her with the lower part of her torso.

Too late, she realized her mistake.

With his free hand, he raised the back of her skirts up, over her outthrust buttocks, to a level above her hips, shoving the thin folds of silk under the waistline of her gown. Then, as she tried to twist away from him, she heard the sound of his belt unbuckling, and a moment later, she felt the hot, swollen shaft of him against the cool, bared skin of her bottom.

"Here is my claim on you, Brittany," he rasped as the full, rounded tip of him paused at the juncture of her thighs, beneath her buttocks. "Here, where you've begged me to stake it so often before!"

And with a hard thrust, he drove the shaft home.

She moaned as she felt his complete possession of her, not only because of the manner in which he took her, but because all at once she realized that his intrusion had found her wet and ready for him. Too late, she recognized her body's responses to the power he seemed to have over her flesh. But more than that, she realized that he could never have gained such power if it weren't for the fact that she loved him, damn his miserable hide! She loved him!

Bryce heard her moan, felt, at the same instant, her sweet liquid warmth encase him, and knew she wanted him as much as he wanted her. And at that moment, all the anger died out of him, replaced by a slowly growing awareness that he was ashamed of his treatment of her. She was a proud, spirited woman with a keen mind, and yet, here he was, treating her no better than a—a *thing*, an object to be bullied about and—

"Oh, Christ!" he swore, dropping her wrists and pulling out of her, then grabbing her by the shoulders and turning her about to face him.

Her eyes as she gazed up at him were brimming with unshed tears and the *look* in them—*what did it mean?*

"Christ!" he swore again, feeling her shoulders trembling as he held them. "Brittany . . . ah, Brittany, I'm—I'm sorry," he whispered, his eyes never leaving hers. "Forgive me . . ."

With a muffled cry, she went into his arms, feeling them enfold her, feeling the soft fabric of his shirt absorb her tears.

Bryce held her tightly to him, bending his head to bury his face in the hair above her ear. It smelled of violets.

"Forgive me, love, forgive me," he was saying again. "I don't know what comes over me sometimes when—ah, Brittany, I know there's no excuse for such anger, but—'tis just that when I learned you deliberately invited that redcoated popinjay tonight, I—"

He broke off as Brittany pulled suddenly back from the embrace and eyed him incredulously.

"*I* invited . . . ?" Her eyes were wide with disbelief. "You believe that *I*—"

"Well, of course. Your stepmother said that—"

"Althea." Comprehension and contempt laced her tone.

"Aye, Althea," he confirmed, examining her face for a clue as to the significance of this.

"Oh, Bryce," she said, not knowing whether to laugh or cry, "no wonder you were angry! But she lied to you, Bryce. 'Twas she who invited Edwards, with no prior warning to Father or me."

"But—"

"She knows about you, Bryce—or at least about your aristocratic background. I overheard her talking to Father about some scrap of paper he found aboard the *Louise*—a letter, I think. And when she learned you were a nobleman, she immediately set about making plans for Melody to—to have you."

"*Melody?* That tepid schoolgirl? The chit would go gray and lined before I'd offer for her!"

Brittany's winged brows rose a fraction at his declaration. "You certainly gave a different impression this evening," she sniffed.

Dawning comprehension lit his eyes, and the corners of Bryce's mouth curved upward. "You were *jealous*," he told her, the grin in full evidence now, "and believing me to be smitten with your sister, you pretended to be taken with that—"

"Jealous? *I?*" Her tone was outraged, but she didn't meet his eyes.

Taking one of his hands that still held her loosely about the waist, he tucked the knuckles lightly beneath her chin, forcing her to look at him. "Aye," he said softly, "but no more so than I, when I believed

you to be taken with Edwards and thought to repay
you by pretending interest in your sister."

"Oh, I—*oh* . . ."

He nodded, his green eyes intent on hers. "We
were both duped and playing the same game, love,
but 'tis nothing to be ashamed of. Jealousy is a brand
new emotion for me," he smiled.

Slowly, hesitantly, she smiled back at him. "A-aye,
and so 'tis with me."

But as she gazed at him, she noticed his look had
altered. His eyes dropped to her gaping bodice and
the lush charms revealed there, then traveled back
up to her face, roaming hungrily over it, fastening at
last on her mouth. She heard a change in his breathing and felt her own increase.

"Brittany," he whispered hoarsely, then lowered
his head to capture the ripe, parted lips his eyes had
feasted on. "Ah, sweet," he breathed, just as he
claimed them.

Her head swam with giddy anticipation as she
opened her mouth to receive his questing tongue,
felt his knowing hand cup her breast while, with the
other, he traced the curves of her bare buttocks, then
pressed her tightly to him. Dizzy with longing, she
reached eager arms about his neck, clinging to him
as the only solid thing in her reeling world.

And Bryce, his head spinning with the implications of a sense of deepened closeness between
them, growing out of the honesty they'd just shared,
felt he couldn't get enough of her. His hands were
everywhere, cupping a lush curve here, tracing a
hollow there, savoring the sweetness of her, intent
on making both of them mindless with mutual pleasure.

He was in the throes of trying to decide whether to
take her there, standing up, as he craved, or carry

her to a more private place, and had just parted his mouth from hers to ask how she felt about this when, suddenly, he stiffened.

Then Brittany heard it too. *Voices*, coming from somewhere beyond the dining room: "I tell you, madam, 'twas nothing but the wind you heard."

"*Father*," Brittany gasped, her fingers clutching her torn bodice.

"Quick," Bryce urged, as he began to fasten his breeches. "Where does that door lead?" He indicated a dark oaken door beyond the fireplace wall.

"To the buttery," she whispered, at the same time moving toward it. "But there's a servants' staircase at the far end. 'Twill take me above to my chamber."

The voices were growing nearer now, and they could make out Althea's strident tones: "A fine lot your precious undisturbed sleep would reap us, should we wake to find our silver gone!"

Bryce was opening the door for Brittany, but as she would have passed through, he caught her shoulders gently and turned her to him for a light kiss.

"Sleep well, love," he whispered. Then, as his hands touched briefly on her hips, he chuckled and hastily lowered the skirts he'd raised earlier.

Feeling the heat rise to her face, she stammered a good night and turned into the buttery.

"Oh," she murmured, half turning to glance at him over her shoulders, "what will *you* do?"

"Try to head them off while I stay hidden in the shadows," he grinned, glancing down at his front. "Damn these tight breeches, anyway!"

Brittany followed his glance, then blushed furiously before she saw the door close, his soft laughter echoing in her ears.

She made it into the darkened buttery none too

soon, for on the other side of the door, she heard him speak in a voice that convincingly conveyed surprise.

"Why, Timothy ... madam, what brings you down here at this hour? Did you awaken, like me, to find you had a terrible thirst? 'Twas likely the wine at dinner. An excellent vintage, mind you, but a bit tangy, don't you think? Here, allow me to fetch you some of this lemonade ..."

Brittany quickly found her way to her chamber in the darkness. Once inside, she struggled out of her torn clothes by the light of the guttering candle, which she'd left burning on her nightstand, then hurriedly stuffed the ruined gown and shift into the blanket chest at the foot of her bed. She made a mental note to dispose of them with the trash in the morning, then rummaged through her chest of drawers for a light cotton night rail, and slipped it on.

The candle had gone out, and for a moment she contemplated her tester bed in the dim light afforded by the waning moon. Too keyed up by the events of the past half hour to sleep, she moved to her dressing table where she sat and picked up her hairbrush. Slowly, with long, sweeping strokes, she began to restore order to her disheveled mane of hair as she let her mind wander over the encounter with Bryce.

That she loved him, she had no doubt. She now realized she'd preferred their interactions even in those moments when he'd been fiercely angry with her, over the terrible hurt and emptiness she felt when he'd appeared so distant and uninvolved, earlier in the evening.

A small smile hovered about her lips, barely visible in the darkened mirror above the dressing table, as she dwelt on the source of his anger. He'd been jealous of her attentions to the colonel—*jealous!* Surely a man who feels jealousy is one who has come to *care?* Hadn't her own encounter with that emotion been born out of her newly awakened love for him?

And he'd *admitted* his feelings, spoken openly of them to her! It took a man of considerable honesty and courage, a man, confident with a sense of who he is, to acknowledge such things, she felt. There was a flash of white in the mirror as her smile broadened. More and more, she was beginning to understand how she could have fallen in love with Bryce Tremaine Avery.

She pulled the brush through her hair with a long, final stroke, yawning as she debated whether to plait the heavy tresses, for she was at last feeling sleepy. Deciding to forego the task, she set the brush down when, suddenly, she heard a muffled sound behind her.

Her eyes darted to the mirror, and she stiffened in terror as she made out a tall, dark form coming up behind her. She turned, half rising from the stool as she opened her mouth to scream, but before she could, a hot, dry hand cut off the sound, clamping tightly across the lower part of her face while, at the same instant, an arm grabbed her from behind, pinning her own to her sides as her assailant jerked her roughly to her feet.

She had a terrified moment to register how different from Bryce's this one's touch was, how repugnant the scent of his unwashed flesh unsuccessfully covered by an unfamiliar cologne; then, as she struggled against the man with a rising sense of panic, she felt her arms released for a moment before a sharp pain tore through her skull.

The last thing she saw as total darkness engulfed her, was the glimmer of a pair of yellow eyes in the mirror.

CHAPTER 22

LENORE MADDOX CAST HER EYES APPROV-
ingly over the large, opulent drawing room of her
house on Sophia Street. Richly appointed, as
brothels went, Sophia's Chateau represented a
dozen years of hard work and a careful husbanding
of the monies she'd earned in her rooms above the
Rising Sun Tavern, but it had all been worth it. Hers
was the fanciest establishment of its kind in the
Southern colonies and, more importantly, as the
madam, she no longer had to sell her own favors
and split half of each night's take with that greedy
owner of the Rising Sun.

Her cool gray gaze roamed the drawing room
again, taking in the dozen or so elegantly clad gentlemen who sat or stood about, each engaged by a
beautiful, suggestively attired young female. On a
wine red satin sofa before the marble-faced fireplace
sat Daphne, former mistress to the governor of a
nearby colony, but content, now that her former
lover had found a new light-o'-love, to barter her
honey-blond charms under the protection of Len-

ore's roof. In the far corner, perched beside a red-coated major from one of His Majesty's regiments, was lovely, sloe-eyed Yvette, lured by the promise of a wealthier clientele from the premises of Lenore's arch-rival, Mimi Poitiers—the French bitch! And standing by the intricately carved, gilded newel post at the base of the stairs, preparing to lead young Lord Fairfax to her chamber above, was dusky, almond-eyed Desirée, who'd arrived from New Orleans just last week, after her young protector had been killed in a duel and she'd suddenly found herself without any means of support; Desirée was one of the town's beauteous quadroons, raised by her protective mama from birth for the express purpose of becoming a *placée*, a white man's skilled mistress.

Lenore frowned. It had taken a pretty penny to buy the mother's consent to Desirée's placement in a Virginia brothel following the duel. Even though Desirée was no longer a virgin, a condition the young Creole hotbloods demanded of the quadroon *placées* they took, the crafty old mulatto mama had driven a hard bargain, knowing, Lenore supposed, that Desirée's exceptional looks—and talents—would sustain it. More than that, she'd somehow sensed that Lenore's establishment was in dire need of some new flesh, which had been true. That foolish Marie-Isabelle had run off with a sailor who'd promised to take her back to her native Spain (Ha! There was a fool born every minute. She was likely lying in chains below decks on his ship right now, on her way to some crib in Morocco or Algiers!). And then, on the heels of that, the bewitchingly beautiful Cherokee, Summer Rain, had taken ill and died of the fever she caught from a patron.

Lenore's eyes moved in irritation to the figure of a small, slender man who stood by the door to the front entry foyer. With skin as fair as her own, Étienne was an octoroon whom she'd bought in New Orleans as her slave two years ago, when she'd opened Sophia's Chateau. He'd belonged to the owner of the Full Moon, a notorious brothel there, having been carefully trained by its owner in the art of procurement. In fact, it had been Étienne who'd made the deal with Desirée's mama.

Lenore's eyes narrowed. The miserable little wretch had been charged with finding *two* new girls, and thus far, he'd only turned up one—the costly, though valuable, Desirée. And Lenore had immediate need of another whore! Why, business was so brisk, she could fill every one of the two dozen chambers upstairs with an eager patron several times each night. Yet one of those chambers sat unoccupied at this very moment, lacking a female employee to work it!

She watched Étienne step into the foyer to answer the door, then return a few moments later with a pair of satin-coated, periwigged gentlemen in obvious high spirits. Ah, yes, the Thorntons' ball had been held this evening, and these two were probably fresh from it, looking for a less tame finish to their evening. And here she was, without a girl to spare! Sighing, she met Étienne's eyes and gave him a barely perceptible nod before advancing to greet the two gentlemen.

As she moved across the room, she caught Étienne's discreet retreat to the rear of the house. Good. He'd understood her well enough, then. He was going out back to check for the arrival of the beauty he'd sworn to produce tonight.

Of course, she could have done the arranging herself. She'd known the gentleman Étienne was meeting for some time. But the man owed her money (a debt he hoped to erase with the girl he was bringing tonight), and she found it distasteful to haggle with debtors. She thought briefly about the elegant gaming room to the left of the main drawing room she traversed now, a smile hovering about her painted lips. No, let Étienne deal with those who owed her money from their gambling there. 'Twas a duty that went well with his procuring. Of course, she was just a bit curious over the girl that would arrive tonight—had *better* arrive tonight, she amended—but time enough for that after Étienne and the gentleman had settled his notes.

Hmm, she mused silently as her smile widened for the benefit of the two periwigged patrons she approached, *I think they said she was a redhead . . . It's been a while since we've had a redhead . . .*

Reaching the end of the gangplank, Tansy stepped off, then turned and waited for O'Leary to join her. Up on deck, Will Thatcher stood smiling at her, and she smiled back, almost wishing she hadn't promised Brittany she'd return tonight.

She thought Will had never looked handsomer; now that his full, dark hair had grown in a bit, he appeared years younger, and there was something about his face these days that was youthful, too. Brittany had said it was the softening aspect she thought came with a person's knowing that he was loved, and now, as she gazed at him, Tansy was inclined to believe her. She sure did love him, the big darlin'!

"I 'ope that dreamy smile on yer lovely face 'as somethin' t' do wi' the time we just 'ad t'gether, Tansy, love," Will called to her.

Feeling her face grow warm, Tansy cast a glance about to see if anyone had heard him. "Shh!" she said, placing a finger to her lips. "Will Thatcher, don't you know anything about dis—dis—"

"Discretion?" he prompted, his grin white in the moonlight.

"Hmph!" she grumbled. "He knows the word but he doesn't know *it*!"

Her lover chuckled, then grew somewhat serious. "Are ye certain ye won't be needin' me t' 'scort ye 'ome, lass? 'Tis awful late, and—"

"Will Thatcher, you know we went over this before," she said in a voice louder than she'd intended on the silent dock. "O'Leary's all the protection ah'll need, and then some, and, besides, you're on—"

"I ken, I ken—I be on watch t'night, but, lass, mind ye take care just the same—promise?"

She gave him a ready smile. "Promise. Now ah'd best be off." She blew him a kiss. "See you around noon!"

"Aye," he smiled, wishing it were late morning instead of less than an hour after midnight, "and Tansy . . . ?"

She turned, placing a staying hand on O'Leary's collar as she looked at Will questioningly.

"I love ye, lass."

Grinning helplessly, Tansy mouthed the words, "I love you, too," then turned and walked off, a dreamy expression on her face.

Sophia Street ran along the river, and she planned to take it as far as William, then turn left toward the Chambers house, but as she got about a block away from where the *Lady Beth* was docked, she began to wonder whether another route might not have been better.

Walking along the docks by the river was somewhat eerie. Numerous ships loomed beside her, their tall masts appearing like specters in the moonlight, their spars and rigging creaking with the movement of the current. A fog was rolling in, and at various points she stopped, listening to the furtive scurryings of unseen creatures she hoped were only river rats. At the corner of Charlotte Street she stopped short, holding her breath while a gray shadow crossed her path, but when O'Leary's growl elicited a feline hiss, she relaxed, realizing it was merely a cat.

"O'Leary," she said then, "this is silly. Ah just told Will there was nothing to worry about, and here ah am, acting scared as a—"

She broke off, tuning her ears to the sound of a horse's hooves hitting the cobblestones from some distance away. Looking up ahead, she thought she spied a shadow moving a couple of blocks away, but she couldn't be sure because of the increasing fog rolling in from the river.

Deciding not to take any chances, she looked about for a place to hide. Strangely enough, there was a fine looking mansion on the far corner, appearing oddly out of place in this section of town. She thought of running for the shelter of the walled courtyard before it, but she then saw that there were several carriages and mounts tethered there, and lights were blazing in many of its windows. She decided against it, not wanting to run into some party guest and having to explain herself.

At last she opted to hide behind a pile of kegs across the street from the mansion, on the river side, pulling O'Leary along with her and managing to hide both of them just as a large bay gelding came into view, out of the fog.

As he neared the house known as Sophia's Chateau, Richard Avery was well pleased with himself. Before him, slung face down, across the front of his saddle, was his erstwhile fiancée, Brittany Chambers, unconscious and completely at his mercy—the arrogant bitch!

He thought of the brief exchange of words they'd had, after she awakened from the tap on the head he'd given her. Why, the slut hadn't so much as blinked when he informed her that his father had killed himself over their disgrace! And it was a disgrace brought about by *her*, the faithless bitch!

Glancing down at the long red hair that nearly trailed to the ground, he gave a grunt of satisfaction. Whatever had been in that potion Étienne had given him, it had dispatched her nicely, only seconds after he'd forced it down her throat. He only hoped it wouldn't take too long for her to come around after he installed her at Lenore's; he had every intention of using her well himself tonight before releasing her to her new "profession."

A sinister laugh broke from his throat as he turned his mount's head into the courtyard in front of Sophia's Chateau. Lenore didn't know it yet, but this hot little package wasn't going to be at her disposal forever—oh no! He'd wait a few months, to be sure the shrew was thoroughly ridden and broken in spirit, if not in body. Then he'd pay for her use one night and offer to rescue her, provided she marry him. She'd do it, just to be free of Lenore (the greedy witch!), and Lenore would agree to it because he'd offer her enough of the shrew's dowry gold to make it worth her while.

Suddenly Richard frowned. He'd always meant to take a virgin to wife, just like any other gentleman. He supposed now he'd have to wait some months before getting an heir on her, once they were wed.

All at once a leering grin replaced the frown. For

the moment, for just another hour or so, Brittany Chambers was still an innocent, and, by heaven, he meant to have her! He had a special little ritual for deflowering virgins . . .

Tansy stood stone-still as she watched the bay gelding disappear into the courtyard. The fog curled and eddied around her, but she didn't move, so horrified was she at what she'd just seen. Brittany Chambers in the hands of that scumsnake, Richard Avery— how was it possible?

But she knew she'd never mistake that long red hair on the woman she'd just spied slung across Avery's saddle. It was Brittany, all right. But how had he managed to steal her right out from her daddy's house, and, what was more, where was he taking her?

Again she eyed the strangely misplaced mansion across the street. There was something funny about the place, something—

Suddenly her eyes flew to an upstairs window of the house. It was well lit from what must have been numerous candles burning inside, and she could see people moving across the opening; there were three of them.

All at once, Tansy froze, a sickening feeling churning her insides. There, naked as the day she was born, except for a red ribbon about her neck, was a young blond woman. In the front of her was a half-clothed man, and he was fumbling crudely with her bare breasts while behind her was another man; he was as naked as she and he was—*oh God!*

"Sweet Lord, have mercy!" Tansy cried, then she alerted O'Leary and the two of them began to move swiftly, but silently, toward William Street. She'd briefly considered going back for Will, but she knew he had his watch duty, and besides, she had a feeling Captain Bryce would want to be the first to be told about this. Now, if she could only alert him *in time*!

Bryce lay in the comfortable Chippendale tester bed in his host's guest chamber and tried to sleep, but found it impossible. Dancing through his head were images of Brittany and the way she'd looked tonight, both in the elegant cinnamon silk gown she'd worn to dinner and in the tattered remnants he'd made of it later, in the kitchen. With the latter image, he felt himself go rock hard with wanting her, and, with a groan of frustration, he turned and pounded his pillow, aware of the need to focus on something else if he wished to sleep at all tonight.

But still his mind was filled with Brittany—only Brittany. The corners of his mouth lifted in a smile as he thought of the extremes of emotion she was able to inspire in him.

First, there was the alarming intensity of the anger she could provoke, alarming because it wasn't like him. Hell, he thought, no woman had ever been able to engender anything more than annoying irritation in him! What was it about that minx that had him acting like a bear with a thorn in its paw?

He smiled in the darkness, thinking of another, vastly different state of emotional chaos she could invoke. No woman had ever stirred his senses so much. And then there was the jealousy he'd been consumed with this evening. Why, it had been an emotion so foreign to him, it had taken most of the evening—and some dire behavior, he admitted ruefully—before he began to recognize it for what it was.

And Brittany Chambers lay at the root of it. Why?

He felt the answer to these questions lay close at hand, buried, but attainable if he would only take the time to sort them out. Like a navigator entering uncharted waters, he examined what he assumed to be the clues, sure he'd soon be able to make sense of them. That the solution eluded him because his approach was wrong didn't occur to him; he never realized that what he sought lay not in external signs, but within himself; and so, again and again he felt his answer tease him, lying just beyond his grasp.

The delicate chime of the timepiece on the mantel told him it was one o'clock, and he cursed softly in the darkness. Turning to find a more comfortable spot on the feather mattress, he realized he was still hard. Damn, but he wanted her!

He wondered if she were having this much trouble as she lay in her bed down the hall. He toyed briefly with the idea of going there to find out, among other things, but rejected it. He'd had a difficult enough time throwing Timothy and her stepmother off the track earlier, and he had no wish to tempt fate again. He had far too much respect for the hellion to compromise her under her father's own roof.

But the notion had been tempting... incredibly tempting...

Tossing and turning for several more minutes, at length he sat up and swung his legs to the floor, intent on a decanter of brandy his host had placed at his disposal on a table near the fireplace. He'd just begun to move toward it when, all of a sudden, he heard a noise outside in the hallway. Then he watched the handle on the door turn slowly, so as not to make a sound.

He was in the process of flattening himself against the wall that would be hidden by the door as it opened, when he heard Tansy's frantic half whisper.

"Captain Bryce?"

He pulled the door ajar and looked down at her. "Aye, lass, what's amiss? Is Will—?"

"Oh, Cap'n!" she exclaimed, lapsing into the thick patois that took over when she became overwrought, "It ain't Will! It be Miz Britt'ny! Dat snake done stole her away! He done took her into dat fancy house an'—"

"Hold on, lass, take it slowly," Bryce urged, reaching for the breeches he'd worn earlier in the day. "*Who's* taken what *where*?"

It was only then that Tansy realized he was naked, and she squeezed her eyes tightly shut, muttering, "Oh, Lawd!"

But in the next second she forced herself to take a calming breath, remembering who needed her—and why. "Captain," she said in a clear voice as she looked somewhere over his head, "Richard Avery has Miz Brittany. Ah saw—"

She froze at the sound of animal pain that tore from Bryce's throat, then braced herself for the onslaught of his grip as he took her by the shoulders and looked into her face. Daring to meet his eyes, she saw they appeared silver in the moonlight, and at the fierce emotion she saw in them, she felt herself tremble. Not for all the wealth in the world would she want to be standing in Richard Avery's shoes this night.

"*Where? How?*" The words, as they rushed out in a controlled rasp, sent further chills down her spine, but she forced herself to answer clearly.

"Down by the river. Ah saw them as ah was coming back from the *Lady Beth*. She—she was unconscious on his horse, and from where O'Leary and ah hid, ah could see he was taking her to—to—oh, God, Captain Bryce! It was a bawdy house!"

Tears were choking her speech, now, but Tansy swallowed them down, adding, "Ah can take you there, Captain, but, please, we've got to hurry!"

But Bryce was way ahead of her, yanking on his boots in record time, not bothering to fasten the buttons on his shirt as he tore open a drawer in the chest where he'd stashed his things and pulled out a pistol.

Strangely enough, the sight of the weapon, which should have terrified her, gave Tansy a strange sense of comfort. What was terrifying was the look in his eyes as she met his gaze before he urged her silently out the door.

CHAPTER 23

THE DISCREET HUM OF REFINED CONVERSA-
tion surrounded Lenore in the drawing room as she
moved about, seeing that things ran smoothly in the
establishment on Sophia Street. Its atmosphere was
genteel because of the high standards she set, in
terms both of the kind of patrons she went out of her
way to attract and of the type of female she employed to attract them. None of her girls were the
crude, unwashed sort, oh no. She had Étienne take
great pains to see he procured only those who were
well-spoken and well-mannered, as well as young
and beautiful.

Lenore frowned. She used whores who appeared
to be ladies, yes, but that did not extend to employ-
ing women who actually *were* ladies. Like the redhead lying upstairs right now in Marie-Isabelle's old
chamber.

Lenore was worried. A glance in a gilt-framed mirror she passed reminded her to erase the frown from
her smooth forehead; at thirty, she still passed for a
beauty, her face unlined and her carefully coiffed

sable hair showing not a trace of gray, but it didn't pay to frown and encourage wrinkles in the flawless white complexion she'd always prided herself on.

Nodding approval at one of her footmen, who passed with a tray bearing several glasses and a decanter of the finest French brandy, she gave the mirror a final glance and went over the events of the past half hour in her mind.

Étienne had summoned her to view the unconscious girl he'd installed in the vacant bedchamber along with Avery, who'd refused to leave her. She remembered well her astonishment at the redhead's beauty; the girl was incomparable. Both her face and the lush body that was revealed after they'd stripped her of that demure night rail were flawless.

But when, upon being questioned, Richard Avery had told her that the girl was a common tradesman's daughter who'd run away from home, something hadn't rung true to Lenore's carefully attuned ears. After all, she hadn't clawed her way to the top of her profession by being naive where the two staple ingredients were concerned: money and people. And with the beauteous redhead, her "people sense" had buzzed loudly in the back of her brain; there was something familiar about the chit . . . something that recalled a rumor or story she'd heard somewhere.

Upon confronting Avery and questioning him as only she could, she'd finally gained the truth: the redhead was the infamous Brittany Chambers, otherwise known as the Fredericksburg Shrew. She'd been ready to throw both Avery and the girl out, then and there.

But then Richard had proposed striking a bargain with her. Pointing out that the girl was a virgin (as, of course, why should she not be?) he indicated the problem her shrewishness would pose. A virgin was a valuable commodity to a brothel owner, but a shrewish one might be more trouble than she was worth, he said. His offer was to tame Brittany Chambers, deflowering her in the process, to produce a biddable whore who would be enormously profitable to Sophia's Chateau in the following months. But then, he went on, he meant to return and *wed* her! Urging his explanation right past Lenore's incredulous reaction, he'd gone on to remind her that Brittany Chambers was an heiress, and her dowry was large enough (he'd cited a staggering sum) to allow him and Lenore to split it evenly, after which each would still remain handsomely rewarded.

It had been tempting. It still was. Lenore had retreated to the drawing room to ponder the offer, leaving Étienne with Richard and the girl, with strict instructions to protect the chit's virginity at all costs; Étienne was extremely skillful with the knife he wore on his slender person at all times.

Now, as she considered her options, Lenore examined her main fear—that the girl's family would search for her and find her here. After all, the girl was well known in the area, and news of her beauty, not to mention her exact identity, might soon be bandied about.

Of course, there were ways of disguising a whore. She remembered Barbara, the little actress from Charleston, who'd been so concerned about being recognized and thrown into prison for the debts she'd skipped out on. They'd purchased her an excellent wig and had her wear a jewel-studded demimask whenever patrons were about. The mask had actually become her highly lucrative trademark!

And Avery had promised to engineer a false trail to lead her family into thinking she'd run off with someone. He'd even guaranteed he could force the

chit to write a letter to that effect, having her be purposefully vague about her lover's identity, so that
when she showed up in a few months with Richard as
her groom, they would believe that she'd decided to
accept her erstwhile fiancé after all. (Oh, yes, he'd told
Lenore and Étienne all about the broken engagement!)

Hearing horses in the courtyard outside, Lenore
signaled the first footman to attend the door in
Étienne's absence and resumed thinking about her
alternatives. She was sorely tempted by the fat purse
Brittany Chambers's dowry would bring her, but she
could ill afford the scandal of the family's tracing the
girl here; despite precautions, things sometimes had
a way of going awry. God's Boots, if the authorities
were brought in, it could well spell the end of Sophia's Chateau!

But there was another option. Étienne might be
able to sell the girl to their New Orleans contact. As
a virgin, she would command a high price, not to
mention what her beauty would add to that. (They
needn't mention her shrewishness). The problem
was, in that endeavor she would have to bypass
Richard Avery, and that could prove dangerous. She
could still see the lust gleaming in his nasty yellow
eyes, and the eyes weren't all that was nasty about
him. Crossing Richard was inviting trouble . . . ugly
trouble. Lenore shivered.

Then, out of the corner of her eye, she caught
sight of the stranger who'd just been admitted by her
footman, and the problems awaiting Lenore upstairs
vanished from her thoughts.

He was utterly the handsomest, most virile, most
arresting man she'd ever seen. Raven hair curling
casually over a well-formed head . . . straight nose,
well-proportioned in a strong, angular face dominated by high cheekbones and a square, determined

chin . . . a firm, masculine mouth framed by grooves that were dimples when he smiled, as he did now, at Daphne, who was giving him the eye—but, then, there was not a woman in the room who was not eyeing him.

Lenore was just taking in his great height and breadth of shoulder when he nodded at a whispered remark from her footman and moved in a graceful, catlike fashion, straight toward her, and then she noticed his eyes . . . green, the color of leaves in the shade, or old emeralds in candlelight. . . . Lenore felt something stir deep in her woman's core, something she hadn't felt in years.

"Mistress Maddox?" The crisp accent of the English upper classes met Lenore's ears, but then, she'd known he would be a gentleman. Even dressed casually as he was, wearing a coatless riding outfit, rather than the formal evening clothes the other patrons wore, she'd known from his bearing that he was upper crust, perhaps even a nobleman; her "people sense" was ticking nicely.

"Aye," she answered, touching a black silk fan to her chin and smiling, "though I fear you have the advantage over me, sir. I do not—"

"Bryce Tremaine, madam, here in the colonies on business for my father, the marquis of Clarendon."

"Ah. I knew it," purred Lenore with obvious satisfaction. "I can spot an aristocrat nine times out of ten. Well, my lord, welcome to Fredericksburg." Here her voice lowered suggestively, adding, "And its . . . pleasures."

Bryce was acutely aware of the iron control he exerted over his emotions as he bestowed a lazy smile on the painted whore in front of him. Beneath this careless facade, his mind and senses were tightly coiled, ready to pick up any clue they could seize on to help him determine where they were holding Brittany. Sweet Jesus, even now she could be—

With a silent click, he shut out the maddening thought and concentrated on his purpose. Tansy had gone ahead to fetch Will, who was to wait in the yard behind the mansion with the horses Bryce had borrowed from Timothy's stable, as well as all the remaining gold he had left on the *Lady Beth*. He would get Brittany out of here, no matter what, but he preferred to use the persuasive power of gold rather than violence to gain that end; Brittany might be hurt through the latter. Mentally, he checked on the pistol he'd secreted in the waistband of his breeches, well camouflaged by the loose, full-sleeved shirt he wore.

"Well, my lord," the madam was saying, "how can we help you tonight, hmm?" She made a discreet gesture, indicating a pair of young women who had drawn near, their eyes avidly taking him in; they were wearing gowns cut so low, their rouged nipples were showing. "A blonde, perhaps, or are the sultry charms of a brunette like Maria, here, more to your liking?"

Bryce flicked his glance over the pair of young whores, before returning it to the madam. "Neither, I'm afraid, though these ladies are quite charming." He took the time to send the pair an indulgent smile. "But I seem to have a particular yen for a redhead this evening."

It was a calculated risk. He knew there could be several with that hair color in a house such as this, not just the woman he so desperately sought, but he had to start somewhere. "In fact," he added, "the yen is so strong, I'd be willing to pay handsomely to have it satisfied."

Lenore was just about to express dismay at having been caught without the thing he wanted, but at his last words, a shrewd expression crossed her face and she asked him, "Handsomely, my lord? How handsomely?"

Bryce appeared to be absorbed in canvassing the women in the room. "'Tis a pity . . . I don't happen to see any about who would—"

A black silk fan touched his sleeve, and he looked into Lenore's cool gray eyes.

"*How* handsomely would you be willing to pay, my lord?"

He made a negligent gesture and then, in a bored tone of voice, mentioned a sum he knew to be vastly greater than such an establishment would charge, even if it were located in the most expensive section of London. "Money should be no object when a man's yens are at stake," he smiled, "don't you agree?"

Lenore barely succeeded in suppressing a gasp at the figure he cited, and then her eyes narrowed calculatingly. At first she hadn't even considered the Chambers chit in this discussion; after all, she was hardly ready for employment at the moment. But this man was obviously used to spending lavishly to achieve his pleasures, and her "money sense" was operating in high gear.

"Truth to tell, my lord, I do not actually have any . . . experienced employees who fit your, ah, yen, but—" Her voice lowered conspiratorially, "how would you like to taste a *virgin*?"

He hadn't been expecting it. In his awareness of Brittany, she was the woman who had given her virginity to him—nay, *insisted* he *take* it—but as he looked into the shrewd gray eyes of the woman before him, he knew without a doubt that it was Brittany she was offering him; to the rest of the world, Timothy Chambers's daughter was a well-protected, carefully reared young virgin.

He smiled, careful to hide his excitement. "A redheaded virgin, madam?"

"But of course," smiled Lenore. "You are interested, then?"

"Lead the way, madam," said Bryce, declining with a brief gesture the brandy tray her footman offered.

"Ah, not so fast, my lord," murmured Lenore, eyeing the expensive tailoring of his riding clothes, the fine, top-quality leather of the boots, "for I haven't yet explained one inescapable fact I must point out to you."

"And that is...?" Bryce forced the words out slowly, doing all he could to maintain a grip on his patience.

"The fact is, virgins command a somewhat higher price, my lord, for, after all, once they're—"

"Name it," Bryce said, hoping any eagerness in his tone would be taken for something induced by lust, and when she whispered an outrageous figure, he merely gave her a silent nod and looked at her as if to say, "Your move."

A cool one, thought Lenore, *and choosy, too, but, then, with looks like that and an apparent abundance of wealth at his disposal, he can afford to be*. Well, she had never been one to miss an opportunity where she found one.

Suddenly the thought struck her that the redhead might still be unconscious—or worse, hissing and spitting. She'd have to be cautious.

"Ah, my lord," she purred, "I must point out that I can guarantee only two things: that your redhead is beautiful and virginal. Beyond that, you are on your

own. Virgins often have a way of being...
recalcitrant, you know, and—"

Bryce forced a grin that had the suggestion of a
leer about it, and watched her visibly relax.

"And payment will be in advance," she smiled.
"Ah, how did you plan to—"

"My man awaits in your yard with enough gold to
satisfy what we've agreed on. Once I've seen the girl
and ascertained her comeliness, I'll give you my demand note and you may send someone to him to
collect payment. Does that satisfy, madam?"

Lenore's eyes signaled greedy anticipation. "Wait
here," she said, turning toward the wide staircase
near the entrance.

Bryce placed a hand on her perfumed shoulder,
staying her movement. "Not for too long, I hope,"
he told her meaningfully. "I can be an impatient
man, madam, and when I am toyed with, my gener-
osity has been known to dwindle. Do we understand
each other?"

Lenore read the adamantine look in the green eyes
and gave him a quick nod. "Aye, my lord, of
course."

He released the shoulder and watched her hurry
toward the stairs.

As she headed for the chamber where they held Brittany, Lenore's mind raced with plans. The Englishman's offer was too lucrative to refuse. She would
sell the girl's virginal favors to him tonight and then
have Étienne spirit her away to New Orleans in the
morning. The total amount she received would be
less than her share of the dowry sum, but making a
profit this way would be fraught with far less risk
than going Avery's route. Her mind was made up.

The only problem was Avery, but she had a plan.

She would signal Étienne to serve him a drugged brandy. (Étienne was so good with those voodoo concoctions he'd picked up from his mother in New Orleans!) When Richard awoke in the morning, they would tell him the girl had escaped, then pay him a fairly generous sum—in gold (she could afford to be generous—now) to recapture her, saying Lenore was eager to go the dowry route with him. There was some risk, but she knew Avery was desperate for ready cash, and she was willing to wager his greed would take care of the rest. Ah, yes, there was nothing like desperation, and a little greed, to quell a man's suspicions.

But when she opened the door to the silken opulence of the bedchamber at the rear of the mansion, all of Lenore's carefully laid plans crumbled.

There, out cold on the red Turkey carpet, lay Étienne, a brass candlestick beside his head indicating the source of his unconscious state. And on the bed, breathing hard as he wrestled with the redhead, was Richard Avery.

The girl struggled fiercely, but she made no sound, and then Lenore saw why: a man's linen handkerchief had been tied about the lower part of her face and head to gag her. Moreover, one of her wrists was tied to a bedpost by a silken drapery cord. Another such cord lay on the rug near the opposite post; it appeared as if the girl had perhaps awakened and surprised Avery while he was in the midst of binding her.

Avery panted and cursed violently as Brittany fought him. When she narrowly missed his groin with her knee, he hissed an obscenity and twisted to one side. It was then that Lenore saw his breeches were unfastened and he had a full erection.

"*Richard!*" Lenore shrieked, looking about for

something she might use to beat him off. *He was about to ruin the fattest profit of her career!* Spying the brass poker beside the fireplace in the far corner, she ran toward it, then frozen as her hand touched the handle.

Flying through the door she'd left ajar came a tall, muscular mass of human rage. It was the Englishman. He must have followed her upstairs!

With an exultant smile, Lenore backed into the shadows. Perhaps she wouldn't have to take care of Avery now; her wealthy client would do it for her!

She watched as Bryce fell on Avery with an enraged snarl, seizing him by the shoulders and pulling him off the girl in one motion, then, despite Richard's goodly size, flinging him to the floor like a rag doll.

Avery hit the floor with a yowl of pain, as his head glanced off the edge of the candlestick he'd used on Étienne. He twisted and tried to grab it, but Bryce was too quick for him. With a growl that was animal-like in its intensity, he hurled himself at the prone man, knocking the candlestick out of reach as his knees landed on Avery's midsection.

"*Argh!*" cried Richard, but in the next second he drove his fist into Bryce's shoulder. Bryce grunted; then, before Avery could repeat the action with his other fist, he landed a crunching blow to Richard's chin with his right, following it with one to the nose with his left, sending the blood gushing.

"No more!" whined Avery. "Don't! I—I yield! Don't hurt me again!" He had both hands up before his face in a protective gesture.

"I'll do more than hurt you, you swine," Bryce snarled. "*I'll kill you!*"

"Bryce, no!"

It was the first sound made by the girl on the bed

since the Englishman had entered. In the shadows, Lenore's head went up, her eyes moving from the vanquished Avery to Brittany. *Bryce? She knew him!* What had they gotten themselves into?

"He deserves killing, Brittany," Bryce was saying between breaths that showed he'd exerted himself physically, but was hardly winded. "The vermin deserves it for even daring to touch you, let alone—"

"Bryce, he's your *brother*!"

At this Lenore's eyes widened, but her reaction was nothing compared to Avery's. Shock gave way to stunned disbelief, before cold denial registered in the yellow eyes.

"The bitch is crazed," he sneered.

"Shut your slimy mouth!" Bryce threatened, and in a tone so ominous, Avery had the good sense to remain quiet.

Stepping agilely to his feet, Bryce gave Richard a look of disgust and then a prod with his boot. "You have thirty seconds to make yourself decent. There's a lady present, or I'd tell what I'll do to it if you tarry."

Richard blanched, then half-rose and fumbled with the fastenings of his breeches while Bryce stood over him with clenched fists.

On the bed, Brittany finished untying her wrist and wrapped herself in a white silk sheet.

When Richard was finished, he spied a splotch of blood that dripped onto his leg and made a whimpering sound while he used his sleeve to wipe his bleeding nose. Then he looked up, giving Bryce an accusing look.

"I don't know why you're so bloody fierce about this, Tremaine. 'Tis not as if you're a member of her family or anything. And, besides, I was going to wed her, truly I was. She had no call to break with me and—"

"No call?" Bryce questioned menacingly. "No call to break with a man who beats innocent women and brutalizes his people and animals? No call to break with a man who would have wed her only for the dowry she could bring to save the estates he'd squandered away through reckless gambling? And then perhaps for the purpose of abusing her the way his father did his mother?"

"Leave my mother and father out of this!" cried Richard. "The dead should rest in peace."

Bryce started. "What's that you say? Your mother and fa—Surely you meant just your mother."

"Nay," said Richard, "my father, too. He killed himself two days ago. Drowned himself in the river when we learned we were ruined."

Bryce was stunned. He stood there in silence as the news sank in. So Edmund was dead . . . and by his own hand. He wondered why he didn't feel anything more than a strange kind of numbness.

Richard took the reprieve to drive a point home. "Aye, when we were ruined, and 'twas all the fault of that redheaded bitch there. I—"

A growl of outrage cut him off. "*Get up*," Bryce ordered, not waiting for him to comply, but hauling him to his feet by his collar and shirtfront.

"Now," said Bryce, still holding onto his shirtfront with menace, "I'm going to tell you whose fault it really was . . . *brother!*"

And then, as Richard listened in horrified silence, Bryce told him the story of Beth Tremaine and his sire. The words came rushing out, as if he couldn't work fast enough to exorcise the drive for revenge that had been eating him alive all these months and years. As if, having been robbed of the chance to tell it to the sire, he must heap it upon the son—his brother, God help him.

Then, when he had finished, to his enraged disbelief, he saw Richard's blood-caked lips actually begin to curve in a sneering smile.

"Is that all?" Richard questioned, his yellow eyes alight with amusement.

"Damn you!" cried Bryce, his hand reaching into his open shirt for the pistol he'd concealed. He whipped it out and held it on Avery. "I knew I'd have to kill you."

Brittany had seen the look of pain and outrage in Bryce's eyes at Richard's reaction and braced herself for his fury, but at the sight of the pistol, she cried out to him, "Bryce, don't! He isn't worth it! Don't you see he's only trying to goad you?"

But it was as if Bryce hadn't heard her. His thumb cocked the firing pin on the pistol as he leveled it at Avery, who could only shake his head desperately as he saw the hell in the green eyes.

But at that moment, unbeknownst to all three of them, Étienne was stealthily withdrawing the lethal-looking knife he always carried strapped to the inside of his boot. Unaware of what had gone on during the time he was unconscious, he only knew that a stranger had entered the chamber and was threatening madam's latest prospect. It was probably he who had knocked him out, and not Avery, as he'd supposed when first awakening. If he valued his life, he must remove this threat to the girl. With a steady hand, he raised the knife and aimed.

Brittany caught the movement, as well as the gleam of candlelight on metal and screamed: "Bryce!"

Then everything seemed to happen at once. Bryce jerked the pistol toward Étienne, and Richard, seeing his chance, moved toward him to grab it. His hand on Bryce's arm caused the shot to go wild, but no matter; Étienne's knife had already left his hand, sailing through the air to hit, not Bryce, but Richard, whose body interposed. It sank, to the hilt, into Avery's throat. Eyes wide in disbelief, he fell slowly to the ground. He was dead.

Bryce heard the commotion his shot had caused below. Quickly, he thrust the pistol into Avery's hand, then looked at Étienne.

"If you're wise, you'll tell them he threatened you with the pistol, and it was self-defense." He saw Étienne nod, then strode to Brittany on the bed, removing his shirt as he went.

"Are you all right?" he asked worriedly.

Brittany tore her gaze from the corpse on the floor, where they'd been riveted, looked at him and nodded.

"Good lass," Bryce told her, then pulled her from the bed and ushered her toward the open window, wrapping his shirt around her as they moved.

He could hear multiple footsteps thudding up the stairs. "Head them off," he told Étienne. They were unaware of Lenore, standing in the corner in the shadows.

Étienne quickly did as he was bidden, closing the door behind him.

At the same time, Bryce looked down through the window and grinned, seeing Will carrying a huge barrel over to the area beneath them, two floors down.

"I take it we'd better 'urry," grinned Will as he set the barrel in place, then leapt up and stood on top of it.

"You take it right," said Bryce. He picked up Brittany and gently lowered her into Will's waiting arms.

After that, it was less than a minute before he, too, was safely on the ground and they were running for the horses Will had waiting.

A wide-eyed, tearful Tansy threw her arms around Brittany before they mounted. "Lord have mercy, Miz Britt," she cried, "ah thought you'd been took straight to hell this time!"

Brittany hugged her tightly, then glanced at Bryce. "Maybe I was, Tans," she said softly, "maybe I was . . ."

CHAPTER 24

BRYCE ALLOWED THE BIG GRAY FILLY they'd borrowed from Timothy's stable—Brittany's filly, as it turned out—to pick her way slowly over the cobblestones on the way back to the Chambers house. He took care to see that Brittany wasn't jostled as she dozed in front of him on the horse, her head against his shoulder; behind them, on Timothy's big black gelding, Will followed with Tansy.

They'd gone straight from the brothel to the *Lady Beth*. Among other things, Bryce had wanted to be sure they weren't followed before returning Brittany to her father's house. He'd also wanted to give Brittany a chance to calm down after the harrowing experience she'd been subjected to, and he'd figured the *Lady Beth* was the best place to accomplish this.

A smile flitted briefly across his face as he recalled the scene that had occurred when he'd presented her with the third reason he'd chosen to stop at his ship: a change of clothes. He'd taken her to his cabin, then left her there with Tansy, but not before going to the large seachest where he stored his spare clothes and withdrawing a pink silk gown.

"What, pray tell, is that?" she'd asked as he laid it on the bed.

"Why, a gown, of course," he'd answered blandly.

She'd bristled. "Of course 'tis a gown. Any *fool* can see 'tis a gown!" Then, her lovely eyes narrowing to deep blue slits, "But what I should like to know is, *whose* gown?"

He hadn't been able to resist grinning. "Why, 'tis yours . . . now. After all, I do owe you one, don't I?" Then, before she had time to recover from her blush and issue a scathing retort, he'd taken her gently by the shoulders and planted a kiss on the tip of her pert little nose, saying softly, "Truth to tell, sweetheart, I can't even recall her name, so 'tis hardly worth fretting over. Don it, and we'll be off, for I can hardly return you to your father wearing nothing but my shirt, now can I?"

Then he'd left the cabin, but as he closed the door, he heard her snap, "Pink! Have you ever seen a redhead with an ounce of brains in her head wearing *pink*?"

Brittany stirred in his arms, bringing Bryce back to the present. *She must be exhausted*, he thought. *She's been through so much—indeed, through hell, as she'd characterized it to Tansy, earlier.* Damn! If he let himself think about it, he'd wish the Averys alive all over again so he could—but, no—that way lurked disaster, or at least the kind of near-disaster he'd rescued Brittany from tonight. His revenge was behind him now, though he wondered at the tinge of a bad taste he was left with, spoiling the satisfaction he ought to be feeling, now that both Averys were dead. Well, he would put his demons to rest. There was a world of living to be done, something he hadn't taken the time even to think about while the fires of revenge were burning him up inside. But *now*...

He bent to press a kiss on the top of Brittany's head, savoring the faint scent of violets that lingered in her hair; then he let his thoughts settle on the most significant thing that had happened while they were on the *Lady Beth*.

His brain was still spinning from what he'd learned. Making his way from the companionway toward his cabin where he'd left the two women alone so that Brittany might dress, he'd heard their exchange coming through the door, which he'd inadvertently left slightly ajar.

"But, Miz Britt, what are you going to do?" Tansy's voice. "You still don't know yet, do you?"

"I'm not exactly sure, Tans, but 'tis certain I'll have to think of something soon." Brittany's voice had sounded weary ... and troubled.

"Well, ah still think you ought to tell Captain Bryce. After all, he's the father, and—"

"No, Tans! I told you before—this is *my* problem, and I shall handle it—alone."

A sigh issued from Tansy, loud enough to reach Bryce's ears as he stood, frozen, in the passageway beyond the door. "Well, ah hope you don't mean that the way I think you mean it, Miz Britt. You're not the first woman to be carrying a babe without a husband, and ah want you to know ah mean to help all ah can! Will and ah are marrying soon and ..."

Moving noiselessly back toward the companionway, Bryce had left them to finish their discussion alone, his head reeling with the implications of what he'd overheard.

Brittany carried his child! And what was more, judging by their conversation, she'd known about it for some time, yet she hadn't said a word to him—and wasn't planning to, either, apparently. *Why?*

Even now, when he thought about it as he listened to the sounds of their horses' hooves echoing on the cobblestones, Bryce was hard put not to rouse her and shake the answer out of her. *Why?* Why was she so determined to keep this news from him and to go such a difficult route alone?

But, even as he asked it he felt he knew the answer. Brittany was the most stubborn, free-minded woman alive, and she'd go to any lengths to safeguard her precious, hard-won independence.

But, damnit, there were other things to be considered here! And the life of her child—*their* child—was foremost among them. He admired her spirit of independence, truly he did, but did that mean he was to sit blandly by and allow her to bring another bastard into the world?

His mind flitted back to the day when he'd turned five and William and Olivia had sat him down to explain the meaning of the word *bastard*. A disgruntled crofter's wife had hurled it at him when he had accidentally splattered her wash with mud while galloping his new pony too close by. Perhaps she'd guessed at his true parentage, William had surmised, as several in the village had when they'd seen the green eyes of the lord's adopted son—green eyes that were exactly like Beth Tremaine's.

And no matter that William and Olivia's explanation, along with the story of his birth which accompanied it, had been unstintingly kind; he still recalled, with the vivid clarity of remembered childhood pain, the anguish he'd felt as he heard the truth for the first time. A bastard—he'd been born an unwanted bastard!

Of course, time and the healing power of William

and Olivia's love had soothed the wound, but that was beside the point. Did he want a child of his subjected to the same kinds of taunts and hurts? Then, as he turned the filly's head toward William Street, Bryce suddenly knew what he intended to do.

As she felt the filly make the turn, Brittany awoke from the catnap she'd been taking and opened her eyes long enough to recognize where they were. Soon they'd be reaching the big brick house up the street; pray God they'd be able to enter unobserved. She could well imagine the scene and all the explaining they'd have to do if they didn't! And she was weary . . . bone-weary, not only from the emotional exhaustion of the night's events, but also, she suspected, because of the burden she carried.

A sweet burden, she thought, savoring the idea of the child, the wee babe nestled deep inside her, that she already loved beyond telling.

Thoughts of her condition brought into focus the reality of her problem once again. Tansy was becoming more and more vocal about her feeling that Bryce should be told, but Brittany was adamant in her decision to keep him out of it.

If anything, the unsettling discovery that he'd carried a woman's gown aboard ship with him drove the point home. Surreptitiously glancing down at the pink silk, she grimaced and quickly shut her eyes.

But in her mind's eye, she pictured a blonde wearing it . . . or perhaps a brunette . . . aye, that was it, a dark-haired beauty who'd been invited to come to him while his ship was in port, or perhaps who'd travelled with him when—

Enough! her mind cried out as her eyes snapped open with a look of chagrin. Merciful heaven, why did she torture herself with these thoughts? It was enough to be reminded that Bryce Tremaine Avery was a handsome bachelor with mistresses aplenty, most likely, and she just the latest among them. He'd enjoyed her body (as, indeed, she'd enjoyed his, she had to admit) but he'd never declared a single word of love amid the enjoyment, and she'd be damned if she'd surrender herself in marriage to a man who cared no more for her than—than a woman in a pink gown whose name he couldn't even recall!

And that was supposing he'd even offer for her if he knew. After all, he was a nobleman, due to inherit a peerage someday, while she was a mere colonial tradesman's daughter. But the last thing he was going to do was find out, because if the knowledge that she was with child should prompt him to offer marriage, she'd know it was only to give his child a name, and that she couldn't bear. Wed him because he felt obligated? *She'd rather die!*

Settling this once and for all in her mind, she turned her thoughts toward the future. As she'd told Tansy, she'd have to come up with some kind of plan—and soon. A lot depended on how much money she could expect to see from what remained after the twins resold the very expensive tobacco they'd used to lure the Averys; she certainly couldn't—*wouldn't*—go to her father and Althea for a way out of her dilemma, oh no. They'd marry her off to the very next suitor who ambled down the lane!

No, she'd have to secure some funds and leave . . . but for where? Some distant town or city where she could settle in, pretending to be a widow, she supposed, but . . .

Oh, she was so tired, she wasn't really thinking clearly right now . . . tomorrow, aye, in the morning, after she'd had some sleep . . . for now, it was all just too much to contemplate . . .

Closing her eyes, Brittany began to doze again.

At the same moment, Bryce swore softly, under his breath. They were passing the Horse's Head right now, and up ahead, through the trees lining the lane, he could see the Chambers home. It was ablaze with lights.

"Looks like we're in fer it now," grumbled Will behind him. "'Pears the 'ole 'ouse-'old's up, and at nigh three in the morn, I don't fancy they're 'avin' tea!"

Bryce added another oath to the string he'd sworn, and reined in, signaling for Will to do the same. Running toward them was a man they recognized as Ned, the groom in charge of Timothy's stable.

"'Ere, now, chaps," called Ned, "whut d' ye mean by—oh, 'tis you, Cap'n Tremaine!" Then he caught sight of Brittany. "Mistress Brittany! Cap'n, is she—is aught amiss with the young—"

"Nay, Ned," said Bryce, "all's well, thanks to the use of these two fine horses you've kept so fit, for we got there in time. Sorry we didn't alert you when we borrowed them, though. We—"

"Oh, that don't matter none now, Cap'n," Ned told him with a shy grin that indicated his pride in the compliment paid him. "So long as the young mistress is safe, we can all rest easy, sir, but it did give us quite a turn, findin' 'er and the 'orses missin' and all." He glanced back at the house. "Ah, 'er pa be awful worried, though. Mayhap I—"

"We'll take care of it, Ned," Bryce told him as he signaled the filly to move toward the house. Then he checked her movement for a moment as he glanced back at the groom. "Oh, and Ned?"

"Aye, sir?"

"I'm sure her father would be grateful if news of this were to be kept—"

"Oh, ye can count on me, Cap'n! I ain't seen nothin' this night, no sir, nothin' at all!"

"Good man," Bryce told him, then moved toward the house.

Will and Tansy dismounted first while Bryce gently awakened Brittany. He had just finished helping her down and was dismounting himself when the front door flew open and Althea ran out.

"Young woman, where have you been? We've been sick with worry! Your father—why, Captain Tremaine, we certainly didn't expect—"

"Althea, what is it?" Timothy's voice cut in as he appeared behind her in the doorway. "Have they found Brittany? Is she—"

"She's safe and well, sir," Bryce told him as he handed the filly's reins to Ned. He looked down at Brittany, who hadn't uttered a word and was looking as if she'd rather be anywhere but there at the moment. "She's a bit tired, but otherwise unharmed. May we go inside?"

"Ah, of course," Timothy answered, looking somewhat bemused. What was going on here? First, Ned had come to awaken them, saying two of the horses had been stolen, one of them Gray Mist, Brittany's filly, the other, Black Dan, his own mount. And since his headstrong daughter had occasionally been known to sneak out at night for a riding spree in the fields behind the town when she was younger, they'd checked her chamber and found she was missing. They would have put two and two together, assuming she was on another one of her escapades, except that with such an assessment they couldn't account for Black Dan's disappearance. And now, after an hour of pacing the floor, and just as he'd been wondering if he should send men out looking for her, here was Brittany, and in the company of Tremaine and his man, not to mention the little abigail they'd assumed to be asleep in her own chamber! Well, there'd be some hard questions asked tonight, he decided as he ushered them into the house where, among the staff, only Preston was awake, thank the Almighty! Preston, at least, could be trusted to keep his mouth shut!

He led them into the drawing room, indicating they should all sit while the butler went for tea.

"Ah, sir," said Bryce, still standing, with his arm about Brittany's shoulders, "perhaps you ought to send for something stronger." He looked at the older man meaningfully. "I have a feeling you're going to need it."

Timothy blinked, then nodded in Preston's direction before nervously adjusting the belt on the long dressing gown he wore and taking his seat, gesturing for Bryce and Brittany to do the same.

Brittany was dead tired, but she took one look at Althea in her wrapper, pinch-faced and rigid on the settee where Bryce would have seated her, and decided to remain standing. She glanced up at Bryce and gave him a slight negative shake of the head.

Having followed her glance, Bryce nodded and remained where he was, his arm sliding unobtrusively down Brittany's back and about her waist, ready to give the support he felt she might need. She looked extremely tired and, given her condition, he would have preferred sending her upstairs to her bed, but one glance at his hosts told him they expected her presence during the explanations that were forthcoming, and he dared not suggest otherwise.

Seeing no help for it, he plunged in. "Sir, madam, let me begin by telling you that my full name is not

Bryce Tremaine, and that I am not merely a ship's captain."

He watched Timothy and Althea glance at each other with a conspiratorial look of smugness.

"Indeed, I must now admit to you," he continued, "that I have been visiting these colonies under false pretenses. I am actually the adopted son and heir of the marquis of Clarendon, and my full name is Bryce Tremaine Avery."

There was another mutual look of smug satisfaction before Timothy started and shifted his glance to Bryce. "Eh? What's that? Avery, you say? But wasn't that the name of Brittany's fi—"

"Exactly," said Bryce. "Now, if you'll permit me to explain from the beginning . . ."

He went on to tell them, then, beginning with the circumstances preceding his birth, of the long, involved story of his revenge, leaving out only those details that were not pertinent to the moment in which Brittany decided to enlist her cousins' aid and intervene, "bent on helping me, out of her own altruism" (here he received a surreptitious poke in the ribs from Brittany and saw the corners of her mouth twitch) "and her desire to spare us all unnecessary violence."

At this point, Timothy's eyes fell on his daughter with a mixture of awe and incredulity, and he reached swiftly for the snifter of brandy Preston held on a tray before him, downing it in one gulp.

Althea was more vocal. "I knew it!" she crowed. "You never intended to wed that Avery person from the beginning! 'Twas all a ruse to aid you in some more of your usual high jinks!"

"Nay, madam," said Bryce, "for if you'll listen further, I think you'll find nothing 'usual' about it—or about what's happened since . . ."

He finished the story, then, relating what had happened after Brittany broke with Avery and they returned to Fredericksburg, ending with the hair-raising tale (though he took pains to make it as bland as possible) of what had occurred that evening. When he came to the part about the house on Sophia Street, it was Althea who bolted down a brandy, and at his recapitulation of Avery's death and their narrow escape, Timothy reached for his second.

"So you see, sir, madam," said Bryce, "your daughter has been through a great deal, but she has come out of it essentially unharmed." He glanced at Will and Tansy, who were both nodding their heads emphatically at this statement, but a shriek from the settee brought everyone's focus on Althea.

"*Unharmed!* Unharmed, you say? Our daughter involves herself in the most outlandish, dangerous scheme I've ever heard of, gets herself kidnapped in the bargain and taken to a—to a"—she couldn't say it—"and you say she is *unharmed*? What about her reputation? Her good name? Oh, if word gets out about any of this, I'll perish! The entire family will be ruined! Oh, Melody, my poor Melody—what hope will there be for her then?"

"Now, now, my dear," soothed Timothy, patting her on the shoulder, "it may not come t' all that. After all, the captain did say he took pains t' see they were unobserved and not followed when they left— when they left—" He couldn't say it, either.

He turned to Bryce. "But, see here, sir, ah, yer lordship, the lass has been through a great deal that is, ah, shall we say, highly improper, when ye consider her upbringin'. I mean, sir, 'tis not right, what ye've involved her in, and"—his glance shifted to his daughter—"and although I can quickly guess as how she may have had more t' do with this than ye're lettin' on, still, ye're a man, mature and fully responsible. Ye ought not t' have let her—"

"Sir," Bryce interrupted, taking a step toward him and raising a placating hand, "I agree that all you say is true, but if you'll hear me out, I believe I may be able to set this all to rights with what I have in mind."

Timothy looked at him with a mixture of hope and skepticism. "Aye, sir—ah, yer lordship, and what would that be?"

"Indeed," Althea echoed, "what could it possibly be?"

Bryce glanced briefly at her, then at Timothy. "I should like to request the honor of having the hand of your daughter Brittany in marriage."

There was a chorus of surprised exclamations from everyone in the room—except Brittany.

Brittany fainted.

CHAPTER 25

Brittany finished emptying the contents of her stomach into the chamber pot, closed the lid with a shudder, and pressed to her lips a dampened square of linen. She didn't know why she bothered with breakfast anyway these days. Even the weak tea and dry biscuit Tansy had brought her didn't stay down.

Snapping a leaf off the sprig of mint that lay on her breakfast tray, she nibbled at it gingerly, anxious to dispel the horrid taste that lingered in her mouth. As she nibbled, she began to pace with short, angry strides. Now that her nausea was taken care of, her thoughts revolved around the events of last night and this morning.

How *could* she have fainted? Of all the asinine, ill-timed things she'd ever done, that was the worst! She'd never fainted before in her life!

But the worst part of it was that, coming when it had, her fainting had caused her to be carried up to her chamber and put straight to bed—by Will, she'd learned from Tansy this morning—leaving Bryce to remain below to answer her father's questions, prevaricating to Timothy (a willing dupe) until the two of them had her wrapped up in a neat little parcel, ready to be signed, sealed, and delivered—to the marriage altar.

"Ye've discussed this with the lass?" Timothy had asked Bryce. (Tansy had even mimicked their speech patterns correctly.)

"Aye, sir."

"And—and *she's agreed*?"

"She has." *Oh, the duplicity!*

A whoop of joy had issued from her father then, and in the next moment he'd ordered champagne to be brought up from the cellar by Preston and they'd all toasted the betrothal, even Will and Tansy, who, when she learned the facts from her friend this morning, had apologized profusely:

"Ah'm plumb sorry, honeychile. Ah thought you reconsidered your options and told him about the babe when the two of you were riding on that gray horse together and that he asked you to wed him then. After all, he made it sound so convincing."

"I'll just *bet* he did!" Brittany had fumed. "And of course Father needed no convincing. He just jumped at the chance to see me led down the aisle at long last!"

"But, Miz Britt," Tansy had told her as she was about to leave for the ship to join Will in arranging her own wedding, "might be this is for the best. After all, you didn't know what to do about the babe, and now ... well, it's been decided for you. Think of it as Providence, honeychile. The good Lord working in one of His mysterious ways."

"Hmph!" muttered Brittany now, kicking at one of her discarded slippers, which got in the way of her pacing. "It's been decided for me all right, but there's nothing mysterious or providential about how it came about!"

Her mind flicked back to those pre-dawn moments when, after the others had at last gone to their beds, Bryce had stolen into her room. Exhausted as she was, some unconscious sense must have told her he was there, for she'd awakened suddenly from her deep sleep to find him at her side, hovering over her in the moonlight, his arms braced on either side of her on the mattress as he looked down at her with concerned eyes.

"Bryce . . . ?" she'd questioned, unsure of whether he was real or a figure of her dreams.

"Aye, sweetheart," he'd murmured, and when he kissed her tenderly on the forehead, she'd known the warmth of his lips was real and this was no dream. Still she made no response, her semi-awakened state making her strangely passive when she ought to have been asking him about the marriage proposal he'd put to her father before she'd fainted.

Perhaps Bryce had felt he had to say something to her by way of explanation, for his next words touched on it: "You need someone to take care of you, hellion," he said, a strange, tender smile playing about his lips.

"Take care of me . . ." she'd echoed drowsily.

"Aye." His green eyes grew deep with concern as they held hers. "How are you feeling, little one?" he'd questioned.

And then Brittany had known—known that *he knew*. Somehow, somewhere, he'd discovered the truth of the secret she'd taken such pains to keep from him. He knew she was carrying his child!

Fighting the panic that rose in her chest, she'd sought to remain calm, for she was determined not to let him see that she realized he knew. Hoping it would pass for a weary plea, she'd murmured, "Feel fine ... sleepy ..." and closed her eyes.

There was a brief silence in the darkness before she'd felt the mattress sink deeper on either side of her as he leaned down and softly touched each eyelid with his lips.

"Sleep well, little one," he'd whispered, "You'll need your strength when we have it out tomorrow." And he'd quietly left the chamber.

"Aye, Bryce Tremaine Avery," Brittany fumed now, her pacing growing ever more agitated, "you might well have expected to have it out today—now that my first shock is behind me and my brain no longer befuddled by sleep!"

But when she'd uttered this imagined retort to her "betrothed," Brittany stopped her pacing and stood still, suddenly realizing the words would never be said. No, not today or any day, for it suddenly became clear to her what she must do. And with this realization came a sadness such as she'd never felt— a heavy, dark, oppressive thing that welled up from the heart of her, filling her breast and weighing down her limbs until she felt as if she could neither move nor breathe.

With an enormous effort, she moved toward the high tester bed, climbed the three-stepped stool beside it, and flung herself across the rumpled coverlet. And then came the great, wrenching sobs that shook her slender frame while hot tears assailed her eyes, pouring out the pain that came with her decision: She must never see Bryce again.

It was dark when she left the house, a light cloak covering the thin muslin walking gown she wore as she let herself out through the servants' entrance near the summer kitchen. Reaching the cool green garden, she breathed a sigh of relief at the ease with which she'd escaped undetected.

They were all at supper now, the servants busy with attending the meal, the diners no doubt discussing the contrary young woman they still believed to be upstairs in her chamber, refusing to come out. She'd played the game all day, steadfastly declining their entreaties to unlock the door, insisting she needed time alone to think about all that had happened.

Her father had been puzzled by her behavior but had finally accepted it for what she let him think it was: the nervousness of a young woman newly betrothed and frightened by the implications of the vast step she was taking.

Althea had been more suspicious, carping at her through the closed door that she had better not be having second thoughts, for the wedding *would* take place, whether she'd gotten cold feet or not; Bryce had invited the entire family to his home in England following the wedding, and though Timothy wouldn't be able to get away, Althea had accepted on behalf of herself and Melody "and you are *not* going to ruin Melody's chances to meet the kind of young men Lord Bryce can introduce her to, d' ye hear, Brittany? You are not going to spoil your sister's chances again!"

The only other person who'd spoken to her from beyond the door had been Bryce, for Tansy and Will, she'd learned, were elsewhere in Fredericksburg, deep in the throes of arranging their own marriage.

"You'll have to come out sometime, sweet," Bryce had called to her, and she'd heard the amusement in his voice. "But take your time, m'love," he'd added, "for now that I know you'll soon be mine in every way, I find I have all the patience in the world."

She purposely hadn't answered him, but before he left she heard him chuckle and add, "Get plenty of rest, Brittany, for I promise, you're soon going to need *all* your energy . . . in our marriage bed!"

As she stood in the garden now, the muted sounds of the sultry August night throbbing around her, Brittany swallowed the sob that threatened her resolve. She adjusted the hood of her cloak, realizing, as she felt the first trickle of perspiration run down her neck, that it was far too warm for such a garment. But she knew she had to wear it: they'd be searching for her when her absence was discovered (*Please, let it not be soon!* she prayed) and her red hair would be a readily identifiable clue when they questioned anyone who might have seen her.

Her plan was to make her way toward the docks on foot, pretending to be a ladies' maid who'd been sent on an errand for a mistress in the city. She thought regretfully of the sleek gray filly standing in the stable not twenty yards away, knowing she dared not ride her; Ned would probably be doubly alert now, with last night's equine abduction fresh in his mind, and she couldn't risk being seen by him.

She fingered the heavy chamois bag she'd stashed deep in the pocket of the serving apron she'd taken from a hook in the pantry and donned to make her disguise more plausible. It contained all of the jewels she'd inherited from what was left of her mother's estate, and while the thought of parting with any of them was deeply distressing, she knew she must; they were her passport to the future she'd carefully carved out for herself and her unborn child during the long hours in her chamber today.

Last night, as they'd left Bryce's ship, she'd seen a vessel in port that was familiar to her. It was the *Virginia Belle*, a schooner whose captain, a man named Tyler, was known for somewhat unorthodox dealings—"a self-styled soldier of fortune," Timothy had once called him, grumbling that the man dealt in everything from contraband to runaway slaves, if the price was right.

Well, thought Brittany as she slipped noiselessly among the shadows beside the house, feeling the weight of her mother's jewels against her thigh as she moved, *the price will be more than right, Captain Tyler, and you will have a new passenger tonight!*

It was nearly two hours later when Brittany, footsore and taut with nerves that were ready to snap from the tension of moving through the streets without calling attention to herself, arrived at the old stone warehouse on Sophia Street. Diagonally across from her, resting quietly at its mooring, was the *Virginia Belle*. She leaned against the stone facade of the warehouse and concentrated on calming her nerves as she planned her next move.

All was still aboard the ship and, indeed, about the docks themselves, the loudest sound being the gentle lapping of the river against the hulls of the dozen or so vessels in port. She knew that, if she wished, she could make out the familiar outline of the *Louise* far to her right, down by Frederick Street or, just a hundred yards or so to her left, the dark silhouette of the *Lady Beth*, but she carefully kept her eyes averted from these familiar sights. Her past had to be put behind her now; ahead was the future — and the new life she would make for herself and the child.

She was just trying to decide how to go about making her presence known to the sailor she could now see standing on watch on the deck of the *Virginia Belle* when her ears caught the sound of male laughter echoing on the river. It was hard to tell where it was coming from because of the way sound traveled on the water, but its source seemed to be directly across from her, on a vessel docked next to the *Virginia Belle*.

Pressing herself against the warehouse wall, she remained perfectly still, hoping she blended adequately with the shadows as she listened. There it was again, more laughter, and this time it was joined by a second outpouring of mirth while, at the same moment, a lantern began to glow on the top deck of the unknown ship.

Brittany swallowed hard, sure her senses were playing tricks on her. The laughter—it sounded *familiar*! Then, as she gazed at the deck of the strange vessel with disbelieving eyes, she caught sight of two figures beneath the glow of the lantern, even as she heard their laughter peal out again across the water. They were of equal height and stature, and they each bore an unmistakable head of *bright red hair*!

"Toby," roared a beloved voice filled with laughter, "if you don't stop, I shall wake the dead with my mirth! But you cannot mean he actually fished it out of the broth and held it aloft by its tail?"

"Oh, aye," laughed his twin as the two of them made their way down the plank, "and the innkeeper merely fixed him with a sober eye before telling him 'twould cost him tuppence more—*for having extra meat in his soup!*"

There was a double roar of laughter from the pair of them then; they had reached the street and were half doubled up with it, Tony wiping at his eyes with a square of embroidered linen, Toby holding his sides as he repeated the last part of the humorous anecdote his brother had told him and exploded with another outburst of laughter: "Meat in his soup! Aha—aha—ho—ho! Oh, I say! 'Twas—'twas—aha —ha!"

"—famous, brother! 'Twas truly famous!" echoed Tony, his laughter matching his twin's.

Brittany stood watching them for several seconds, all her carefully laid plans falling like a house of cards. She had no idea what they were doing on a strange ship in Fredericksburg, but every instinct told her to step out of the shadows and go to them. Toby and Tony had always stood by her and kept her secrets, and she wondered if she dared take the chance that they could be trusted to do so now. Their dear faces and wonderful laughter suddenly made her realize how awful it would be to leave everyone and all that was familiar and beloved behind, never to be seen again, and so, after another moment's hesitation, she left the protective shadows of the warehouse and stepped into the street.

"Gentlemen!" she called, lowering the hood of her cloak. "Guess who!"

"Damn me, I still don't believe it!" said Tony as he sat facing Brittany across the table in the well-appointed cabin of the ship he and his brother owned. "I cannot actually credit your being here!"

"Oh, come now," Brittany replied as she sipped the sherry Toby had just handed her, "you really shouldn't be surprised. After all," she added with an attempt at a careless smile, "it isn't as if, ah, unorthodox escapades on my part are anything new to you."

"Oh, coz," said Tony, "'tis not that which dumbfounds me. 'Tis—'tis—"

"—'tis the nature of it," supplied his twin as he took a seat beside Tony. "You see," he added with a tender smile as he took her hand across the table, "while we are quite inured to your escapades, we've never seen you in one where you were . . . giving up . . . running away."

"Aye, running away," echoed Tony, "instead of standing your ground and fighting the matter out. 'Tis unlike you, Britt."

Brittany heard the disappointment in the voices but noticed also that while their words were accusing, their eyes were filled with gentle concern and a need to understand.

After their initial shock and surprise at meeting her in such an unsavory place as the docks at night, they'd greeted her joyfully and escorted her onto this ship, the *Briar Rose*, one of several, they'd informed her, which they employed to take advantage of the commercial opportunities growing out of Sweetbriar's expanding profits. And as they'd sequestered themselves with her here in this cabin reserved for their own use, she'd told them only as much as she'd figured she had to: that she was running away to avoid a loveless marriage to Bryce Tremaine Avery.

Of course, they'd caught her on that.

"Loveless?" Toby had questioned shrewdly.

"As in 'neither given *nor* returned?'" Tony had followed up, as both pairs of identical gray eyes pierced hers, reminding her of the times in their childhood when the two young imps would be satisfied with nothing less than total candor from her, and she from them.

"No," she'd murmured then, her eyes lowering as she added brokenly, "loveless on his part, but—but quite the reverse on mine."

Tony's eyes had been filled with sympathy when

she raised hers to look at him then, but Toby's response had been more vehement.

"The bloody sod! He's always been of the first water in my book, but now I'm inclined to think Bryce is a damned fool if he doesn't return your affection."

"Aye, a damned fool," Tony had seconded, "but tell us, if the man doesn't love you, how did he come to propose marriage?"

She'd gone on to tell them, then, of the terrible events of the night preceding the engagement, beginning with her abduction by Richard Avery and ending with her rescue and return home following Avery's death. The twins had listened with growing horror and outrage at Avery's ruthless behavior, jointly coming forward and wrapping their arms about her in a compassionate hug when she finished the tale.

And it was her memory of their compassion, as well as the recollection of the candor they'd always shared, that prompted her to answer the querying looks in their faces now.

"Very well, you two," she said softly, "I should have known I couldn't keep anything back from you." She met their eyes squarely and took a deep breath before plunging ahead. "The reason I'm not acting entirely myself—and running away, as you put it—is that I no longer have only myself to worry about. I am with child."

There was a joint exclamation that hovered somewhere between sympathy and dismay as both men reached out for the white-knuckled hand she clenched on the table and covered it with their own.

Brittany gave them each a shaky smile and rushed on, eager to tell them everything now. "I haven't told Bryce, but I have reason to suspect he knows, and I feel sure that that is the sole reason he's offered for me."

She gave a brittle little laugh. "I cannot even be sure 'tis my honor he's concerned with, I'm afraid. Having been born a bastard himself, he may merely be determined to see that his own child does not suffer the same fate. At any rate, there certainly haven't been any declarations of love on his part."

There was silence in the cabin, punctuated only by the creaking of timber far above their heads and the sound of a dog barking in the distance. Both twins looked at her, their faces a double study in compassion, as they waited, knowing there was more.

"The two of you are aware of the reasons I've avoided marrying. My wish for a modicum of freedom and the hope of having some control over my own life are nothing new to you. But, and I tell you this truly, those reasons have little to do with my current plans. If—" She felt her eyes fill with tears, her lips tremble, but made herself continue. "—If Bryce were to l-love me, I would glady surrender all that brave hope for independence and . . . and wed him. But the fact is, dear cousins, that he does not, and so I must leave and make a new life for myself and the babe. You see," she said tremulously, "the one thing I find I cannot surrender is *myself* . . . to a man who cannot give *himself* in return."

They watched her dash her tears away with an impatient hand and look at them, her expression determined.

"Will you help me?" she asked in a steady voice.

Toby glanced at Tony, Tony at him; then both looked back at their cousin. "Aye," came the dual response.

CHAPTER 26

NO ONE NOTICED THE TALL, CLOAKED man who made his way among the fine carriages and handsome mounts waiting in the courtyard in front of the house on Sophia Street. He kept to the shadows, avoiding the various grooms and drivers who stood about seeing to their masters' vehicles while the masters pleasured themselves within the brightly lit mansion. Gaining at last the privacy of the bricked walkway that led to the back of the building, he quickened his pace and headed for the rear entrance, which was reserved for certain select patrons who didn't wish to be seen coming and going from Lenore Maddox's establishment.

"Sir?" queried the footman who opened the door upon hearing the signal known to a privileged few: two quick raps and a pause, followed by three more raps.

"Show me to the blue room and summon your mistress," said an authoritative voice emanating from between the turned-up collar and severely lowered tricorn of the man at the door.

The footman opened his mouth to question the identity of the caller but then thought better of it. There was something forbidding about the man, something that warned he would not tolerate being questioned in such a manner, and even though the rules of the house demanded that a patron using this entrance make himself known, if only by a pseudonym, the footman wisely held his tongue. After all, the stranger's words and manner had indicated well enough that he'd been there before, hadn't they?

Moreover, there was something else about the cloaked figure that didn't invite too close an examination, something... *sinister*...

Feeling the hairs rise on the back of his neck, the footman nodded with sudden alacrity. "Right this way, sir. If you'll follow me..."

Standing at the top of the staircase, Lenore Maddox looked over the well-groomed heads of the men and women in her drawing room, heard the soft murmur of polite conversation which swirled and eddied about the elegant chamber, and congratulated herself. Despite all of her fears, the incident of last night had had no nasty repercussions. Here she was, less than twenty-four hours after Richard Avery had met his death in that upstairs chamber, carrying on with business as usual.

Of course, in the minutes immediately following that unfortunate incident, she had not been sure she would even have a business in the future. She could still remember with absolute clarity the icy feeling that had crept through her bones as she'd gazed in shock at Avery's still form with the blood spurting from his neck, while outside in the hallway, a mixture of male and female voices clamored for entrance—and explanations.

But Étienne—ah, dear, valuable Étienne! (She must remember to give him a reward)—had saved the day. Spying in the crowd the local magistrate, Sir Geoffrey Carstairs, he'd recalled that Avery owed Sir Geoffrey a good sum of money, the result of gambling losses suffered here, in this very house, a few months back. So Étienne had pulled the magistrate aside and quickly constructed a story which was sure to enlist his sympathy: Avery had arrived earlier in the evening and demanded access to the tables but had been refused by Madame, who told him she could not allow him to play further until he settled his current debts, both to the house and to those patrons to whom he'd incurred obligations while gaming here, whereupon Avery became enraged and threatened Madame with a pistol; alas, Étienne had had to act quickly; armed with only his humble knife, he'd saved Madame's life—and perhaps that of anyone else on the premises to whom the crazed Avery owed money.

The effect had been immediate. Ordering the crowd to disperse in his authoritative voice, Sir Geoffrey had entered the chamber with Étienne and verified the "facts." By then Lenore had stepped forth from the shadows, still somewhat in shock, but alert enough to catch Étienne's gesture to remain silent while he handled this.

The most surprising thing to her, now that she thought about it, was that Étienne had even been aware she was in the room. After all, he'd been knocked unconscious when she arrived, and she'd been hidden in the dim recesses of the room during all the horror.

Ah, but Étienne had always been a discerning fellow, and he *had* known—and had seized upon the added sympathy generated by a tale that featured

Avery threatening a woman, rather than Étienne himself. It had been brilliant! (She really must remember that reward . . . hmm, what should it be? His freedom? She knew he would like that . . . but then he'd be free to leave her at will, and he was far too valuable to lose. . . . Hmm, perhaps a gold snuffbox like the one owned by Lord Sotheby . . .)

Just as she was mulling this over in her mind, the object of Lenore's thoughts signaled her from the base of the stairs.

"What is it, Étienne?" she asked as she reached the bottom step.

"Stokes informs me we have a visitor in the blue room, Madame. He wishes to see you."

"Who is it?"

"He wouldn't give his name—or Stokes was afraid to ask. I—"

"*Afraid to ask?*" Lenore was outraged, but kept her voice low as she headed for the rear of the house, Étienne at her side. "The *idea*! He knows the rules. And why—"

"I am not sure, Madame, but I can tell you this," murmured Étienne as he touched her sleeve to halt her progress.

Lenore paused, looking at him expectantly.

"I have never seen Stokes looking quite so upset before. He's normally unflappable, as footmen go, but just now he was acting . . . almost fearful. And Stokes says the caller has been here before. He knew the knock and to ask for the blue room. But why wouldn't a regular leave a name? All of our most discreet regulars have their aliases and—"

"Wait here," said Lenore abruptly. She started to move but again felt Étienne's restraining touch on her sleeve.

"Do you think it wise to go alone, Madame? After all, the man—"

"Your concern touches me, Étienne," she said, giving him one of her rare smiles that was not merely a simulation of warmth. (*Yes, a gold snuffbox it will be,* she thought. *He's earned it!*) "But I fear I need you to oversee things in here. I daresay we're busier tonight than we've ever been." She lowered her voice conspiratorially. "Perhaps a bit of notoriety is good for business."

Lenore started again for the blue room, then paused one more time, meeting Étienne's eyes. "Put a footman outside the door of the blue room. If he hears anything untoward, he is to fetch you at once."

Étienne nodded and watched her glide away from him, the swaying movements of the paniers beneath her skirts the only indication that she was moving more quickly than usual.

A few moments later, Lenore entered the lavish sitting room that was decorated in varying shades of blue, from the deep blue velvet draperies covering the windows to the predominantly blue Turkey carpet underfoot. Standing with his back to her at an elegant fireplace that was faced with fine Carrara marble, was a tall, cloaked figure wearing a tricorn over a white powdered wig. The man turned as he heard her enter.

Lenore could note nothing familiar about his appearance, for his tricorn was pulled low over his face and the turned-up collar of the cloak hid the rest of his features. "Sir . . . ?" she questioned.

"Sit down, Lenore," said the tall figure, "but before you do, make sure that door is shut behind you."

Lenore froze. That voice!—*she knew that voice*. But it couldn't be! He was—

"I said *shut it*!" came the chilling command.

Lenore found herself trembling, but she quickly turned to obey, then whirled to face him again. Disbelieving, yet fascinated, she watched as tricorn and cloak were cast aside and Edmund Avery stared back at her, his pale blue reptilian eyes as cold as she'd ever seen them.

"No, m'dear, I am not a ghost," he said with a smile that never reached his eyes.

"*Edmund*," she breathed, "we thought you were—"

"Exactly," he snapped, gesturing for her to sit. "'Twas just what everyone was supposed to think, a tale concocted by me to provide a cover, so that I might work my revenge."

"R-revenge," stammered Lenore, her thoughts flying to Richard Avery and the untimely death he'd met here last night. Surely Edmund couldn't mean—"

"Disabuse yourself of any notion that 'twas fashioned for your benefit, dear Lenore," Edmund told her in that tone of voice that made her blood freeze. "Richard was yet quite alive when 'twas hatched."

She watched him move toward a small sideboard containing a silver tray bearing a brandy decanter and several glasses. Licking her lips in a nervous gesture as she watched him pour brandy into two of the glasses, she tried to force some calm into her thoughts. She was by no means mollified by his assurance that his faked suicide was not for her benefit, for he'd also let her know he was aware of his son's death, and she had good reason to fear his placement of blame. Why else would he be here? Trying not to panic, she wondered if she could in some way alert the footman Étienne had placed outside the door by now. Oh, she would give anything for Étienne's presence right now, even his freedom!

Edmund walked to the settee where she sat and handed her a brandy, then lowered himself into a chair opposite her. He took a sip of the golden brown liquor, then stared pensively at the glass as he began to speak.

"My son knew of the suicide hoax. 'Twas he who pretended to find my hat floating on the river and who gave out to the authorities that I'd drowned myself, being distraught over irreversible financial losses and my wife's recent death. The reason for this was to enable the two of us to split up, each seeking—I, covertly, Richard a bit more openly—retribution from those who were responsible for our financial losses."

"Brittany Chambers and her friends," Lenore whispered involuntarily.

Edmund's head jerked up, his eyes narrowed into pale blue slivers. "How did you know that?"

"Why, I—" Licking lips which had gone totally dry beneath their paint, Lenore felt herself hypnotized by the reptilian stare. She forced herself to look away, and raised the glass of brandy to her mouth, taking a large swallow. Then, helpless under Edmund's relentless stare, she proceeded to answer his question. She told him everything that had happened the evening before, including the unbelievable tale that the Englishman Tremaine had related to Richard. She was about to relate, with particular care, the part about Richard's death at the hands of Étienne being an accident, when Edmund interrupted.

"William's adopted 'foundling' . . . I can hardly believe it! All these years I've been sitting here thinking

the brat I'd heard about was some orphan, taken in
to spite me, when all along my brother was harbor-
ing a viper under his roof—a viper sent to hunt me
down—and for what? The 'honor' of some sniveling
peasant slut I supposedly wronged! It tries my reason!"

Somewhat relieved to see his anger directed elsewhere, Lenore felt emboldened to ask, "If—if you
were unaware of this Tremaine's purposes, then you
were only after the girl?"

"Aye," he nodded, "the Chambers bitch—and her
dandified cousins, the Wakefields!"

"The Wakefields? You don't mean Tony and—"

"They are exactly whom I mean! They contrived
with her to deliberately ruin us, I'm sure of it, only,
until now I wasn't exactly sure why." His glance
moved from the glass he held to Lenore. "You say
the girl and Tremaine were thick?"

Lenore nodded. "Perhaps even lovers, now that I
think on 'it. There was a ... certain familiarity between them that a woman of my particular background comes to recognize."

"That's it, then," said Edmund, nodding his head.
"She and my bastard were lovers and schemed the
whole thing, enlisting those redheaded fops in the
bargain. Hmm ... 'twould seem I have my work cut
out for me."

Lenore took another swallow of brandy. She still
wasn't completely assured of being free of Edmund's
wrath, but she had to know. "Wh-what will you do
now?"

Edmund smiled that blood-chilling smile she'd
come to dread. "Well, that all depends, m'dear. Finish the work I began when I followed those dandies
upriver, of course, and then take care of the others."
The smile became an ominous grin. "'Twill actually

serve a double purpose, that, for with the adopted heir out of the way, William's lands and titles will again fall to me."

Lenore watched him sit back in his chair as if savoring the prospect, then nearly jumped as his gaze suddenly fell on her again.

"But," he said as his face hardened, "there's still the matter of the loss of my son. You know, Lenore, 'tis all well and good that I shall get my rightful inheritance back, but what, beyond that, is good about it when I have no son to leave it to?"

"'Twas an *accident*, Ed—your lordship—I swear it! I was about to tell you of it before, but—"

"An accident?" said Edmund silkily. "A man loses his only son and the woman responsible for it tells him—"

"'Twas not *I* who was responsible!" Lenore nearly shouted in her rising panic. "He—he came in the way of a knife meant for your bastard. I swear it! Here," she added, jumping up from the settee, "I'll summon Étienne and you can ask him. He was there. He—"

"Sit down, Lenore."

She took one longing look at the door, then seemed to crumple. Listlessly, like the cobra's victim she fancied she was, she obeyed.

"Much better," said Edmund. "Now, tell me, how important is it to you that I believe what you say is true?"

"Oh, I—"

"Important enough," he interrupted, at the same moment reaching into the pocket of his coat and producing what looked like a black velvet drawstring pouch, "for you to pay me the *total value* of these jewels that belonged to my late wife?" He opened the pouch and dumped a pile of jewelry onto a small side table. There were a pair of diamond necklaces, numerous earrings studded with rubies and emeralds, rings bearing similar precious gems, and a heavy gold bracelet encrusted with perfectly matched sapphires.

Ignoring Lenore's gasp, he went on. "I found these sewn in the hems of several of my late wife's gowns when we were searching for suitable clothes to bury her in. The bitch kept them secret from me all these years. I wish I'd—"

He checked his rising temper and made a casual gesture at the jewels. "They're worth many thousands of pounds, I know. The goldsmith I visited when I arrived this afternoon indicated as much. But I also know that his offer had, as a matter of course, to be less than half of their actual value, else how would he ply his trade and make a profit in their resale?

"Now, I am asking you once again: Will you buy them from me *at full value*, in exchange for my, ah, acceptance of your story?"

Sweat was beading Lenore's brow and upper lip as she reached slowly for the jewels. Turning the pieces over in her hands, she examined them one by one, occasionally holding one up to the light thrown by a pair of candelabra on a table beside the settee. At last, she returned the gems to the pouch and looked up at him.

"I haven't the cash at hand for the likes of these, but, if you'll give me some time, I believe I can come by it."

"How much time? Even now, Tremaine may be making plans to return to England. Once he's there, he and William—hmm," he mused, his voice grown suddenly unctuous. "William . . . my dear brother who couldn't wait to see me displaced from my patrimony. . . . Perhaps—

"See to it that you take no more than a few days," he snapped. "I suddenly find myself eager to visit the country of my birth, and purchasing, or even hiring, a ship takes time."

"Of course, your lordship." Lenore rose, ostensibly to see him out.

But Edmund merely reached for the pouch and returned it slowly to his pocket, then took up his unfinished brandy. Lazily, like a man who had all the time in the world, he swirled and sniffed the liquid in the glass, then ran heavy-lidded eyes over her.

"Going somewhere, m'dear?" he questioned.

"Why, I—"

"Because if you were, I suggest you rethink it."

Lenore waited.

"I require a whore," he said.

Lenore's face broke into a relieved smile. "Well, why didn't you say so directly? I'll see if Jeanette or Desirée is fr—"

"But I do not want Jeanette or Desirée."

Lenore's carefully plucked brows drew together in a perplexed frown. "But they are my best! Who then?"

The grin that preceded Edmund's answer made her shiver.

"You," he told her.

CHAPTER 27

"WHAT NEWS?" ASKED TIMOTHY OF THE small group of men that rode up to the Chambers house.

The first to dismount was Ned, and his brown eyes looked troubled as they met his employer's. "Sorry, sir, but nary a trace. 'Tis as if she's vanished t' thin air."

Several of the young men with him in the search party which had been hastily formed that morning of various Chambers servants—footmen, stable boys, and the kitchen lad—nodded their heads and murmured agreement.

Timothy shook his head sadly, a worried frown creasing his brow. They'd been searching for Brittany all day, ever since her little abigail, the last to pound on her door and receive no answer, had convinced them to break it down, fearing Brittany was no longer being recalcitrant but was ill or even injured and incapable of responding.

He'd been reluctant at first, having been subjected to an earful of his wife's harping that the girl was merely being "disobedient and contrary and ought to be left without food or drink for a day or two—Let us see how willful she is on an empty stomach!" Althea had urged.

But thank God the little black woman had prevailed! When they'd broken into the chamber, Lord Bryce among them, it had been empty, and a quick search had turned up the fact that not only were a light cloak and frock missing, but the jewels inherited from Louise as well. The valuables box Timothy had long ago hidden for her under a loose floorboard, and to which only Brittany had a key, was empty.

Timothy had been alarmed, Althea sorely vexed, Tansy dismayed; but his lordship's reaction had been the severest of all, though he'd said very little. Timothy watched the blood drain from his face as he took in the empty chamber, then saw him go perfectly still while, behind him, Melody and several of the housemaids who'd learned what happened had begun weeping and wringing their hands, filling the air with female hysteria. Then, before Timothy could think what to do, Lord Bryce had turned and headed, grim-faced, for the door, pausing only to bestow a parting comment on Timothy:

"I'll find her," he 'd said tautly.

But now it was nearly dusk. These men he'd sent out this morning had been gone all day with no sign of her, and the man she was to wed hadn't returned yet, much less sent word that he'd found anything. He knew Lord Bryce had gone to his ship to enlist the aid of the crew, for Will Thatcher had come by at noontime to tell Timothy he and the seamen were searching, but with ill luck thus far. Even Tansy and the other female help had joined the hunt, accompanied by that huge dog, their hope being that some

clue might be found through the network of intelligence that passed through the town as the servants'
grapevine.

Where had she gone? And, more important, why
would the lass *wish* to run away? Had her betrothed
lied to Timothy when he said Brittany agreed to the
marriage? Somehow, Timothy just couldn't give credence to that. The man was honest if he was anything, regardless of that business of hiding his
identity while he sought to restore his family's
honor; that was different, and Timothy knew it. A
man understood these things. And Timothy also understood something about people's characters; he
hadn't made his fortune in a merchant's trade all
these years without learning to read people.

Suddenly Timothy heaved a sigh as a bitter
thought struck him. Aye, he'd learned to read people, all right, all but one! And the one who'd managed to escape him was the one he loved best in all
the world: his elder daughter. But it hadn't always
been so. Ah, when her mother was alive, they'd
been thick as thieves! Brittany had been the sun-
niest, happiest little lass alive . . .

When had he begun to lose her? The answer came
to him slowly, like an ache in the night, something
he'd been sleeping with all these years, but had been
too unaware—too busy—to notice. He'd been too
wrapped up in his damnable business to stay close to
the lass, too tired and preoccupied to do anything
more than hand her over to Althea. He winced, at
last acknowledging the lack of wisdom in *that*.

No wonder she'd really begun to be difficult when
the matter of finding her a husband had arisen.
Making a "proper match" had always been his wife's
passion, not his . . . and clearly not the child's, he
thought sadly. He had to allow that Althea's notions

of rearing a daughter were far more rigid than Louise's or his had ever been. Brittany, his dear little free spirit, the elfin child he remembered so well, had likely chafed under her stepmother's restraining hand, so much so that she would do anything to secure the independence she was always talking about.

Why hadn't he listened? And why did he have the feeling now, as if he were making up for all the blindness he'd displayed over the years, that he at last understood only too well why she'd run away this time, instead of fighting them with that fierce temper she'd developed? Because, as he thought on it, he would have sworn there was something solid between Brittany and the Englishman; this time she'd let her heart get involved. It wasn't anything he could put his finger on . . . a smile here, an exchanged glance there . . .

But *because* she was involved, she wasn't running from the man; this time Brittany was running away from *herself*.

Shaking his head again, Timothy thanked the men for their efforts and sent them to take their suppers, saying he'd send word when he decided what to do next. Then, feeling older than he had in years, he walked slowly back toward the house.

Bryce entered the noisy, smoke-filled common room of the Rising Sun Tavern, letting his eyes adjust to the diminished light, for, although the sun was setting outside, the tavern's interior was dimmer by far; the tiny panes of glass at its few windows were coated with soot, and the handful of tallow candles that graced the heavy oaken tables did little to brighten the atmosphere.

Casting wearily about for a free table, he made his

way toward the far end of the room where a pair of British officers were just leaving. His weariness wasn't really from physical exertion, although he'd been on and off horseback since mid-morning, covering the fields where Timothy told him she liked to ride, visiting the homes of her friends, both in town and on the outskirts, and combing the streets and lanes in general. But he was beginning to feel an emotional exhaustion, the kind that came from keeping one's hopes up only to have them dashed time and time again. Someone had seen a "redheaded lass" entering the chandler's shop; it had turned out to be the parson's wife—forty, if she was a day. Another had spied a heavily veiled, cloaked female leaving St. George's Church; when he'd caught up with her outside Hugh Mercer's apothecary shop, he'd found a woman recently widowed and in mourning, as she sadly told him when he'd been bold and, he supposed, ill-mannered enough to inquire about her wearing such a costume in the heat. Aye, he'd had numerous disappointments.

A smiling barmaid came up to the table and asked his pleasure. She was pretty and quite young, probably too young to be wearing a dress cut so low—it exposed much of what nature had endowed her with. Ignoring the way she brought this home by her bold glance and her manner of bending unnecessarily low before him, he ordered an ale and, as an afterthought, a bowl of fish stew, recalling that he'd eaten nothing all day.

The wench went for his order and he was left alone with the smoke and the noise . . . and his thoughts. Where in God's name was she? By now he and Will's crew had torn most of the town apart, yet nothing, not a trace. For the thousandth time that day he reminded himself that she'd obviously left of her own accord, deliberately, with enough wealth in jewels to see her comfortably gone from here; she'd run away and was not, like the night before, the victim of foul play. And, also for the thousandth time, he tried to forestall the images of her lying wounded, perhaps worse, in a ditch somewhere, the victim of a robbery, or worse; he told himself, made himself remember, that Brittany was an intelligent, resourceful woman who would be far too keen-witted to plan an escape that wasn't carefully thought out and laced with safeguards.

But most of all, he found himself just thinking about her; the exciting, alive, warm, never-boring, passionate, contrary, delightful, true-to-herself woman he'd committed himself to marrying. Having reiterated all these qualities to himself, he had to smile. It amazed him to think that in the space of less than a summer, she'd come from being simply "the hellion," to meaning all those things to him. And something nibbled at the back of his mind, something he'd chased before and found elusive. Only now, in his fear that she might have slipped out of his life as suddenly as she entered it, that he might never see her again, he sensed he was closer to the answer than ever.

Slowly, like someone searching the pages of a picture album, hoping to find a familiar face, he examined all the hours they'd spent together over the last days and weeks. He recalled their first meeting and how he'd provoked her, and not only then, but at other times as well, only to find the provocations a double-edged sword that cut back to catch him in its arc. He remembered that first heady physical joining, where he'd tutored her virgin body, and had himself been taught untold lessons by her passion. He saw her laughing with Tansy, the little black woman she called her friend, daring the world to say otherwise.

But he remembered, too, the image of Brittany in the storm, falling from her horse, and the sick feeling in his gut when he'd thought her—he wouldn't think it, not now. And then there was the terror he'd felt at the news that Avery had her. Dear God, he'd never known he could feel such *terror*! Only now, even as he sat here, he could feel its ghost rising again, for there was every possibility that she was again in danger and—

No. He *must* not let himself think it. Avery, both Averys, were dead and he was free. Never again would he have to fear that one of them would reach out to harm someone he loved. He—

Suddenly the words of his inner voice hit him like a thunderbolt: *Someone he loved*.

He *loved* her! For a long moment he sat perfectly still, savoring the remarkable truth of this, the miracle of it. Across the room two barmaids shouted insults at each other before being reprimanded by the innkeeper; at the next table a guest laughed heartily at his companion's joke; everywhere about him there was the drone of human voices, the sounds of people unwinding at the end of the day, but Bryce never heard them, so caught up was he in the wonder of the moment.

He loved her. More deeply and more fervently than he'd loved anyone or anything before. *That's* what had been eluding him all this time! What had slipped by him as he'd sifted through his images of her, trying to fathom her grip on him, had been his blindness to his *own* emotions; he'd been in bondage, so caught up in his passion for revenge, he hadn't had the freedom to feel love. But now that he *was* free, he was able to see into his heart, and he *knew.* Sweet Christ, how he loved her!

But what about her? What did she feel about him? *Damn,* the answer was plain enough. She'd run from him, hadn't she? Any fool could see how obvious it was that—

Or was it? He tried to imagine himself in her place. She carried their child. He paused for a moment, closing his eyes as he fastened on the wonder of that miracle, too.

But then he moved on, trying to fathom Brittany's mind, how she viewed herself, as well as the man who'd fathered the child . . . *the man who'd never given her a single indication that he cared about the mother.*

The enormity of this fell on him like a boulder smashing a flower. *Christ,* he was little better than Avery! Oh, it was true he'd offered to wed her, but in what manner? In the most high-handed, impersonal manner one could wish for! And while it was also true that he'd only come to recognize his own feelings just now, this was only an excuse he could offer himself; no one had offered it to Brittany.

Poor sweetheart, he thought, *what have I done to you?*

"'Ere's yer ale, guv'nor," said the barmaid, startling him out of his reverie. She thrust a tankard in front of him and gave him an arch smile. "'At'll be thruppence, and yer stew's arrivin' shortly, ah, unless there wuz somethin' *else* ye wanted?" The smile broadened to a suggestive grin.

"Thanks, sweetheart, but no," said Bryce, digging some coins out of his pocket, including enough for a generous tip.

The girl's face dropped with disappointment, but quickly revived when she saw the extra coins. Tucking them into her well-displayed cleavage, she gave him a saucy wink and departed, nearly bumping into the innkeeper, who brought his stew.

"'Ere you are, sir, nice and 'ot," said the big, cheerful man, who reminded him of Timothy.

Bryce nodded and began to eat. The stew was excellent, and he was well into it when an exchange between his host and the barmaid caught his ear.

"You, Emma, 'oo's ordered these other two bowls o' stew?"

"Oh," said the barmaid, "'tis those two red-'eaded blokes over there. Twins they are, like two peas in a pod, and, Lord, would ye look at them purple coats!"

Bryce set down the crude pewter spoon he'd been given and jerked his head in the direction the barmaid was indicating. And there, three tables away, sat Toby and Tony Wakefield! What in hell were they doing in Fredericksburg?

Wasting no time, he got up and headed for their table. Their host had gotten there first, blocking their view of him, but when the big man finished serving them and moved away, the twins froze as they recognized him, their spoons held aloft in surprise.

"Bryce!" they exclaimed as one.

"Good evening, gentlemen," said Bryce. "Fancy meeting you here."

"A-aye . . ." said Tony.

". . . fancy that!" added Toby.

There was an awkward moment of silence, so fleeting that Bryce wondered if he'd imagined it, before both men rose and stretched out their hands.

"How are you, Bryce?"

"Join us, won't you?"

Bryce shook hands with each and took a seat, gesturing to the barmaid to bring his tankard and bowl from the other table.

The three ate and drank companionably for a few minutes while they traded pleasantries and Bryce was caught up on the news from Sweetbriar. There was a brief exchange about the deaths of both Averys, with the twins expressing less surprise than he would have expected at the news of Richard's demise, and asking no details. In fact, they were quick to pass that by, moving on to an explanation of their business in Fredericksburg. Bryce suddenly began to realize that both men were acting a bit strangely—uneasy, he thought, if not a trifle nervous. And then it dawned on him that they hadn't made a single inquiry about Brittany and her family.

I wonder . . . he mused; then, aloud: "But I haven't told you my news, gentlemen, and good news it is, too." His eyes moved from Toby's to Tony's. "Brittany and I are to be wed."

Did he imagine it, or did the two exchange a pregnant glance before they fell into congratulating him with hearty enthusiasm?

"Well, that's the best news . . ." said Toby.

". . . we've heard in years!" Tony added.

Toby ordered another round of ale, and Tony proposed a toast when it arrived:

"To the happy couple!" he said, and they all raised their tankards when Toby added, with an assessing glance at Bryce: "And to the man who fell in love with our cousin!" He kept his eyes on Bryce as the latter nodded solemnly, pointedly giving his own addition to the toast before they drank:

"Aye," he said, as green eyes met gray, "I love her."

The ale was duly drunk while Bryce caught several glances exchanged between the two, who then suddenly remembered they were due at their ship for a briefing with their captain. Wishing him final congratulations on his forthcoming nuptials, they paid their bill and quickly got up to leave, saying they would call on him soon at the Chambers house.

Bryce waited only long enough to see them disappear through the door to the street before rising and moving after them. Convinced they knew where Brittany was or, even more likely, that they were hiding her, he set out to follow them, his heart thumping wildly in his chest as he prayed this was not yet another false lead.

Aboard the *Briar Rose* Brittany thanked the cabin boy who brought her supper tray and bade him good night. The lad reminded her of Harry, and suddenly she felt like crying—again.

Why was she so weepy these days? Then she recalled that Tansy had told her mothers-to-be often had sudden shifts of mood that included tears. Tansy.... Now she really was going to cry. How could she ever face not seeing her beloved friend again?

She wondered if Tansy and Will had set the date for their wedding yet, and, touching on the word *wedding*, she clutched the embroidered handkerchief Toby had given her and stifled a bitter sob.

"Fool," she murmured, "one would think you'd have cried yourself out by now!"

Have you? an inner voice mocked, *and who will hold your hand when this child is born, and stem the tears when you are alone?*

Thoughts of the child had some of that very effect now, and she angrily wiped her cheeks dry, determining to sit down and address her supper; she had to think of the child, and weeping and foregoing meals would never do.

But as she uncovered the tray and looked at the

plump crabmeat cakes accompanied by an array of succulent summer vegetables and a mound of fluffy rice, she knew she wasn't hungry. She forced herself to take a few bites, knowing she had likely been given Captain Josiah Quimby's own dinner, just as she occupied his cabin on the *Briar Rose*.

Upon being introduced to her by the twins as their cousin who was to travel aboard the *Briar Rose* on an unexpected holiday, the jovial, white-haired captain had insisted she take his cabin while they were in port, until one of the seldom-used passenger cabins could be cleaned and refurbished, making it more suitable for a lady. She'd protested, but Quimby would have none of it, and now, as she looked around the handsomely furnished chamber, with its thick Turkey carpets underfoot and a large, masculine-looking bed in one corner, she was grateful. The room was spacious and the bed comfortable, which was a plus, considering all the time she'd spent weeping there, once the twins had left.

Thoughts of her cousins nearly sent her into another round of tears. They'd been so wonderfully kind, installing her on their ship and asking no further questions, once they'd learned her full reason for leaving home. And they'd spent last evening and most of the day today going out of their way to distract her by making her laugh with one funny story after another.

So this evening, when Captain Quimby had casually mentioned his surprise that the young gentlemen were not taking advantage of their stay in Fredericksburg by making their usual "gentlemen's entertainment rounds" of the town by night, she had gone to them and insisted that they do so. At first they had demurred, saying they preferred to keep her company instead, but when she had lavishly admired their new purple coats with the puce linings, saying it was a shame they weren't going to be able to show the garments off, they'd gotten a familiar glimmer in their eyes and allowed her to persuade them.

And she'd politely refused Captain Quimby's invitation to join him and the other officers in the dining room for dinner, telling him she was feeling a bit peaked from the August heat. The dear man had been instantly solicitous, even sending up from the hold the ship's splendid brass bathing tub, which was promptly filled by several seamen with soothing, tepid water.

Of course, she'd had no fresh clothes to change into, having decided she could not afford to take any baggage when she left, as that might call too much attention to her, but even there the twins had come to her rescue. They'd donated a pair of their newest silk, monogrammed nightshirts for her to sleep in, and Toby's cornflower-blue silk robe as well, explaining to the captain that her baggage would be arriving shortly—something they also took care of by sending her measurements and a description of her coloring to their tailor in the city with instructions to "find a proper seamstress and have her assemble a small traveling wardrobe in a hurry or risk losing our patronage—forever!"

"Somehow," Brittany had laughed when she heard, "I know I shall be receiving new clothes in record time!"

But as she thought of their extravagant gesture (for they'd adamantly refused to let her pay for the wardrobe with any of her jewels), she knew a moment of chagrin; soon, none of those garments would fit her!

She placed her hand over the still-flat abdomen beneath Toby's robe and closed her eyes: "Let me have strength," she prayed softly. "Please, God, let me have the strength to bear the course I've chosen!"

A short while later, Toby and Tony stood outside the door to their cousin's temporary cabin and debated in whispers:

"She's got to be told," said Toby.

"But what if we're wrong?"

"We're not wrong," replied his brother. "You heard his answer to my toast as well as I. The man's besotted! You could see it in his eyes."

"It certainly seemed so," whispered Tony, "but if we should be mistaken, Britt will carve us up for fish bait."

"Nonsense. That shrewish temper's merely a ruse, remember? To stave off unwanted suitors?"

"Aye," said his twin with a grimace, "and his lordship may yet prove to be one, with us as his false advocates!"

"Courage, old man. We've got to take the chance. It might well be the last our cousin and her babe will get!"

"Aye, you're right," said Tony.

"Of course I'm right," said Toby.

They both reached out and rapped on the door as one, but there was no answer. Trying again, a bit more loudly, they still got no response. Casting a worried glance at each other, they tried the door and found it unlocked, but when they stepped inside the cabin, they found Brittany on the huge bed, fast asleep.

With tender smiles, they crept quietly back into the passageway, closing the door softly behind them.

"We'll tell her in the morning," said Tony.

"After she's had a good night's rest," affirmed his brother.

And with satisfied smiles, the two made their way

back to the companionway and up on deck. *Their* night had barely begun!

But before they descended the gangplank, they chatted briefly with the young seaman on watch, the seaman who'd missed seeing the tall shadow of a man who'd slipped silently into the companionway through which the twins had just passed.

CHAPTER 28

BRYCE QUIETLY LET HIMSELF INTO THE cabin he'd seen the twins leaving. There was a soft glow coming from a gimbaled lantern fixed to the wall beside the bed, and when his eyes fell on the handsomely carved piece of furniture, he let out a quiet sigh of relief.

There, curled up with her arms about one of the pillows, was Brittany, her magnificent hair tangled from sleep and swirling about her slender frame like a burnished copper cloak. Moving closer to the bed, he drank in every detail of her, from the wild beauty of her hair to the still perfection of her features in sleep, pausing to savor the rose petal softness of her lips, barely parted in slumber, the exquisite proportions of her delicate, straight little nose and finely chiseled cheekbones, the sweep of winged auburn brows over eyes whose mahogany lashes fanned lightly against—

He stopped his eager assessment as his eyes fell on the fragile skin beneath her eyes and he saw the unmistakable trail of dried tears.

"Oh, sweetheart," he whispered, his voice thick with emotion, "I promise you, after tonight, you won't ever cry yourself to sleep again!"

Or sleep alone again, he vowed.

Leaning forward as he braced his hands on the mattress on either side of her head, he bent to kiss her eyes, and then the telltale evidence of her pain.

"Never again," he murmured.

She stirred at his gentle touch, and he saw a smile curve her lips, transforming her face with an expression of such sweetness, he caught his breath.

Memories stirred in him, of all the times he'd seen that smile and had been similarly transfixed, and he wondered if it had been her smile he'd fallen in love with first, a prelude to the woman herself.

And as he stood, mesmerized by those lips whose passionate responses he also recalled, he felt a tightening in his loins and he knew he couldn't last a moment longer without tasting their heady wine.

Swiftly straightening, he bent to remove his boots, and when he had cast them aside, shrugged quickly out of his jacket. His cravat soon followed, but he never noticed where these landed, for Brittany had stirred again, exposing a long length of shapely thigh; his eyes were riveted to the creamy expanse of flesh.

Then, as his hands went to the fastenings of his breeches, he suddenly heard her cry out:

"*No, Tansy!* I couldn't bear it if he wed me for the child! 'Twould kill me to be pitied and bound to him out of duty and—Oh, God! I love him too much to tie him to me thus!"

Bryce froze, his elation at this unconscious confirmation of her feelings toward him warring with his dismay at the vehemence of her conviction that he wanted her only because she carried their child.

What if he'd been wrong to come here like this? What if she didn't believe him when he told her he loved her?—which was the first thing he'd planned to say to her, once he kissed her awake.

Hell, he thought, running his hand through his hair in agitation, *she's liable to come up hissing and spitting, telling me to take my uncredited avowals and damnable presence out of here, so she can get on with the business of leading the independent life she's always craved!*

His eyes fell on the perfectly flat expanse of her belly beneath the blue robe and his mouth hardened. *No, hellion*, he thought, *not with our child, you won't! And not in the face of the love I bear you, either!*

That settled, he tore off his remaining clothes, intent on pursuing his original plan, with one addition: He would use every power of persuasion at his command to convince her it was her he wanted—*in love*—and only then, the child they'd created—also in love, whether they'd recognized its fragile beginnings at the time of conception or not!

Brittany felt she was dreaming. Warm male lips covered hers, familiar lips—Bryce's. Oh, but why did they seem so real if this was only a dream? But they did, and so did the strong, gentle hands that cupped her head to hold it still while he worked the tender assault on her mouth. Even the scent of him was real, a mixture of leather and clean sweat and horses and the sandalwood soap he used.

Dreamily, she succumbed to the heady arousal that was taking place. She stretched her arms out lazily, as a cat would, then moved them into place about her dream lover's neck, even as she felt herself shiver when his gently questing tongue touched hers. She felt his lips move to her ear, and then to the sensitive spot beneath it, and sensed a tendril of something familiar coil at the base of her belly.

But when the deft fingers parted her robe and found the already aching, already swollen nipple of her breast, teasing it until she felt an answering jolt of pure pleasure at the juncture of her thighs, she suddenly realized the wetness she felt there was no dream . . .

And neither was the man in her arms!

Her eyes snapped open, taking in the face that had haunted her, dreaming and awake, ever since she'd left, and for a moment she knew a joy so extreme, she thought she could die of it.

But in the next second, as lazy green eyes met her own, she stiffened and closed hers, turning her head aside on the pillow.

"No," she groaned.

Bryce had felt her stiffen and was ready for it. "Listen to me, Brittany," he told her, carefully taking her chin and turning it, forcing her to face him, and when her eyes remained shut, he kissed each one, murmuring, "Open your eyes, love. I want you to look at me."

There was a moment's hesitation, and then she complied, knowing that to wait would only prolong the agony of what she must face.

Bryce's eyes locked with hers, seeing the pain in them. "I love you," he said simply, and then, partly because of her dumbfounded look, and partly because of his need to hear himself say the joy-filled words again, he repeated them: *"I love you."*

Hope warred with disbelief in the face of all the negatives she'd lived with for so long, and disbelief won. Turning her head again, Brittany choked on a sob. "'Tis the child you love," she murmured brokenly.

Bryce caught her face gently between two hands and forced her to look at him. "Aye," he breathed, his green eyes intense as they held her gaze, his hand travelling to her belly, "I love our child, but I love the mother first."

He took his other hand and bent the forefinger to catch the shimmering tear that traced its way down her cheek, as he gave her a queer, tender smile. "Beloved hellion," he whispered, "don't you know I'm so in love with you, I can't think straight? Why else would I have behaved like such a fool, offering for you before I'd even had time to sort out my own feelings, let alone speak to you, telling you of my intent?"

"Because of the—"

"No! Not because of the child—because of *you*, sweet, darling idiot! The child was only a catalyst to bring me to my senses...." He took a shuddering breath "...that and the terror I felt all day today, when I feared I had lost you."

Brittany heard the honest fervor in his voice and searched for the truth in his eyes. "Y—you really . . . do . . . *love me*?" she hiccoughed through her tears.

"I swear it," he said solemnly, "and on this little one's head, if need be," he added, pressing lightly on her belly.

A new rush of hot tears stung her eyes as she heard the truth in his words and read it in his face. "*Oh, Bryce,*" she cried, feeling she could touch his soul with hers just then as she threw her arms about his neck, "I love you too! I never knew I could love anyone so much!"

And Bryce enfolded her in his arms as he closed his eyes, just holding her and savoring her, and the sweetness of the moment.

They remained that way for several long

caught up in the piercing joy of having found each other—of having found their hearts. But soon, as each of their senses became filled with the other's presence, the scent, the touch, the sound of quiet breathing, something new began to work between them.

Feeling the texture of her hair beneath his lips, aware of the rounded fullness of her bare breasts against his chest, Bryce succumbed to a renewed stirring of arousal in his loins and quickly heeded its call. Pressing her gently into the mattress, he breathed her name, his warm breath ruffling the tendrils of hair about her ear. Then his mouth slid to the silken skin of her neck, kissing the pulse there, finding it suddenly quicken as his hand cupped her breast and the long length of his thighs pressed against hers.

Brittany answered with a tremulous sigh and then a gasp of pleasure when she felt his thumb brush across her nipple. She saw him raise his head to look at her, his green eyes locking with her own as the thumb continued its devastating work. Below, in her woman's place, a tension began to build with each deft stroke, and she knew Bryce could read this in her eyes as he made his magic.

And as he watched her eyes change from their sapphire brilliance to pools of deepest blue, saw her flush with the realization of his intimate awareness of her body's responses, Bryce rejoiced in the knowledge of the pleasure he could bring her.

Then his gaze dropped to her lips, which were parted in passion, and he lowered his head to claim ~~~ with his own. The kiss was by turns urgent, ~~~ ntle, then teasing, his tongue rimming the ~~~ r lips, touching the corners, then slip- ~~~ to graze her teeth and lightly fence with her tongue, and all the while Brittany was aware of the building of a soul-tearing tenderness; this was a kiss that said "I love you" in a language more thorough than words.

When he moved his mouth to blaze a trail of fire down her neck and shoulder, culminating at the aching coral bud that had been neglected thus far, Brittany cried out softly with the pleasure of it, taking her fingers and threading them through the curls at the back of his head, pressing him closer, never wanting him to stop. When he sucked and nibbled, teasing the peak to throbbing hardness, she moaned deep in her throat. And when his hand left her other breast to trace the indentation of her waist and approach, with devastating slowness, her triangle of auburn curls, she began to twist and writhe beneath his touch, gasping his name, crying out for more.

Bryce's low, pleased laughter met her ears as he eagerly gave her what she wanted; placing his hand on the shallow indentation above the nest of curls, he pressed down gently, raising his head at the same time to watch her reaction.

"Oh!" breathed Brittany, feeling a rush of pleasure at her center. "Oh!"

Bryce smiled knowingly, then quickly moved until he was straddling her legs; the one hand continued to press while, with the fingers of the other, he found the warm, moist opening of her and stroked it, touching at last the tiny swollen bud above.

"Oh . . . ohhh!" cried Brittany as sweet spirals of delight issued from the core of her. She began to thrash wildly on the bed, reaching out her arms to him, begging him to take her.

Bryce felt a singing in his veins, his blood stirred to a violent throbbing as he beheld the eager passion of this woman he adored, but he forced himself to deny the satisfaction he, too, had begun to crave.

"Easy, love," he murmured huskily, his eyes intent on her face, "for we've time enough . . . and more . . . all the time in the world . . ."

Bent on prolonging her pleasure, knowing it would increase the pleasure of the end they sought together, he took his time with her, delighting in the abandoned cries she uttered.

Over and over again, he murmured her name and his love for her as his fingers prepared her; he delighted in the slippery wetness of her when he slipped one inside, loving her tightness; he felt the blood pounding in his ears when she answered with a sharp cry of need and opened her thighs.

Soon he moved to bend over her, his head lowering until his tongue traced the outline of her navel; then, placing his hands beneath her, cupping her buttocks to raise her hips, he moved his mouth downward, to the place where his fingers had played.

Suddenly Brittany sensed what he was about and with a gasp of denial, pressed her thighs tightly together. *No!* she thought. *'Tis too intimate, too—*

But then Bryce's mouth found her, and all protests flew from her mind. As his tongue stroked her pulsing nub, she again opened her thighs to him, her hands tightening in his hair.

Tenderly, oh, so tenderly, he made love to her through the most intimate of kisses, tasting her, loving the clean, sweet scent of her as it mingled with the faint musk of her womanliness.

"That's it, love," he rasped as her hips arched toward him, "give yourself to me . . . give me all of you . . . you're as beautiful here as anything I've ever seen . . . ah, love . . ."

He kissed and probed, entering her with his tongue...once...then again, until he felt her quiver beneath him, heard her sob with pleasure, and then he knew he himself could wait no longer.

With a groan, he moved to take her in his arms, cupping his hand about the back of her head as he looked into her eyes.

"I love you, Brittany," he breathed, his voice a husky caress.

Brittany answered him in kind, the words a joyful whisper before she felt his mouth close over her own and tasted herself on his lips and tongue.

And as she wound her arms about him, clasping him to her with fervent need, she felt his hardness probing the joining of her thighs; then, with a sharp cry of his name, she felt him drive home.

Bryce felt her velvety tightness encase his swollen shaft and the last vestiges of control left him. With a harsh cry, he moved his hands beneath her buttocks and pulled her closer, probing her depths to the fullest, then withdrew slightly to plunge again...and again.

Brittany picked up the rhythm, following it with an instinct as old as time, arcing to meet him, falling back, arcing again, feeling the building of something powerful and rare.

And then they found it, that sweet, soaring ecstasy that comes when flesh and will are one with heart and mind and soul. Bryce gave a fierce cry that was her name, feeling her climax beneath him, feeling his own shuddering release as Brittany's cry of rapture filled his ears. It was a moment of the purest shared passion, one that can only happen when love is at its core, and they reveled in the wonder of it.

A long time later, when each had cooled to the

point where speech was possible, Brittany stirred in his arms, whispering, "Are you still alive?"

"Aye," she heard him whisper against her ear, and she could tell he was grinning.

"I'm not so sure about me," she said, a grin also beginning. "I think a person could die from so much happiness."

Bryce broke away to raise himself up on an elbow and look at her. The grin was still in evidence. "They call it 'the little death,' you know. Some delightful nonsense about how we die a little each time we—"

A slim hand shot up, the fingers closing lightly over his lips. "Nay," she said, "never say so, for I can associate nothing but life with such a wonder."

Bryce closed his hand over her fingers and kissed them. "Well said," he murmured, and then his hand traveled to her belly, pressing it gently. "And when I think of the wonder of this life we've created . . ."

He shook his head and smiled at her. "And the wonder of you, and that I should love you so. . . . I am a whole man at last, tonight, Brittany. Before I met you, learned to love you, I was only half alive—less, when I consider how I almost let my vengeance destroy me."

The smile was gone now, a look of solemn intensity in the green eyes. "You *are* my life, Brittany," he told her.

Brittany closed her eyes, feeling a joy that was so fierce, it was almost painful. "Oh, Bryce," she murmured, suddenly close to tears, "'tis the same with me! But when I think that I almost—"

"Shh." He stilled her lips with a kiss, then went on to kiss each eye, her nose, her chin, and then her lips again.

"Now, m'lady," he said with mock solemnity,

"what say you, we make plans to make an honest woman of you?"

"Oh, aye," she grinned, "for 'tis sure our son will appreciate it!"

"A son, is it?" he grinned back. "And here I had my mind bent on a daughter...a lovely, laughing little minx with red hair like her mother's." He picked up one of the yard-long tresses and kissed it.

"Well," said Brittany, dimpling, "if she has green eyes, I'll allow it."

"Hmm, bossy wench, aren't you?"

She pulled a face, making him laugh, but all at once his face grew serious.

"I'm reminded of something I wanted to tell you, love," he said, taking her hand. "I want you to know I've never taken lightly your fears of losing your independence."

Brittany began to interrupt, but he silenced her with a light touch on her lips with his forefinger.

"And because your wishes are important to me," he continued, "I want you to know that I've already seen a solicitor with the aim of having him draw up papers—part of a marriage agreement—that will see you left in full control of your fortune."

Her eyes grew wide with surprise.

"Moreover," said Bryce, "I tell you right now that I have no intention of making this marriage a one-way process. I plan to discuss with you all matters involving the two of us and our mutual interests, from the naming of our children to the company we keep, to the way we spend our free time. And that is not to say we won't have individual lives in many respects, either.

"You see, I happen to believe you have a wonderful brain in your head, and that you should use it for more than deciding which gown to wear to tea. Do I make myself clear?"

The love shining in Brittany's eyes was his answer, and Bryce gently touched his knuckles to her cheek. "I adore you, hellion," he whispered.

And then their mouths met, and the fires began to burn again, and it was far into the night before either of them slept—or cared to.

In the morning Bryce awoke fairly early, by habit. He spent several long minutes looking down at Brittany as she lay sleeping, curled up with her back nestled against him, as she had during the night—when they'd finally found sleep. Quietly, he studied her, finding her the most exquisite creature he'd ever known.

Her long hair was tangled about her, catching a beam of sunlight that streamed through the porthole and turned the fiery tresses to molten copper. And that face—dear God, was it really his to wake up to every morning for the rest of their lives?—her incredibly beautiful face, with its creamy complexion lightly flushed in slumber, the lush lips slightly curled in the beginnings of a smile and still swollen from his lovemaking, the ethereal perfection of nose, brow, and cheek—it was the face of a woman who knows she is loved and cherished, he knew, and he wondered if others would see this with the certainty that he did now.

The thought reminded him of his plans for the day, and reluctantly, after pressing a kiss to her temple, he rose and dressed, being careful not to awaken her. Then he went to pay a call on her cousins, in the cabin she'd told him they were using.

Having gotten in not more than a couple of hours earlier, Toby and Tony were less than thrilled to be

awakened by Bryce, but when he told them of what
had transpired between him and Brittany during the
night, they broke into delighted smiles, and there
was a round of well-wishing that far exceeded their
forced responses of the evening before.

And when he informed them of a decision he and
their cousin had made, they were beside themselves
with pleasure. Because of the child, among other
things, he told them, he and Brittany wished to wed
immediately, and rather than request a special li-
cense, he asked if they would persuade their captain
to take the *Briar Rose* out to sea for the purpose of
performing a marriage ceremony there. Estimating it
would take a day or so, they'd decided to invite only
Will and Tansy, and the twins, of course, sending a
note to Brittany's family that would explain something to the effect that though Brittany had been
found safe and sound, in their eagerness for each
other, the young couple hadn't been able to wait,
and would return wed—and soon, to prepare for
the trip to England.

He asked Toby and Tony to help by paying a visit
to their tailor to pick up at least one suitable gown
from the wardrobe they'd ordered for Brittany—and
they were only too glad to do this, as their heads
filled with visions of selecting suitable "wedding attire" from the half dozen new sartorially splendid
suits they also happened to have on order. Then
Bryce prepared to locate his first mate and Tansy,
and to secure suitable clothes for himself from the
Lady Beth.

And so the day passed quickly, with all of the par-
ticipants from Captain Quimby to the laughing bride
(who "no more resembles an 'ellion than my sainted
mother," said Will) doing their parts. And in mid-af-
ternoon, catching the tide with a good wind behind

them, the *Briar Rose* set out for the waters of the Chesapeake, its happy, excited wedding party aboard.

Meanwhile, unbeknownst to them, in a tavern in Fredericksburg, a tall, aristocratic figure nodded at the man across the table from him.

"'Tis arranged, then, Captain Monroe. You are to outfit your vessel for my trip to England at once. No one is to know you sail for anyone other than yourself. For all intents and purposes, you are simply making one more voyage as part of your routine business and trade. Am I clear?"

The grizzled sea captain regarded the man across from him. *Cold lookin' devil,* he thought to himself. *Gives me the willies, 'e does, wot with them pale eyes of 'is starin' all the time. Why, fer my money I'd jest as soon not take 'im on!*

But Ezra Monroe knew he could not afford to be choosy these days. Since the tea tax had been imposed, those who plied their trade in the sea lanes between England and the colonies were hurting— independents like himself most of all. So, pushing his misgivings aside, Captain Monroe looked at the man who'd just leased his ship, the *Chesapeake Star,* for a handsome sum, and nodded.

"Aye," he said, "but wot wuz that ye said about wot t' watch fer, t' determine the time we sail?"

A look of impatience crossed the haughty countenance. "You are to keep a careful watch on the vessel I shall point out to you when we leave here, and alert me in my rooms the moment she prepares to weigh anchor. We sail in her wake."

"Very well, sir," said Monroe, rising at the same time his companion did, "and wot would the name o' this 'ere vessel be?"

His future passenger gave him a predatory grin that made Monroe suddenly wish he'd reconsidered this assignment after all.

"Why, the *Lady Beth*," said Edmund Avery unctuously, "the good ship *Lady Beth*."

CHAPTER 29

BRITTANY STOOD BEFORE THE HANDSOME
looking glass in Josiah Quimby's cabin and stared at
her reflection with wonder. Was the elegant creature
looking back at her really she? It didn't seem possible, and at times neither did this dreamlike wedding
cruise. Beginning at two in the afternoon, it had
taken them more than nine hours to reach the open
sea where Captain Quimby had told them his authority to perform a wedding ceremony would become valid.

So, here she was, with the clock having just struck
eleven, dressed in the most beautiful gown she'd
ever imagined, waiting for the gentlemen, whom
Tansy had gone to fetch, so that the ceremony could
begin.

Feeling she might have to pinch herself to be sure
it was all real, she made a graceful pirouette before
the glass, a happy bubble of laughter escaping her
lips. The gown she wore, an extravagance only the
twins could have thought of, she realized, was a
filmy, layered concoction of the thinnest ivory sar-

cenet, its wide, paniered skirts parting in front to reveal a heavier silk underskirt of the palest blush coral, a shade she'd once seen inside a large, curled seashell in a dockside shop.

The ivory sarcenet bodice, with its deep, square-cut décolletage, had an inset of the same blush coral at the neckline, worked into the tiniest pleated ruching she'd ever seen, and the inset was edged, at the place where it met the bodice proper, with exquisite ivory lace.

Ivory lace also fell from the narrow sleeves that ended at her elbows; attached to the sleeves, above the lace flounces, was a modest bow made of a narrow satin ribbon in the blush color; matching bows caught up the wide hems of her overskirts at intervals, to let the underskirt peek through. And, finally, tiny ivory seed pearls were scattered about the overskirt, their creamy opalescence catching the candlelight as she moved.

There were matching seed pearls scattered tastefully in her hair, which Tansy had worked into an elaborate cluster of curls at the crown of her head while a large hank of the hair beneath it was left to curl down her back. Ivory satin slippers completed the outfit, and her mother's pearls, the simple necklace and earrings she treasured, were in place.

"Well, O'Leary, how do I look?"

Tansy's "black Irishman," as she called him, was the only other occupant of the cabin at the moment. The big hound had found a place of honor in all their hearts since the day he'd so courageously defended Tansy and Brittany from Richard Avery, and they'd been reluctant to leave him behind. He loved the sea, which doubly endeared him to Will, and the only reason he wasn't up on deck right now was that the crew had a pet parrot, a noisy, squawking crea-

ture named Oliver, who, from the moment O'Leary
had come on board, had been bent on giving him
grief. Flying about him, cackling at him with a
human voice, trying to hitch a ride on his head, the
big green bird had pestered the giant hound so mer-
cilessly, they'd finally taken pity on O'Leary and sequestered him below.

Now, at Brittany's query, the dog put his head between his paws and gave her a long-suffering look.

"Poor O'Leary," said Brittany, "you miss looking at
the waves, don't you? And 'tis such a lovely, calm
night out there, too!"

As if he understood what she was saying,
O'Leary's dark eyes rolled toward the cabin door,
then fastened plaintively on Brittany.

"Well, you needn't look so soulful about it! You
know the crew would stash him away in the hold for
you for a few hours—if only they could catch him!"

What she said was true. In fact, O'Leary, with his
majestic size, had made such a hit with the crew at the
outset that they'd spent the better part of an hour
trying to coax Oliver down from the rigging (where he
loved to sit—when he wasn't annoying the bejabbers
out of some unsuspecting innocent, that is) but to no
avail. He'd merely fluttered from ratline to ratline, in
between forays at the beleaguered hound, jeering at
them with a perfect imitation of human speech in
phrases that ranged from "Ahoy, there!" to "Let's 'ave
another round o' rum, mates!"

Brittany bent to bestow a commiserating pat on
O'Leary's head, murmuring, "Poor dog, we'll save
you a piece of the wedding cake they've been baking
in the galley."

Just then there was a sound of voices in the passageway, and a knock at the door.

"Miz Britt, we're here!" called Tansy.

Clasping her hands to contain her eagerness, Brittany bade them enter, and in filed Tansy, Captain Quimby, and the twins. Tansy looked absolutely stunning in a gown of pale apricot silk, its sleeves and bodice trimmed with ecru lace, its wide paniers barely fitting through the doorway. She looked, except for the lack of a powdered wig, like a fashion plate as she stood beside Captain Quimby, who was very impressive, dressed in his formal sea captain's attire, his cockaded hat folded and held under his arm.

But, as she might have expected, it was the appearance of her cousins that captured and held her attention. *Lord, they've really outdone themselves this time!* thought Brittany as she took in their matching cloth-of-gold coats.

Preening like a pair of proud peacocks, Toby and Tony stopped just inside the door, knowing they were being assessed. Gold-embroidered, azure blue waistcoats rested beneath the cloth-of-gold coats, whose filigreed gold buttons each boasted a small sapphire in the center. Each man wore a snowy white linen stock, accompanied by a black velvet solitaire, the black tie that was worn over it, and they'd opted for their own hair, powdered and captured behind in a bag wig.

Thank God they didn't overdo it on the breeches! thought Brittany, noting the simple white satin these were made of, but as her eyes travelled the length of them, beyond the masculine calves encased in pristine white silk hose, she saw their shoes had rescued the "plainness" of their lower torsos. High-heeled and constructed of fine black leather polished to a fare-thee-well, they were topped with the world's most prodigiously ornamented gold buckles, glittering with sapphires and rubies, making for a king's ransom in footwear!

"Well, Coz?" queried Tony, balancing his gold-headed walking stick before him.

"Will we do?" finished Toby, affecting an identical pose.

Her back to them so they couldn't see her, Tansy rolled her eyes, but Brittany merely laughed, saying, "Of course you'll do! What would my wedding be without my own dear cousins decked out in sartorial splendor?"

Taking this to be a compliment, the twins grinned at her and came forward, each placing a kiss on one of her cheeks.

"And you look absolutely radiant," said Tony, "which is exactly how a bride *should* look!"

"And ravishing," added Toby with a comically suggestive leer, "which is exactly the way the groom wishes the bride to look!"

"Speaking of my groom . . ." said Brittany, gazing toward the open door with a question on her face.

"Oh, he's coming," said Tansy. "He just had to help Will with some last minute nerves."

"Whose nerves?—Will's?" Brittany was puzzled.

"Aye," grinned Toby, "You see, we have some great news, Coz! We've convinced Tansy and Will not to waste this splendid cruise, with its lovers' moon riding in the sky, so—"

"—Will and Tansy are to be wed by Captain Quimby tonight, too!" Tony finished.

Opening her mouth in surprise, Brittany turned eagerly toward Tansy, who stood, grinning at her like a smitten schoolgirl. "*Are you?* Oh, Tans!" she exclaimed, hugging her small friend delightedly. "A double wedding for us! Nothing could make me happier!"

"Except the presence of your groom, I hope," said a deep male voice at the doorway.

She turned, and the sight of Bryce standing there made her heart give a little lurch. He was, oh, so handsome, dressed in a dove gray formal coat superbly tailored to fit his wide shoulders; a white satin waistcoat with understated silver embroidery set this off perfectly, as did the black satin breeches that met the white silk hose which drew her eyes to his well-muscled calves. The black leather of his shoes was as highly polished as the twins', but any resemblance stopped there, for the simple buckles were fashioned of unadorned silver.

Running the virile length of him, her eyes moved slowly back up to his face which, above the snowy white cravat, looked tan and impossibly handsome as he stood there smiling at her, the deep grooves of his dimples framing even, white teeth which contrasted startlingly with the bronze of his face. His dark hair, which was still damp from bathing, curled negligently over his forehead, giving him an almost boyish look, and that, coupled with the green eyes which were focused on her so intently, made her succumb to a delicious shiver coursing down her spine.

He was the most attractive, most masculine thing alive, and she was about to tell him so when Bryce strode across the short space that separated them and took her hands.

"You," he murmured, his green eyes running hotly over her, "look too delicious to be *real*! My God, woman, if you grow any lovelier, I'll have to spend our married life calling other men out; as you look now, no man will be able to keep his eyes off you!"

Brittany felt a blush stealing from the tips of her toes to the roots of her hair and glanced surreptitiously about to see if the others had heard; it wasn't Bryce's words that nonplussed her so much as the

avid look of sexual hunger in the green eyes. It was a
look she'd seen from him in their private moments,
but never like this, before others—even if the others
were their friends!

But no one seemed to have noticed, or, if they
had, they were too discreet to show it. Instead, they
all suddenly turned back toward the doorway, where
Will Thatcher's big frame dwarfed the aperture.

Ducking his head, he came into the cabin, then
stood silently, his eyes sliding with nervous hesitation toward his diminutive bride-to-be.

"*Sweet mercy,*" muttered Tansy, as she took in the
appearance of her groom; added to this came the
sound of murmurs of approval from the others.

Will's formal clothes were almost identical to
Bryce's in cut and fabric except for the colors; where
the younger man's dress coat was done in that soft
dove gray, Will's was a pale butternut color, and instead of black, his satin breeches were a deep chocolate brown. But aside from the positive change the
well-cut formal clothes rendered, the most astonishing transformation in Thatcher's appearance came
from the beautiful head of tightly curled black hair
he sported, its soft downiness handsomely covering
a head that had always been well-shaped. Long
enough now to be queued at the nape of his neck
and tied there by a narrow black velvet ribbon, it
gave him a fashionable, utterly civilized look, despite
the gold earring he wore. Moreover, it made him
look a good ten years younger, and handsomer, by
far, than he'd ever appeared before.

Pride and adoration shining in her eyes, Tansy
stepped closer and made a low, sweeping curtsy before him. He extended a hand to help her rise, a shy
grin beginning to spread across his face.

"Mm-mm, Coffee Man," Tansy murmured softly, "you'll do. . . . You'll do just *fine!*"

In the next instant Captain Quimby was urging them to take their places, and the wedding ceremony got under way. Brittany and Bryce were the first to take their vows, followed shortly by Tansy and Will, the two men taking the role of best man for each other, one twin giving each bride away.

Then, once congratulations and good wishes had been passed around, all of them went up on deck, where the crew had a celebration in store for them.

It was a quiet, star-spangled night. The winds that had brought them downriver in record time had died down a couple of hours earlier, so the crew had been able to set up a banquet table on the open deck; it was made of a pair of wide planks balanced across some water barrels, the unused spare canvas they brought up from the hold serving as a simple, but serviceable, tablecloth. The food, ranging from succulent Chesapeake Bay oysters to a three-tiered wedding cake carefully decorated in the galley by the French-trained chef the twins employed whenever they sailed, was served buffet-style, with barrels here and there functioning as seats for the men, and a pair of captain's chairs carried up for the brides.

French, too, was the champagne that had been destined for the cellars at Sweetbriar, and that delicious bubbly liquid flowed freely for all—except the unfortunate sailors who'd drawn duty for the skeleton crew which was, even then, turning the ship around and sailing back.

Music found its way into the celebration, with the appearance of three members of the crew who played tolerably well on hautboy, flute, and fiddle. Soon both bridal party and crew were dancing one lively quadrille after another, with an awkward minuet or two in between (the homely talents of the musicians being less adept at this stately form).

About an hour and a half into all this revelry, one of the ship's officers happened to look up from the champagne he was sipping and exclaimed in a robust voice to the boatswain who was standing nearby:

"Great Neptune, Watts, will you look at that!"

An old sailor overheard him and, the piece of wedding cake he'd been about to eat poised in mid-air, he cried, "Blimey, now I've seen all!"

The musicians, on hearing him, turned to look in the direction he indicated, and the music stopped dead as their jaws hung slack with amazement; with the cessation of the music, all eyes were suddenly bent in the same direction, dancers and diners alike, frozen where they stood.

Coming slowly toward them, in a movement that could only be called ambling, but in an *S*-like, weaving pattern, was O'Leary, his great head bent low to the deck. At least they thought it was his head, for, perched on it in regal fashion was the parrot, Oliver, his head tilted oddly as he eyed them all.

"O'Leary!" cried Tansy, breaking away from the other dancers and moving toward her hound, "What's wrong, baby?"

O'Leary did his best to look at her, but the effort was so costly, he gave it up and sank slowly to his haunches and then further, until he was flat on the deck, his four legs splayed out, bug-like, away from his body.

"He's foxed!" said Tony, recognizing the signs.

"They're *both* foxed!" said Brittany, as they

watched Oliver lose his balance and slide down O'Leary's nose.

"Awk! Foxed!" cried Oliver. "Bring out the rum!"

A crewman came running from the stern section, holding a cracked, empty champagne bottle. "Er, beggin' yer pardon, Cap'n," he said to Quimby, "but I jest found this rollin' around the deck near the 'atch there." He gestured in the direction from which the hapless O'Leary (and companion) had come. "There be a wet stain on the boards nearby, and a pair o' green feathers stuck to 'em," he added, eyeing the lurching parrot who was trying his best to remount the wolfhound's head.

"Someone take these sots below," ordered Quimby, trying hard to stifle the laughter that threatened his composure, "and I suggest it be the men who so carelessly dropped a certain bottle of France's finest!"

A pair of young seamen stepped forward sheepishly and made for the undignified looking pair of animals.

"'At does it, ye scurvy green devil!" muttered the first, a young man of no more than twenty, as he grabbed the reeling parrot. "Now I ken why ye flew at me 'ead when I wuz luggin' up them bottles! Ye're spendin' the night in the *brig!*"

"Come along with ye, O'Leary," said the second seaman, a burly redheaded youngster who spoke in an Irish brogue. "And didn't ye know better than t' let that feathered Sasenach lead ye t' ruin? 'Tis ashamed o' ye, I am, me boyo!"

He led the weaving hound away to the sound of an explosion of laughter from the celebrants, some of whom, at the sight of Oliver, (now hanging upside down from the first seaman's arm as they disappeared from sight) were soon doubled over and weak from their efforts.

"P-poor O'Leary," laughed Brittany. "I h-hope he won't suffer too much for it!"

"Not to worry, m'dear," said Toby as he wiped tears of mirth from his eyes, "so long as no one tries to cure his 'morning after' with the standard remedy."

"And what would that be?" asked Tansy.

Toby glanced at Tony, who winked as he supplied the reply. "Why, some 'hair o' the dog,' of course!"

It was about an hour later when, after everyone else had retired, Brittany and Bryce stood alone on the deck, drinking in the brilliance of the night sky. They watched it as lovers do, holding hands, content with their silence and each other.

"Oh, look, Bryce!" exclaimed Brittany, breaking the silence suddenly. "A shooting star!"

Bryce followed her gaze and nodded. "Then you must make a wish. 'Tis a lucky omen, you know."

She closed her eyes, smiling. "I wish—I wish... that we may go on like this forever, for, truly, I've never felt such peace... and joy!" She opened her eyes and looked up at him. "There, will that do?"

"'Twill more than do, love," he murmured as he released her hand and placed both of his on her shoulders.

Brittany felt a quickening someplace deep inside her at the more intimate touch.

"But you must know," he continued, a smile lurking about his chiseled mouth as he held her eyes with his, "that I would wish for more than merely remaining as we are. The essence of life is change ... and growth... and I would fancy us twenty... thirty years hence, gazing at this selfsame sky with

what we share now multiplied a thousandfold. Tonight is only a beginning, beloved wife, a prelude, I
think, to things more rare than we might ever have
imagined . . . miracles, in fact . . ."

His hands came up to lightly cup her face, and his
dark head lowered to claim her mouth.

Brittany closed her eyes and gave herself up to the
languid sensuality of his kiss, her arms stealing
about his neck as she stood on tiptoe to press her
yielding body against his.

Slowly building in its intensity, the kiss was deepened, the sensitive tips of their tongues touching
and catching a sweet promise of fire, the taste of
each other making them giddy with longing.

Bryce's arms came around her, pressing her waist
and hips closer still, and his head reeled with the
knowledge that she was truly his. She was his wife
and wanted him, loved him, as much as he did her,
and this was the first miracle.

And Brittany felt she could drown in the exquisite
joy of this moment. A beginning, he'd said. *Oh, aye!*
her heart cried out, *and every shared minute from now
until forever, an eternity of wonder!*

When at last they broke apart, breathless and
eager, Bryce pressed his lips to her temple, murmuring huskily, "'Tis always like this for me, love. The
moment I touch you, I'm hungry for you—all of
you."

"I think," breathed his wife, between little gasps
as his lips found her eyes, her lips, her hair, "'tis
time . . . we found . . . our bed."

And she reveled in her husband's low, delighted
laughter as he swept her up into his arms and carried her below.

CHAPTER 30

LADY BRITTANY AVERY LOOKED OUT OF the mullioned windows of the spacious bedchamber she shared with her husband at Clarendon Hall. Her blue eyes swept the vast lawns and distant acreage of the estate that would be Bryce's and hers and their children's some day, drinking in lush greenery under a blue dome of early October sky. Stretching languidly, like a well-fed cat, she turned and smiled at the rumpled linen sheets of the enormous canopied bed where she and her husband had spent yet another enchanting night.

She was in no hurry to ring for the ladies' maid Lady Olivia had assigned her. Her thoughts were still consumed with the attentiveness of the husband who had just left her to meet with Lord William over some matters of the estate.

Dreamily, she walked over to the satinwood dressing table in her dressing alcove, sat, and picked up a silver repoussé hairbrush, part of a set that was a gift from Olivia. As she pulled the brush through her tangled curls, a slight smile curved her lips.

Her husband was proving to be an insatiable lover, and she couldn't have wished him different. Constantly surprised by the ardor he invoked in her, she knew she matched him, hunger for hunger. In fact, on each of the three days since they had arrived here, they had retired early and arisen late, much to the fond amusement of Lord William, the father-in-law she already loved for his gentle ways and quiet humor, and to the delight of her own father.

Yes, much to Brittany's astonishment, Timothy had accompanied them to England along with Althea and Melody. In fact, after their return home following the wedding cruise, Timothy had greeted the newlyweds with praise and laughter, instead of the admonishments Brittany had been expecting after her disappearance and subsequent elopement.

And there had followed a wonderful hour alone with her father. Timothy had sequestered her with him in his study and proceeded to talk to her in a warm, fatherly way, telling her of his love and of the aspirations and dreams he had for her happiness, inviting her to confide in him her deepest emotions —her fears, her joys—and confessing his own feelings in return.

Asking her to forgive him for what he termed "my preoccupation and neglect of you over the years," he begged her to allow him to think it might not be too late to make amends, and father and daughter had wept together over what they had lost and then laughed together over what they realized they had rediscovered: a deep and abiding love and the knowledge that never again would they allow themselves to drift apart.

It was a Timothy she hadn't known since those early years when her mother was alive, and when he informed her that he would be accepting Bryce's invitation to go to England, "my business concerns be hanged," Brittany knew it was a Timothy who was here to stay.

And oddly enough, despite their vastly different backgrounds, he and Lord William had gotten on splendidly from the moment they'd met—the two of them companionably smoked their pipes together as they discussed the political turmoil brewing in the colonies—each sympathetic to the American cause, each dreading what might soon happen if men of sense and reason did not prevail.

As for Althea, her nose had been put slightly out of joint at news of the elopement, which made her realize she had been robbed of the chance to dazzle tidewater society by staging the "wedding of the year," impressing her friends and acquaintances with her stepdaughter's alliance to a British lord. It had taken some doing on Bryce's part, but after informing her that he would hear no further criticism of his wife—*"from anyone,"* he had presented her with a lovely silver tray engraved with the Avery coat of arms, and her stepmother had been mollified.

And although she and Melody had succumbed to severe seasickness for the entire duration of their voyage aboard the *Lady Beth,* Lady Olivia's tender, solicitous care of them when they arrived here had done much to put Althea at last into excellent spirits, especially when Olivia promised to hold a glittering ball at which she would introduce Bryce's new wife —and her family—to the cream of British society.

Brittany paused in the brushing of her hair, her eyes straying to the gilt and enamel jewelry box lying open on the dressing table. The box was a wedding gift from her husband, but that was not the whole of it; resting inside, on a bed of midnight blue velvet, was the most exquisite necklace she'd ever seen.

Made of heavily filigreed gold worked around eight large matching diamonds, four on either side, it gave way to an even larger diamond that dropped from the center, its multifaceted brilliance winking at her in the sunlight that poured into the room.

She'd been dumbfounded, and then overcome with tears, when Bryce presented it to her on their wedding night, telling her that he'd purchased it from a Fredericksburg merchant who vowed it had once belonged to Charles II's favorite mistress. And then Bryce had kissed away her ecstatic tears saying, "'Tis a fitting emblem of a promise I make to you this night: *You* are the only mistress I shall ever have, Brittany, and whenever you wear it, I wish you to think on that. . . . Dearly beloved wife, for me there will be no other."

Smiling at this recollection, Brittany carefully closed the lid on the box, her glance resting on the enormous sapphire of the ring on her finger; surrounded by a glittering circle of diamonds, the deep blue stone adorned yet another gift she'd received from Bryce, this two nights ago. A belatedly bestowed betrothal ring, it had been handed down in the Avery family for nine generations and had been kept here at Clarendon Hall, where it had rested in William's valuables box since his wife had passed on, awaiting the day when his heir would bring a wife to wear it.

It has certainly been a time of gift-giving, she thought, recalling her astonishment when the twins, on seeing them off in Fredericksburg, had presented her and Bryce with the ownership papers to Saracen, and the promise that they would ship the stallion to England on the first packet that had accommodations suitable for such prized horseflesh.

But perhaps the grandest gift of all, at least in

terms of its power to overwhelm, had been Bryce's wedding present to Will and Tansy. The future marquis of Clarendon, vowing he no longer had the need or urge to roam the sea—and claiming he had selfish motives in mind, for he wished to see more of them once they settled in America—had on behalf of himself and his bride, presented them with the title to the *Lady Beth*!

Brittany could still see Tansy's smiling tears as the little black woman realized what this would mean to her new husband; she could still picture Will's eyes, suspiciously moist as he clasped Bryce about the shoulders and gruffly muttered his thanks.

And that had meant that they, too, had accompanied Bryce and Brittany to England, for Will was to take the schooner back to the colonies under his own hand. The black couple was, right now, honeymooning in a private, richly furnished hunting lodge on William's estate, their visit to last yet a fortnight; at that time they would purchase what merchandise they could (though definitely not *tea*!) from the generous amount Timothy had given them as a wedding gift, and return to Virginia to "make our profit and build our nest."

Oh, if I grow any happier, I'll explode! thought Brittany as she finally rose to ring for her bath. She planned to share a late morning repast with Timothy in the breakfast room (Timothy, since leaving his business affairs happily in the hands of his solicitor and a manager they'd hired, had been shamelessly enjoying his newfound habit of arising late); then she would write a few letters, most notably a reply to Aunt Amelia, whose delighted congratulations had arrived by yesterday's post; and after that, she would join Bryce for a ride on the estate, finishing with the picnic he'd promised her "at a *very* secluded spot!"

* * *

A few hours later she found herself riding beside her husband on the fine chestnut barb mare he'd selected from William's stables for her use until Saracen arrived. True to his promise, Bryce carried a picnic hamper, and it was filled with a host of tempting morsels. They were approaching a little glen that was shaded by a heavy copse of oak trees when Bryce slowed the big bay stallion he rode and turned to her, saying, "Before we go any further, love, there's a stop I wish to make. It won't take long, and then we can head for our picnic spot. Do you mind?"

"Of course not, silly!" she said, suddenly curious about the nature of this spot. Something about his tone suggested it was important to him.

They threaded their way through the trees, following an old bridle path which was half covered by the autumn leaves that had already begun to fall. Presently they came to a small clearing, and Brittany gasped with delight at the beauty of the place. Surrounded by tall oaks, it was perhaps twenty yards across at its widest point. A small, babbling brook erupted beside a giant rock at one end and meandered off into the trees at the other, its crystal clear waters no more than a foot deep as they ran over the stony bottom. Ferns and mosses at the water's edge gave way to lush green grass that was dotted with clumps of wildflowers: cowslips, eglantine, moss roses, and wild thyme; also, although they were well past blooming, she could see the heart-shaped leaves of violets, her favorite, at the wood's edge.

Then, upon closer inspection, she noticed across the stream on the far side, beneath the trees, an irregular row of curved white stones—Why, they were headstones!

Turning to Bryce with a question on her lips, she

saw him smile, but there was a serious look in the green eyes.

"The final resting place of my mother and her family," he said. "This spot used to be a favorite of the children, my mother and her young brothers—a place to splash and cool off during a respite from chores in the heat of summer—and after my grandfather's death, we buried him here, along with his children, whose remains we had moved from the churchyard in the village. 'Twas his last request."

He dismounted, set aside the picnic hamper, and helped her down before continuing.

"I came here briefly the afternoon we arrived—you remember . . . you were overseeing the unpacking, and I disappeared for a while—largely to see if the place was well-tended and not overgrown, as sometimes happens. After all, William had been ill and perhaps unable to see to all the details of the estate."

He took her hand and began walking toward a shallow spot in the brook where three stepping-stones provided a crossing.

"Of course, I had another reason as well . . ."

"A moment alone with them before you brought me here?" Brittany asked softly.

"Aye," he said, looking at her and smiling. "I had to see if all my devils were truly exorcised before sharing this with you—something I wanted to do very badly."

Brittany paused and laid a hand gently on his sleeve. "And were they?" she asked, her eyes searching his for any hint of pain.

"Aye," he said, "they were."

Then he reached out and wrapped his arms about her, holding her head tenderly against his shoulder as he stared across the top of it, at the headstones. "I thought I'd rid myself of them the night I learned of Edmund's death and then saw Richard slain, but now I'm not so sure."

He released her slightly, keeping his hands on her shoulders as he looked into her eyes. "I think the real healing came when I realized I loved you, Brittany . . . and that you returned my love."

"Oh, Bryce . . ." she murmured, emotion making her voice quaver.

"I know . . ." he whispered thickly, ". . . we're both awfully lucky, love . . .

"But come," he said in a brighter voice as he kissed her lightly on the forehead and took her hand again, "let's take a closer look."

She let him lead her to the stream, where he stopped and swung her up into his arms to carry her across, despite her laughing protests.

When he'd set her down again and would have gone straight to the gravesite, she asked him to wait, and, darting here and there she quickly gathered a bouquet of the wildflowers she saw, rejoining him only after she had a satisfactory number.

When Bryce saw what she was about, he stood very still, a surge of emotion blurring his eyes as they followed her. When she came running up to him with her simple bouquet, her heart in her eyes, he gathered her up into his arms, just barely avoiding crushing the flowers as he buried his face in her hair, murmuring, "*I love you so!*"

They stood that way for a long moment, with nothing but their soul-binding silence between them and the murmur of the brook about them, its music a poem to their love.

And when at last they broke apart, Bryce let her lead the way, and she approached each humble grave, laying a blossom upon it, until she reached the last, which read simply:

ELIZABETH TREMAINE
1727–1743

And before this she knelt and placed the remainder of the flowers, murmuring a brief prayer before she raised her head to look at her husband.

Standing beside her, his eyes on the flowers and then on his mother's name, Bryce said in a clear, firm voice, "I'm here, mother, and this is my wife, Brittany. She brings you flowers, and soon she'll bring a child— your grandson or granddaughter—into the world you left too soon. And we'll bring our child here someday, mother, and tell it of a lass named Beth."

Brittany blinked back the tears that threatened, and Bryce helped her to her feet when, all at once, they heard a sound break the stillness—a sound so chilling, it didn't seem real.

From the other end of the row of tombstones, in the deep shadows behind the large one over the place where Bryce's grandfather rested, came a bark of ugly, maddened laughter, its evil staccato echoing across the glen.

Brittany had time to glance at Bryce with fearful eyes before he pushed her behind him, making himself a physical barrier between her and the threatening malice.

And then, springing out from behind the tombstone and looking like a true ghost, came a tall, cloaked figure.

Brittany peered around Bryce's shoulder at the same moment and—*It couldn't be!* Oh, God!

Edmund Avery's pale blue eyes locked with those

of the man he'd sired as he leveled a pistol at him. The ugly laughter died away as suddenly as it had come, and he spoke:

"So . . . thought you'd seen a ghost, did you? Well, I regret disappointing you both, but as you can see, I am very much *alive* . . . which is less than I can promise for the two of you shortly, my *dear conniving son and daughter-in-law!*"

Bryce's body tensed as his brain searched desperately for a way out, a way to save his wife and unborn child, as he kept his eyes on the pistol and tried to stall for time.

"Avery, listen to me," he said. "I know you think otherwise, but Brittany is not to blame for your troubles. I'm the one you want. Take me and let her go."

The laughter again—a short, malicious barrage.

"What? And let her live to tell a tale?" Avery sneered. "That is, even if I believed you, *which I do not*! The bitch is too clever by far *not* to have been involved. Too much of what occurred centered about the actions of our fair Mistress Chambers—and her foppish cousins.

"Well, I shall be dealing with *them* later! As well as my dear brother, William! But now, for the two of you . . ."

He raised the pistol slowly, as if savoring what he was about to do, when all of a sudden, a pair of shots rang out, almost as one.

Bryce recoiled at the sounds, fanning his arms behind him as if to provide an added shield for Brittany, and then he watched incredulously as Edmund, his smoking pistol still in hand, dropped to the ground, a bullet through his heart.

"I say! Good shot, that!" called a familiar voice.

"And just in time, too!" echoed another.

"Tony! Toby!" cried Brittany as she and Bryce

whirled to see them crossing the brook. "How did you—"

"Followed the blackguard here!" said Toby.

"Couldn't let him work his nasties on our favorite cousin!" added his brother.

The two approached wearing, as usual, impeccably tailored apparel, this time riding clothes in appropriately subdued English colors. They embraced Bryce warmly, then hugged Brittany, who murmured her tearful gratitude.

"Don't cry, Coz," said Tony with a smile.

"You were never in any real danger," added Toby. "We've been following the bounder for weeks now, even traced him to this very spot, three days running."

"You've been here all along?" Brittany questioned in bewilderment as they watched Bryce check Avery's body. "But then why didn't you—"

"Didn't want to alert the scum by letting him—and therefore you—know we were in the neighborhood," Tony explained matter-of-factly.

"He'd have known something was up when we appeared on this side of the Atlantic," his twin added, and then went on, alternating with his brother in their typical fashion, to explain what had happened since the last time they'd seen them.

It seemed the twins had visited Lenore Maddox's establishment themselves, it being a favorite "resting place" of theirs whenever they spent a night on the town in Fredericksburg. And from Lenore, who now had reasons of her own to hate Avery, they'd learned he was still alive, that his suicide was only a sham. Discovering his deadly plans as well, they'd followed him across the Atlantic on the *Briar Rose* and dogged him stealthily when he went straight to Clarendon Hall.

Evidently Avery had followed Bryce here when he had come on his first visit, but had decided to bide his time until he could catch Brittany with him. William was to have been killed in his bed that night—with a knife, a more silent weapon.

"I think," said Bryce when the twins had finished, "that Edmund learned, in the most final way, the lesson that I was only partly spared—that revenge is a double-edged sword, quite capable of claiming the wielder as well as his victim. It robs a man of being able to live"—his eyes fell on Avery's body—"in one way or another . . ."

They were all silent for a moment, and then Bryce suggested they retrieve their horses. The authorities would have to be summoned, "and besides," he added, smiling down at Brittany, "I am sorely in need of spending some time alone with my wife."

"Only once you've made us known to the marquis, your father!" scolded Tony with a grin.

"Indeed!" Toby seconded. "We've heard the marquis has the best tailor in London and—*Oh! Oh—oh —ohh!*"

At his outcry all heads turned.

"I've been *wounded*!" he shouted.

"Wounded!" queried Bryce. "What—?"

At this Toby held out the spotless tricorn he'd removed at the graveside. There, near the crown, his finger poking through it to emphasize his loss, was a decidedly large bullet hole.

My God, thought Brittany as the reality of the close call came home to her. *He could have been killed!* And with that, she fainted—fortunately, right into Bryce's arms.

Tony glanced at her, and then at his brother. "Don't blame her!" he said. "'Twas a very fine hat!"

EPILOGUE

Somerset, England, March 19, 1774

BRYCE SMILED AS HE LOOKED DOWN AT the tiny infant he held. Four-week-old Tremaine Anthony Avery, his firstborn son and heir, stirred briefly in his father's arms before relaxing again into the dreamless sleep of the very young. Nearby, in an ornate cradle festooned with blue ribbons, Tremaine's brother William Tobias, lay wide awake, his baby blue eyes trying mightily to focus on a satin bow dangling from the cradle's hood. Younger than Tremaine by twelve minutes, Wills, as they'd dubbed him, was definitely the more active of the twins, "as if," his mother had joked, "he's trying to make up for the extra time he spent waiting to come out."

They were in the temporary nursery that had been set up, at Brittany's urging, in the chamber adjoining theirs, so that when the twins awoke to be fed at night, their mother, who'd insisted on nursing them herself, could reach them quickly. Bryce chuckled to himself as he recalled the appalled shock on Althea's face when she learned her stepdaughter would be her own wet-nurse.

"But it simply isn't done among those of our class!" Althea had protested.

Ignoring her stepmother's appropriation of the class distinction that, in point of fact, only Brittany, as the wife of a lord, was entitled to, Brittany had merely laughed. "But I *choose* to have it done, and with my husband's blessing, for we wouldn't dream of missing the warmth and intimacy we share in this endeavor."

"You—you mean that you actually *allow* your husband to be present when—when—" Althea had gone speechless with shock, glancing, red-faced at Bryce as he'd stood there, taking this all in.

Bryce felt himself warmed all over now, as he recalled the intimate look his wife had thrown him before answering her stepmother: "Aye, he watches—and participates!—holding Tremaine whilst I nurse Wills, or burping Wills whilst I feed Tremaine...as I said, 'tis a very intimate sharing..."

And it had been just such a time they'd shared not a half hour ago, laughing, talking together desultorily while the twins had their "dinner," before Brittany left for her dressing alcove, to change and make ready for the christening that was to take place in an hour.

Brittany's family, with the exception of her cousins, who had pressing concerns at Sweetbriar, had stayed on at Clarendon Hall until after the birthing. Timothy had been especially eager to be close to his daughter at this momentous occasion in their lives. And Althea had been anxious to stay on as well, though perhaps for other reasons; she'd seen

Melody introduced to the cream of London society, with the result that, at this very moment, Brittany's sister had no less than five handsome offers for her hand. (The only problem, Bryce thought with amusement, was that little Melody had taken a cue from her sister's past behavior and wasn't sure she'd be having any of them. "After all," she'd told her incredulous parents, "Brittany made a splendid match at one-and-twenty, and I'm not yet seventeen!")

As for the Wakefields, both the twins and Amelia had crossed the ocean to be present for the christening. Tony and Toby, in particular, had been eager to attend; not only were they to be godfathers, but the second names of the infants were their own.

And Will and Tansy had arrived, too, though just last night. Their crossing had been easy enough (and thank heaven, for Tansy was carrying Will's child), but they'd been detained, in London, since Will had used the trip to export some colonial goods, as well as to visit their friends.

Tensions between England and her American colonies had been increasing at an alarming rate, especially since news of a certain incident had reached London on the nineteenth of January. At that time, a colonial ship named the *Hayley*, owned by one John Hancock, a New Englander, had come with the news that, on December sixteenth of '73, a group of men disguised themselves as Mohawk Indians, boarded East India Company ships at Griffen's Wharf, Boston, and threw three hundred and forty-two chests of tea from the London firm of Davison and Newman into Boston Harbor. The tea was valued at almost ten thousand pounds!

Parliament and populace alike had been outraged (the few exceptions, most notably William Avery, the marquis of Clarendon, notwithstanding), and officials at docks from London to Land's End had begun to closely monitor colonial trade ships of all kinds. Indeed, Will had told them, though he'd reached the London Hole nearly a fortnight ago, he and Tansy were lucky to be here even now!

A soft sound drew Bryce's attention away from his musings and he looked up to see his wife standing in the doorway that connected their chamber to the nursery. She was more beautiful than ever, the deep azure folds of her velvet gown accentuating a figure that was just as slender as when he'd met her, but grown somehow more softly rounded with the advent of childbirth. She was the center of his life. The love they shared grew deeper with each passing day, as he'd known it would, as he'd told her that night when they'd confessed their love for each other. Theirs was a love to cherish and nurture, just as they would cherish and nurture these blessed infants born of it, a special thing   rare, and beautiful, and fine . . .

"Tuppence for your thoughts, darling," said Brittany as she came forward with a grin.

"Tuppence, is't?" he queried dryly, then lightly tweaked her nose as she bent to relieve him of Tremaine.

She pulled a face at him, then grinned. "Well, Father says the cost of everything is going up," she quipped, adding, ". . . um, thruppence?"

"No," he laughed, standing and giving her a light kiss on the mouth, "not even the worth of all the tea in Boston Harbor, for I was just thinking of how much I love you, and would deem that priceless."

Brittany paused and looked up at her husband, all the love she bore him in her eyes. And then, when she saw the sudden leap of fire in Bryce's green-eyed gaze, she felt a familiar ripple course through her.

It had been a long four weeks since the twins had been born, not because of her health, for the birthing had been relatively easy, but because the midwife and Olivia had cautioned them to "abstain a fortnight or two" after the births (Olivia's blush making it perfectly clear as to *what* they were to abstain *from*!). So they'd had to curtail their ardor, making do with embraces and kisses that were all too chaste... *until now,* she thought giddily, then reminding herself that they had a christening to see through, she amended, or until *tonight*!

Bryce saw her seductive smile and quirked one handsome eyebrow. "Thruppence for *your* thoughts, love?" he queried with a bold grin.

"Ah," said his wife, forcing herself to remember the christening, "not for all the tea in China... but," she added with a promise in her eyes, "ask me again tonight, love.... Aye, tonight should do just fine..."

Veronica Sattler welcomes letters from her readers. Please address them to

> Veronica Sattler
> c/o SMK
> St. Martin's Press
> 175 Fifth Avenue
> New York, NY 10010

Sweeping from the wild Scottish Highlands to tapestried castle halls, from court revelries to battlefields, from the unstoppable desire for power to the unquenchable hungers of the heart—they struggled passionately toward a triumphant destiny.

HEARTSTORM

ELIZABETH STUART

"A vibrant tapestry of highland castles and lochs, of passionate love and conflicting loyalties."
—**Elizabeth Kary, author of *Love, Honor and Betray***

HEARTSTORM
Elizabeth Stuart
_____ 91527-6 $4.50 U.S.   _____ 91528-4 $5.50 Can.

Publishers Book and Audio Mailing Service
P.O. Box 120159, Staten Island, NY 10312-0004

Please send me the book(s) I have checked above. I am enclosing $_____
(please add $1.25 for the first book, and $.25 for each additional book to cover
postage and handling. Send check or money order only—no CODs.)

Name _____

Address _____

City _____State/Zip _____

Please allow six weeks for delivery. Prices subject to change without notice.

HEARTS 10/89